PENGUIN BOOKS

Island Reich

Praise for *Island Reich*

'Highly entertaining . . . The plot is splendidly complicated.
Like most good adventure novels set in recognizable history,
Grimwood offers readers an enticing "what if?"' *SCOTSMAN*

'A rip-roaring yarn that is totally credible. Excellent' *Sun*

'Jack Grimwood matches Robert Harris, Joseph Kanon, Ken
Follett and John le Carré thrill for thrill in this breath-taking
WWII story of atmospheric suspense, daring espionage
and political intrigue, set in the tense depths of
Britain's Darkest Hour' *Glasgow Life*

'Top notch . . . the suspense never wavers' *Crime Time*

Praise for Jack Grimwood

'A fine book . . . for those who enjoy vintage le Carré'
Ian Rankin

'The new le Carré . . . an absolutely brilliant page-turner . . .
if you love thrillers, Jack Grimwood is a name you need
to remember' BBC Radio 2, *The Sara Cox Show*

'Mesmerising . . . something special in the arena of
international thrillers' *Financial Times*

'So atmospheric, so elegantly written . . . I just disappeared
into it totally' Marian Keyes

'A blizzard of exciting set pieces, superbly realized'
Daily Telegraph

'The rejuvenation of the espionage thriller continues apace'
Guardian

ABOUT THE AUTHOR

Jack Grimwood, aka Jon Courtenay Grimwood, was born in Malta and christened in the upturned bell of a ship. He grew up in the Far East, Britain and Scandinavia. He's written for national newspapers, is a two-time winner of the BSFA Award for Best Novel, and was shortlisted for Le Prix Montesquieu 2015. His work has been translated into numerous languages. He is married to the journalist and novelist Sam Baker. *Island Reich* is his third thriller.

jackgrimwood.com
jonathangrimwood.com
j-cg.co.uk
@joncg

By the same author

Moskva

Nightfall Berlin

Island Reich

JACK GRIMWOOD

PENGUIN BOOKS

PENGUIN BOOKS

UK | USA | Canada | Ireland | Australia
India | New Zealand | South Africa

Penguin Books is part of the Penguin Random House group of companies
whose addresses can be found at global.penguinrandomhouse.com

First published by Michael Joseph 2021
Published in Penguin Books 2021

001

Typeset by Jouve (UK), Milton Keynes
Printed and bound in Great Britain by Clays Ltd, Elcograf S.p.A.

The authorized representative in the EEA is Penguin Random House Ireland,
Morrison Chambers, 32 Nassau Street, Dublin D02 YH68

A CIP catalogue record for this book is available from the British Library

ISBN: 978–1–405–93670–5

www.greenpenguin.co.uk

Captain J. P. (Jack) Grimwood RN
1921–2020

Born into a world ravaged by war and Spanish Flu. Died in a world haunted by Covid. Sailed out of Rosyth and Aberdeen, sunk sailing home from the Faroes, fought in the Far East. Signed up for the Navy as a very young man. Never really left. I'm sorry we weren't allowed to say goodbye.

Author's Note

No facts were killed in the writing of this book – but I don't doubt a passing historian might consider they'd been given a hard time.

Island Reich is a novel. A work of fiction woven around real events and real people. Bill O'Hagan didn't exist. A number of the people Bill meets did.

Historical events happen in *Island Reich* on the day they happened in life. Where possible, I've kept faith with the truth. Occasionally, I've cheated, and invented an incident, implied a motive, or shifted a tide or weather pattern for narrative convenience.

A number of memoranda occur throughout the book. A few are real, many are simplifications or paraphrases, and the rest are made up. All relate to real events and the dates of those events are correct.

(If not, the mistake is mine.)

In my defence, Herodotus did say, 'Very few things happen at the right time, and the rest do not happen at all. The conscientious historian will correct these defects . . .'

How could a conscientious novelist do less?

In the Beginning . . .
Late May 1940

I

The teenager stumbled as her mother threw her into a muddy ditch.

'Stay there,' the woman ordered.

Her voice was so fierce that her daughter obeyed. She huddled, hands over her ears, as a Stuka bomber dived like a hawk on the line of refugees. The next few minutes were filled with the thud of bullets hitting flesh, and the howls of an old man, and women and children taking too long to die. A French girl lay in a sewer mouth, face down, with blood flowing from a gash in her back. Yanking her aside, the girl scrambled in, pulling the body after her. She wanted it to stop.

The dead girl had a bag so she stole it.

The girl was dead so it wasn't stealing, not really.

There was no money. That would be asking too much. There were papers, though. Papers naming her as Mignon du Plessis and the girl took those. She also stole the crucifix from the girl's neck, hanging it round her own.

II

Settling himself under the pine, the young German officer unslung his captured Lee–Enfield .303, and jacked a round of English ammunition into the breech. He had one shot and it was the most important of his life.

In a matter of minutes, the Duke of Windsor and Wallis Simpson would be travelling along the road below in their unmistakable Canadian-made Buick. A Rolls-Royce would bring up the rear, laden with Wallis's luggage.

Captain Keller knew what he had to do and knew he was the man to do it. This shot guaranteed his future. His mother had been English. That was a black mark against an ambitious young intelligence officer.

This shot was his chance to wipe that mark away.

This shot was the shot of his life.

Putting his eyes to the cross hairs, he picked off refugees on the road below one at a time in his head, as he readied himself to take it. He was behind enemy lines. He was dressed as a civilian. He would be shot if he was captured. It was a risk worth taking.

III

A tramp steamer was waiting at the docks. First stop Belfast, second stop Dublin. Bill O'Hagan would be getting off there, although he'd signed on for Cardiff, Liverpool and then back to Glasgow, where he was now.

Bill hadn't presented references but there was a war on and ships were under attack. A working boat on a trip like this might as well have painted a big red target on the deck and a sign saying *Sink Me.*

They'd been glad to get him.

He was heading for Kingston docks when he saw the houses. A row of them. The kind of houses lived in by people who'd never had to worry about money. The kind of people he despised. One last burglary to fund his new life in Southern Ireland.

What kind of fool would turn that down?

He chose a boat that looked empty, but for a window in the attics, which was open and had a curtain flapping. Its front door was up five grey stone steps, its lock was a Chubb and new. The lock on the back, once he'd scaled the garden wall, was older and simpler. It took no time to pick at all.

IV

Grabbing a schnapps from the built-in cabinet between chauffeur and passenger, Colonel von Neudeck considered his options.

At his age, and having already lost one arm in the last war, his chances of throwing himself from a speeding Mercedes and living were zero. Even if he did remember to roll when he landed on the pristine surface of one of Herr Hitler's new autobahns.

Bullet-proof glass separated him from his driver. The man was half von Neudeck's age, and twice his fitness. The kind of shaven thug who'd take having someone try to wrestle the steering from him badly, even if this had been possible.

Sitting back, von Neudeck helped himself to a second schnapps and wondered how much it would hurt to die by firing squad. He didn't bother to wonder what he'd done wrong. These days you didn't have to do anything. All the same, he did wonder why they'd dragged him from his castle instead of simply shooting him on the spot. That's what he would have done.

He did miss the old days.

A soldier hurried from a guard hut, saluted the Mercedes and lifted a barrier. The Mercedes purred its way along an oak-lined drive towards the courtyard of a newly redeveloped hunting lodge.

Von Neudeck blinked at the man waiting on its steps.

'Ernst,' the man said. 'How lovely to see you.'

The second most powerful man in Germany held a hunting rifle and was dressed in fetching shades of brown, set off with a flowing loden cloak.

'Perfect timing,' Hermann Goering said. 'I'm hunting boar. Why don't you join me?'

V

Wallis Simpson stared at the bombs dropping from a distant plane and flinched as the first exploded. 'Stop right now,' she demanded.

The Buick slammed to a halt. The Rolls-Royce behind braked sharply to avoid running into the back of them. The road was narrow and they'd been going too fast anyway, forcing oncoming refugees off the road.

'You said the front wouldn't have reached this far,' she said accusingly.

'I'm sorry, madame.'

'Turn back,' she ordered.

The driver glanced in his mirror and the Duke of Windsor nodded. The Stukas were already peeling away, loads dropped and bullets emptied on to the refugees below. The fall of France was happening faster than anyone could imagine.

'We can turn there,' the duke said, indicating a lay-by in the shadow of pines half a mile ahead. The Buick moved off, pushing through refugees, who banged on the car as it tried to get by.

'Really,' Wallis said.

But the duke wasn't listening. His attention was on a girl crawling from a sewer pipe. For a moment their gazes met. Then the Buick pressed on.

'Remember that afternoon with Hermann?' Wallis asked, and the girl was forgotten. Referring to a Nazi general by his first name in front of their British driver was unwise, the duke felt, but he kept that to himself.

'Of course I do, darling. How could I forget?'

The Return

I

October 1937, Berlin

'Daisy,' the new Duchess of Windsor said. 'I didn't expect to find you here.'

The American dipped a curtsy. 'We're just leaving,' she said regretfully. She turned to the bearded Englishman beside her. 'Aren't we?'

The man grunted, remembered his manners and bowed, then bowed more deeply to the duke, who was coming up the steps behind.

'William,' the duke said.

Sir William Renhou took the out-thrust hand.

'Just going?' the duke asked.

'Afraid so, sir. Flying out to Kenya this afternoon. Can't say I'll be sorry to go, except for the present company, obviously.'

Their exchange was watched by Hermann Goering, who stood in the doorway of his manor house, smiling widely. 'Come in, come in,' he told the duke and duchess. The Renhous were forgotten already.

The fat man in a flamboyant white uniform herded his guests towards a new painting that showed him in his substantially thinner youth, standing in front of an Albatros D.III, the biplane he'd flown when leading Jagdgeschwader 1, the fighter wing once commanded by Manfred von Richthofen.

'Very striking,' the Duke of Windsor said.

Goering had been an air ace before he was wounded in

Hitler's abortive Beer Hall Putsch, rode the Führer's coat tails to power and found himself head of the German air force and one of the most important men in the new Reich.

The man in the painting wore both the Blue Max, the old empire's highest award, and an Iron Cross First Class. Goering was wearing both now, but in a slightly mocking way that suggested he knew he'd reached an age and level of power where he could indulge his love of dressing up.

'I'm afraid I don't speak German,' Wallis Simpson said.

'I'll try to speak English.'

'No. Don't, Hermann. My husband likes to practise.'

'If he's as fluent in German as he is in other languages, I'm impressed.'

'My mother. You know.'

Mary of Teck, the ex-king's mother, was fluent in German, English and French, and had become queen in 1910, four years before George V went to war with most of her family.

This visit to Carinhall was the best bit of their visit to Germany yet. The newspapers back home were being beastly about it. Even some of the American press were being horrid. Jewish owners, the duke said.

'I used my German in the Great War,' the duke said proudly.

Field Marshal Goering tipped his head to one side, like a small child making a show of listening. Given that his jowls and his bulk already made him look like a big baby, the effect was unnerving.

'Questioning prisoners.'

'I thought you were in the lines, sir?'

'Only once. I made William, the man who just left, take me forward so I could say I'd been under fire. I was a major in the Grenadier Guards, for God's sake. Being in the line was my duty. You know the real insult? They gave me the Military

Cross simply for going forward when others were expected to fight there and die.'

'I've never seen you wear it, sir.'

'Damned if I'm going to wear a medal I didn't earn. My father allowed me to question captured officers as a consolation prize.'

'Was that interesting?'

'Very. Mostly they were happy to talk. Not about plans or their own defences. But about pretty much everything else. And when they discovered who I was . . .'

'They were even keener?'

The duke smiled. 'There was one man . . . He'd lost his arm a year before and insisted on returning to his regiment. We picked him up after the wind turned and he'd almost mustard-gassed half his men.'

'He was dying?'

'Far from it. He led them to higher ground behind the trenches the moment he realized what was happening. We found them breathing through socks they'd pissed on to make impromptu gas masks.'

'What was especially interesting about this man, sir?'

'Who said he was interesting?'

'You remember him. With respect, sir. How many of those you questioned do you remember?'

'Just that one,' the duke admitted. 'We talked, we played chess, we discussed war, and he told me nothing. He answered every question. I doubt he ever lied. And yet he said nothing of military value at all. Neuberg. Neuman . . . Something like that. Makes me wonder what happened to him.'

'You disliked the man?'

'Far from it. There's an art to keeping yourself that private.'

Goering glanced at an ormolu clock on the huge over-mantel and sighed theatrically. 'Our time is up, your royal highness. Much to my regret. Unless I can persuade you to stay longer?'

'I can't. I'm having a drink with Ogilvie-Forbes.'

'Not your ambassador?'

The duke shot him a look.

'I'm sorry,' Goering said. 'I couldn't resist. I'm not saying your chargé d'affaires isn't a good man, it's just a pity that Ambassador Henderson's unexpected departure should coincide with your arrival. But, before you go, there's something you must see . . .'

Papers spilled across Goering's desk, and an open window let in an October breeze and the rustle of huge oaks outside. The fat man nodded to a newly framed map on his wall.

'Beautiful,' Wallis said. Bending, she took a closer look. When she straightened up, Goering was smiling.

'There's no border between Germany and Austria,' Wallis said.

'Nor should there be. Austria will decide soon that it wants our countries to be united, to become one.'

'I haven't heard about this,' the duke said.

'It hasn't happened yet, sir. There will be a vote. It will be overwhelming.' Goering searched through the papers on his desk, coming up with a sketch map of the world. 'We have other changes in mind too.'

The entirety of French North Africa had been added to Berlin's empire, which was shown stretching all the way from Deutsch-Südwestafrika to Tangiers on the Mediterranean coast. The eastern edge of Africa, from the Cape to Arabia, was coloured a red that swept across Persia and Afghanistan to join up with India, Burma and Malaya beyond. London had also acquired the Philippines and the Dutch East Indies, which would surprise both the Americans and the Dutch.

The British Isles themselves were now entirely red; the Irish Free State having been folded back into the United Kingdom. 'The prime minister will not agree to it,' the duke said. 'And my brother would never approve.'

Goering chuckled. 'The PM won't be given a choice. And it isn't your brother we intend to discuss this with.'

2

Spain, Saturday, 22 June 1940

Her passport said her name was Gretchen Schmidt. It was a lie. It said her nationality was Swiss and that was a lie too. She was American. Her German was good enough to pass for *Schweizerdeutsch* though, and her looks helped.

Adjusting her sights to two hundred yards, Lilly Black fixed the cross hairs on the Duke of Windsor's elegant temple, steadied her nerves, readjusted her aim and took a deep breath, releasing half of it before tightening her finger.

A fraction more pressure would see her target dead.

Behind Lilly, a three-quarter moon hung ghostly in an afternoon sky. Below, in a dusty Castilian courtyard, the duke gripped the door handle of a 6.6-litre Hispano-Suiza belonging to Colonel Juan Beigbeder.

The colonel was Spanish, one of Generalissimo Franco's finest officers. Not that you'd have known it from his flamboyant Arab robes and silver dagger jammed in his sash. Today, though, he was acting for Berlin.

If the duke decided to climb into Beigbeder's car, Lilly would shoot. America couldn't allow the duke and duchess to fall into German hands. Mr Standish, her boss, had been clear on that.

The man who'd briefly been Edward VIII wasn't in the habit of opening his own doors. But this meeting was a discreet one. A hill town far enough from Madrid for the few people who mattered to even know it existed, never mind have visited.

Releasing her breath as she'd been taught in sniper school, Lilly took another breath and held it. *Open the door, or don't,* she thought, refusing to let her cross hairs waver. All the bloody man had to do was make up his mind.

Spain was non-belligerent, not neutral, in the war that had swept Europe. There was a difference and the difference mattered. Spain's loyalties lay with Germany, as Portugal's lay with Britain.

Reaching for his coffee, Colonel Beigbeder sipped it carefully. They were seated at a table in front of the café. The duke had decided he'd rather stay here.

'A simple broadcast,' Beigbeder said. 'That's all Berlin asks. Von Ribbentrop would fly here to ask you himself, but he didn't want to be misunderstood.'

'By whom?' the duke demanded.

'*Darling . . .*' At his side, the woman for whom he'd given up his throne touched her hand to his arm and he sat back reluctantly.

Wallis Simpson and Joachim von Ribbentrop had been friends before the war, when he was Berlin's man in London. There were those who said they'd been lovers but Wallis never dignified gossip by acknowledging it.

'What could my husband say anyway? If he did broadcast.'

'The truth,' Colonel Beigbeder said firmly. 'It's an absurdity for London and Berlin to be fighting each other. Both countries hate Bolsheviks. Both share a common culture. Their aims and beliefs are near identical. For God's sake . . .' He allowed a slight exasperation to show. 'The British royal family is of German origin. The Führer regards your husband's abdication as a tragedy. The common people in Britain miss him. They'll listen to what he says . . . Sir, you must know this?'

'At least think about it, darling,' Wallis said.

'Your Excellency . . .'

Colonel Beigbeder scowled as his driver pushed himself away from the wall, his hip catching their table's corner. He'd been watching the roofs and now his gaze was fixed on the town hall. 'Permission to relieve myself, sir.'

'If you must.'

But I locked that.

Lilly Black had time for one thought, before the colonel's driver began advancing on her. He was holding a silenced Beretta and it was aimed at her head. The last time she'd noticed him, he'd been leaning against the wall behind his colonel.

Lilly reached for the rifle she'd been ready to pack away.

'Don't,' he said. 'It's over.'

So much for going to Paris to patch things up with Daisy, Lilly thought.

So much for the life she'd been planning to live when the war in Europe was over. Not being taken was more important than staying alive. Pulling a miniature camera from her pocket, Lilly snapped the man's picture. A final act of defiance before stepping backwards off the roof. The passing American tourist who took the camera from Lilly's dead hand vanished before a crowd could form.

'What just happened?' the duchess demanded.

'A workman fell from a ladder, your highness. The police and an ambulance have been called.'

'He was badly hurt?'

'A broken leg, your highness.'

'Lucky it wasn't a broken back.' The duke considered the cloudless sky. 'Must be bloody working in this heat.'

'I imagine they're used to it,' Wallis said.

It was time to let the duke go. He was getting restless. Always a sign that his patience was at an end. Although Beigbeder knew the suggestion must come from him. 'One final thing, sir,' he said. 'London has installed listening devices throughout your suite in Madrid. They're recording every word you say. You might want to consider changing hotels.'

'Everywhere?' the duke said.

'Afraid so, sir.' Turning to Wallis, Beigbeder met her gaze. 'I'd have liked to have known you in London,' he said. 'Joachim speaks of your soirées, drinks at the Savoy, teas at the Ritz. He misses those days.'

The duke and Wallis said nothing. They didn't need to. Their expression said it all.

They missed those days, too.

Hotel Ritz
Plaza de la Lealtad
Madrid

Saturday, 22 June 1940

My dearest Joachim,

Thank you for the flowers. They were lovely as ever. I
am forwarding you this via your ambassador, whose
discretion I'm assured I can rely on.

You know how I feel about this war. That we should find
ourselves on opposite sides is intolerable. The way the new
king is treating my husband is intolerable. This running
from country to country like some refugee is intolerable.
Tomorrow is my husband's birthday. He will be miserable. I
know he will be miserable.

I miss having you to talk to, and you know how hard I
worked to try to dissuade my husband from abdicating.
Usually he will listen to reason, but when he engages his
stubborn streak . . .

This is not the life I wanted for him. An empty title,
barely any money and no influence. If he was still king
none of this would have happened. He wouldn't have
allowed it to happen. I wouldn't have allowed it to happen.
Your friend with the robes tells me the English have
installed listening devices throughout our room. It's too
late to change hotels tonight but we will do so first thing
tomorrow.

I hate them. I hate them all. I look forward to better days.
I know you do too.

Write to me.
Wallis

To: Joachim von Ribbentrop, Reichsminister of Foreign Affairs

3

HM Prison Barlinnie, Glasgow, same day

Bill O'Hagan woke in an underground cell in Glasgow's Barlinnie Prison and for a second thought he'd gone blind. The darkness was so absolute he touched a finger to his eyes to check they were still there.

He needed a drink and he needed a piss, and he had no memory of how he'd ended up in solitary. Not willingly, if the swelling to his jaw was anything to go by. He hoped the damage wasn't permanent.

Lock-pickers could be as ugly as they liked. But his other job was as a con man, and you needed your looks for that game. In the last fifteen years he'd been a missionary, a Flying Corps officer down on his luck and an Irish baronet burnt out by rebels. The last two had been surprisingly profitable.

Forcing himself to his feet, Bill staggered three steps and met a wall. Turning, he headed in the other direction. Halfway across he hit something at knee height and fell. 'Shite . . .'

He didn't need lights to know it was a safe.

A Cosmos Deluxe. He could tell that from its handle, a cross bar gripped in a metal fist. The Cosmos wasn't a new model, but it was a good one. And he didn't need to think twice to know what was expected of him. So, Bill O'Hagan was required to crack a lock in pitch darkness. Well, he'd done it before . . .

In many ways it was where he came in.

4

Edinburgh, February 1910

The lock on the back door of the rectory opened with a click. Stretching up, Bill tried to reach the bolt he'd been pushed through a tiny window to free.

He was too short.

Dragging a chair across the kitchen, he clambered up and yanked at the bolt with both hands. He wasn't worried about waking anyone. The old priest was dead and the new one hadn't arrived.

'What took you so long?' his uncle growled. Pushing Bill aside, he ordered Cousin Pat in, slammed the bolt into place and made to turn the key.

'Where is it?' He glared at Bill, who shrank back.

'There wasn't one,' Bill protested.

'Then how the hell . . .'

Bill scrabbled in his pocket for a lock pick. It was small, rusty, slightly bent.

Backhanding Bill to the floor, Uncle Roy stood over him, glaring. He seemed to be wondering whether to add a kick to the mix. 'We don't steal from our own,' he said heavily. 'Who did you take that from?'

'Maxie. A week ago. Bit more.'

'And you taught yourself?'

He had, too. Bill had lifted a lock from a hardware shop and taken it apart to see how it worked and what was inside. After he'd put it back together, he'd spent every minute since jiggling the pick until his fingers hurt. It had taken days before the levers started to do what they were told.

'I said . . .'

Bill put an arm across his face in case Uncle Roy intended to slap him again. But nothing happened. When Bill risked a peek, his uncle was looking thoughtful.

'So. You could do it again?'

'Aye,' Bill said. 'I could.'

'Well, I'll be damned,' Uncle Roy said, his eyes alight. 'You'll either die rich or you'll hang.'

5

Lying full-length on the filthy floor, Bill put his ear to the safe's cold door, turned the dial five times to reset the tumblers, and began. Within seconds he was gone, lost to the sounds of the mechanism within, listening for silences and clicks.

In an ideal world he'd have a notebook to record where on the dial those silences and clicks fell, and enough light to read his notes and draw a graph that revealed the combination when he read off where the lines crossed. However, he'd been doing this long enough to read a dial with his fingers, visualize the graph and keep the numbers in his head.

He worked in the silences on both sides of an agonizingly slow drip from the ceiling of his pitch-black cell. Three drops of water later he heard the faintest double click he'd been waiting for. He had the last of the numbers. Now all he had to do was stop his relief wiping the earlier ones from his mind.

That had happened before.

Thirty-three left, 15 right, 70 left, 25 right. He felt an almost unimaginably slight hesitation and knew he was there. The safe was empty. Of course it was. The bastards didn't want him to open it so they could retrieve something. They just wanted to see if he could.

'I've done it. All right? I've done it.' The darkness swallowed his words.

If there was anyone listening, they didn't answer.

To His Majesty's Ambassadors,
Spain, Portugal & Switzerland
From Lord Halifax, Foreign Office

Date: 22 June 1940
<u>Confidential</u>

<u>Hospitality</u>

The Comptroller of the Royal Household at the orders of His Majesty wishes me to remind you that His Royal Highness The Duke of Windsor, and Her Highness The Duchess, are travelling as private individuals.

As such, while the duke is to be accorded the full respect due to a member of the British royal family, the private nature of his travel means that he may not draw on embassies for funds or accommodation.

Nor, in this time of war and privation at home, are banquets, parties, soirées or luncheons to be given in his honour. Any breach of this will be regarded as a disciplinary matter.

6

The United States Office of Information, better known as the Department of Unintended Consequences to those who knew it existed at all, occupied the corner of an upper floor in the National Archives Building on Pennsylvania Avenue, Washington DC. A building not yet completed and already overcrowded. The shelving set aside for archives had proved so inadequate it was being extended, with architects, foremen and workmen coming and going at all hours. Ideal cover for an office that didn't officially exist, and liked it that way.

Charles Standish III's official job was to keep America out of the war.

A time might come when the president decided war was inevitable, and put his intelligence-gathering on an official basis. That time might be soon. But it was not yet. It might not even be for another year.

If America was lucky, it might be never.

Standish's unofficial job was to ensure that President Roosevelt was in full possession of all the facts and in the strongest possible position should war be declared on America, or America decide to declare war on anyone else.

His specialty was facts. 'Eliminate all other factors, and the one which remains must be the truth.' Standish was a great believer in Conan Doyle.

Wallis Simpson, Baltimore's most famous social climber,

was currently swanning round the bits of Europe that weren't yet at war. Since she was proving an intractable problem, Standish turned his thoughts to the woman he'd had shadowing her. Lilly Black was dead. He needed to decide if her sister, Daisy Renhou, could replace her.

Flipping open Daisy's file, he checked her arrest warrant, court transcript, juvenile detention record and the crimescene photo of the boy she'd shot five times in the groin. All before the age of fifteen. Quite impressive in its way.

'A natural-born killer.'

For the psychiatrist that had probably been a negative. To Standish it sounded like the start of his ideal CV. These days, Daisy was a notorious Nazi sympathizer and the mistress of a Parisian gangster, having bolted from her thug of a husband. All of which had been recorded in the scandal sheets. What the scandal sheets didn't know was that she was also Standish's sleeper agent.

Leaning back, he pulled the blinds shut and set a projector running.

On his wall, twenty thousand members of the German American Bund gave jerky Nazi salutes as their *Bundsführer* took the podium in Madison Square Gardens, backed by a huge poster of George Washington and swastika banners.

After attacking the Jewish press and insulting blacks, their leader mocked Standish's boss as the Jew-loving President Frank D. *Rosenfeld*, before encouraging his followers to batter a left-wing protester.

All of this watched hungrily from the front row by an immaculately dressed Aryan blonde who might have been film star Marion Davies – if Miss Davies hadn't had alcohol problems and been the mistress of William Randolph Hearst, a man twice her age and far too jealous to let her out in public. Standish tried to put himself in Daisy's head. He hoped she'd understand how important it was she took her sister's place.

If not, he'd have to make her understand.

7

Paris, Sunday, 23 June 1940

'We should have a victory parade, my Führer.'

Reichsmarschall Goering had come through on a telephone line reserved for matters of critical importance.

'Hermann . . .'

'I'm disturbing something?'

'Work,' Hitler said. 'Always, work.'

Papers were spread across his desk, a map of Western Europe was open, with red lines that advanced inexorably to the French coast and the English Channel.

'No victory parade,' Hitler said firmly.

'But Paris has fallen,' Goering protested.

'No grand parade. Not in Paris. Not at home. Not yet.'

'I don't understand . . .' Reichsmarschall Goering sounded crestfallen.

'Hermann,' Hitler said. 'You will get your parade. I promise. But first I must have victory. When London falls, then you can have your big parade.'

8

Paris, same day

A few minutes after Daisy took a call from the US embassy in Madrid to say her sister was dead, a paper-wrapped parcel arrived in the foyer of the apartment block she shared with her Parisian lover. In the sent-by box was her sister's name. As Lilly and Daisy had no contact, Daisy knew this was a lie.

Taking yesterday's baguette from a paper bag in Pierre's kitchen, Daisy checked the fridge for cheese. She settled on a block of Comté and removed a bottle of Veuve Clicquot as an afterthought. She owed her sister that much at least.

Taking two glasses, Daisy filled both and toasted her endlessly irritating and now forever-absent sister. What hadn't Madrid told her? Her sister didn't do accidents: she wasn't the kind of person.

'To Lilly . . .' Raising her glass, Daisy drank it down, barely tasting the champagne.

Then she swallowed her sister's glass and refilled both, emptying each in turn. The alcohol didn't make her feel any better. Lilly had hated Daisy's current lover. She'd hated all of Daisy's lovers. Lilly hadn't blamed Daisy though. Not for the mess she'd made of her life recently. That, she blamed on William Renhou.

The stiff, unbending Kenyan settler Daisy had unexpectedly wed on one of his brief trips to Europe.

'You were right, Lil,' Daisy said. 'Terrible idea. Awful man.'

Inside the parcel was a badly battered little camera. Flipping open the back, Daisy realized drunkenly that she'd just ruined any film inside. Only, there wasn't. Also, no letter, no note. She didn't even recognize the handwriting on the wrapping. Sighing, she poured herself another champagne and it drank down.

'I should eat something, shouldn't I?' she told herself.

She could hear Lilly's tart agreement.

The baguette was hard and the cheese mouldy. She was wondering if there was anything else to eat when the entry bell rang.

It wasn't Pierre the Rat, so named from his days with a Marseille gang. Last she'd heard of it, her lover was in Biarritz, fleecing refugees. Taking one of his revolvers from the desk, she stamped her way down to the lobby.

'Yes?' she demanded through the door.

'Lady Renhou?' a man asked.

'I don't use that any more.'

He rattled the handle.

Daisy eyed it with disinterest.

'You need to open this,' he said eventually.

'I don't need to do anything of the sort,' she snapped. All the same, she yanked free the bolt, stepping to one side as the door swung open. The man in the doorway wore a homburg and a pale jacket. He was clutching his briefcase to his chest in a slightly protective way.

'You're still here,' he said.

'Where else would I be?'

His eyes widened when he saw the revolver.

'What do you want?' Daisy asked.

Reaching into his jacket, he produced a card. *Howard Bennett — US Trade Representative.* The name was solid, forgettable; the job title made him sound like someone's assistant. Daisy recognized him for what he was. Both name and job title were lies.

Mr Bennett faltered when he saw what remained of the mouldy cheese and the almost empty bottle of champagne. 'There's a little left,' Daisy said. 'If you'd like?'

'It's about your husband . . .'

Daisy froze. She couldn't help it.

'I understand things were difficult between you?'

She was staring at him, she realized. Not just staring, glaring. Taking a deep breath, Daisy uncurled her fist.

'What about him?' she said.

'According to London, he went absent without leave at Dunkirk having shot one of his own men. They were wondering if you'd seen him lately?'

'No,' Daisy said. 'I haven't.'

'Would you tell me if you had?'

Daisy snorted. 'If I thought there was the slightest chance they'd hang him I'd lead you to him myself. I thought you were here about Lilly.'

'Lilly?' Mr Bennett sounded puzzled.

'She's dead. Things were difficult between us, too.'

Mr Bennett noticed the two champagne glasses. 'I'm sorry,' he said. 'I should have asked. Are you alone?'

'A glass for me. A glass for my sister.'

'I see,' Mr Bennett said, frowning in a way that suggested he didn't.

'What do you actually want?' Daisy demanded. 'And don't tell me you're here to ask if I've seen William, because I'm the last person he'd contact. London might not know that but you certainly do.'

'We want you to do something for your country.'

Daisy laughed.

Reaching into his pocket, Mr Bennett slid a garishly enamelled silver dollar across the table between them. 'Mr Standish says wakey-wakey.'

'About bloody time.'

Reaching into her bag, Daisy produced its twin.

9

Washington DC, same day.

The line between Paris and Washington was crackly – there was an echo, an intermittent delay, and once it cut out altogether. But it was what there was, and Standish was old enough to remember when spycraft relied on cryptic telegrams, letters in invisible ink, and obscure clues snuck into the crosswords of the *Washington Post*.

'She knew about her sister, sir.'

'How did . . . ?'

'Some schmo in Madrid.'

Standish sat back in his leather chair and regarded the Capitol Building through the dust-stained window of his corner office. A temple to freedom built, at least partly, by slaves. He doubted many people noticed the irony.

'What did he say? *Exactly*.'

'A fall. An accident.'

'I said we were to say it was a motor-vehicle crash.'

'It's always a fender bender. Perhaps they thought there'd been too many.'

'That's mine to call.'

'Of course, sir.'

'What did you tell her?'

'It was a homicide. She was to take Lilly's place.'

'You bring up Sir William?'

'Right at the start. I thought: Let's get him out of the way.

That'll make it easier to get her to return to the Channel Islands and his family home.' He paused. 'Only thing . . .'

'What?'

'She's not Lilly, sir.'

'Same father, same mother, same upbringing.'

'Can we trust her?'

Standish considered the question. He didn't trust anyone. It was his job not to trust anyone. But if he had to trust someone it would be one of the Black twins. And this man was right. She wasn't Lilly. Lilly had to be taught to kill.

Daisy had taught herself.

'It's just,' the man on the line said, 'she was drunk. It wasn't yet lunchtime. She met me at the door holding a .38. There was an empty bottle of French champagne and two glasses on the coffee table. She looked like she'd been out on the tiles.'

'Daisy always could inhabit a part.'

'That's what worries me, sir.'

'She'll be fine,' Standish said. 'Besides, we haven't got much choice.'

He shut Daisy's file, and wondered what to say in that afternoon's meeting. Just enough to convince the president he was on top of things. Not enough to start him asking awkward questions.

10

Glasgow, same day

No lock picks, no clues as to the make, no lights . . .

For Christ's sake. Bill O'Hagan wanted to punch something he was so furious. Not least because this safe had no dial.

Instead, a lock plate slid up to uncover a keyhole.

He traced the keyhole with his finger and tried to imagine the size and weight of the key. This safe was smaller than the previous one but still too heavy for one man to lift. Even if he'd had anywhere to take it.

Solitary confinement was designed to break you. Bill knew that. He'd been in solitary before. If anyone had been willing to talk, he'd have pointed out that he was broken already, one way or another. This was a test. It had to be. It was too baroque to be torture.

And if it was a test, then it could be passed. If it could be passed, then his reward would probably be being let out of solitary. Assuming he wasn't simply given another test. He needed to be out to have any chance of escape.

Bill thought hard. If it was a test, the means to pass it must be hidden in his cell. And if it wasn't a test but some kind of mental torture? He still had nothing to lose from looking.

Bill began in the corner he'd been using as a latrine. The flagstones were slimy under his fingertips as he searched, and he found nothing.

Slowly, methodically, he checked the rest of the floor. A nail was the first item he found, in the far corner. It was sharp enough to be new. The next was a panel pin near the door. He found the length of wire last, because it had been left tight against the rear of the safe, along the floor.

Using the nail to put a bend in the wire, he inserted the wire into the keyhole and felt for the first lever; then he set about working out the lock's internal shape.

Bill had no idea how many hours passed before he had it open.

For a moment he just sat there, then he pulled back the door, reached inside and found safety matches. Warders must have been watching, because the moment he struck the first match, the door smashed open and in they rushed.

One warder jerked him to his feet; another gripped his arms to hold him still. It was the third man, the one in the white coat, who slammed a needle into his neck.

11

The Somme, November 1916

In a second Bill was back in a collapsed dug-out at the Somme, knowing he should do something and not knowing what because of the screaming in his ear. It rose and rose, and then, when Bill thought it could get no higher, rose again. It was the sound of his last comrade dying.

'Help me. Help me.'

There was no help. Not here, in the autumn of 1916, with men half mad from endless bombardment, and water rising in the trenches, from rain that never ceased and overflowed earthworks meant to keep it from rising to their waists and sometimes their necks.

'Peter . . .'

'He's dead,' Bill said.

One of Bertie's legs was missing. Bill had tied the stump off with his belt. Bill checked the man's other leg, and the screaming changed register. That leg was broken and crushed by ceiling boards and sodden earth.

The water was rising faster.

In the gaps between Bertie's screams, Bill could hear planks, posts and pit props creaking as they fought to hold the weight. When the last of the roof fell in Bertie and he would die with it.

Bill couldn't move his pal. He wouldn't dig his own way out and leave Bertie to drown; that was wrong. Most of the boy's shoulders were under water now. It would reach his chin in minutes, and drown him soon enough, if the roof didn't cave in first.

'Hush now,' Bill said. 'I'll help.'

Putting his hand over the Bertie's mouth, he drew his bayonet and drove it into Bertie's chest. It took two goes before Bertie's struggles stopped.

12

Paris, Sunday, 23 June 1940

Having accepted France's surrender in the same railway carriage that France had used to accept Germany's surrender twenty-two years earlier, Hitler allowed himself a whirlwind tour of Paris. All he required of the city in advance of his visit was that statues of the generals who'd delivered France's victory over Germany in the Great War be taken down.

The Parisians responded to this in the only way they knew how: by pretending it wasn't happening or they didn't know who he was.

At l'Opéra, the greatest of Garnier's buildings for Napoleon III, the caretaker refused Hitler's tip on the grounds that it was his job to welcome tourists. And when the three Mercedes carrying Hitler's entourage reached Montmartre, the cars had to slow while an elegant woman in a black hat finished crossing the road in front of them. None of them noticed the woman climb into a black Citroën Avant, glance contemptuously towards Hitler's Mercedes, and turn her car's nose for Place du Tertre and the suburbs beyond.

Daisy Renhou drove carefully, wondering what she'd do if she hit a roadblock. She hoped that telling the Nazis she was an American would suffice. If it didn't, she could always tell them she used to party with Hermann Goering, Wallis Simpson and Albert Speer. It might work. After all, it had the advantage of being true.

Luckily, the streets were clear and Daisy drove on.

The sky was a deep summer blue.

The refugees from Belgium and northern France had been and mostly gone, heading south for Spain. Behind them they'd left ample evidence of their misery and a trickle of those too weak to travel faster. Daisy passed discarded carts, horses turned loose, fuel-starved cars, forsaken motorcycles and half a dozen broken three-wheeled vans.

Stopping at a café beyond the city's edge, she noticed a dark-haired child huddled over a bowl of soup in one corner. When the girl saw Daisy notice her, she looked away.

'Where are you heading?' Daisy asked in French.

Bag in hand, the girl was half out of her seat before Daisy stopped her. Putting a hand on the child's shoulder, she pushed gently. 'Sit.' The child's arms were thin, her collarbone sunken inside the neck of a dress that had once been expensive. Now it was simply filthy. She did as told, but Daisy could see she was ready to run.

'Away from here,' the child said.

'Where are you from?' Daisy asked.

'Lille.'

'And before that?'

The girl hesitated.

'It's all right,' Daisy told her. 'You don't have to say.'

She ordered the *plat du jour* for them both, letting the girl eat most of her steak too, and only telling her to slow down once. 'Antwerp,' the girl whispered, when the steak was finished. 'We used to live in Antwerp.'

And before that? Daisy wanted to say. Instead she asked a simpler question. 'Where are your parents?'

'My father was sent to a camp. My mother took me and ran. There was an attack on the road, Stuka bombers. She said hide, so I hid. I should have gone back.'

'No,' Daisy said. 'You shouldn't. You did the right thing.'

She covered the girl's hand with her own for a moment, while the child steadied herself, and removed it before contact became embarrassing. The girl's story was written in the size of her pitiful bundle, the filth on her face, the dirt under her nails. She'd fled towards Paris because she had to go somewhere, and arrived to find it full of the people she was fleeing.

'You speak good French,' Daisy said.

'And Dutch, some English, a little German.'

She sounded proud of her accomplishments. For a second Daisy had a glimpse of the well-brought-up girl she'd probably been. 'What did your father do?' Daisy asked. It was the wrong question. The girl's face closed down.

'Give me a lift,' the girl demanded suddenly.

'Where to?'

'Wherever you're going.'

13

Paris, same day

Coffee would run out soon, and quite possibly food too, but there was enough for now and Daisy intended to be somewhere else before it was gone. Catching the waitress's attention, she ordered two black coffees. The refugee girl was watching. Waiting anxiously for her answer.

'Have you paid for your soup?' Daisy asked.

The girl sat shamefaced.

'No money?'

'I was hungry.'

On the edge of starving, more like, with dark shadows round her eyes and her cheeks hollowed to the bone. It gave her an unnerving, pietà-like beauty. Daisy didn't blame her for ordering food she couldn't pay for.

'What do I call you? It doesn't have to be your real name.'

The girl gave a slight smile. 'Mignon,' she said.

'OK,' Daisy said. 'You're Mignon Black, my niece. We're travelling together.'

'You mean it?'

'I never say things I don't mean. Except to men. That's different. You're allowed to lie to them. They're pigs. It's practically compulsory.'

The girl gaped at her.

In a deserted courtyard outside, Daisy unscrewed the number plates from her Citroën and stole some from a tatty Peugeot baker's van. It had been Daisy's intention to give the girl a lift ever since she spotted her hunched over her bowl. It was important, though, that the girl was the one who asked.

Alone, Daisy was too conspicuous. Much safer for both of them to be travelling together. The girl was eating the last of Daisy's bread when Daisy returned.

'He was a jeweller,' Mignon said. 'He traded diamonds.'

They drank their coffees in silence, and then Daisy told Mignon to wash her face in the café bathroom and do something about her filthy nails, and went to pay their bills. She gave the proprietor an extra fifty francs to wipe his memory. They hadn't been there; no one had seen them.

'You're hiding from the Germans? he asked.

'From my husband.'

Husband. Lover. It made little difference to him. He nodded his understanding. 'You're taking her with you?' He pointed to the door through which Mignon had vanished.

'Yes,' Daisy said. 'I am.'

'She couldn't pay for her food.'

'You knew that?'

'Of course I knew. You think she's the first? They've been coming through for weeks. God knows where they end up.'

'And now it's over.'

His glance was sharp.

'Your government has surrendered,' Daisy said.

He spat, crossly. 'This isn't where it ends,' he said. 'This is where it begins.'

14

France, same day

On a long tree-lined road beyond Alençon, having turned west after Paris to cut through miles of forest on her way to St Malo, Daisy slowed the Citroën and reached behind her, rummaging in her case. Mignon was the deal. The deal to stop the devil getting Daisy's soul. Take a life, save a life. Mignon was the life saved.

Daisy was banking this one in advance.

'Wear this,' she ordered.

Mignon considered the crucifix that Daisy had pulled from her jewellery roll. It looked old and expensive. 'I have one,' she said.

'It doesn't suit you. Take this one.'

'I like mine,' Mignon said. She pushed out her jaw and her face set. Daisy imagined there'd been a time she'd behaved like that. Probably around the same age.

'I'm trying to save your life,' Daisy said.

'What's wrong with mine?'

It's cheap and it's nasty and I don't care who you stole it from but you should probably have remembered to wash their blood off its chain.

'Mine's bigger,' Daisy said.

Mignon took the cross reluctantly, hesitating before fixing it round her neck. She handed her old one over when Daisy held out her hand, and gasped when Daisy threw it out of the window.

'Now,' Daisy said. 'Do you know the Lord's Prayer?'

'No. I don't.'

'Right. Repeat after me. "Our Father, who art in heaven . . ."'

To the Right Honourable Winston Churchill
From Sir Samuel Hoare,
His Majesty's Ambassador to Madrid

Date: Monday, 24 June 1940

I've just been told by Her Highness The Duchess of Windsor that I should consider her and her husband homeless, penniless, possession-less, virtually refugees.

Yesterday, being the duke's 46th birthday, they had a quiet dinner on the veranda of the Ritz in Madrid, in full view of all passing photographers. This afternoon they're changing rooms to one the duchess likes better.

They've fixed drinks with Doña Sol, fascist sister of the Duke of Alba for next week. The week after they intend to dine with Prince Alonzo, one of the duke's cousins and a senior officer in Franco's air force. The last time they met him, Alonzo regaled them with details of the tanks, aeroplanes and troops that his hero, Herr Hitler, has at his disposal.

I have informed the duke and duchess of your suggestion that they return to England as soon as practicable. The duchess expressed her delight and her hope that Fort Belvedere in Windsor Great Park be put at their disposal, 'As I miss it dreadfully.' (Put bluntly, she swings between desperately wanting to be accepted and being furious she isn't.)

For his part, the duke was less amenable. He declares his absolute loyalty to his brother while refusing to return until he's given a job worthy of his status as ex-king, and until he has the new king's assurance Wallis will be received at court. Until then he'll stay where he is.

I fear we're in for a long battle, sir. On more fronts than one.

Monday, 24 June 1940

My dear Fruity,

God, this war is a disaster. I had a letter from Joachim von R (this is in confidence) saying how much he'd respected my judgement when he was ambassador to London and I was king, and how none of this would have happened if I was on the throne. The terrible thing is I suspect he's right. If Britain refuses to negotiate it will be invaded and the Germans will win, as they have won everywhere else.

Joachim reminded me how much my people, the ordinary people, loved me for caring about their lives. How heartbroken they were when I had to abdicate. This whole war has been got up by Bolsheviks and Jews. One just knows it has.

Anyway, we arrived in Spain eventually, after a squabble with some ghastly little clerk at the border. The trip south was horrific. Every peasant in the country has loaded their lives on to horse-drawn carts and fled. Mattresses, bathtubs, buckets. Several thousand of them are camped like gypsies on the Spanish border. Filthy, hungry, disease-ridden. Something must be done, but dear God, I understand why General Franco refuses to let them in.

Now, again in confidence. I have been ordered home! *Ordered.* Obviously, I have no intention of obeying until

Wallis's position at court and my inheritance are settled. Wallis agrees. She sends her love – or would do. She's in her room with a migraine after a trying few days.

Yours sincerely,
Edward

PS I know you had your doubts about Joachim but Wallis assures me it was only ever friendship and I believe her in this, as in everything.

To: Major Edward Metcalfe, MVO, MC

15

Spain, same day

'Carefully . . .'

Wallis's voice was sharp enough to be heard inside. When the duke hurried into the corridor with a letter he'd been writing still in his hand, he found her standing beside the lift, her face aghast.

A Spanish chambermaid had just tried to balance a box of Lalique glass on top of three black Dior jackets Wallis had found draped over a pigskin beauty box.

'This is impossible,' she said furiously.

'There's a war on.' The duke regretted saying the words the moment they were out of his mouth. He watched her face tighten. 'Anything they break we'll buy again,' he said hastily. 'I promise.'

'With what?' Wallis said. 'We're running out of money. Isn't that what you said? Just because I wanted that little leopard brooch with the rubies.'

'Darling . . .'

'Yes. I know. This is neither the time nor the place.'

'Tell me where you want your things and I'll help.'

'They can do it. It's what they're here for. All I want is for them to do it properly. Is that too much to ask?' She stopped to take a closer look at the duke. 'Where's your other cufflink?'

'I don't know,' he said, sounding frustrated. 'It's not in my cufflink box, and I can't find my Reverso.' He shot his cuff to show her a gold Omega. 'I've been wearing this for days.'

'Have you had breakfast?'

'Toast,' he said. 'That's all there was.'

'I had grapefruit.'

'I don't like grapefruit.' The duke scowled. 'I've lost my cufflink, my favourite jacket's dirty and all my shoes need reheeling. How am I expected to dress when London's conscripted my bloody valet?'

'Come inside,' Wallis said. 'We'll find that cufflink . . . Careful,' she said furiously to a boy who'd appeared with a pile of Sèvres plates, piled high as if just removed from a pantry. 'Have you any idea what those are worth? They need to be wrapped,' she added. 'Individually wrapped.'

'Do we really need a full dinner set?' the duke asked, eyeing the tottering pile of plates in the boy's arms.

'Yes,' Wallis said. 'Twenty-four of everything. That's not the kind of set one should break up.'

'My love. We only have two motorcars.'

'That's not my fault.'

16

Bill O'Hagan woke in a clean bed, in a room with flowers in a vase but bars over the window. If it was a prison it wasn't like any he'd been in before. The rattle of a key in the door told him it had been locked. A second later, a man in brogues, red cords and a tweed jacket came into his room.

'You're awake,' he said. 'Good. To business. We need your help.'

'Doing what?' Bill demanded.

'You're an intelligent man. You tell me.'

'Opening safes.'

'Opening safes,' he agreed.

'Why me?'

'Do you know better?' The man sounded interested.

'I'm hardly going to give you names . . .'

'If they're in prison I'm sure they'd jump at the chance to earn time off for good behaviour.'

'The good ones aren't in prison.'

'You were in prison. Well, you were, until I pulled you out.'

'I fell off a wall,' Bill said crossly. 'It's hard to run from the polis with a buggered ankle.'

Having settled himself into an armchair, the man puffed at his pipe as he considered this point. Bill had the feeling he was waiting to see if Bill would fill the silence and seemed gratified when he didn't.

'Right,' he said finally. 'Here's the thing. The Nazis are about to invade the Channel Islands. We started evacuating them, realized we couldn't do it in time and changed our minds. We've taken the children from Jersey and Guernsey, and emptied Alderney altogether. Which is useful, because Alderney's our target. We need you to go there and crack a safe. That's the right word for it, isn't it? Crack?'

'Aye,' Bill said. 'That's the right word.'

Patronizing bastard.

'Wouldn't it be simpler to bring the safe here?' Bill asked.

'If it was there already, then yes. Much simpler. Unfortunately, it isn't. Not yet. Anyway, rule of law has passed to the Island Bailiffs, with instructions to carry on as normal after the invasion. They're not to welcome the Germans; neither are they to resist.'

'*Christ,*' Bill said.

'Indeed. Since the islands can't be defended with any likelihood of success, London has decided there's no point trying.'

That wasn't why Bill was swearing. He'd realized why the safe wasn't yet there. The Nazis would bring it with them. This man wanted him to parachute into enemy territory or be there before they invaded.

'There's a new moon in a week,' the man said. 'That gives us enough time to brief you and train you. You'll take a radio so you can let us know when the job's done. We'll pick you up the moment you tip us the wink.'

He sat back, looking smug.

'Not a chance,' Bill said.

'It's their invasion plans, troop numbers, aircraft details, vectors of attack, landing sites. Vital information.'

'I don't believe you.'

'You don't . . . ?'

'Why would it be there? Why wouldn't it be in Berlin? It

makes no sense. Someone's lied to you. Either that, or you're lying to me.'

'What happened?' the man demanded.

Bill stared at him, thrown.

'A sergeant in the Great War, medals beyond the obvious ones, mentioned in dispatches. How does a man like you become a thief?'

I was born one.

'All property is theft,' Bill said.

'Gods. You're a Bolshevik?'

'They wouldnae have me. I still believe in the redistribution of wealth, though.'

'You're Robin Hood. Is that it? You expect me to believe those you stole from deserved it?'

Bill thought of the big houses, the new cars, the maids and chauffeurs, all the trappings of a happy life and a war spent getting rich while his friends screamed out their last, hanging like fallen scarecrows on the wire of no man's land.

'No,' he said. 'They deserved far worse.'

17

Edinburgh, December 1918

The story was simple enough. On the morning of Friday, 20 December 1918, sixteen-year-old Annie McLean went down with Spanish flu and by that evening was dead, her newborn baby sucking desperately at her cold breast.

Recently returned from the trenches, her first love did the only thing he could think of. He stamped his way through Edinburgh's Old Town to Queen Mary's Wynd, with her child wrapped in a blanket.

Bill had no idea if the bairn was his. He hadn't asked and Annie hadn't said different. The dates of his enlistment and return made it possible, more or less. Edinburgh wasn't a good city to be born poor. Not for him and not for Annie. Now he hated the place. Even its most familiar streets felt wrong. The war had slaughtered his pals and the few who did come back were changed.

Turning into the Wynd, he headed up worn steps into a bitter wind, and tumbled his way through the door of The Traveller.

'Is that for sale?'

'There's a market for bairns?'

'For everything.'

'No,' Bill said firmly. 'It's not.'

Mary was behind the bar, tiredness in her eyes. She didn't seem thrilled to see him. 'You survived,' she said.

'More or less.'

'What are you having, then?'

'I didn't come for the ale.'

'What else would bring a man here?'

'This,' Bill said, pushing the baby across and watching Mary's nose wrinkle at its stink.

'What am I meant to do with that?'

Bill looked at the straining buttons on her dress. She had a new one of her own. He knew 'cos Annie had told him.

'Feed it.'

'Who told you I could?'

'Annie did.'

Mary opened her mouth to say something cutting and Bill shook his head.

'She's dead,' he said. He thrust the child at her. 'Please.' He wasn't above begging.

Maybe it was the tears in his eyes that did it. When she turned away it was to fumble at the buttons of her dress. When she turned back, he was gone.

To Chiefs of Staff – Army, Navy, Air Force
From Generaloberst Wilhelm Keitel,
Chief of the Armed Forces High Command

Date: Tuesday, 25 June 1940
<u>Secret</u>

<u>The Channel Islands</u>

I write at the Führer's instruction.

He has decided to launch his final invasion of England from the Channel Islands, which you will see from your maps is a small archipelago just off the north-west coast of France. As such, he will be invading mainland Britain from British soil.

There are symbolic, strategic, political and propaganda reasons for this.

Although technically British, the islands owe their loyalty direct to the king and not to parliament. The Führer is entirely certain that, having usurped his brother's position only three years ago, the new king will want them defended to the last.

You should expect each island to be heavily fortified and plan accordingly. Capturing them, the first British territory to be taken, will be a huge propaganda coup. As such, he has ordered Leni Riefenstahl to film the invasion for worldwide distribution by our press agencies.

The islands are our stepping stones to the conquest of Britain.

As soon as Field Marshal Goering has delivered him the skies, the Führer will personally command the Reich's victorious attack from Alderney, the island closest to English soil.

18

Scotland, Tuesday, 25 June 1940

Bill looked enough like the man in the photograph to shock him. There the similarity ended. The expression on the face of the man he was meant to impersonate was sneering, his attitude arrogant, smug and entitled.

He was everything Bill despised.

'You're saying . . . not only do you want me to crack a safe under Nazi eyes, you want me to do this while pretending to be Sir William Renhou, a wife-beating fascist who thinks we'd be better off killing Bolsheviks than fighting Hitler?'

'Not pretending,' Colonel Welham said. 'Becoming . . .'

Bill had a name for his visitor now.

'No harder, I'm sure, than playing an out-of-luck Anglo-Irish officer burnt out by Fenians; or a bishop returning from the Congo, both of which I believe you've been, quite successfully.'

For a while Bill had done well in the gentlemen's clubs of London, where the porters prided themselves on knowing every member by heart, and let him in with his dog collar and discreet pectoral cross, because they couldn't admit they might have forgotten him.

'You don't think Renhou's friends might notice?'

'He's lived in Kenya most of his adult life. The only time he went back to Alderney was to bury his father and settle his estate. He stayed six months, talked to nobody and hated every minute of it.'

'His wife then . . .'

'She's in Paris.'

'Earlier,' Bill said, 'I heard a man screaming.'

'A Nazi,' Welham said. 'Someone we've been questioning.'

'What happened to the Geneva Convention?'

'He wasn't a prisoner of war. So it doesn't apply.'

'He's British?'

'There are no British Nazis. You'd do well to remember that.'

'If he wasn't British and he wasn't a prisoner of war, who was he?'

'A courier we kidnapped in Portugal.' Welham said this as if kidnapping foreigners in neutral countries and shipping them to Scotland to be tortured was entirely standard.

'Did you get the information you needed?'

'Not as much as we'd like. Right. Are you in?'

'No,' Bill said. 'I'm not.'

'It's for your country.'

'I've fought one war for this country already. The War to End All Wars. Look how that turned out. I'll take my chances in prison.'

'Wrong answer,' Welham said.

19

Washington DC, Thursday, 27 June 1940

Mr Standish, being a confirmed bachelor from Ohio, would have preferred to be from Boston. Still, it was too late now. Weighing the little camera in the palm of his hand, he turned it over. Lilly Black's camera had been based on this one.

A Latvian subminiature that took tiny rolls of 16-mm film.

Standish had arranged for it to be stolen from a factory in Riga. He was quietly proud of that. Kodak had been contracted to make seventy-five copies, thirty-three of which had been shared between Special Ops in England, Norwegian Intelligence and the Deuxième Bureau in France. He imagined the French models were now in German hands. Quite possibly the Norwegian ones too.

Putting it down, Standish picked up a paper knife and slit the envelope he'd been avoiding, spilling its contents across his desk. This was the point at which he wished he was the kind of man who kept a bottle of bourbon in his drawer.

If he hadn't known the first photograph was taken in Spain, he'd have thought the village square was in Mexico. The second showed the Spanish foreign minister, the third a Nazi officer. The fourth, the Duke of Windsor and Wallis Simpson.

Proof that the ex-king of England had met with his country's enemies. Proof that Franco's man had facilitated it. Not simply proof, evidence. At best the duke was misguided, at worst treasonous.

Should this be shared with London?

Most definitely.

Would it be? Not yet, if Standish had his way.

The second-to-last shot showed the Nazi officer, his face twisting in fury as Lilly stepped to her death. It was the one after that, the one taken by the woman Standish had had shadowing her, he dreaded. Lilly lay broken, eyes open, blood spreading under her head. He made himself stare at it for a long time. He'd been fond of Lilly Black. Her death was his responsibility and he would repay it. He just hoped the death of Lilly's sister wasn't the price.

20

Madrid, same day

Count Ciano hesitated at his end of the telephone line. 'I thought you should know,' he told Wallis Simpson, 'that the British foreign minister, Lord Halifax, has approached Il Duce about Italy brokering peace between Berlin and London.'

'Thank God,' said Wallis. 'About time London showed some sense.'

'Oh, it's not going to happen,' the Italian foreign minister said. 'Churchill's blocked it. He'd rather lose than negotiate. He's threatening to have Halifax replaced for daring to suggest it.'

'I hate them all,' Wallis said.

The crash of a whisky glass against a wall stopped her in her tracks.

'I'd better go,' she said.

'Is everything all right?' Count Ciano's question was light, his voice amused and only slightly accented. 'Wallis . . . ?'

'Someone just dropped something.'

'You can't get the staff.'

It was an old joke of theirs. Ciano was Mussolini's son-in-law, and one of Wallis's early lovers. It didn't feel so much of a joke now. She'd had to abandon her house in Paris, and her villa on the French-Italian border. Her husband had had tears in his eyes as he bade farewell to his terriers. These days, they were making do with one driver, and whatever staff hotels could provide.

'You shouldn't have telephoned me.'

'I know,' Count Ciano said, sounding not the slightest bit

abashed. 'It was obviously inappropriate. What will you tell your husband when he asks who was on the telephone?'

'The truth,' Wallis said tartly.

'What an interesting marriage.'

Wallis scowled at the glittering shards of a whisky tumbler.

'That was Waterford,' she said.

The duke pushed a piece of paper at her, and Wallis recognized the Royal Household letterhead. She skimmed the words, tripping on the arcane language and the palace's habitual obliqueness.

'What does it mean?'

'It means, not content with taking Fort Belvedere from us, having promised it would remain ours, my brother has given it to the army as a training base. They'll ruin it. He knows they will. That's why he did it.'

The duke was close to crying.

'He knows how much I love the place. He knows I rebuilt it, that I had the gardens landscaped. He knows I used my own money. He knows it's where we first met. He's doing it on purpose. Sanctimonious little shit.'

Fort Belvedere was a Gothic Revival castle in Windsor Great Park the duke had been given by his father in the 1920s, and made his own. It was the place he'd been happiest. The duke's younger brother, now king, had written a few months before to say the royal warrant allowing the duke to use it was being withdrawn and the duke's possessions put into storage. At the time George VI said he needed it for himself. He'd said nothing about passing it to the army.

'Come to bed,' Wallis said. Some days that was the only thing that worked where her husband was concerned. She didn't know what she'd do if they ever reached a point where it was no longer enough.

To Eberhard von Stohrer,
Reich Ambassador, Spain
From Joachim von Ribbentrop,
Reichsminister of Foreign Affairs

Date: Thursday, 27 June 1940
Confidential

My dear Eberhard,
A small task, if you would.
By diplomatic bag I am sending a magnum of good
Krug, and a handwritten card to be attached to exactly
seventeen carnations, which you will need to supply
yourself. The card, the carnations and the Krug should
be delivered to the Duke and Duchess of Windsor's hotel.
I'm sorry to ask this of you but the prince and his wife
remain our friends and it is imperative they know it.
(Between ourselves – as men of the world – the
number of carnations represents the times the duchess
and I have enjoyed each other's company. Something of
which the duke remains, and must remain, blissfully
unaware.)

21

Berlin, same day

Sitting back, von Ribbentrop reached into his desk for an ivory card with the Nazi eagle embossed in gold leaf at the top, then stopped, selecting a plain card instead. Removing the top from his fountain pen, he wrote quickly. It would be best if the brief note appeared dashed off between other business: 'With admiration and respect. I trust you will get some rest. You deserve it.'

He signed the note J, and added a single x.

He was in favour of gestures that were both elegant and deniable.

22

Washington DC, Friday, 28 June 1940

'Darling. You must. It's for the best . . .'

That was Wallis Simpson. She called him darling a lot.

Reaching for his Chesterfields, Standish dragged a glass ashtray closer and lit the first of what he feared would be too many cigarettes. It was just past midnight and Washington DC was a parade of darkness and neon beyond his window. The tape was three years old, recorded in the final weeks before Edward renounced his throne.

'I'd rather die than live without you.' That was Edward, obviously. 'They can't make me give you up. I'm king . . .'

Such a brat, Standish thought.

'No,' Wallis said. 'You mustn't abdicate. You can't. It would be wrong. You must renounce your plans for us to marry. Tell the archbishop you've listened to reason. I won't let you do this.'

Her words could be read two ways. Selfless, or utterly self-ish. Standish knew which his money was on.

'It's my decision,' the king said.

'Don't do this just for me, darling.'

'I'm not. I'm doing it for us.'

You could hear Wallis gather her thoughts. At least you could if you'd listened to the tape as often as Standish had.

'Darling. You mustn't give up the throne for me. It's dear of you. Incredibly dear but it's too much. You were born to be king. We'll remain lovers. Isn't that what we've always been?'

'I don't want to be king.'

This was where stubbornness crept into his voice. The point at which Wallis Simpson lost, although she hadn't realized it yet. The man meant it. At least, he did in that moment. Trapped in Buckingham Palace, with Wallis having retreated first to Fort Belvedere, then to the south of France to escape his family's hatred, he no longer wanted his throne.

'Darling. You don't mean that.'

'Of course I do. They've all turned against me. My mother's being beastly. You know what she's like. Now she's worse. My brother's furious. Let's see how he likes it when he's the one who has to do all the work.'

'You'll consider what I've said?' Wallis asked.

'There's nothing to consider. If the archbishop won't marry us then I refuse to remain king. My father said I'd make a bloody hash of it and he was right.'

To All Ministers
From War Cabinet, London

Date: Friday, 28 June 1940
<u>Top Secret</u>

We will fight them to the last. We will fight them as no country has fought them before. This is our darkest hour and the invasion is upon us.

Three days ago, we took the decision to withdraw British troops from the Channel Islands and cancel the evacuation of Guernsey and Jersey.

In an effort to preserve morale we decided against announcing this. News now reaches us that Nazi bombers are attacking the islands. We can be certain the Germans will launch a ground assault next.

An invasion of the British mainland will undoubtedly follow.

We have issued orders that the attack on the Channel Islands is not to be announced before we have prepared the ground. The BBC will begin by announcing the islands have been declared open; and that rather than risk civilian losses, our forces have been withdrawn.

Only after this will we announce they have been attacked.

23

Channel Islands, same day

A Guernsey steamer pushed smoke at the heavens as a bomber flew overhead. The setting was so perfect that the four-man crew of the Dornier Do 17 might have been looking at a picture postcard. The blue of the English Channel reminded its pilot of home, although the waters of the Baltic were paler.

Below him was a French boat.

He passed close enough to see a fisherman, a woman with a black hat, and a girl who huddled with her arms wrapped round her head. The woman seemed to be trying to reassure her. Then his target was ahead.

Fishermen stopped folding nets; carts skewed across the quay as horses shied. And as a back line began dropping from the Dornier's bomb bay, the crowd by the bus station realized what was happening and ran.

Flipping the catch on his trigger, the plane's gunner saw the line of military trucks he'd been told to look for and opened fire. High above him, Stukas took their cue and dived, wing sirens screaming like banshees. The harbour café was machine-gunned, the port's telephone box blown to pieces. Fifty of the tomato trucks misidentified as troop carriers went up in flames.

Unarmed, unable to defend itself, Guernsey saw its capital destroyed.

At nine o'clock that night, too late to save those killed or injured, the BBC announced the islands' demilitarization.

The German raid was not revealed until later.

'You're safe,' Daisy promised. 'You're safe.'

Mignon sat huddled in the bottom of the fishing boat Daisy had hired in St Malo, sobbing her heart out. Liquid puddled between her feet from where she'd wet herself. The child was crying.

'You said it was over,' she sobbed.

'In France,' said Daisy, staring at the smoke rising from St Peter Port. 'This isn't France. These are the Channel Islands.'

The fisherman's price for not turning back was her pearls, which were probably worth more than his damn boat. They were the last of the jewellery given to her by her husband. She wasn't upset to see them go.

Thousands of gannets clung to cliffs stained white with guano. Their noise was incredible, even from a distance.

'So many,' Mignon said.

'The islanders used to eat them,' Daisy said. 'When times were harder.' She nodded a few minutes later to a squat fort joined to Alderney by a causeway. 'Clonque,' she said. 'And that's Tourgis.' She pointed to a bigger fort inland. 'Both built a hundred years ago to keep Napoleon III at bay.'

She was talking to take Mignon's mind off what was happening behind them. It seemed to be working, too. The girl was leaning out of the boat, watching Alderney's shoreline, and occasionally glancing at the slopes beyond.

'It's not very big,' she said.

Daisy laughed. 'I have friends in Africa whose farms are larger.'

Mignon managed a smile. A breakwater lay ahead of them, constructed at the same time as the forts. A hamlet of six or seven houses clustered round its inner harbour.

'It looks deserted,' Mignon said.

Daisy peered. The girl was right.

'Everyone fled,' the fisherman said flatly. 'They locked their houses, shot their dogs, turned out their cows and ran away . . . It was the talk of St Malo,' he added for Daisy's benefit, seeing her scowl.

'You didn't tell me.'

'You didn't ask.'

'Drop us over there,' Daisy said. 'We'll walk round.'

Mignon took in a sandy bay, another Victorian fortress beyond, a stone hut at the start of a rough track, and the gorse blocking the mouth of a quarry, obviously abandoned years before.

'You're sure this is the right place?'

'Absolutely,' Daisy said. She indicated an islet just offshore, with a fortified house dug into its side. The house was dark, squat and heavy set, with walls of black granite and a single turret at one end.

'See that? That's home.'

24

Scotland, same day

Two guards bundled Bill along the walkway of Bridewell, otherwise known as Duke Street Prison, Glasgow. The walkway was empty apart from them. The cell doors were steel lined and thick, the air thicker still. A women's prison Bridewell might have become, but it was here the famous gallows were kept.

And it was here they hanged men.

Bill wondered if anyone had heard him arrive. Seconds later, when banging began from every cell – inmates hammering metal mugs against their doors to acknowledge the condemned – he had his answer.

'Come on then,' one of the guards said. 'Let's get this done.' They pushed Bill ahead of them as he waited for a kick that never came.

'In here . . .'

A door slammed behind him and he found himself in a cell. Colonel Welham stood by the window. He was holding an open file that he examined with grim satisfaction. 'That big house you robbed not ten miles from here? The old man you hit died. That makes it murder.'

'He was fifty,' Bill said. 'Fifty-five at most. I barely touched him.'

'No wonder you were trying to flee the country.'

'You can't do this.'

'Of course I can.' Welham mimed a judge putting on the

black cap. Then he reached into his leather briefcase to extract a sheet of paper. 'You had your chance to help your country. You refused. We hang traitors in this country.'

You'll either die rich or you'll hang.

Uncle Roy said that when Bill was nine. At fifteen he'd thrown Bill to the polis to buy his own freedom. Everything had been leading to this point, even then.

Bill didn't even blame him.

25

Edinburgh, January 1916

'I know you're in there.' The policeman held an oil lamp in one hand and a truncheon in the other. 'I said . . .'

Pushing himself deeper into the shadows, Bill tried not to breathe. Opposite him, his cousin Pat did the same. Uncle Roy had ducked behind the counter. Safely out of sight of the polis. His glare said *don't speak*.

Bill had turned fifteen and could jemmy a sash as easily as Pat. He wasn't as good at dipping pockets, but he was ace at picking locks, even fancy ones. Tonight's had been to a posh chemist's on Dundas Street.

'He's gone,' the policeman said.

'No,' another said. 'He's here.'

That's when Bill discovered there were two of them.

Williams & Sons catered to New Town ladies and their rich husbands. Morphine for tiredness. Tonic for the nerves. Pills for male vitality. Opium for stomach upsets. Laudanum for women's business. There were silver-handled hairbrushes, ivory shoehorns, badger-fur shaving brushes. It was the drugs Uncle Roy wanted, though. Drugs and poisons. There was a ready market for those.

'It's empty.'

'I tell you it's not.'

Uncle Roy had been out of prison a month. The judge wouldn't be any kinder this time. Not to Uncle Roy. Not to any of them. There was a war on. The Kaiser was trampling little countries all over Europe. Men were dying in the trenches. Uncle Roy should have been among them. He caught Bill's gaze in the half-darkness and jerked his chin towards the door.

Hop it, his gesture said. 'Take the wallopers with you.'

The justice of the peace was in his seventies. A sour-faced man who stared at Bill through wire-framed glasses. 'O'Hagan,' he said. 'That sounds like a Fenian name to me. What happened to your face?'

'I fell, sir.'

Bill knew enough not to say he'd had the shit kicked out of him by the polis for making them chase him halfway across the New Town.

'How old are you, O'Hagan?'

'Fourteen,' Bill lied, hoping for sympathy.

'Eighteen, sir,' the policeman said loudly. 'I know him.'

'Why haven't you been conscripted?'

Bill could feel the trap closing in.

'Too young, sir.'

'Sergeant White doesn't think so.'

'He's got me muddled with someone else.'

'There's a war on,' the old man said. 'Brave boys dying. Brave boys who need the medicines you tried to steal. This is a serious crime. I'm minded to refer it to a court able to hand down the severity of sentence a crime like this deserves.'

'Five years,' the sergeant muttered. 'Ten.'

'Of course,' the magistrate said. 'Were you to decide . . .'

'The sergeant will walk me down to the recruiting office?'

The old man crumpled the charge sheet and dropped it into a basket beside his desk. 'I'm sure he will.'

26

Alderney, Friday, 28 June 1940

'Wait here,' Daisy told Mignon.

Heading for the hut at the slope, where her husband kept his car, she removed a key from above its lintel and vanished inside, reappearing a few seconds later with a bigger key. Mignon was trembling.

'There's someone on that slope,' she said. 'Watching us.'

Daisy scanned Aldoy Head, seeing only gorse, seagulls and a thorn-covered ruin. No sign of an intruder. Although that didn't mean anything. There were a thousand places to hide on Alderney. She'd run every zigzag and path on the island in the six months her husband stayed here when his father died.

'You're imagining it,' she said firmly.

Removing her shoes and then her stockings, Daisy put both in her case, which she lifted above her head before turning to the causeway. Typically, the tide was in and they were going to have to wade.

'That's Renhou?' Mignon said.

'The *hou* comes from *holm*, Norse for a small island. Technically, it's an islet. Now, follow me.' The water was warmer than Daisy expected.

'How deep is it?' Mignon asked.

'Keep to the middle and it won't rise above your knees. Step off and it's over your head.'

'Isn't there a boat?'

'Yes. Over there.'

It was tied to a far jetty, and from the way it listed had taken in water. They were halfway across when Daisy heard a splash. Turning, she saw Mignon surfacing, wet through, her hair slicked to her face and close to crying.

'*My things*,' Mignon said.

'Where are they?'

The child shrugged miserably.

'I suggest you find them if you want them.'

The scowl suited Mignon better than tears. She ducked under, came back up for a breath and disappeared again. She found her case eventually, its cardboard misshapen and bulging in the wrong places.

'It'll dry,' Daisy promised. 'If it doesn't, I'll find you another.'

'It's what's inside that matters.'

'Then you're fine,' Daisy said. 'Aren't you?'

The word *Renhou* could be used to describe the house, the islet or the family. In Daisy's opinion, its multiple use suggested life on Alderney had been simpler at one time. Either that, or her late husband's family had always lacked imagination.

From Comptroller of the Royal Household
To Winston Churchill, Prime Minister of the United Kingdom

Date: Friday, 28 June 1940
<u>Confidential</u>

His Majesty has had sight of a communiqué from your office about his brother, His Royal Highness The Duke of Windsor, regarding flying boats being sent from RAF Coastal Command to Lisbon to facilitate the return of the duke and his wife. The fifth line of this communiqué refers to 'Their Royal Highnesses'.

This is, as I'm sure you understand, a severe breach of protocol and I am instructed to ensure that this mistake does not reoccur. At His Majesty's orders, I remind your office that the correct form of address for His Majesty's brother and his wife is 'His Royal Highness The Duke of Windsor and Her Highness The Duchess'. Wallis Simpson (as was) does not have royal standing.

27

Glasgow, same day

The cell for the condemned in Bridewell had a barred window, set high enough to stop prisoners beating the public executioner and hanging themselves before due time. Its floor was paved with slabs big as gravestones, and its walls glazed with the misery of those who'd spent their last nights there.

'What about food?' Bill demanded.

'You won't need it where you're going.' The guard slammed the flap shut and all was silence.

Bill hadn't expected to live this long, if he was honest.

He'd watched his pals die in the mud, one after another, and every day since had felt undeserved. In the years after the war, he'd cheated, lied and stolen from bankers, stockbrokers and profiteers when what he really wanted to do was hang the bloody lot of them for what they'd done to his friends.

In the years after that, he became less choosy about whom he stole from, although Uncle Pat's slap stayed with him and he never again stole from his own. Sometimes life seemed a circle. Endlessly coming back to where it began.

And now it was going to end here too.

He could remember his first visit to Glasgow. That had also been on a Friday. Morning rather than night though. He'd come for the riot everyone knew was waiting to happen. Thousands like him did. Eighty-one days after the end of the Great War. The wind had been bitter, but not bitter enough to chill the fury of the crowd.

28

'Run,' the boy next to Bill said.

Bill shook his head and fixed his feet. Ahead of him a double row of City of Glasgow police had their truncheons drawn and faces set.

'They're going to charge,' the boy said.

'Aye,' said Bill. 'I know.'

Priests were already denouncing Bolsheviks from the pulpit, and headlines screamed 'REVOLUTION' . . . Rumour said English tanks would be here by evening. And Glasgow's George Square was full of strikers demanding an end to shite wages, worsening work conditions and a fifty-seven-hour week.

'You go,' Bill said. The boy did.

Bill chose his target carefully, punching for a policeman's throat and twisting the truncheon from his grip. He used the truncheon, hard and fast, on the polis directly behind. Many of those he fought beside had returned from the trenches. And after you'd faced charging Huns . . . well, polis uniforms, and truncheons beaten into the palm of calloused hands in unison, no longer impressed them.

The wall of blue discovered that when the crowd drove them back, and the streets around George Square filled with running battles.

Bill found the boy a few minutes later, unconscious and propped up by a wall. A docker jerked his thumb towards the public gardens. 'There's a nursing station. Lassies from old field hospitals . . .'

So that was where Bill took him.

A dark-haired girl glanced up and scowled. She was folding crêpe bandages, which struck Bill as the most pointless pastime he could imagine.

'This boy's injured.'

She rolled her eyes at the stupidity of his statement and pushed back her chair. 'Carry him in then.' Her words were abrupt. Her accent foreign.

'Your brother?' she asked.

'Some kid.'

She stared at him, reassessing.

Bill waited while she lifted the boy's eyelids and examined his pupils, took his pulse and prodded a lump on his skull.

'Not broken.'

'That is.' Bill indicated his nose.

Gripping it, she wrenched it back into place, ignoring grating cartilage and the boy's abrupt cry.

'He's awake,' Bill said.

'He is now.'

'Where did you learn that?'

'Vienna. Riots everywhere these days.'

Her name was Miriam, and she was Jewish, an anarchist and a volunteer at the impromptu hospital set up by the dockers' union. Until three months before she'd been nursing soldiers on the other side.

They lived together for the next seven years.

To Lord Halifax,
Secretary of State for Foreign Affairs
From Sir Samuel Hoare,
His Majesty's Ambassador to Madrid

Date: Friday, 28 June 1940
<u>Top Secret</u>

We have discovered that Admiral Wilhelm Canaris, head of Abwehr/German Intelligence, is to meet the Spanish caudillo Francisco Franco within the next week to ask for Spanish backing for a German invasion of Gibraltar. This meeting has been brokered by Eberhard von Stohrer, Berlin's ambassador to Madrid, on Herr Hitler's direct orders. If Gibraltar is taken, I fully expect Germany to give it to Spain, and Spain to enter the war on Germany's side.

It thus becomes imperative that the Duke of Windsor be persuaded to leave Spain as swiftly as possible. With this in mind, the Palace needs to break the current impasse between the king and his brother that is preventing His Royal Highness's relocation. The implications of the duke falling into enemy hands are horrific.

29

Glasgow, same day

A knock at his cell door woke Bill from dreams of Miriam.

A young priest peered in nervously. 'Am I disturbing you?' he said. The man wore a clean dog collar and carried a shiny-looking bible. When he glanced round the cell, Bill had a feeling he was trying not to shudder.

'Fuck off,' Bill said tiredly.

He blinked at Bill. 'You want me to go away?'

'Oh, for fuck's sake. Of course I want . . .'

'Before I do could you tell me if you're Catholic or Protestant? The governor doesn't know and your forms don't say.'

'I have forms?'

'Oh yes,' he said. 'You can't hang someone without paperwork.'

The young man seemed entirely serious – touchingly unaware that this might not have been an appropriate thing to say.

'In you come,' Bill said.

'If you're sure.'

'Do it,' Bill said, voice harder. 'Before I change my mind.'

The young man tried to work out where to sit, and when Bill shifted up on the bed, sat so tentatively that Bill stood with a sigh and settled himself on the flagstones, his back to the wall and his knees under his chin.

'Catholic or Protestant?'

'Neither,' Bill said. 'I'm an atheist.'

'Oh . . .' The priest sounded shocked. 'It's just, it's

traditional to have a priest. Some men like to talk, you know. It's meant to help. So, if you want to confess . . .'

'To what?' Bill demanded. 'I have as many sins as the next man. But none of them put me here.'

'My son . . .'

The priest had the grace to blush when Bill glared. He was in his late twenties at most, possibly younger.

'I didn't do it,' Bill said.

'The first step to absolution is repentance. The first step to repentance is an acceptance of your sins.'

'Of which, as I said, there are many. However, they have fuck all to do with why I'm here.'

'Would you like me to comfort your family afterwards?'

'I don't have one,' Bill said. 'I had a child once who might have been mine, and another who definitely was. I gave the first away, and her mother took the second when she left.'

'How old would that child be now?'

Bill did the sums in his head. 'Fourteen? Fifteen?'

The prison clock struck and Bill counted its single chime. They'd reached the wrong side of midnight. He wasn't hanging tomorrow. He was hanging today. Maybe, if the priest had been someone else, they could have talked and time would have passed that way. Only Bill had nothing he wanted to say, and the young priest wasn't practised enough to draw out confidences. Bill was on the point of sending him away when he had a better idea.

'Did you bring playing cards?'

'No,' the priest said. 'But I'll get some.'

His hammering brought a guard who returned five minutes later with a pack that turned out to be battered and greasy but also complete.

'Right,' Bill said. 'I'm going to teach you to cheat.'

*

Bill taught the priest how to mark, memorize and palm cards. How to shuffle a deck without really shuffling, so that the aces remained where you wanted them. All of which the young man learned slowly but doggedly. He seemed to be enjoying himself.

For a while, until his face had become known, Bill had made a decent living playing poker on the transatlantic liners. And Bill shuffled the deck with a lazy ease he'd learned while being someone else.

'You're better at this than I expected,' he said eventually.

Between them, they killed the dead hours between darkness and dawn.

30

Alderney, Saturday, 29 June 1940

It was morning, early enough to still be dark, and Daisy worked by the light of a hurricane lamp, not wanting to use the electric in case using it started the generator and the noise woke Mignon.

Using a chisel, she cracked the handle from a Sabatier, tossed its broken bits into the kitchen bin, and ground the blade to a length she liked. Then she headed back to her room, slipped on a black singlet, stepped into gym shorts, pulled on navy plimsoles and tucked up her hair, pulling a cap low over her eyes.

Smear dirt on her limbs, and she'd be invisible in the nautical dawn: the second of those liminal periods before sunrise, when night shifts from astronomical, through nautical, to civil dawn, which was what people whose lives didn't depend on the first two thought of as dawn.

Sprinting across the causeway, she hurled herself up the path to Aldoy Head, stopping at the top to check her pulse. It was steady and her breathing regular. So, either she was fitter than she thought or she should have run faster.

Dropping to a crouch, she rubbed the dirt into her arms and legs, put a line of it across her face and checked her hair was still inside her cap. In the distance St Anne's stood in darkness. Perhaps the island really was as deserted as the St Malo fisherman said.

At Fort Tourgis she stopped her run.

Death was in the air. She knew its smell well enough.

Three Alsatians, cleanly shot, left in the corner of a field behind the fort. She examined them by the light of her Ronson, lighting a cigarette to help mask their smell. The brass from their shooting lay on the grass. Small-calibre, civilian-issue, British-made.

All three were emaciated. And apart from their single, front-on gunshot wounds, there was no signs of mistreatment. She was looking at mercy killings. If she and Mignon really were the only people on Alderney, then someone had come from another island to put the abandoned pets out of their misery.

'You're back.'

'I'm back,' Daisy agreed.

'You locked me in,' Mignon said.

'And put the key through the front door so you could let me in when I got back,' Daisy said. 'I went for a run. I needed the exercise.'

Taking the key from Mignon, Daisy locked the house behind her.

'I need a bath.'

'The water's freezing.'

'Freezing is fine,' Daisy said.

31

Glasgow, same day

'William Edward O'Hagan?'

Bill looked for Welham but the colonel wasn't there. In his place a bulldog-faced man in a shiny suit was flanked by two warders.

'Who are you?' Bill demanded.

'I asked you your name.'

'And I asked you yours.' The man's glare said he had little time for murderers or traitors and he'd be glad when this was done. Bill held his stare until the man turned away.

'This is where we say goodbye,' Bill told the priest firmly.

'I should come with you.'

'No point,' Bill said. 'I've taught you all I can.'

The two warders walked Bill into a white-walled room, with the governor following behind. A simple gallows had white lines below it marking the trapdoor. A small man beside the scaffold eyed Bill with a hangman's eye. He adjusted the rope and widened its noose a little.

The warders positioned themselves either side of Bill in case he struggled or tried to make a run for it. They indicated the painted square and Bill began walking, each step harder and slower than the one before. He was shocked to realize his whole body was shaking. His throat was so dry he could barely speak.

'Any point saying I've changed my mind?'

The governor sounded exasperated. 'You want the priest after all?'

'No. I'll go.'

'You'll go where?'

'Tell the colonel—'

'Enough.' The governor nodded to a warder, who yanked Bill's hands behind his back, fixing a strap round his wrists. His plea was swallowed by a hood. The world became dust and darkness and Bill stumbled as they manhandled him into position. Then he felt the warders release his arms, and, before his knees could give way, they stepped back, the trapdoor opened beneath him, and he felt himself fall . . .

1940 Executions in the City and County of Glasgow					
Name and Surname	When and Where Died	Sex	Age	Name, Surname and Rank or Business of Father	Cause of Death
———				———	———
Profession and whether Single, Married or Divorced				Maiden Name of Mother	By Whom Certified
William Edward O'Hagan	1940 June Twenty-Ninth 8 a.m. Bridewell Prison, City and County of Glasgow	M	41		Hanging
———				———	———
Thief Divorced (Jewish woman. Foreign.)				Mary O'Hagan	James Ferguson, prison doctor

To War Cabinet, London
From Winston Churchill

Date: Saturday, 29 June 1940
<u>Strictest Confidence</u>

This country is losing merchant ships faster than it can stand. Sixty-one vessels, comprising 313,000 gross tons, in the last month alone. Add to this the loss of battleships, destroyers and frigates sunk protecting our merchant marine and we must accept we cannot stand the losses much longer.

The German U-boat campaign has depleted our food reserves and brought some in this country close to starvation. Without food we cannot muster an army against the forthcoming invasion. I know there are mutterings among MPs that we should accept Berlin's offer to negotiate. We have held out, these people say. We have shown Berlin who we are. Now we must compromise.

I need from each of you a clear statement of where you stand.

Should the weight of intelligent, informed opinion be that negotiate with Herr Hitler we must, then I will stand down as prime minister, but I will not stand in the way. My view is that we must fight to the end. This is His Majesty The King's view too.

32

Glasgow, same day

'You're a fool.'

Welham dragged the hood from Bill's head, leaving him staring up at the open trapdoor above. It was indeed a long drop. The shock of it had slammed his knees into his body and knocked the air from his lungs. He heard the click of a revolver hammer and felt the touch of its muzzle to his temple.

'No one would hear,' Welham said. 'No one would care.'

He let Bill consider the second of those.

'You're ours now, William. Understand?'

Bill nodded.

'Good. You'll spend today having a medical, getting a haircut, visiting a tailor to have clothes made. Tomorrow we'll do photographs for your new passport, etc. The day after you're on your way.'

'Where?' Bill managed to croak.

'Arisaig.'

'Never heard of it,' Bill said.

'I should hope not.'

Holstering his revolver, Welham undid the strap fixing Bill's wrists. 'RAF Section 14, the Naval Research Bureau, the Ministry of Supply, Secondment Decision.'

Bill was bemused.

'The Special Operations Executive.'

'The name means nothing to me.'

To Joachim von Ribbentrop,
Reichsminister of Foreign Affairs
From Colonel Juan Beigbeder

Date: Sunday, 30 June 1940
<u>Top Secret</u>

Spanish intelligence has identified the woman who
committed suicide as American intelligence operative Lilly
Black. Masquerading as Gretchen Schmidt, a Swiss-
German journalist, she was travelling with a fake Swiss
passport. A sniper rifle was retrieved from a roof
overlooking the square and we believe her mission was to
assassinate the duke.

To Colonel Juan Beigbeder
From Joachim von Ribbentrop,
Reichsminister of Foreign Affairs

Date: Sunday, 30 June 1940
<u>Top Secret</u>

Please establish who identified Lilly Black's body, and under what name it was identified. Our files show that Black's father ran the Shanghai desk of the US Office of Information in the 1920s when Wallis Simpson was flitting between lovers in that city and perfecting her famous 'Shanghai squeeze'.

(By contrast, her sister Daisy, the self-styled 'black' sheep of the family, married a friend of UK fascist Sir Oswald Mosley, left him and moved to Paris as the mistress of a French gangster. Her current whereabouts are unknown.)

To Joachim von Ribbentrop,
Reichsminister of Foreign Affairs
From Colonel Juan Beigbeder

Date: Sunday, 30 June 1940
<u>Top Secret</u>

'Shanghai squeeze'? We really must have that drink sometime!

33

Arisaig, Monday, 1 July 1940

A wiry-looking officer in a Black Watch kilt waited on the platform.

'Call me Angus,' he told Bill, offering his hand.

'Where am I?' Bill asked. 'Or is that a secret?'

Angus pointed at a big house in the distance. 'Arisaig,' he said. 'You're one of ours now. We're not fussy. We employ murderers and thieves, arsonists and anarchists, forgers and fakes.'

'Anarchists?'

'The older ones are good at bomb-making. The young ones are happy to hate the Nazis more than they hate us. We're not picky . . .' Angus caught himself. 'Actually, we're very picky. We're just not fussy about whom we pick. Right, you'd better fetch your baggage.'

'I don't have any.'

'Excellent,' Angus said. 'That's the spirit.' Pulling an envelope from his pocket, he shook out a signet ring engraved with a wild man rising from the waves. 'This is yours. You wear it at all times.'

Bill slipped it on to his little finger.

'Good,' Angus said. 'Let's get you started.'

'Lesson one,' Angus said, leading Bill down to the gardens . . .

'This is Lieutenant Fairbairn. He will instruct you in silent killing. That is, with your hands or a knife should you lose your sidearm.'

'Which you shouldn't,' Fairbairn said. 'Ever. It's also for when firearms might raise an alarm.' The man was wiry, wizened. Too old to be a lieutenant. Too old to be in the army at all. Scars covered his wrists, his fingers, his thumbs, the bits of his forearms that were visible.

'Shanghai,' Fairbairn said. 'Riot squad. Lost track of the number of knife fights I've had. Now, pay attention. Chivalry is irrelevant. The Queensberry rules don't apply. Prisoners are better dead. Understood?'

Bill nodded.

'Good.' Fairbairn told Angus. 'I'll take it from here. Off you go.'

Fairbairn walked Bill to the loch edge, spinning round to sweep Bill's feet from under him the moment Angus was out of sight. He raised his boot to stamp on Bill's throat. 'You're dead,' he said.

Bill picked himself up from the shallows, his uniform sodden, his elbow bleeding from where he'd crashed into the rocks on his way down. Fairbairn's gaze was sourly amused. 'I suggest you concentrate,' he said.

Holding up his hand, the fingers together, Fairbairn indicated the edge from little fingertip to wrist joint. 'A hard strike with your hand held like this will kill. All strikes should be hard. Hard, fast, unexpected.'

He struck at Bill's throat and, as Bill blocked, stabbed for Bill's kidneys with his other hand. Bill dropped. 'Get up,' Fairbairn ordered.

Bill climbed to his feet.

'Always get up. Get up fast. Do everything fast. Pray your enemy isn't faster . . . Right. Points to strike, in order. Back of the neck, either side of spine, from the bridge of nose to the base of throat, either side of head and throat, from base of throat to temple, upper arm, upper forearm, kidneys.'

He pointed at a scarecrow standing in a stony field.

'Attack that,' he ordered.

Bill did. He attacked in the order given. It was more solid than he'd expected. A canvas dummy filled with sand.

'Both hands,' Fairbairn ordered.

Bill used both.

'I didn't tell you to stop.'

Bill kept going, feeling his hands numb and his muscles knot.

'Repetition,' Fairbairn said. 'It's how you learn . . . Right. Now, grab my wrist.'

Bill did and shrank back as Lieutenant Fairbairn's knee rose for his balls, and his fingers went for Bill's eyes, both stopping just in time.

'Don't waste time on releases. Attack. The purpose of freeing yourself is to attack. Make the movement that frees you violent. Preferably fatal.'

He tossed Bill a knife. 'Describe it,' he ordered.

'Sharp point, double-edged, razor sharp either side.'

'Why?'

'To stop someone grabbing it.'

'Good,' Fairbairn said. 'You'd be surprised how many recruits don't understand that. Now, switch it from hand to hand, while using your disengaged hand to feint and parry. The abdomen is your primary target, so slash for the face, wrist or forearms, then go for the gut. Don't let the Hun see it coming.'

Bill nodded.

'Now, stab your friend over there.'

Bill did, slashing and jabbing the dummy until sand bled from canvas. When Fairbairn called, Bill turned and only just avoided a short length of tarred rope spinning towards his face.

'That's a knife,' Fairbairn said. 'Attack me.'

Bill tried to slash at Fairbairn's brutally scarred arms, while dodging the blows Fairbairn aimed at his neck and throat and gut. By the end Bill's chest was heaving, and he found it hard to see for the sweat in his eyes, but he was landing blows.

'No idea what your job is,' Fairbairn said. 'Don't want to know. But it must be important to put you at the top of my list. If I don't see you before you go, good luck.'

His handshake was as firm as Bill expected. Bill felt bruised, exhausted and slightly shaken. As he watched Fairbairn walk away without looking back, he realized the older man felt none of those things.

34

Spain, same day

The second of the meetings between the Duke of Windsor and Colonel Beigbeder, Franco's foreign minister, was a quiet one, taking place on the terrace of Beigbeder's dilapidated palace two hundred miles from Madrid. The most important person on the terrace, at least in his own mind, was the duke, who exhibited all the languid boredom that Beigbeder expected from an English aristocrat.

As well as the duke, Wallis Simpson and Beigbeder, the meeting included a first secretary from the German embassy. This man hadn't introduced himself and the Spaniard had led the duke and duchess to believe he was a junior official on his own staff. The German had orders to say nothing and simply observe.

This he did, with the hunger of a hawk.

As high commissioner for Spanish North Africa, Beigbeder was the man who had brought fifty thousand Moorish troops to support General Franco's revolt against Madrid. A known Anglophile, with a taste for English women, he was pragmatic enough to have offered his services as go-between for Berlin and the duke.

It was the German's job to decide if the duke could be turned. If he could, good. If not, Berlin would make other arrangements to ensure his compliance.

Wallis Simpson was holding court.

Beigbeder insisted she'd be the one to make the decision.

The German disagreed. You only had to look at her husband's sullen mouth to know this was a man who liked to make up his own mind. However, both he and Beigbeder knew it didn't matter which of the Windsors made the decision so long as it was made.

'I'm told London insists on your return?' Beigbeder said lightly.

Wallis ignored a warning glance from her husband. 'He's already told them he won't go. Not until—'

'There are certain matters of protocol,' the duke said abruptly. 'In addition to financial matters, which are not for discussion.'

Beigbeder felt that comment was aimed at the duchess.

From the set of her mouth she thought so too.

'They tried to assassinate us,' she said fiercely. 'A month ago. On the road out of Paris. Do you know, the British Mission in Paris told my husband he was "no longer needed"? They suggested we head to La Croë, say goodbye to the servants and shutter our house until the war is over.'

'That was earlier,' the duke said. 'And there's absolutely no suggestion it was them.'

'Who else would it be?' Wallis demanded.

'Them . . . ?' Beigbeder asked.

'London. The English. His bloody family.'

35

Outskirts of Paris, late May 1940

Wallis scowled at the refugees blocking the road in front of their Buick, then scowled at her husband, who had his head in his hands. 'You can't still be hungover,' she said.

The duke thought back to the previous night's drinks with Baron di Vituso while Wallis was overseeing the packing, and Fruity Metcalfe was *still* sulking because the duke had asked him, months before, to deliver Wallis's terriers to the château at Le Croë to keep them safe until the war was over.

Fruity Metcalfe was his aide-de-camp and meant to be his friend. Some friend. Anyway, it was Raffaele, Baron di Vituso's fault for turning up unannounced like that. And Fruity's for letting him in.

God, the Italian ambassador could drink.

'Strange times,' Vituso had said, letting himself into the duke's study. 'Thought you might like company.'

'Fruity's sulking,' the duke told him. 'Wallis wants to take two full sets of china, all her summer clothes and her hairdresser. I'm hiding in here because I can't stand another argument with either of them.'

'You're leaving?'

'I can hardly stay.'

The German army had swept round the gun encampments of the Maginot Line – as the duke had said they would, before having his certainty thrown back in his face by the Head of the

British Mission in Paris, who had done nothing but sideline him, patronize Wallis and try to keep him away from official functions and out of the public eye. Bloody man.

Well, the duke thought, *I was right, wasn't I?*

The Maginot Line might not have existed for all it did to stop the Wehrmacht, and now they were sweeping through France, and England would be next.

Vituso nodded towards the whisky decanter. 'Don't suppose I could bother you for one of those?'

'Pour yourself a large one,' the duke said. 'Pour me one while you're at it.' He pushed across a packet of Chesterfield, and followed it with a heavy silver desk lighter. 'Help yourself to a cigarette while you're at it.'

'Chin chin,' Vituso said.

The duke raised his own glass.

He'd said things he shouldn't have. Quite a lot of things actually. Vituso was a man one could talk to. A man of the world. He understood how hard abdicating had been. How furious the duke was with his family for how Wallis was being treated.

Look at them now, crawling through refugees as they fled the city they should have been able to call home. It wasn't self-pity. He despised people who pitied themselves, but really . . .

'What did you and Vituso talk about anyway?'

The duke thought of his fury as he told Vituso what he thought of his parsimonious, sanctimonious prig of a brother and the mess he was making of being king. Britain should never have gone to war with Germany. The very idea was absurd. As for his brother's dreadful hausfrau of a wife and their simpering brat. *Shirley,* Wallis called her. After Shirley Temple obviously.

'Nothing of import,' the duke said.

'Nothing?'

'Well, he did suggest we move to Rome. Then he changed it and said he thought you might like Naples better. He offered to find us a palace and have Mussolini pay. As ideas go, I've heard worse. At least Italy's still neutral. For the moment anyway.'

'You think that will change?'

'If I was Benito' – the duke spoke as if Il Duce was a close friend – 'I'd declare war on France in time to get a seat at the table when it comes to dividing up the spoils.'

Wallis looked at the stream of refugees. 'France is already defeated.'

'True,' the duke said. 'But it hasn't yet—'

Before he could say *surrendered* a bullet hit.

It exited its barrel at 2,500 feet per second, drilled through the Buick's windscreen and passed between the duke and Wallis before either realized what had happened. As Edward swore and Wallis flung herself sideways, the car lurched to a halt. Having checked that both his passengers were unharmed, their driver scrambled out and hurried to the rear.

Removing fuel cans strapped to the back, he opened the boot. The round had drilled through the rear seat, smashed the teapot of a twelve-piece hand-painted Sèvres tea set, ripped through a pigskin beauty case containing Her Highness's cosmetics and flattened itself against the chassis.

The driver couldn't be certain but it looked disconcertingly like a standard .303, British issue. Deciding not to mention that, he dropped it to the ground.

36

'How appalling,' Beigbeder said when Wallis Simpson had finished describing how difficult it had been to find a garage capable of replacing the Buick's shattered windscreen.

'Of course,' Wallis said. 'Churchill's a drunk.'

'A drunk?'

'A bottle of brandy a day,' she said. 'And he soaks his cigars in port before he smokes them. More than a bottle a day. Probably two bottles.'

Beigbeder looked so shocked and horrified at the thought of it that she sat back with a grim smile.

'And then this.'

'Wallis . . .'

'Show him. How can he help us if you won't show him? It arrived this morning, brought by some nauseatingly self-satisfied little man.'

Who probably hadn't used her title, Beigbeder imagined. He glanced at the duke, seeking permission to read the note Her Highness pushed across. He knew what it said, because he had spies in the British embassy, but it would hardly do for him to let them know that.

Even for a note it was terse to the point of rudeness.

It should not be necessary to remind you that, as a serving officer, lastly on secondment to the British Mission in Paris, you are subject to military discipline, up to and including court martial. You are to leave for Lisbon immediately. Any failure to do so will be regarded as a breach of a direct order.

'Who does Churchill think he is?' Wallis demanded.

A man trying to play a complicated game of chess, while suspecting that one of his major pieces might be about to change sides. Also, the leader of a country at war. Beigbeder kept those thoughts to himself. 'Outrageous,' he said. 'Unthinkable. He must know that His Royal Highness's only interest is the good of his country.'

'You would have thought so, wouldn't you?' the duke said.

The duke's voice was as the world remembered it from his abdication speech, but tinged with bitterness. The same could be said of his face. He was still handsome, instantly recognizable. Although he lacked the drop-dead good looks of his youth.

'My wife's family has a house in Portugal,' Beigbeder said.

'That's kind,' the duke said. 'But I've just made other arrangements. Do you know Ricardo do Espírito Santo e Silva?'

'A wise choice.'

Beigbeder hid his sigh of relief. Portuguese or not, Espírito Santo was a banker who'd been of use to Madrid before now. It was widely accepted that Don Ricardo was a man whose sympathies could be relied on.

To Eberhard von Stohrer,
Reich Ambassador, Spain
From Joachim von Ribbentrop,
Reichsminister of Foreign Affairs

Date: Monday, 1 July 1940
Burn the attached. Make no copies.

Foreign Office
Willhelmstraße 76
Berlin

Monday

My dear Eberhard,

I have had a report from our friend in Madrid about his meeting with the duke and duchess. Apparently, they're stewing nicely.

I know you understand this, but please ensure that everyone around you understands it too. It is vital that at all times we are seen to believe that all the duke wants is peace, and his sole desire is to spare his country the pain of a brutal invasion.

Whatever we may think privately – that he is driven by hurt pride, greed and hatred for his brother (and she by fury that he stepped down from his throne) – our public position is that the duke is entirely honourable. This man can give us Britain and we can return his throne. It is a seduction and we must tread carefully.

Wallis is your greatest asset. Her obsession with haute couture clothing and high-end jewellery is well known. Use it. Use her. I could make an indecent joke here, but we're both men of the world so I'll leave you to imagine it.

Joachim

To Charles Standish III, US Office of Information
From Alexander Weddell, US Ambassador to Spain

Date: Monday, 1 July 1940
<u>Top Secret</u>

I had drinks with the Duke of Windsor last night.

The meeting was brief, cordial and perhaps a little too frank on his part. He feels that the war is an unmitigated disaster for the British empire, that Britain itself is on the brink of a humiliating defeat and that the empire will not survive an extended war, no matter how it ends.

I do not believe, having talked, that he is being paid by the Germans. He is, however, fascinated by fascism, certain of Hitler's victory, and believes it his own duty to bring about the least-damaging peace possible.

I have not mentioned any of this to Sir Samuel Hoare, the British ambassador here. Although, as one of Neville Chamberlain's right-hand men and a known appeaser, I don't doubt that, like many in his country, he would quietly agree.

37

Arisaig, Tuesday, 2 July 1940

'You're late,' the woman said.

Bill wanted to say he'd had four hours' sleep, missed breakfast and woken to find he was expected to strangle a pig with piano wire. 'I'd have been earlier,' he said, 'if I wasn't vomiting.'

'This isn't a place for people with delicate stomachs.'

'This isn't a place for people with delicate anything,' Bill snapped.

To his surprise, the woman smiled. 'As long as we're both clear about that. Now, the fact you speak German is one of the reasons we chose you. How well do you speak it?'

'Well enough.'

'Well enough for what?' she demanded. 'To pass as a native? Order a beer? What does "well enough" mean?'

'I spent a year in a Hun prison camp,' Bill said, switching languages. 'And several years in Vienna.'

'Doing what?'

'Messing up my marriage.'

'Your accent's grim but you'll do.'

She indicated a chair at the table in front of her and Bill sat. There was a map of Alderney on the table. From one prison to another, because that's what Alderney was. A prison, just with water in place of bars.

'You're lucky,' she said. 'It's been evacuated. The only Channel Island that has. So, unless you're very unlucky, anyone who knows you're a fake will be here, while you'll be there pretending for the Germans. We've briefed Mrs Beecher, your old housekeeper. She'll be returning from Jersey to keep house.'

'Why haven't I been evacuated?'

'You're in hiding. You went AWOL after shooting your own ADC. As of today, there's a warrant out for your arrest.'

'Christ. Did he?'

'You,' she said. 'Yes, you did.'

'They'll intern me. The Germans.'

'Make sure they don't. Mention your arrest warrant. Tell them you're pals with Sir Oswald Mosley and share his views on Slavs, blacks and Jews . . . What?' she demanded, seeing Bill's expression.

Bill was thinking of Miriam. 'My wife was Jewish. My daughter too.'

'You don't have a wife,' the woman said. 'You did, but she ran off with a French gangster. You very definitely don't have a child.

'Now, remember . . . Drop comments about drinking with the Duke of Windsor, your wife's friendship with Wallis Simpson, your visit to the Goerings at Carinhall . . . Hell,' the woman said, 'you're a white settler. You spent most of the thirties whipping blacks, stealing land and shooting elephants, a hundred in a single year. You like nothing better than putting bullets through things. They should love you.

'Right,' she said. 'Place of birth?'

'Renhou,' Bill said dutifully.

'Date of birth?'

'The fourteenth of November 1898.'

'What year did you marry Daisy Black?'

'Nineteen thirty-six.'

'What year did she leave you?'

'Nineteen thirty-eight. The marriage lasted eighteen months.

Which, from the sound of things, was several months longer than it should have done.'

'Where did you go to school?'

'Eton.'

'Obviously.' Her voice was sour. 'You failed to get into Winchester. Not intelligent enough.' The questions were endless, and by the end, when Bill began to fumble his answers, she grew impatient.

'I've only been here a day,' he protested.

'And you only have a couple to go. This is the stuff that will keep you alive. Study it tonight and we'll go back to it tomorrow.'

'I'm probably killing pigs tonight.'

'You're done with pigs,' she said tartly. 'If you're doing anything it's learning to stuff dynamite up the arses of dead rats to make booby traps.'

'I won't need to booby trap anything.'

She stared at him. 'How do you know?'

38

Arisaig, same day

A battered leather case on Bill's bed contained a radio, with telegraph key, headset, transmitter, power supply and receiver. Its knobs read *Volume, Waveband, Crystal selection* and *Tuning*. A note was taped to the top. It read: 'Remember: The enemy will try to pinpoint your location by the process of triangulation. Every use brings the Nazis closer.'

Beside it, Bill found a tape recorder, with a note saying it should stay here when he went. Plugging it in, he pushed play. A voice he instantly hated drawled an introduction to *A Letter from East Africa*, an occasional programme from the BBC Empire Service. 'This is Sir William Renhou in Mombasa, sitting on my veranda and watching night fall over the Indian Ocean . . .'

Without even thinking about it, Bill set his face to mimic every judge who'd ever sneered down from the bench while passing sentence on him. He could do an upper-class English accent. He'd never make matinée idol, but in a better life he could have been a character actor.

'This is Sir William Renhou in Mombasa,' he repeated, 'sitting on my veranda and watching night fall over the Indian Ocean.'

While listening to the tape, Bill flicked through his new passport, and found two tiny, carefully-aged photographs inside. He wore a safari jacket in both and his stare was convincingly arrogant. Welham's make-up girl had fixed him a false beard for these, which she'd removed the moment the shoot was done.

Renhou had been required to shave the moment he went back to active service.

Inside were entry and exit stamps for Kenya, Tanganyika, Northern Rhodesia, Southern Rhodesia, South Africa . . .

'All right for some,' Bill said sourly.

Sir William's *Letter* was a reassuring and unlikely litany of the benefits the Sir Williams of the world brought to an area substantially larger than Europe. Nowhere did it mention native villages burnt out so farms could grow or Sir William's part in shooting blacks who wanted their grazing returned.

'This is Sir William, drunk as a skunk, lying in his teeth and watching night fall . . .' Bill signed off with his own version of the introduction and turned to the wireless's instruction booklet. How to tune a crystal, how to make sure the headphones were working, how to use Morse code.

He already had his own instructions.

Wait for the safe to arrive, crack it, let London know. But what if he couldn't contact London because the invasion had happened, and the Germans had already taken the capital? The woman with the map hadn't been able to answer that one.

To Charles Standish III, US Office of Information
From Alexander Weddell, US Ambassador to Spain

Date: Wednesday, 3 July 1940
<u>Top Secret</u>

The Duke and Duchess of Windsor left for Portugal this morning.

The duke and I managed one final drink during which the duke admitted he would have fallen into line, returned to London and taken whatever post was offered if only his mother, brother and sister-in-law agreed to meet his wife. Apparently, Churchill tried to arrange it. His brother and mother refused.

Since then, the duke's position has hardened. We have to accept that he has started to think of his family as the enemy. Our biggest problem is that Berlin is using promises and London threats.

We both know which the duke likes best.

To Alexander Weddell, US Ambassador to Spain
From Charles Standish III, US Office of Information

Date: Wednesday, 3 July 1940
<u>Top Secret</u>

If Britain falls, and the Nazis' Molotov-Ribbentrop
Pact with the Soviets holds, Europe will be divided
between the fascists and the communists. In which case,
America's isolation deepens. It is the president's view this
cannot be allowed to happen. It must not be allowed to
happen. London must ask for help, though. Mr Roosevelt
cannot act unless London requests.

39

Algeria, same day

Late on the afternoon of Wednesday, 3 July 1940, a British battle fleet off the Algerian coast opened fire on French ships at anchor in Mers-el-Kébir.

The *Bretagne*, a French battleship, took a shell to its magazine. Metal ripped and flesh melted. Despite the carnage, its sailors kept returning fire until the end. Their bravery cost them a thousand lives.

'You're sure?'

Standish stared through his office window in Washington at workmen extending the archives. He was glad that almost everything that passed across his desk was either burnt or microfiched. There was more than enough paper in the world.

On the other end of the line, Standish's contact assured him he'd had it from the harbour master at Mers-el-Kébir himself. The English had attacked their allies.

'Well, I'll be damned,' Standish said.

The last he'd heard, London had agreed to respect the French fleet's integrity in return for a binding promise it wouldn't be handed to the Germans. If the *Bretagne* had just been sunk by HMS *Hood* it meant Churchill believed he had nothing left to lose.

He must believe the invasion imminent.

From the German News Bureau
To All Agencies

Date: Wednesday, 3 July 1940

Following today's attack by British warships on French vessels at anchor at Mers-el-Kébir, we are releasing documents captured during the recent events in France relating to Operation Pike, a British plan to bomb Soviet oil fields. Proof, if proof were needed, of London's willingness to attack without warning not only old allies but countries with which it has no cause for war.

Hôtel Ritz Paris
15 Place Vendôme
1er Arrondissement
Paris

Wednesday, 3 July 1940

<u>Secret</u>

My dear Ernst,

Well, the damn treaty with the French is signed and I'll be on my way back to Berlin all too soon. I trust you have reached Alderney by now, and I hope you feel reconciled to your new posting. Dragging a senior officer out of retirement to oversee a tiny island would be an absurdity if that island was not the stepping stone for the Führer's forthcoming invasion.

As soon as Admiral Dönitz has swept the Channel of British shipping and I have cleared the sky of their wretched planes, the invasion begins. We will be victorious. We are always victorious. You know how savagely we were stabbed in the back at Versailles after the last war, when France and Britain forced us to sign that iniquitous treaty. It is our duty to make Germany great again. Everyone's duty.

Even yours, old friend.

I will be sending you a special guest. I cannot yet say whom, but you are a clever man. Who would we want standing at the Führer's side as he leads his troops into London? I know you will work it out.

Do not let me down.

In haste,
Hermann

To: Colonel Ernst von Neudeck, Iron Cross First Class

40

Arisaig, same day

'If you'd come with me, sir.'

The others in the mess at Arisaig glanced up from their after-supper brandies, realized they shouldn't be inquisitive and looked away. They were a motley collection, Bill included, all of them out of place in the panelled room Angus had turned into a mess by pushing a mahogany table to the wall and filling the floor with a collection of rotting armchairs.

'Where are we going?' Bill asked.

'For a walk, sir. For a walk.'

Liverpool, Bill decided. Originally Irish, but not for a generation or so. Not new to the army, though. He'd been in long enough for marching to become second nature. Bill adjusted his step.

'I'm told you can't swim?'

'That's right,' Bill said.

'I'm also told you fear water?'

'Flanders,' Bill said. 'Nineteen sixteen. A collapsed dug-out with a rising flood.'

'That would do it.' The man walked to the loch's edge. 'As I don't have time to teach you to swim, I'm going to teach you to float.'

Bill stepped back.

'Bodies float. Unless you weigh them down.'

'I'm not sure there are going to be bodies,' Bill said.

'Of course there are,' the man said. 'You're a rush job.

You've been bumped to the head of the queue. There's bound to be bodies. Right,' he said. 'In you go.'

Bill started to strip.

'No. As you are.'

The water was colder than Bill expected, his uniform heavier. His boots like weights. 'If you go in fully dressed,' the man said, 'kick off your shoes, then rid yourself of your jacket. Unless it's really cold. Mind you, if it's really cold the water will kill you anyway.'

An hour later Bill could float on his back. An hour after that, he could manage several strokes of rudimentary breast-stroke without swallowing water. 'I've taught worse,' the man said. 'Not many, mind you. Still, if you get yourself killed, with luck it won't be by drowning. Now, let's teach you to paddle a canoe . . .'

To Brigadier Oswald Harker, Director MI5
From Winston Churchill

Date: Wednesday, 3 July 1940
<u>For Your Eyes Only</u>

I have arranged with Major Hardinge, His Majesty's private secretary, for you to be received by His Majesty The King at Windsor Castle this afternoon at 4 p.m. His Majesty is expecting to be briefed on the extent of Nazi infiltration into the upper echelons of British society. Major Hardinge has been told the real reason you are attending.

I need you to broach the unthinkable. What do we do if the Duke of Windsor is not to be trusted? It would be best if you framed everything in terms of Wallis Simpson's evil influence rather than the duke's own inclinations.

(The king will find that easy enough to believe.)

The king will take it from you because he knows of your department's work rooting out fifth columnists. In particular, members of the Right Club at the Russian Tea Rooms. He also knows that Anna Wolkoff, owner of the tea rooms, was ex-couturier to Wallis Simpson, and is in the Tower for treason while we decide whether or not to hang her.

You should not suggest directly that the duke is a traitor. At the same time the king must be left in no doubt that if his brother comes under Berlin's control, he will be used as a fig leaf for the invasion.

(That the duke will need to be dealt with should this happen must not be mentioned. His Majesty will need to arrive at that conclusion for himself.)

Thursday, 4 July 1940

We are pleased to appoint His Royal Highness The Duke of Windsor as Governor of the Bahamas with immediate effect. His Royal Highness, and Her Highness The Duchess, will take up this post without delay.

George R. I.

To the Right Hon. Winston Churchill, Prime Minister
From Major Hardinge, Private Secretary to His Majesty

Date: Thursday, 4 July 1940

His Majesty asks that you make arrangements to collect His Royal Highness The Duke of Windsor, and Her Highness The Duchess, from wherever they are currently residing and return them to London, for onward passage to the Bahamas where the duke should take up his governorship without delay.

If necessary, remind the duke that it is his duty to obey.

41

Alderney, same day

The pub in Braye had a couple of tables on the street, a rudimentary terrace at the back and a patch of gravel to the side. The only interesting thing about it, apart from the terrace overlooking Alderney's harbour, was an open-topped blue Mercedes parked on the gravel.

Its one-armed owner was inside the public bar, trying a pint of English beer. So far Colonel von Neudeck wasn't impressed by his new posting. For an island once described as two thousand alcoholics clinging to a rock, its alcohol left much to be desired.

He liked the view better. The Admiralty breakwater at Braye had been commissioned in the age of sail and finished in the age of ironclads, by which time the ships it was intended for were already too big to enter. There was a moral in there somewhere.

'Why does the air smell sour?' he asked the man who served him. He asked in English. Better English than the islander expected.

'Does it?' The barman Michael considered that. 'I hadn't noticed.'

'Also, why are you still here?'

'I missed the boat.'

'Is that true?' von Neudeck asked, as if he somehow expected the barman to say, 'No, not really.'

'Absolutely.'

'But you have a boat?'

'Yes,' the man said, his voice neutral.

'To fish, and to smuggle?'

Michael looked puzzled.

'I read FitzHerbert's *History of Alderney*. You islanders are famous for your silver mines, and smuggling.'

'The mines are worked out and no one smuggles any more.'

'That's good,' von Neudeck said. 'I'd only have to shoot them . . . You can see France from Alderney,' he added. 'It didn't say that. It looks close. Close enough to swim.'

'It's eight miles. The current would kill you.'

The German smiled. 'Don't worry,' he said, tapping his empty sleeve. 'I wasn't intending to try . . .'

Carry on as normal, the Bailiffs of Guernsey and Jersey had told the islanders. Von Neudeck was glad. This was to be a model occupation. A model occupation as a dress rehearsal for the occupation of Britain.

He imagined the islander knew that.

10 Downing Street
Whitehall

Thursday, 4 July 1940

<u>Most Secret and Personal</u>

Dear Roosevelt,

Belgium has fallen. Holland has fallen. France has fallen. Denmark has fallen. Norway has fallen. The Soviets have taken Lithuania, Latvia, Estonia and Bessarabia.

It is obvious that under the Molotov-Ribbentrop non-aggression pact Berlin and Moscow have every intention of dividing Europe between them. The choice is between a free Europe, or a Soviet and Nazified Europe. Civilisation's hope rests on Britain's survival. We need your help.

We need it now.

With all good wishes and respect,
Churchill

To: President Franklin D. Roosevelt

42

Portugal, Friday, 5 July 1940

'That must be Espírito Santo.'

A thick-set man, sweating slightly in a beautifully cut suit, stood in the doorway of Casa de Santa Maria, the pink stucco house that had been found for the Duke and Duchess of Windsor's stay. The woman standing beside Espírito Santo was both thin and chicly dressed. Wallis approved.

'Highnesses.' The man bowed as the driver climbed from the Buick to open the duke's door, then hurried round for Wallis.

'It's beautiful,' Wallis said.

The villa was the size of a small hotel, set on the edge of a wide bay that curled round to the small town of Cascais in the distance. The sea was as blue as the sky, and palm trees lined a distant promenade.

'I am Ricardo do Espírito Santo,' the man said, as if Wallis didn't know. 'Welcome to our summer house. We are delighted you can use it.'

The men shook hands. 'I trust we're not inconveniencing you,' the duke said. 'Where are you staying?'

'I have an apartment in Lisbon.'

'I'm sure it's hot,' the duke said. 'This is really very kind.'

'You have a swimming pool,' Wallis exclaimed. 'How divine. David loves a pool.'

'David?' Senhora Espírito Santo sounded puzzled.

'I know. I know,' Wallis said. 'Why David when he was Edward, Prince of Wales, and King Edward afterwards?

They're like popes, his family. The name they're christened with isn't what they're called. And, of course, if they're in line for the throne then often they rule under another name entirely.'

'I'm not sure I understand,' Senhora Espírito Santo said.

'You're not meant to. That's the point. You're either in the family or not.' She nodded at her husband. 'He was at the very heart of it. Now he's on the very edge and I'm outside.'

'*Wallis.*'

'You know it's true.'

'What should I call him?' Senhora Espírito Santo whispered.

Wallis sighed. 'Your royal highness the first time, sir thereafter. That's what I had to do. They're as obsessed with their titles as they are with their names. Well, not my husband obviously. If he was, he'd still be king-emperor, and I'd be in America licking my wounds.'

If Senhora Espírito Santo was trying to conceal her shock at Wallis's candour, she failed. 'It's a very small house for a prince,' she said anxiously.

'It's beautiful,' Wallis replied. 'It has a swimming pool, it looks out over the sea and its walls are my favourite pink. I think it's wonderful.'

As the duke continued to talk to Espírito Santo, and servants appeared to help unload the Buick, Senhora Espírito Santo led Wallis inside. Her first surprise was the man waiting for her.

'Your highness,' he said.

Wallis's lips tightened at the lack of royal between those words but she forced a smile. 'What a pleasure.'

Her husband had turned to Sir Samuel Hoare in the early weeks of the abdication crisis. These days he was London's man in Madrid. So, what was he doing in Portugal?

'I didn't expect to see you.'

Sir Samuel was put out. 'I helped arrange the house. Is the duke . . .'

'I'm here,' her husband said.

Turning, Wallis saw the duke, with Espírito Santo behind him. Neither of them seemed thrilled at Sir Samuel's presence.

'Your royal highness.'

Her husband rated his full title with a deep bow, Wallis noticed. Of course he did. She was the one worth no more than a quick bend and a truncated *highness*.

'I trust it was a good drive?' Sir Samuel said.

'Certainly better than the one from Cannes to Perpignan. Or from Perpignan to Madrid, come to that.'

'You stopped off for a few days in Barcelona, I believe?'

'Wallis needed a break.'

'Understandable,' Sir Samuel Hoare said, obviously meaning the opposite. 'And while in Madrid, I believe you made some trips outside the city?'

'How could we not?' the duke said. 'Spanish culture is so rich. Almost as rich as Portuguese,' he said smoothly, turning to Espírito Santo.

He was at his most charming. Worry and tiredness held at bay while he filled his role as grateful guest, man of the world and gracious prince. He did it well, Wallis knew. No one watching would have known how hard the poor dear found it.

'Now,' the duke said to Sir Samuel, 'you'd better introduce me to your staff.' He nodded at two young men behind the ambassador.

'Not my staff, sir. These are the pilots.'

The duke looked blank.

'From RAF Coastal Command, sir. They flew out yesterday. They're here to collect you. We thought perhaps first thing tomorrow.'

Wallis shot her husband a look.

His face had closed down.

'Tomorrow?' Wallis said.

'Or the day after,' Sir Samuel said wearily. 'If you're too exhausted to make the flight until then.'

'I think we need a word,' the duke said firmly. He steered the ambassador towards what was obviously a library and closed its door with a bang. The two pilots were left looking after him.

'Perhaps Mr Santo could show us the rest of the house,' Wallis said brightly.

'I've already told the PM that I will not return to Britain until my own wife is accorded the same respect as my brothers' wives.'

'Sir . . .'

'No,' the duke said sharply. 'You will listen. You may tell Winston that I'm happy to return the moment the king gives his assurance that he, and his wife, will grant me, and my wife, an audience.'

'Sir. You can't expect me—'

'Until I have that assurance,' the duke said, speaking over him, 'I will not return to Britain and neither will Wallis.'

'Sir, the flying boats are waiting.'

'Send them home.'

'I can't possibly do that.'

'Then it's your responsibility if those two boys waste their time here when they'd rather be doing their duty.'

'Speaking of duty, sir . . .'

'Speaking of duty, sir, I am entirely happy to do mine the moment my brother remembers his.'

43

London, same day

Colonel Welham found Bill at a corner table in the café at Waterloo Station, with a cup of tea in front of him. A folded copy of *The Times* rested on the seat beside him. The RAF had bombed Hamburg. There'd been scattered raids on the South Coast. In response to the French surrender, Britain's allies in Iraq had cut off oil to Tripoli. The Norwegian king was in hiding.

'Quite the country gent,' Welham said, pulling out a chair.

Bill was in lightweight tweeds entirely unsuited to the city. His brogues were tan, handmade and equally out of place. His tie was knitted and his shirt worsted. Everything he wore was suitable for the real Sir William. He could have been the poor relation of a duke, or a parson, if not for the ill-disguised anger with which he greeted Welham. He'd woken to find an armed guard outside his room. *For his own protection*, he'd been told.

'You need to stop fiddling with that,' Welham said.

Looking down, Bill discovered he'd been turning Renhou's ring.

'It's uncomfortable.'

'You'll grow used to it . . . Tea,' Welham said to the waitress who materialized at his shoulder. She disappeared towards the silver urn at one end of the counter, and they heard a clatter as she found him a cup.

'They're going to ration tea,' Welham said. 'From the end of this week.' He picked up his biscuit. 'They'll be rationing these next. Right,' he said. 'In, do the job, call us. If you don't call us, we'll swing by with a sub before dawn on the twenty-ninth. We'll expect you to have cracked the safe by then. Make sure you have.'

'And if I'm not there?'

'We'll assume you're dead. A word of warning. Don't think of bailing on us. Wherever you go, whoever you become, we *will* find you. We're hanging traitors every week. We've been doing it all year. We will win this war and if you run, we will find you. And hang you properly this time.'

'Is that a challenge?' Bill said.

Welham failed to conceal his shock.

'Because if it is, I don't respond well to threats. Also, as of today I outrank you. Remember? I'm a brigadier now. Brigadier Sir William Renhou. If we meet again in public I expect you to call me sir.'

Pushing back his chair, Bill thanked the waitress, told her the colonel would pay and picked up another packet of biscuits on his way out.

44

Alderney, same day

Captain Keller didn't expect his new commanding officer to be at Alderney Airport to greet him. But he did expect the man to be at his own HQ.

Still, the island had a better airstrip than he'd imagined. And field engineers were already knocking down walls in the Island Hall to create something resembling a functioning Ops Room. His new boss, meanwhile, was apparently drinking in a tavern on the edge of Braye.

The tavern was as shoddy as Keller expected, with a twee English telephone box outside, poorly painted benches and half-dead flowers in barrels. Keller's mother had been English. A fact he'd not been allowed to forget.

Drinking here showed a lack of decorum.

A scar-faced sergeant and a soft-looking boy whose gloves suggested he was von Neudeck's chauffeur took one look at Keller and came to attention. The burns on the sergeant's face were horrific, and not recent.

'Spain?' Keller demanded.

'Jarama, sir.'

'It was a tough battle.'

The man's expression stayed neutral.

'I was there,' Keller said. 'We held; most didn't. From the look of it you held too.' He waited for von Neudeck's driver to realize he should get the door.

*

'Heil Hitler.' Keller raised his arm and the colonel replied in kind. The captain couldn't help noticing his salute was substantially less enthusiastic.

'Good flight?' von Neudeck asked.

'Wonderful,' the captain said.

The colonel nodded absent-mindedly. 'Remind me again why you're here?'

Keller flushed.

As if realizing his question might be tactless, von Neudeck shrugged. 'It just seems strange. I don't doubt you're competent. You're probably ambitious, you're young to have risen to the rank of captain. This island has me. I'm not sure why it would need you as well.'

Keller checked to see if he was being was mocked, but the colonel seemed entirely serious. 'Alderney is . . .'

'Hitler's stepping stone. Yes. So Hermann keeps telling me.'

The Reichsmarschall? Trying for a more respectful attitude, Keller said, 'I imagine the Führer will need a full staff when he arrives.'

Von Neudeck's glass stopped halfway to his mouth.

'The Führer, himself? Here?'

Keller smiled.

Issued by the Ministry of Information
on behalf of the War Office and
the Ministry of Home Security

(Printed in England)

STAY WHERE YOU ARE

If this island is invaded by sea or air, everyone who is not under orders must stay where he or she is. This is not simply advice: it is an order from the Government, and you must obey it just as soldiers obey their orders. Your order is 'Stay Put', but remember that this does not apply until invasion comes.

Why must I stay put?

Because in France, Holland and Belgium, the Germans were helped by the people who took flight before them. Great crowds of refugees blocked all roads. The soldiers who could have defended them could not get at the enemy. These refugees were got out on to the roads by rumour and false orders. Do not be caught out in this way. Do not take any notice of any story telling what the enemy has done or where he is. Do not take orders except from the Military, the Police, the L.D.V. and the A.R.P. authorities or wardens.

What will happen to me if I don't stay put?

If you do not stay put you will stand a very good chance of being killed. The enemy may machine-gun you from the air in order to increase panic, or you may run into enemy forces which have landed behind you. An official German message was captured in Belgium which ran: 'Watch for civilian refugees on the roads.

Harass them as much as possible.' Our soldiers will be hurrying to drive back the invader and will not be able to stop and help you. On the contrary, they will have to turn off the roads so that they can get at the enemy. You will not have reached safety and you will have done just as the enemy wanted you to do.

How should I prepare to stay put?
Make ready your air-raid shelter. If you have no shelter prepare one. Advice can be obtained from your local Air Raid Warden or found in 'Your Home as an Air Raid Shelter', the government booklet that tells you how to prepare a shelter in your house that will be strong enough to protect you from stray shots and falling metal. If you can have a trench available in your garden or field, so much the better, especially if you live somewhere there is likely to be danger from shell fire.

How can I help?
You can help by setting a good example to others. Civilians who try to join the fight are more likely to get in the way than to help. The defeat of an enemy attack is the task of the armed forces, which include the Local Defence Volunteers, so if you wish to, enrol with them. If there is no vacancy for you at the moment, register your name for enrolment and you will be called upon as soon as there is. For those who cannot join there are many ways in which the Military may need your help in their preparations. Be ready to turn your hand to anything if asked. If you are responsible for the safety of a factory or some other important building, get in touch with the nearest military authority. You will then be told how your defence should fit in with the Military's organisation and plans.

What shall I do if the Invader comes my way?
If fighting by organised forces is going on in your district and you have no special duties elsewhere, go to your shelter and stay

there till the battle is past. Do not attempt to join the fight. Behave as if an air-raid were going on. The enemy will seldom turn aside to attack separate houses. But if small parties are going about threatening persons and property in an area not under enemy control and come your way, you have the right of every man and woman to do what you can to protect yourself, your family and your home.

Stay put

It's easy to say. When the time comes it may be hard to do. But you have got to do it; and in doing it you will be fighting Britain's battle as bravely as any soldier.

45

Portugal, same day

Compared to Monte-Carlo, Portugal's Casino do Estoril was drab and unprepossessing. A modern white block. If you understood modern in a dated sort of way. As the duke said, it might as well have been a cinema in Surbiton.

'You'll be all right on your own?' he asked.

Wallis smiled thinly. 'I won't be on my own, will I?'

She nodded to two women from the British embassy. Penny Something, who was dark-haired and vaguely pretty, and a middle-aged woman so drab Wallis had forgotten her name already. Wallis's first night in Lisbon, still feeling grubby and tired from the drive, and her husband wanted to play roulette. The embassy had insisted on sending two of their own to help her settle in.

'I can stay,' the duke said.

Reaching up, Wallis adjusted her husband's bow tie, aware of a dozen eyes in the foyer watching. 'Go,' she said. 'Have a good evening. I'll be fine.' Wallis felt Penny Something's gaze as she headed for the restrooms. A second after she entered, the door opened behind her and Wallis turned from the mirror with a scowl.

'Your royal highness.'

The woman was blonde, her jacket was Chanel, her jewellery good. Wallis was almost certain she'd never seen her before.

'Have we met?' Wallis asked.

'Only once, ma'am. In Berlin. At Carinhall. At Field Marshal Goering's party. Frau Metz. You won't remember me.'

'Of course I remember,' Wallis said easily. 'What on earth are you doing in Lisbon?'

'My husband's just been posted here.'

'That must be hard after Berlin.'

The woman gave a slight shrug that managed to look chic rather than rude. 'There are worse places,' she said. 'And everyone's here: assassins, spies, disgraced aristocrats, diplomats, even you . . .'

Wallis smiled ruefully.

'You're not enjoying yourself?' Frau Metz said.

'This is my husband's idea of relaxing. And I have a couple of shop girls better suited to a Lyons Corner House for company.'

'Ouch.'

'Ouch indeed.'

'Do you play bezique?'

'Not well,' Wallis said.

'I'm not sure that matters. If you're not enjoying yourself and feel like a change of company then once you're on the casino floor, turn right and head for the green door at the end. We'll have a private game. The casino will take their cut from the pot.'

'Those two will just follow.'

'Trust me,' Frau Metz said. 'The green door. If you go first, I'll follow a few minutes after. If you'd be willing to grant me a quick word?'

The restroom door began to open and Wallis made a show of drying her hands. It was Penny Something-or-other from the embassy. She'd known it would be. Returning to the foyer, Wallis scooped up her evening bag.

'I'll be through there.' She nodded to the casino floor.

'Your highness . . .'

'You should wait,' Wallis said. 'For your friend.'

46

Portugal, same day

As Wallis approached the green door a flunky stepped forward.

'I'm meeting someone,' Wallis said.

'Forgive me. You know the stakes, senhora?'

'I always know the stakes. I was born knowing the stakes. I don't imagine they're higher than Monaco.'

The flunky's glance took in her Chanel jacket, her diamond ring, her severe but obviously expensive haircut, her expectation that he would open the door and hurry himself about it.

Once inside, Wallis ordered ten thousand escudos in casino chips and signed for them with an easy flourish. Setting the counters in front of her, Wallis told a casino employee what she intended to play. He immediately broke open two new packs, removed all the cards below six and shuffled the remainder.

'A good choice of table, your royal highness.' Frau Metz stood behind a spare chair. At Wallis's nod she sat.

'Now,' Wallis said. 'What is this about?'

'I was hoping for a quiet word.'

'You'd better make it quick.' Wallis glanced at the door.

'They've been turned away.' Frau Metz sneered. 'They were told this was a room for high-stakes games. One of them asked how high.'

'Oh, good God.'

'Quite. Shall we play?'

They played in silence, and Wallis won both games, the pile of chips growing in front of her. When the second game ended, Frau Metz leant in close.

'Joachim sends his love. He asks also for your help. It is obvious your husband is the only man who can save Britain from itself. I ask you this in good faith. What is stopping him accepting Berlin's friendship?'

He's done it, Wallis thought, remembering her husband's comment about bringing Berlin to the negotiating table. What would he want her to say? What did she want to say for herself?

'Duty,' Wallis said. 'Fear of committing treason. Loyalty to his brother, no matter how badly his brother has treated him.'

'It isn't treason to save your country from disaster,' said Frau Metz. 'And I'm surprised he thinks he owes his brother anything. The new king has behaved appallingly to both of you. I'm surprised your husband isn't furious.'

'Oh, he is,' Wallis said. 'Sometimes so furious he finds it hard to control. He blames his father rather than his brother, though.'

'Whom do you blame, your royal highness?'

Here we go, Wallis thought.

'The lot of them,' she said, hoping it sounded candid. 'His thug of a father. His impossible mother. His stammering fool of a brother. That fat, badly dressed little hausfrau his brother married. It all goes back to the will.'

'The will?' Frau Metz pulled her chair close.

'That's how London controls him. Money. Or, in my husband's case, lack of it. Poor darling. He had no idea what was coming. How his father had intentionally poisoned everything by rewriting his will.'

'You were there when it was read?'

'Good God, no. I was at Fort Belvedere. The reading took

place at Sandringham. The three brothers, their damned mother and the late king's . . .' Wallis stopped. 'I'm not sure I should be telling you this.'

Frau Metz touched her finger very slightly to Wallis's wrist. 'It would probably help to tell someone,' she said softly.

'We should meet again.'

Frau Metz smiled. 'I'd like that very much,' she said.

47

English Channel, Saturday, 6 July 1940

The submarine stank. It stank of oil and sweat and urine from where crew members pissed into the bilge drain nearest their stations. It was hot, fetid, over-crowded and impossibly cramped. Bill was hating every minute.

'Someone must be able to help me,' he protested.

The boy commanding the sub shook his head. Glancing round, the lieutenant realized how many of his small crew were listening. Until then, Bill had done what it was suggested he do, kept his head down and stayed out of the crew's way while they took him where he needed to go, so they could go on to more important duties in the Bay of Biscay.

'I really need to paddle myself in?' Bill asked.

Taking a deep breath, the lieutenant said, 'I'm sorry, sir. There seems to be some confusion.' A sub-lieutenant, who looked barely old enough to leave home, was staring now. A warrant officer and a couple of seamen were doing a better job of pretending to be getting on with their jobs.

'Christ, man,' Bill said. 'What if I capsize? I can barely float.'

'You *have* to go in alone, sir.'

'In God's name, why?'

'Because those are my orders. Because the canoe only has room for you and your case.' He took a deep breath. 'Because, even if I could spare a man, he wouldn't be able to get back.'

'Why not?'

'There's a riptide.'

The man kept talking but Bill had stopped listening. There wasn't much that terrified him, but after being trapped in the trenches in a flooded dugout, the thought of drowning did. He opened his mouth to say he couldn't possibly paddle himself in against a riptide and the lieutenant got his words in first.

'Perhaps we should go to your cabin, sir.'

He meant his cabin. It was tiny. The size of a cupboard, with a fold-down shelf for a bed. The lieutenant shut its door firmly behind him.

'Look, sir. Even if I wanted to disobey, I can't. You've seen my boat. It's crowded, it's noisy, and it's no bigger than a sardine can. We're surfacing in ten hours. With all respect, sir, I'll need you off this crate.'

To Joachim von Ribbentrop,
Reichsminister of Foreign Affairs
From Oswald, Freiherr von Hoyningen-Huene,
Reich Ambassador to Portugal

Date: Saturday, 6 July 1940
<u>Top Secret</u>

     My agent met the duchess as suggested and lost a
small sum to her; slightly more than we agreed, but still
modest. She confirms the duchess is as unhappy as you
suggested. Her feeling, for what it's worth, is that the
duchess is utterly untrustworthy, but is unaware of this
herself, since her own self-interest allies so strongly with
what she wants for her husband that she doesn't
distinguish between the two. It seems obvious that the
duke's weak points are greed, pride and a hatred for his
father. Something you already undoubtedly know. Do I
have your permission to build on this?

To Oswald, Freiherr von Hoyningen-Huene,
Reich Ambassador to Portugal
From Joachim von Ribbentrop,
Reichsminister of Foreign Affairs

Date: Saturday, 6 July 1940
<u>Top Secret</u>

Thank you for your report. I was amused by your
astute suggestion that we build on the duke's dislike of his
late father. As it happens, I already have this in hand.

48

Alderney, same day

The air on the island was rancid, the crows never stopped cawing, and that morning's mist had burnt away to leave a naked horizon that emphasized, as if Keller needed it emphasizing, how far from Berlin this posting was.

Seabirds hung at the edge of a cliff on salt-air currents, apparently unmoving. Waves crashed on granite rocks no man could survive if he fell. Captain Keller cared little for gulls, even less about waves and only noticed the rocks because there were too many to miss.

He cared for trees, though. Alderney was strikingly bare of those. The trees he cared for were dark, ancient oaks, found in the depths of the deepest German forests. All good Nazis cared for trees. His previous CO had told him that. He'd liked them ever since.

Had von Neudeck really not been told about the Führer's expected arrival? The old man's shock seemed real. Yet in the last twenty-four hours von Neudeck had started to see nothing but problems in the plan.

Perhaps this was a loyalty test?

If so, Keller's short but impassioned speech after breakfast should help convince von Neudeck of his loyalty to the Reich.

'Take a walk,' von Neudeck said when the speech was done. While Keller was still bristling, he'd added, 'Get to know this island. We might be here a while.'

To Keller that sounded like treason.

The captain had ignored von Neudeck's suggestion he visit the famous gannet colonies, and settled for a walk to Fort Clonque, where he had to leave a path to avoid a dead pony. Clonque wasn't the only part of his new posting to stink like an abattoir. The whole festering place did.

On the way back, he sighted a hotel altogether more to his taste than the cottage he'd been assigned. Through its frosted window he saw a shadow. When he rapped on the glass, the shadow stilled.

Striding for the door, Keller kicked it open to find his way blocked by a teenager, whose eyes had the glitter of a rat that believes itself cornered. When the boy raised a crowbar, Keller shook his head.

'Injure me,' he said, 'and your family dies.'

'I don't have a family. And if I did,' the boy added, 'I wouldn't like them enough to care.'

In spite of himself, Keller laughed. 'Who are you?'

Calculation crossed the boy's face. He was weighing the odds between truth and lying. 'Jimmy Todd,' he said finally. 'Borstal boy. Sent here in the last year of my sentence to help a farmer. Rehabilitation, like.'

He made the last two words a sneer.

'What were you in for?'

'I put someone in hospital.'

'Why?'

'I didn't like him, did I?'

They were negotiating, after a fashion. The teenager probably thought it was for his freedom but Keller knew it was for his life.

'Don't tell me,' Keller said. 'Model prisoner.'

'Didn't put a foot wrong,' the boy said with a grin.

'Why didn't you leave with the farmer?'

'I thought I'd wait for you lot. In the meantime . . .' The boy held up his wrist to show a gold Rolex Oyster. 'You'd be surprised what people leave behind.'

I wouldn't, Keller thought. He'd been the cause of enough people fleeing to know that those who ran unburdened were more likely to survive. 'What do you think we can give you?' Keller demanded.

The boy looked askance. 'Loot.'

49

English Channel, same day

'Wait a second, sir . . .'

The petty officer tightened his grip on the halter that held Bill's collapsible canvas canoe tight to the side of the submarine. The dark waves tried to drag it away again.

'There,' he said. 'That should make it easier.'

Bill's case was already in the canoe, taking the place he'd hoped would be filled by someone rowing him ashore. Bill knew he must look absurd in brogues, twill shirt and light-weight tweeds but night had reduced him to a silhouette and the English Channel to a heaving swirl that rose and sank as he tried to find the courage to climb in.

'When you're ready, sir.'

He'd never be ready. Not for this.

Any hope of a reprieve vanished when the lieutenant clambered down the conning-tower ladder and held out his hand. 'My St Christopher,' he said. 'Thought you might want him.'

'Thank you,' Bill replied.

'Safe trip. Sorry we couldn't row you ashore.'

'I'll manage.'

'I'm sure you will, sir.'

When Bill looked back the submarine was gone. Not submerged, simply swallowed by darkness, as a tidal current carried him away. He dug in an oar, but the water felt like molten lead. Trying to steer was impossible. The best he could manage was to keep himself upright. All around him, black waves boiled and wind ripped foam from their peaks, before turning it to spume that stung like hail.

The sky spun and Bill retched, the unexpected fall of a swell emptying his gut in a single spew. He didn't even notice the Heinkel seaplane until it passed right overhead. When it turned, Bill thought it must have seen him, but instead it circled to where the submarine had been. A flare arced into the darkness. A second flare followed. In their light, the sea raged.

That was when another two Heinkel He 115s swept in. Bill still couldn't hear them above the howl of the wind, but he saw them straighten up and begin their run in the light of the flares. First one, then the other, sowed the sea with depth charges.

Plumes of water rose as they exploded.

One of them was on the turn when its pilot saw Bill.

It swept round in the last light of a flare and Bill had a split second to realize what was happening before it opened fire, bullets ripping across the water towards him. He was out of his canoe ahead of the He 115's machine guns slashing it in two.

Salt filled his throat as a wave swallowed him, and something slammed into his back. Bullets, he thought. I'm dead. But then the rock threw him off, he spun in the current and water closed over him.

He could feel his body fight itself as he choked on water. His chest was bursting and darkness was filling his head. Tumbled by the riptide, he didn't know which direction was up or how to reach air.

The human body floats.

In a loch maybe, not when a current pulls you down.

He tried to remember what he'd been taught. Kick off your shoes, lose your jacket, dump anything heavy. He tried, but the moment he reached to remove his shoes he began sinking again. *You didn't even make it to the bloody beach.*

Bill thought that would be his last thought, and for a while it was.

When the sea finally gave him up, he was several hundred yards along the coast, and the Heinkels were circling away to the side. He had no need to sink his canoe now. They'd done that for him. Sunk his radio, too.

How the hell was he meant to contact HQ without a radio?

With that thought came a realization he was alive. His jacket was sodden, his throat raw, his stomach empty, the knife, garrotte and wireless he'd been given were gone. But he was alive. Bill clung to that thought. And then he heard the crash of waves behind him, twisting round just in time to see jagged rocks race towards him.

He felt himself swept up and knew it wasn't over.

To Sir Walford Selby,
His Majesty's Ambassador to Portugal
From Penny Moony,
Lisbon Embassy (Cyphers)

Date: Saturday, 6 July 1940
<u>For Your Eyes Only</u>

Yesterday evening was uneventful. If anything, the duchess seemed tired from the drive, dissatisfied to be in Portugal and resentful at being required to accompany her husband to the casino. She drank little, smoked without stop, refused my offer of food and didn't touch the olives, bacalao and salted nuts brought with her martinis. She made clear she had no interest in conversation and replied just enough to be polite. I saw no evidence of the witty socialite of popular report.

The only complication arose at the start of the evening when the duchess visited a high-stakes salon from which I was turned away, lacking funds to secure entry. She returned after forty minutes with substantial winnings, having played, she said, an intense hand or two of poker against a Swiss financier, an American industrialist and a Portuguese countess. In the time she was with us, I saw no evidence she entered into any conversations with strangers.

To Sir Walford Selby,
His Majesty's Ambassador to Portugal
From SIS Desk, Lisbon

Date: Saturday, 6 July 1940
<u>Confidential</u>

I believe we need to establish the identity of a well-dressed blonde, wearing an emerald bracelet, who entered the ladies' lavatories shortly after Wallis Simpson and followed her to a salon five minutes later. We will also need funds allocated to allow us access to all salons, high-stakes ones included. I have passed a roll of microfilm to Quentin, who will develop it this morning. The shots were from a distance and I apologize if they are blurred. Q assures me he's inventing a better camera.

50

Bill woke face down on a shingle beach. It took him a moment to remember where he was and why. Remembering didn't make him feel any safer.

Crawling to his knees, he stared at the sea and his guts tightened. In the distance, a huge oil slick was being broken up by waves. He held little hope for the blond-haired lieutenant and his crew. So many lives lost. Bill couldn't imagine what drowning in a cramped, overcrowded tin can, as its sides ripped apart and water rushed in, was like. *He didn't want to imagine.*

His chest tightened at the thought of it.

This time round he heard the Heinkel before he saw it.

Scrambling for cover, he ducked under gorse at the top of the beach just as a He 115 crested Aldoy Head behind him en route for the slick. It made one complete circle of the area and raced out across the blue, so low that its floats skimmed the waves like flying fish. The pilot was enjoying himself, and why not? That didn't make Bill hate him any less.

'Move,' Bill told himself.

He'd reached the shore path before he glanced back and saw a boat rounding a headland behind him. As it drew closer and slowed to avoid rocks, Bill saw two men in German uniform with a boat boy in a fisherman's smock. They had to be heading for the same place as him.

Château Renhou loomed ahead. Uglier than he expected, with heavy walls built to withstand attack from land or sea.

Stumbling on, he lost sight of the house for a moment and walked faster, his breath burning in his throat, his heart hammering, and not just from exhaustion.

He had to get there first.

He had to be at home when the Germans arrived.

He was Sir William Renhou of Renhou. The success of the mission and his chances of staying alive depended on them believing that. Hurrying to a stone hut at the start of the causeway, he felt above its lintel for the key.

It wasn't there.

And the garage door he'd been assured would be locked opened easily. But the key to the château he'd been told would be hanging from a hook inside wasn't there either. Some briefing.

Keyless, he staggered over the causeway and dragged himself up the run of stone steps to the house. His house, he reminded himself. More in hope than expectation, he tried the handle of its huge door and was shocked when it opened.

There were lights on inside. A packing crate stood in the middle of the hall on black and white tiles. It was full of hastily wrapped china. Good-quality china. The door to the cellar was open and Bill could hear a petrol-driven generator.

Bill hesitated. He had no choice but to go on.

'Hello?' he called into the darkness.

When no one answered, he flicked on an overhead light and thudded his way down, so anyone already there knew he was coming. All he found was the generator, and a rack of glass-sided batteries that stored Renhou's electricity. A single bulb on a fraying flex lit the gloom.

'Anyone here?'

His voice echoed off a low ceiling and disappeared through an arch that led to a cellar beyond, and a cellar beyond that, with an end wall filled floor to ceiling with four-gallon cans. Fuel for the generator, which started itself whenever the batteries ran low. The last of the cellars stank of petrol, damp and dead rats.

Removing the oilskin envelope taped to his ribs, Bill broke its seal and extracted his passport, a Rolex, a set of lockpicks, and a crocodile-skin wallet containing five-pound, one-pound and ten-shilling notes. They'd survived the soaking and so had he, if only just.

That was when he spotted a jacket on a peg above a pair of muddy brogues. The brogues stood beside a trug containing secateurs, shears and a pair of tatty cords. Gardening clothes. Bill couldn't do anything about his shirt, but he changed quickly into the rest.

Then he went up to meet the Germans.

51

Alderney, same day

Daisy Renhou glanced up from the tea chest she was preparing to nail shut. For a split second she looked terrified, then she did a double take and her face hardened as she realized Bill wasn't who she'd thought he was.

'That isn't your jacket,' she snapped.

Bill didn't like the way she flipped the hammer round so the claws were facing him. He stepped back smartly.

A plaque next to an empty nail in the hall's oak panelling announced the missing painting as a Redon, purchased by Sir Hugo Renhou in Bruges in 1905. An oblong patch on a dusty table indicated where a carriage clock had been removed.

'You're clearing Renhou?' Bill asked.

'What business is it of yours?'

'You'll have to put it back.'

'Get out.' Daisy stepped forward, hammer in hand when what Bill had feared would happen did. The Germans hammered at the door, the unlatched door swung open and two Wehrmacht officers stood framed in its arch.

For a second everybody froze.

'My apologies,' Bill said into the silence. 'My wife's in a temper.' His German was firm, his voice more confident than he felt.

A colonel and a captain stepped into the entrance hall. The captain had the face of someone who had been handsome in his teens. The colonel was missing one arm, its sleeve neatly pinned. He seemed intrigued.

'Do you and your wife often have arguments like this?'

'I'm not his wife,' Daisy said.

None of Bill's briefings had told him she spoke German.

'As you can see,' Bill said. 'She's cross.'

'This is absurd,' Daisy Renhou turned her glare on Bill and he remembered everything he knew about her. Married for money. A fascist sympathizer. A gangster's mistress. She probably had him down as a looter over from Guernsey. Taking another step forward, she gripped the hammer so tight her knuckles whitened.

The colonel held up a hand.

'You have guests,' he said crossly. 'I am Ernst von Neudeck. This is Captain Keller. We are paying you, and the Dame of Sark, as seigneurs under the king, the respect of coming to you instead of ordering you come to us.' He glanced at the captain and something went unsaid. 'Now, you pay us the respect of making us . . .'

The captain was staring at the tea chests.

'One of you is leaving?' If the man noticed his CO's irritation at being interrupted, he didn't let it show.

'He is,' Daisy said.

'Going where?' the captain asked.

'Anywhere but here,' she snapped.

'Madame,' the colonel said, sounding personally offended. 'We're here on an official visit to introduce ourselves to the Knight of Renhou.'

'*That is not the Knight of Renhou.*'

'Then who is he?' The captain's voice was sharp.

'I've no idea,' Daisy said, her voice equally sharp. 'A thief, I imagine. I've never seen him before in my life.'

To All Editors, Southern Region
From Alfred Duff Cooper,
Chief, Ministry of Information

Date: Sunday, 7 July 1940
<u>For Immediate Action</u>

ONE

British families are **not** fleeing. They are **not**
retreating to safer areas. **Nobody** is panicking.

There have been recent reports in the press of
families relocating to areas they consider safer. These
reports must cease immediately. Any newspaper that
breaks this edict will have its paper allocation cancelled
and its licence withdrawn.

TWO

Tomorrow morning Brighton Beach will be strung
from one end to the other with extra barbed wire. Sappers
will be adding additional tank traps and constructing
several machine-gun posts along the promenade. The
Brighton *Evening Argus* may cover this as inconvenient but
essential. Other papers should simply mention that the
government is taking all sensible precautions to keep
Britain's southern coastline safe.

THREE

You will receive within the next two days a survey showing that the public have total confidence in their government. This will confirm that the majority of the public, although understandably worried by the thought of invasion, understand that it is safer to stay home and leave His Majesty's forces to get on with their job.

Regional newspapers should supply supporting quotations from local residents. National newspapers will use the quotations provided.

52

Alderney, same day

Renhou had two jetties. A wooden one on the Alderney side, with a dinghy used to navigate the causeway at high tide; and a stone one below the terrace that looked towards where England would be. Bill considered the drop between Renhou's sea jetty and von Neudeck's boat. 'Do you need a hand?' the colonel asked him.

'I can manage,' Bill said stiffly. 'All the same, my wife's lying.'

'Why would she do that?' the captain demanded.

'You've never been married, have you?'

They let him climb unaided into the boat, then the colonel clambered after him. Keller followed and the boat boy stepped up to—

'*No you don't.*'

Steaming towards the jetty, a red-faced woman grabbed the bow rope from the boat boy and wrapped it firmly round the rickety post.

'You put Sir William back.'

The colonel stared at her, then at Bill and finally up to the terrace, where Daisy Renhou stood scowling. 'Sir William?' von Neudeck said.

'I'm Mrs Beecher, his housekeeper. I've served this family for forty years.'

'You,' Captain Keller shouted at Daisy. 'Here.'

She looked from Bill to the middle-aged woman, who was telling the boy, whom she was busy calling Eddie, that he wasn't to take the master anywhere. Understood? Sir William was staying here.

Daisy Renhou's fury could have killed.

'You said this wasn't Sir William,' Keller said.

'She's a liar,' Mrs Beecher said firmly, before Daisy could do no more than open her mouth. 'Always has been. They're divorcing.' She met Daisy's glare. 'Not before time either.'

'I thought I'd fired you.'

Mrs Beecher indicated Bill. 'Only Sir William can do that.'

Daisy looked more furious than ever.

53

Alderney, same day

In the entrance hall at Renhou, Captain Keller asked to see Bill's papers in such a way as to appear to ask on his CO's behalf.

So, it was to the colonel that Bill gave his passport.

'William Edward Hugo Giles Renhou . . .' Von Neudeck read the names aloud, then flicked through half a dozen pages. 'You do like travelling, don't you?'

'East Africa in particular,' Bill said, letting in a colonial drawl. 'I don't really regard Alderney as home.'

Daisy might as well have let her mouth drop open. A second later her face hardened. She was assessing. Asking herself questions. Bill got the feeling he wouldn't like any of her answers. She looked like she didn't like them either.

'Do you always carry your passport?' Keller asked.

'Only when expecting invaders.'

Keller didn't look amused. 'May I?' He held out his hand. As von Neudeck handed it over, Keller's nose wrinkled.

'Petrol,' Bill said. 'I've been in the cellars.'

'You have petrol?'

'Electricity too. The only house on the island.'

'We're installing generators.'

'Of course you are.'

'Anything else of interest down there? Perhaps I should look.'

'Perhaps you should,' Bill agreed. 'You'll find glass batteries, broken furniture, a generator old enough to belong in a

169

museum and petrol . . .' He shrugged. 'Oh, and a dead rat. Although you'll probably have to hunt to find that.'

What have I said? Bill wondered, seeing Daisy's face freeze. Other than lay claim to the contents of a house that wasn't his, obviously. He met and held her gaze, and watched her perfect face set and her blue eyes narrow.

Enemies, then. As if there'd ever been any doubt.

'Deutsch-Südwestafrika,' Keller said, flicking through the passport.

'It's called South West Africa these days.'

'It used to be a German colony.'

'Yes,' Bill said. He smiled. 'Who knows? Maybe it will be again. I have mining interests. Manganese and copper. Not as glamorous as farming in Kenya but substantially more profitable. I've got the share certificates somewhere.'

Daisy was staring now.

Hoping his briefing had been accurate on this at least, Bill headed for the drawing room. Even Mrs Beecher seemed shocked when he removed an ugly painting of a shipwreck and rested it on the floor. Behind it was Renhou's safe. An old, not particularly impressive model. Bill had the combination, but he made a point of fumbling the dial.

'Here we go,' he said.

Keller was reaching for the huge and impossibly ornate certificates when von Neudeck stepped in and took them. He whistled at the number.

'Inherited,' Daisy said suddenly. 'It's not like my husband worked for them.'

'You admit he's your husband?' Keller said.

'Not for long. Believe me.'

'When was this?' von Neudeck asked.

Daisy glanced at a silver-framed photograph. They were

in the drawing room at Renhou, pretending none of the previous half-hour had happened.

'Thirty-four,' she said. 'Possibly thirty-three.'

William Renhou, the real William Renhou, brash and heavily bearded, stood over a rhinoceros, with his foot on the animal's head and a bolt-action rifle in his arms. He was as puffed up, arrogant and utterly sure of himself as Bill had ever imagined he would be. More so, somehow.

Bill despised him.

All the same, he adjusted his stance, pushed his chest out a little, and raised his head until he was looking down his nose.

It wasn't Renhou who held von Neudeck's attention though.

'I met him, you know. Years ago.'

Him? Bill checked the photograph.

'The Prince of Wales. During the Great War.'

Either the prince hadn't known the photograph was being taken, hadn't cared or had just been asked a question. He had his head turned to a woman in a white shirt, with shorts slightly too tight for her hips and a pith helmet.

'Who's she?' von Neudeck asked.

'Someone's wife, I imagine,' Bill replied.

'*Someone's wife,*' Daisy mimicked. Her voice was tight. Turning to von Neudeck, she said, 'My marriage was a mistake from the start. And Mrs Beecher's right. We were divorcing . . .'

'Were?' von Neudeck said.

Daisy hesitated, and Bill held his breath.

'Are divorcing,' she said finally. 'And not before time either.'

To War Cabinet
From Winston Churchill

Date: Sunday, 7 July 1940
<u>Strictest Confidence</u>

Malta has come under sustained attack from Italian air bases. This island is our unsinkable aircraft carrier and without it we lose all ability to attack Axis forces in the Mediterranean or cut their line of supply to North Africa.

I have just been informed that Malta's entire defensive force consists of four Hawker Hurricanes and six Gloster Gladiator biplanes, only three of which are airborne at one time.

The bombing by Signor Mussolini's Regia Aeronautica will be terrible. All the same, Malta must hold and I have given orders to this effect. There will be no retreat, no evacuation and no surrender.

To Alfred Duff Cooper,
Chief, Ministry of Information
From Winston Churchill

Date: Sunday, 7 July 1940
<u>In Confidence</u>

<u>MALTA</u>

This is David and Goliath. Please ensure all news stories reference a plucky little island standing proud against almost overwhelming odds. Remember: David won. There is to be no suggestion that Malta might fall to the enemy.

54

Everyone was in the hall for goodbyes when von Neudeck stopped at the front door. 'You're really wanted for shooting your ADC?'

'He tried to surrender.'

'And that's why you're here?'

'Yes,' Bill said. 'That's why I'm here.'

Von Neudeck thought about it. 'What are you doing tomorrow?'

Bill hesitated, aware that both Daisy and the captain were listening. 'Nothing serious. Reading probably. Maybe a light walk.'

'Come and have lunch.'

'On Guernsey?'

Bill's shock amused the colonel. 'I'm based here,' he said. 'Someone else is running Guernsey. Jersey too. I could do with intelligent conversation.' If von Neudeck noticed Keller's flush he ignored it. 'Shall we say twelve? I'll send Otto, my driver.'

Von Neudeck's invitation obviously spurred Keller. 'Since we're extending invitations,' he said, 'perhaps you'd like to accompany me?

It took Daisy a moment to realize he meant her.

'Where?' she said.

'Wherever you'd like to be. Obviously, you can't stay at Château Renhou. Not with things so nasty between you and your husband. And there's no need, I promise you. I know a hotel that's just opened. They can fix you a suite.'

'It might be for the best,' von Neudeck agreed.

The glance Daisy shot Bill was pure hatred. For a second, he thought she'd say she didn't know him after all, but then she gave a curt nod and picked up her handbag. Bill was still wondering why when the boat left with Colonel von Neudeck, leaving Captain Keller and Daisy Renhou to walk.

A blue sky and bright sunshine. Not enough heat haze to ruin a perfect shot. Had Daisy had a sniper rifle, which she didn't.

She was going to have to kill the imposter.

There was rat poison in the cellars, and it wasn't as if Alderney lacked cliffs. Any number of the paths would be dangerous after the recent rain.

She imagined herself in black. Grieving for her broken marriage, despite her better instincts. It would give her gravitas with the Germans.

Add another layer to the disguise.

Who was he anyway, this impressively briefed fraud? To that, Daisy would add, what was he doing here? And, more to the point still, why now? When she'd only been back for a week and a half. It couldn't be coincidence.

'You're very quiet,' Keller said.

'It's been a trying day,' Daisy said, not bothering to sweeten her voice. Then she thought better of it, realizing she might need Keller's support at a later date. 'That man irritates me.'

'Obviously.'

'Why didn't we take the boat?'

They were still on Rue Beaumont, which ran down the spine of the island, from Renhou to Braye Harbour. Little more than a well-worn track.

'Walking is quicker, and besides the colonel prefers his own company. Well, he certainly prefers it to mine . . . This way.' Keller turned on to the road to La Ville, leaving Braye's huge sea wall and deserted harbour behind them.

Ahead was a shuttered hotel.

Daisy's eyes narrowed. 'You said it was open.'

Keller smiled thinly. 'It is. For us, anyway.'

55

Alderney, same day

'Could I possibly see that passport, sir?

The politeness of Mrs Beecher's words was at odds with the firmness in her face. The colonel, the captain and Daisy were gone, leaving Bill and Mrs Beecher alone on the sea terrace behind Renhou.

Opening the passport, she glanced at Bill for a second, matching him to the newly uniformed man in the photograph, then read Renhou's name aloud and flipped to the rubber stamps showing dates of Sir William's entry and exit to half the countries in East Africa.

'Welcome back, sir.'

Bill waited for her to say more. Instead she went inside.

He'd survived first contact with the enemy. He'd survived being denounced by Sir William's wife, who wasn't meant to be here anyway. He had an ally in Renhou's old housekeeper. Against that, he'd been nearly drowned, and had lost his radio, his dagger, his garrotte and most of his confidence. Sitting on a stone bench, he considered his options.

With no way to contact London, a straight hit-and-run on the safe, with a pick-up for the night after, was no longer an option. His only way off Alderney was to trust a submarine would rendezvous before dawn on the twenty-ninth, as he'd been promised.

That either gave him three weeks to become accepted, get to know the layout of the Nazi HQ, wait for the safe to arrive and crack it open. Or three weeks to get the hell out of here, relocate to North Africa and fix a new identity so convincing SOE would never find him. He knew what the old him would have done.

The new him wasn't so sure.

'It's getting late, sir.'

Bill didn't know how long he'd been sitting there. Long enough for the sun to reach the horizon, the sky to darken, and the sea to begin to merge with the sky.

Certainly long enough to accept that coming face to face with von Neudeck had blown his chances of blending in on one of the bigger islands while he worked out how to get away entirely.

'Would you like me to bring you a whisky?'

'That would be kind.' Bill paused. 'I'm slightly puzzled. I'd been told that . . . *my wife* was in Paris. That she was intending to return to America.'

'She was, sir. I'd been at my sister's in Jersey until someone said you were back. They were wrong. It was Lady Renhou. She returned at the end of May, emptied her room of everything valuable, told me I was fired and left.'

'What did you do?'

'Went back to my sister's.'

'Until you were asked to return?'

'Only by then her ladyship had reappeared.'

'She fired you again?'

Mrs Beecher nodded crossly.

56

Portugal, same day

This time the meeting was in a lay-by in Portugal's Serra de Sintra, an impossibly picturesque range of mountains that Diana the Huntress had made her own, if local legends were to be believed. The wind was dry and smelt of herbs, dust and hot metal. Two cars were parked nose to nose. A Buick and a Hispano-Suiza, the latter belonging to a young, blond Swedish count who was acting as Berlin's go-between. The cars were parked outside a café which, in Wallis's opinion, looked more like an abandoned shack.

'Sir,' Count Wadstein said, 'I beg you to reconsider.'

'Impossible,' said the Duke of Windsor. 'Returning to Spain would cause more problems than it would solve.'

'London's orders are that you stay here?'

Wallis thought her husband was about to say he didn't take orders. 'Their request,' he said after a slight hesitation. 'Portugal is an English ally.'

'Historically, certainly. One that's had the sense to stay neutral. Spain is also neutral. As, of course, is my country.'

'Sweden and Spain are not England's allies.'

'Indeed not,' the count said smoothly. 'But Franco's friendship with Berlin makes him well placed to keep you safe.'

'From whom?' the duke said.

'Anyone who might want to hurt you.'

'What have you heard?' Wallis demanded.

The count turned to her. 'Nothing,' he said. 'At least,

nothing firm. I'm told your house is being watched by English agents.'

'To keep me safe,' the duke said tightly. 'I'd expect no less . . .'

Wallis pushed back her chair, and both men stood and watched as she headed for the café. 'Tell them I want a cognac,' the duke called after her.

The slightest of nods said she'd heard her husband's order.

'Your royal highness,' the count said, the moment she'd vanished inside. 'May I speak freely?'

'If you must.'

'I apologize for my bluntness. Germany will win. As it has won everywhere else. We both know this. The Führer wants you at his side for the victory parade in London . . .'

He stopped, silenced by the fury on the duke's face.

'I apologize,' Count Wadstein said. 'I'm simply delivering the message that people who consider themselves your friends have asked me to deliver.'

'Say your piece.'

'Herr Hitler will not negotiate surrender with anyone but you. If you agree, it will not even be a surrender. You will agree the terms between you. It will be an armistice.'

'With a victory parade in London.'

'A state visit. You at his side as you show him your capital.'

'Impossible,' the duke said. 'We're talking about my country here. I cannot be seen at the side of an invader. The people would never forgive me.'

'You are the only man with whom Hitler will negotiate. If you will not agree terms, there will be no terms agreed. Only absolute surrender will be acceptable. You alone can save your people.'

His gaze slid over the duke's shoulder as Wallis returned,

followed by a waiter with a glass of brandy. The duke downed it in one, and sent him back for another.

'What did I miss?' Wallis said.

'Do you think England can hold out?' Wallis asked in the Buick on the way back.

'You mean will we really fight them on the beaches? Will a ramshackle guard of superannuated old men armed with outdated rifles and pitchforks heroically hold at bay the most modern army in the world, where the French, Poles, Czechs, Norwegians, Danes and Belgians have failed? I know, this is the point at which I'm meant to insist we'll never surrender but, in all honesty . . .'

'Then why refuse Berlin's offer?'

'Because Hitler will expect me to reject it. Because he'd think less of me if I appeared to contemplate it even for a second. My only choices are outrage and outright refusal.'

'He'll expect you to change your mind later?'

'He might. But I won't.'

'Darling. What then?'

The duke smiled sourly. 'I expect him to make a better offer.'

57

Alderney, same day

Bill was in the minstrels' gallery when he saw the ghost.

It was after dark and the house was silent. She wore a white nightdress, one button open at the neck to reveal a gold cross, and carried a candle as she glided across the hall below. He watched her vanish. Thin light flickered and he lost her in darkness. He was still telling himself he didn't believe in ghosts when she reappeared.

A board creaked under his foot and he pushed himself into the shadows as she looked up, suddenly still.

That face . . . God, that face.

Dark hair, features lit like a saint by the glow of her candle, and deep eyes that searched the darkness. She was younger than his first love Annie McLean had been when she died in her Edinburgh tenement. Younger than Annie's daughter would be now. The age of his own child with Miriam perhaps.

If she still lived, which felt unlikely.

The candle trembled and he watched wax drip to the floor. She looked at the spill, then back to the gallery, and Bill held his breath.

He watched her walk barefoot to the great stairs, climb steadily to the floor where he had rooms, and continue on up to the floor above, which held Mrs Beecher's room, the guest rooms and the minstrels' gallery where he stood.

Now what? he wondered.

The figure turned for the end of the corridor without

glancing back, her thin shoulders tight under her nightgown. She stopped at a door leading to the attics. It shut silently behind her, and Bill thought he heard a key.

Very carefully, he tried its handle.

The door was locked.

Two floors below, five drops of wax rested on the hall floor. No longer warm but not yet too solid to take Bill's thumbprint.

Not a ghost then.

58

'What do you think the Germans want us to do?'

Jerome, who'd been born on Guernsey, but had travelled to both France and England, and regarded himself as worldly wise, snorted at the question.

'It's obvious,' he told Georgie. 'They demanded stockmen, quarrymen, navvies and mechanics. That means animals, stone cutting, ditches and machinery.' He shrugged. 'At least they're paying us. I didn't expect that.'

'I'm not going to work for nothing.'

'You would if they pointed a gun at you.'

Georgie thought about that. 'We could bash them,' he said finally. 'Steal this boat and head for England.'

'They have guns,' Jerome said patiently. 'We don't. If we sailed to England in a German boat the English would shoot us too.'

'Just an idea,' his friend said grumpily.

Fourteen Guernsey islanders huddled in a boat delivering them to Alderney. It didn't matter what their two guards overheard in the pre-dawn. Georgie and Jerome spoke *Dgèrnésiais*, an impenetrable dialect of Norman French.

'Why not do the work themselves?' Georgie asked finally.

'Not enough of them,' Jerome said. 'Anyway, why would they when they have us?'

*

The islanders smelt the carcasses before they saw them. As the wind changed, and blew straight into their faces, Jerome's stomach heaved and Georgie put his hand to his mouth.

'Nasty,' he said.

Everybody was grim-faced by the time they beached at Crabby Bay. The body of a calf lay just up above the shingle, where it had been shot. Its eyes had been picked clean by crows. Crows that refused to budge when the men approached.

'Pick it up,' the older guard said.

59

Alderney, same day

'I saw a ghost last night.'

Mrs Beecher hesitated, her coffee tray halfway to the break-fast table. Her expression was unreadable.

'Indeed, sir?'

'A young woman in white,' Bill said. 'Perhaps a child. Bare-foot and wearing a nightdress. She had a small crucifix and carried a candle.'

'Did she say anything?'

Bill looked at Mrs Beecher. 'She speaks, then?'

'I'll get you your toast,' Mrs Beecher said.

The attic door was locked when Bill tried it after breakfast. He considered picking it but had a better idea. He knelt for just long enough to establish the lock had a key in it, and that it was on the far side.

'Definitely not a ghost,' he said.

Heading down to meet von Neudeck's driver, Bill stopped off at the kitchens, where Mrs Beecher was stacking bags of sugar.

'From the farm along the way,' she said, seeing him glance at her loot. 'Waste not, want not. If we don't take it the Huns will . . .'

'Our ghost,' Bill said. 'Tell her when she's ready I'd like to say hello.'

'I'm not sure that's advisable.'

'Why not?'

'She arrived with Lady Renhou.'

Bill looked blank.

Mrs Beecher sighed. 'She thinks you're really Sir William Renhou. You can't let her know you're not, and you don't want to terrify her.'

'Why would I terrify her?'

'Because her ladyship told the child the truth as she saw it. That her husband was a monster. That he was like all men, but worse. Now Lady Renhou's gone, and who knows when she'll be back, and she's left alone with you.'

'You're here,' Bill said.

'Given her ladyship's opinion of me, I'm not sure she finds that reassuring.'

'I'm Otto, sir.' The young man reddened. 'Sorry, sir. Private Schultz. The colonel sent me.'

Given that Otto was standing next to a smart blue Mercedes, which boasted a small swastika flapping in the breeze, that much was obvious.

'Where are you from, Otto?'

The young man hesitated, turning the question over as if afraid it might bite. 'Berlin, sir,' he said finally.

'Is this a good posting?'

Otto shrugged. Realized that was rude and nodded too late for Bill to believe him. From the boy's face, Bill knew he had just met the only person on the island who wanted to be there less than he did.

'Doesn't matter,' Bill said.

Renhou and La Ville were half an island apart on the map. Otto delivered Bill there in fifteen minutes, which did more to drum into him how compact Alderney was than any amount of staring at maps in Arisaig might have done.

It also reinforced how he should handle this.

The island was small, he didn't choose to be here, he was subject to other people's whims. The sea was as limiting as any wall and he was already counting down to release. It was obvious, really.

If Alderney was a prison . . . ?

He needed to become a trusty, and fast. One of those tamed prisoners screws regard as one down from useful idiots and one up from furniture. He'd already left it too late to make a break. The best he could do was smile, shape himself to their ends, and keep his thoughts to himself.

Yes, sir. No, sir. Can I help you, sir?

You could hide a whole world of contempt behind a smile.

60

Alderney, same day

'How could they?' Georgie shouted. 'How could they?'

The German guards began moving in.

Jerome held up his hand to signal he'd got this.

'They didn't,' he said firmly. 'The evacuation order for Alderney said no animals. So people killed their livestock and pets. Most people. Some couldn't do it. A group of us came over a week ago to kill any animal that was abandoned and starving.'

'We did this?' Georgie had tears in his eyes.

'It seemed for the best.'

By late afternoon, a dozen rancid dogs and a lot of other animals had been collected by cart and piled into a stinking heap on what looked like a bed of metal logs in the middle of a quarry. The islanders who'd collected them up had nothing left to vomit.

Stencilled *B-1E Elektronbrandbombe*, the logs were the most modern incendiary devices available. They were usually used to burn cities, but most of the cities the Wehrmacht had wanted burning were already in ashes.

The islanders stood back and a soldier ignited the cores.

The flames burnt so fiercely that the quarry's walls crumbled in the heat. Ash rose like smoke and fell across Alderney like snow. Nothing but fragments of bone and scraps of metal remained.

'Right,' the soldier said. 'Now load up the stone, deliver it to the harbour and begin repairing the breakwater.'

From Brighton Wolf

Date: Monday, 8 July 1940
<u>Top Secret</u>

<u>Report. Littlehampton Beach</u>

Concrete tank traps went up today on the slipways, pill boxes on the Promenade, all the road signs were removed to confuse invaders, a slit trench dug into the grass behind the post office, and the church tower left unlocked so it can be used at a moment's notice by snipers. You should tell those coming to restore order and drive out the Bolsheviks to use the other road.

My big news is the size of our Local Defence Volunteers has tripled, again. The bulk are workers from the Coombe Road factory, which produces ventilation fans for submarines. It's the big grey building near the kindergarten if you want to pass that on. I have, under my own initiative, joined the LDV, and being an ex-grammar-school boy now hold the rank of sergeant. Privately, our CO says he expects us to hold for a few hours only, if that.

A third of our group have Lee–Enfield .303 rifles. The rest make do with wooden replicas or pitchforks, bayonets and axes. More rifles are promised but no one has seen them and no one believes it.

We all know Germany will invade. We all expect it to be soon. Whatever lies the BBC tells, everyone expects the Führer to win. I do my part where I can, reminding the CO of our unofficial LDV title – Look, Duck & Vanish.

Forward to victory.

Heil Hitler.

61

Alderney, same day

It was early evening but the sun remained hot and the sea inside Alderney's breakwater was bright with shards of light. Wiping his forehead, Bill wondered how von Neudeck stood his heavy uniform.

'How long?' he asked.

Von Neudeck glanced at the islanders dragging carts laden with stone towards the inner harbour.

'How long, what?'

'How long will you keep them here?'

'Until we don't need them.' Von Neudeck said it so dismissively that Bill was shocked. Then he remembered Sir William wouldn't have been shocked at all and shrugged to show that made perfect sense.

It was a bleak reminder that the man he was imitating had far more in common with von Neudeck and the other Nazis than he'd ever have with any of the locals toiling fruitlessly at the sea wall.

'It won't be enough,' Bill said. He knew from his briefing that the breakwater had spent most of its previous ninety-three years undergoing continuous repair.

'It's all we can do, until we're in a position to replace it with concrete.'

That was an interesting use of *we*. We, meaning the Germans? We, meaning you, when we've conquered you? Bill doubted the colonel even knew himself.

'Walk with me,' von Neudeck said.

'Of cour—'

Out of the corner of his eye, Bill saw movement, heard someone shout a warning and slammed von Neudeck aside without thinking. A rock-filled runaway cart shattered against a wall behind them. Putting his hand to his face, Bill discovered he was bleeding. Exploding stone.

Soldiers from an anti-aircraft encampment near the customs house were already racing towards their fallen CO.

'Are you all right?' Bill asked, helping von Neudeck to his feet.

The colonel stared at the shattered stone and runaway cart, which lay splintered by the wall.

'Colonel,' a breathless soldier said.

'Return to your post,' von Neudeck ordered. Scowling, he watched the soldier depart, taking the others with him. Then he turned to the islanders and unclipped his holster.

Bill beat him to it.

Stalking up the slope, he backhanded the offending labourer so viciously he fell. 'Idiot,' he said, kicking him. 'You nearly killed the CO.'

The man he hit looked dazed. He gestured helplessly at his ruined cart, the blocks he'd been carrying spilled everywhere.

'Georgie's simple,' an islander shouted.

'It was an accident,' another protested.

'Can you prove that?'

The man gaped at Bill.

'Can you?'

'No. Of course not.'

'Pity. It might have saved his life.'

'His life . . . ?'

'He nearly killed a senior German officer. If I were you, I'd be grateful if they don't shoot the lot of you.'

'Sir William,' von Neudeck said.

'Colonel?'

'I'm unharmed.' Turning to the nearest soldier, von Neudeck said, 'Get this cleared up, get the remaining carts unloaded, billet this lot somewhere secure and lock them in for the night.'

'What about that one, sir?'

'Lock him in with the others. I'll deal with him in the morning.'

To Charles Standish III,
US Office of Information
From General Sir Stewart Menzies,
Chief, Secret Intelligence Service (MI6)

Date: Monday, 8 July 1940
<u>Secret</u>

What, if anything, do you know about the relationship,
family or otherwise, between Vichy fascist politician
Raphaël Alibert and Marguerite Alibert, self-styled
Princess Fahmy, widow of the late Ali Kamel Fahmy Bey?

62

Washington DC, same day

Standish had better things to do than answer demands for information from the Chief of British Intelligence, but the timing of Sir Stewart Menzies' question interested him.

Raphaël Alibert was busy establishing a new fascist party in France. Standish wondered if England really thought it could turn on an old ally and destroy one of its battleships at Mers-el-Kébir without there being consequences?

He could have told them exactly what would happen.

But where did an ageing adventuress fit into this? From what Standish remembered of Marguerite Alibert's lurid and unlikely career, if she was involved in what he suspected Sir Stewart thought she was involved with, Sir Stewart was right to be very worried indeed. Marguerite's affairs were carefully chosen and she kept the evidence every time. Her skills as a blackmailer were remarkable.

It was said, with some evidence, that she and the Duke of Windsor had once been very close. He had been very young and she was rumoured to have Paris's largest collection of whips . . .

Standish decided he'd better check on Madame Alibert for himself. After the archivists had gone home. It wouldn't do to attract unwanted attention.

To the Right Honourable Lord Halifax,
Secretary of State for Foreign Affairs
From Victor Mallet, CVO,
British Envoy to Sweden

Date: Monday, 8 July 1940
<u>Confidential</u>

A Swedish minister confirmed this evening that Stockholm has agreed to allow Berlin to route 4,000 Nazi troops a week through Sweden, en route from Germany to Norway, or Norway to Germany. Simultaneously, a treaty is being drawn up to guarantee an increase in the supply of Swedish iron ore to German military factories, vastly increasing German weapons capability.

This, the minister admits candidly, is the Nazis' price for 'respecting' Swedish neutrality. He was mildly apologetic but stressed his government regarded it as a price worth paying.

63

'You saved my life,' von Neudeck said.

'That's a bit over-dramatic, don't you think?' Bill said. 'I pushed you out of the way of a cart. That's hardly taking a bullet.'

Von Neudeck laughed.

He seemed in remarkably good spirits for someone who'd rolled out of bed to watch an execution. This was a different von Neudeck. Focused. Precise. A post had been hammered into the dirt in front of the wall where the cart had crashed; and six privates carrying rifles, and the sergeant with the scarred face, had been dispatched to drag the islanders from the stables where they'd been locked up for the night.

That was something. One post instead of fourteen. Unless he intended to shoot the islanders one at a time.

'You don't have to be here,' von Neudeck said.

'I probably do.'

'*Noblesse oblige*? Your duty as the Knight of Renhou . . . ?'

'Something like that,' Bill said, trying not to feel sick.

'So be it. Here they are now.'

The Guernsey islanders shuffled into view, dragging their feet and looking mutinous. Fourteen of them against nine men on the German side, if you counted Bill, and from their glares the islanders did.

'I'm sure it's policy,' Bill said, fighting to keep his voice light, 'but do you really have to shoot him?'

'We're not shooting anyone.' Von Neudeck patted Bill's shoulder. 'Tactfully put, though. We're treating it as an accident. Who knows? It might even have been one. We're going to flog him, with a warning that we'll shoot the lot of them next time.'

'You tell him,' an islander appealed to Bill. 'You tell him he can't do this.'

'Of course he can do this,' Bill said. 'His men have rifles, you don't. He controls the island, you don't. He can do what he wants. Be grateful your man's not being shot.'

'He's not . . . ?'

'What's your simpleton's name?'

'Georgie.'

'What's yours?'

'Jerome.'

'Listen to me,' Bill said, stepping close. 'Your friend almost killed a senior officer. If he had you'd be dead. All of you.'

He paused to let that sink in.

'If it happens again you will all be dead.' It was meant as a warning but Bill could see Jerome took it as a threat, just as he obviously believed Bill backhanding Georgie to the ground the previous evening had been cruelty. Not a quick-witted intervention that saved the man's life.

Jerome only stepped back into line when a soldier jabbed with a rifle.

Having taken sour amusement choosing where to land his first lash, the scar-faced sergeant raised his whip and brought it slashing down.

Georgie's scream made Bill flinch.

'Gag the man,' von Neudeck ordered.

A trooper pulled Georgie's belt from its loops, jammed it between his teeth and tied it behind his head in a crude knot.

'Continue,' von Neudeck said.

The second blow crossed with the first, cutting a bloody X into Georgie's back as the man arched in agony and fought his ropes.

The belt muted his scream.

If anything, that made Bill feel sicker.

The third blow landed on the first, and piss darkened Georgie's trousers. The next three blows were no kinder, and when a soldier cut him free, Georgie sank sobbing to his knees. 'Stand him upright,' von Neudeck ordered.

The sergeant yanked him to his feet.

'There will be no more accidents,' von Neudeck told the islanders. 'You cannot afford accidents. If there is another, the consequences will be worse. Now, back to work . . .'

To Sir Walford Selby,
His Majesty's Ambassador to Portugal
From SIS Desk, Lisbon

Date: Tuesday, 9 July 1940
<u>Your Eyes Only</u>

So far, I've confirmed who Frau Metz isn't.

She definitely isn't the Swiss trade delegate she told Penny Moony she was when Miss Moony bumped into her in Café Versailles on Avenida da República yesterday evening, and had the presence of mind to say she remembered seeing Frau Metz at the casino. Miss Moony says that Frau Metz seemed in a hurry to get away . . .

Having given her a head start, Miss Moony followed but lost her mark when Frau Metz turned abruptly into a darkened side street and vanished. This sounds altogether too practised and professional to me.

64

Alderney, same day

'I'm sorry about this morning,' von Neudeck said.

'Not ideal,' Bill agreed.

They sat at a pub table in the back room of the Diver in Braye. A half-empty glass in front of Bill and a barely touched pint of bitter in front of the colonel. The labourers shipped in from Guernsey could be seen through the window. On the wall was a cartoon of Hitler listening at a pub door.

'Shall I tell the barman to take that down?' Bill asked.

Von Neudeck shook his head. 'It's not a bad likeness,' he said. Picking up his glass, he stared at it. 'Is it meant to taste like this?'

'Exactly like this,' Bill said.

'Really?' It was obvious von Neudeck wanted something from Bill. Equally obvious that he felt free to take his time getting there.

'*Prost*,' Bill said.

'Cheers,' von Neudeck replied.

The two men smiled at each other. The difference, Bill imagined, was that there was a chance von Neudeck meant it.

'You knew him, didn't you?' von Neudeck said. 'Knew him well.'

'Who?' Bill put down his pint.

'Your file says you were part of his set.'

Who was so decisive a *he* that Bill should know who he was?

'We're talking about the Prince of Wales?'

'As you say. Now your ex-king.'

Bill meant it as a question but von Neudeck took it as a statement. They were indeed talking about Edward, now Duke of Windsor, lately King of Great Britain, Ireland, and the British dominions beyond the seas, and Emperor of India. A man known to his friends as David, just as his replacement, George VI, was known to his family as Bertie. One of the many absurdities of a monarchy Bill thought should long since have been abolished.

'You were close friends?' von Neudeck asked.

In his head Bill ran through what he'd been told at Arisaig about Renhou's set. Nothing complimentary. Spoilt, drunken, over-privileged, given to smashing up restaurants and mocking beggars.

'Sir William?'

'I wouldn't go that far,' Bill said carefully.

Von Neudeck repeated the words back to him, apparently savouring them. 'Would you say he was a difficult man?' he asked.

Bill thought of the abdication, Edward's refusal to compromise, his determination to marry a foreign divorcee. Or, if one believed the papers, his willingness to go along with her desire to marry him. His furious, vitriolic rows with his mother. His open contempt for his brother. His hatred of the new queen.

How could von Neudeck even ask?

'Yes,' Bill said. 'Very.'

'Nervous too?'

Bill nodded, because that was the response von Neudeck expected. Besides, the duke had a nervous face. That sullen mouth, those inward-looking eyes, both framed in a face better suited to a matinée idol than a king.

'What makes you ask?' Bill tried to keep his question casual, but he could hear a tremble in his voice.

'Your file says you knew him. That you were once close. There's a suggestion you argued. The general hopes you might tell me about what.'

'A woman.'

Von Neudeck laughed. 'Of course it was.' Pulling a cigar from his pocket, he lit it and passed Bill one of his own. The colonel was playing for time, watching Bill, judging his next question.

'Wallis Simpson?'

'Good God, no. Someone's wife.'

'Good.' The colonel accepted Bill's answer without question. Chances were it was true. If Sir William had quarrelled with the prince, then some planter's wife in Kenya was probably the reason. Renhou was less than a saint, and the prince's habits well known.

'Would you say you were good friends?' von Neudeck asked again.

'I wouldn't go that far.'

If Bill and the duke ever met, the duke's first words would be, 'Who the fuck are you?' Closely followed by, 'No, you're not . . .'

Bill wasn't liking the way this conversation was going. He wasn't liking it at all. Any situation that brought the duke anywhere near him was only going to end one way. In Bill's exposure, and probably execution.

The best he could hope for was not being tortured first.

'I thought he was in Spain?' Bill said.

'He was,' von Neudeck said. 'In Madrid. Now he's in Lisbon and refusing to come home. Churchill's insisting, and the duke's sticking to his guns. He went there from Spain, and to Spain from France, via Biarritz and the Côte d'Azur. Your prime minister's threatening to court-martial him if he doesn't return. Absent without leave in wartime. Technically that's a capital offence.'

'They wouldn't . . .'

Bill obviously sounded shocked because von Neudeck put a hand to his arm. 'It won't happen,' he promised. 'We'll see that it doesn't.'

'You'll see . . . ?'

'He's at a villa outside Lisbon belonging to a banker called Espírito Santo e Silva, who's not unsympathetic to our aims. We're having the house watched. This is in confidence, you understand? I'm trusting you.'

'Why?'

'You and I have a common culture, a shared heritage. Your royal family is German, whatever they pretend. Our countries shouldn't be at war. The duke himself says that none of this would have happened if he'd remained king.'

'What's my part in this?'

'Would you put Renhou House at his disposal?'

Bill sat back in shock.

Von Neudeck was watching him closely. 'Why do you think we're having the island smartened up?'

'Renhou House is . . .'

'A bit too primitive for a duke and duchess? Don't worry. We'll redecorate if necessary. We have a week or two yet.'

BEWARE

Whether alone or in a crowd,
Never write or say aloud,
What you're loading, whence you hail,
Where you're bound for, when you sail.

—ABOVE ALL NEVER GIVE AWAY
THE MOVEMENTS OF H.M. SHIPS

Careless talk costs lives.

65

Alderney, same day

Putting down his glass, von Neudeck said, 'I'm due to meet a plane . . .'

There was something in the way he said it.

Not the duke though. Thank God. The colonel had just said they had a week or two's grace on that. Who then?

'Someone important?' Bill said. 'Perhaps very important?'

'The Führer? God no. He's busy.'

'Planning an invasion?'

'If London doesn't have the sense to sue for peace.' Sitting back, von Neudeck considered his words carefully. 'Did you hear the speech your king made about the horrors of the last war?'

'*My* king?' Bill said.

'Edward. The real one. The one your archbishop made abdicate. Not his stuttering little brother with the pushy wife.'

'I thought Edward was the one with the pushy wife?'

Von Neudeck raised his eyebrows. 'Have you met Elizabeth Bowes-Lyon?'

'No,' Bill said. 'Have you?'

Von Neudeck smiled, conceding the point. 'Von Ribbentrop has,' he said. 'Apparently he was not impressed. As for the pretender . . .'

It was Bill's turn to raise his eyebrows.

'Come now,' von Neudeck said. 'Who in Britain really thinks

George is the real king? Who agrees with the way his brother was forced out?'

'Most of the country, I imagine.'

'I thought you were Edward's man?'

'Who says I'm not?' Bill said.

Von Neudeck's look was slow and appraising. He nodded to himself and smiled. 'Indeed,' he said. 'Who says you're not.'

'This speech?' Bill reminded him.

'"I speak simply as a soldier of the Last War whose most earnest prayer it is that such cruel and destructive madness shall never again overtake mankind . . ." The duke went on to talk about how terrible the Great War had been. How it destroyed his generation. How nothing like that must happen again. It was widely reported.'

'Not by the BBC,' Bill said.

'No, indeed,' von Neudeck replied. 'Not by the BBC.'

'You're really going to bring the duke here?'

'Hitler's idea. Alderney is to be his *stepping stone*. He hopes for peace, but if that's impossible he will launch his invasion from here. With the duke at his side. The Channel Islands are a Crown possession. They have their own laws. Their own currency. Their own language. They owe allegiance not to parliament but to the king. The Führer respects that. He respects the king.'

'Edward?'

'Who else?' Pushing back his bench, von Neudeck told Bill to finish his pint. 'Come on. General von Hausen is flying in to see what we've achieved here so far. He'll be delighted to meet you.'

66

Alderney, same day

'Who is this? What's he doing here?'

Von Hausen seemed less happy to see Bill than von Neudeck had suggested. Behind the general, a colonel and two majors were clambering from an He III transport model. They wore *Waffenrock*, full dress uniforms. Two NCOs were having trouble with the aeroplane's steps. They were carrying a safe between them. It was all Bill could do not to stare.

'This is Sir William Renhou,' von Neudeck said.

'A local landowner?' The title seemed to mollify the general a little.

'The Knight of Renhou.'

'He owns Alderney?'

'I own Renhou,' Bill said. 'A rock on the north-east corner. It's barely the size of a decent car park.'

'You speak German?'

'I was in a German camp in the last war.'

'You were freed at the end?'

'I escaped and returned to my regiment. I might as well not have bothered. The war ended five days later.'

Von Hausen smiled thinly but the colonel seemed to have been forgiven. When the general's staff headed towards three waiting Mercedes-Benz, Bill headed after them. 'Stop,' the general ordered

Everyone stopped.

'This is the friend of the duke that Goering mentioned?'

'Yes, sir.' Von Neudeck nodded.

'His island. It's to the north of . . .' He clicked his fingers.

An aide said, 'Burhou Island, sir?'

'That's the one.'

'Yes,' von Neudeck said. 'It is.'

'And he has a house there?'

'A castle,' the colonel said. 'It has turrets.'

'One turret,' Bill said firmly.

The general laughed. After that, Bill might as well have been a spaniel for all the suspicion the general's staff showed. None of them questioned his place in the group or tried to stop him taking a seat beside the safe and an NCO in the last of the cars. In prison, the key to becoming a trusty was to be amusing, unthreatening, and useful – preferably all three.

'That looks heavy,' Bill said.

'A new model,' the NCO said patiently.

Bill took a closer look. 'Very impressive,' he said.

Two dials, two handles, huge, heavily armoured hinges, the tolerances of the door and frame so perfect they might as well have been machined by a Swiss watchmaker. Patek Philippe probably.

He'd never faced anything like it in his life.

67

Alderney, same day

The gates to the Island Hall were dragged back the moment the guards saw the first car approaching. Scaffolding covered the front of the building, with swastika banners tied either side of its portico.

Soldiers came to attention as the general was ushered from his car, swept under the portico and stalked through to the stark hall, his staff following hastily. And just like that, Bill was in the Nazi HQ, right behind two NCOs carrying what had to be the safe he'd been sent to crack.

It's not there yet, Welham had said . . .

Well, it was now.

A dour-faced corporal knelt by the front door, wood shavings round his knees. He was replacing the hall's old lock with something tougher. Seeing Bill take a closer look, a major muttered to a staff colonel, who said something to the general. Von Hausen turned.

'Colonel,' he said. 'If you would . . .'

Von Neudeck went to have a word. 'We have business,' he told Bill on his return. His tone suggested he found General von Hausen's qualms tiresome.

'You'd like me to wait outside?'

'Certainly not. You can use the room next to my office.'

The ground and first floors were tidy. The floor above a building site. Internal walls were being knocked out to create a huge Ops Room at the rear. The run of offices at the front overlooking the courtyard were untouched, their doors exiting into the Ops Room along the ghost of a corridor.

'In here,' von Neudeck said, opening one. 'We won't be long.'

The room into which he showed Bill was small, its view obscured by scaffolding and the back of a swastika that blocked out most of its light. Von Neudeck gestured at a shelf of leather-bound books. 'At least you won't be short of something to read.'

'Getting your orders?' Bill asked.

'I have those already.' Realizing he'd been sharp, von Neudeck smiled tiredly. 'Additional orders. No doubt. You know what it's like.'

Hearing the door to the next office shut, Bill checked his surroundings. Even without books, the walls were too thick to let him eavesdrop. On the other hand, the scaffolding behind the banner offered real possibilities. Removing a law book, Bill opened it at random and put it on a chair to suggest he'd been reading. Then he removed the key from the door's newly fitted lock.

It was as intricate as he expected.

He had no clay to take an impression, nor matchbox to keep an impression safe. And if he really wanted freedom to roam, he'd need to discover if all the offices shared a single key. But since he was already here, and the swastika banners meant no one could see him climb on to the scaffolding, it was time to see if he could discover where they'd put that safe.

His money was on von Neudeck's office next door.

68

Washington DC, same day

What, if anything, did Washington know about Marguerite Alibert? Rather more than London might like, Standish imagined.

The first thing out of the envelope on to his desk at the Department of Unintended Consequences was a yellowing cutting from a London newspaper from 1923: 'Not So Easy to Get the Millions of the Rich Husband She Shot'.

A photograph of a masked woman with a cat-o'-nine-tails whipping the naked buttocks of a young English officer followed. The officer knelt at the edge of a bed like a child in prayer. After that came the same young man in bed with what might have been a very young woman, but then again might have been a boy. Their limbs were tangled and sweat varnished their bodies. The final photograph showed the same officer face down on a bed, his buttocks uncovered and a whip on the sheet beside him.

The whip looked carefully positioned and probably was.

A one-time child prostitute, high-class courtesan, blackmailer, con woman, and wife of an Egyptian princeling, Marguerite Alibert believed in insurance policies. In particular, photographs, letters, diary entries, copies of hotel registers and receipts.

Marguerite had been the Duke of Windsor's first lover, and her price for not involving him in a scandal after she had murdered her Egyptian husband at the Savoy on the night of

10 July 1923 was his father the king's protection. In return, she promised not to mention the Prince of Wales or his sexual habits in court.

The prince's engagements had been cancelled first thing next morning, and he'd been bundled off to Canada on a three-month tour with his valet and orders to smile for the cameras and say not a word to journalists.

That she'd shot her husband through the back of his head in a corridor after an earlier argument at a restaurant, and left him on the carpet while she returned to her room for a cigarette before raising the alarm, never got a mention.

At her trial, Marguerite's lawyer painted Ali Bey as a violent, drunken lecher who'd debased an innocent white girl with his depraved oriental lusts. In the end she'd had no choice but to defend herself.

The verdict was never in doubt.

Standish smiled. No wonder London wanted to know how close a relationship existed between Marguerite Alibert, who drank at the Ritz in Paris, where Reichsmarschall Hermann Goering had set up office, and Raphaël Alibert, the Vichy politician who'd just set up the pro-Nazi party, l'Action française.

The thought of Marguerite handing obscene photographs of the young Duke of Windsor to Raphaël, so he could hand them to the Nazis, must be terrifying. Always assuming she hadn't already handed them to Goering herself.

Pulling a tape recorder close, Standish promised London he'd look into it.

69

Alderney, same day

Without giving himself time to hesitate, Bill raised the sash and clambered on to the scaffolding, giving thanks for the arrogance that decided to drape two swastikas instead of one across the hall's façade.

No walk-boards were in place, so he balanced on a cross pole, reached for one above and edged gingerly sideways. He was a safe-cracker, not a cat burglar, and he didn't like heights at the best of times. Unfortunately, this was too good a chance to miss.

Through a crack in badly drawn curtains, he saw officers facing a screen fixed to a far wall. The safe he wanted was to one side of it, mirrored by a bigger, older safe on the other. Probably the building's original.

Von Neudeck sat at the back, cigar in hand. He was working an Agfa projector and a map of France filled the screen. Arrows headed for Britain.

Die Luftschlacht um England. The Air Invasion of England. This was real. It was going to happen. Bill was taking that in when he heard a window slam.

A heartbeat later he realized which window it was.

A moment after that he heard it lock.

Never panic. He'd been told that by an old cat burglar in Saughton nick. On the other hand, the man hadn't just been locked out, with a long drop, and Nazi soldiers circling below.

Bill peered from behind his banner. Two armed guards

below, two more at the gates. Not circling exactly, but heavily armed. Any chance of escaping that way was out.

Edging back to his window, Bill peered through.

His book still rested on a chair. So far as he could see the room was empty. His best bet was to shift the catch with the blade of his lock-knife. He'd just managed to open this one-handed when Daisy's face loomed behind the glass.

Her eyes widened.

Instinct jerked Bill back. He felt his balance go, and reached for the bar above, feeling his fingers miss. Grabbing at a down pole, he came to an abrupt halt, leant right back, on the edge of not being able to stop himself falling.

For a second he teetered there before dragging himself upright, heart hammering so hard that he could feel it beat his ribs.

Daisy was staring at him.

Bill nodded at the lock and she didn't move.

'Let me in,' he mouthed.

Still she hesitated. After which, instead of helping, she drew the curtains abruptly. Bill almost hammered on the glass but a thought stopped him. At Renhou it had been her word against his. Here, all she had to do was do nothing and he'd be caught eventually. She didn't even need to fetch soldiers.

We won't be long, the colonel had said.

The meeting would be breaking up soon. If Daisy wouldn't help, he'd have to help himself. Heart still hammering, Bill slid his blade between the sashes. The curtains twitched and he was staring at Daisy again. Or rather, she was staring at him, her mouth tight, her gaze unreadable. Whatever she was thinking wasn't kind.

'Please,' Bill mouthed.

She glanced behind her.

He pointed at the window lock. For a moment he thought she was going to refuse again. 'For God's sake . . .'

She reached for it, scowling.

70

Alderney, same day

'Who the hell are you?' Daisy demanded, blocking his way.

What was the right answer to that? Lie and say he was a British agent? Lie and say he wasn't? Risk the truth, and say he was a thief blackmailed into being here? Which answer would she hate least?

What if she hated them all?

'The real question', he said, 'is who the hell are you? If you're not the blonde, blue-eyed Nazi I'd been told you were.'

'Who says I'm not?'

'You haven't given me up.'

'Maybe the time's not right yet . . .'

They faced off either side of a half-open window.

'Inside,' Daisy said suddenly. 'Now.'

'General von Hausen's meeting hasn't broken up yet.'

'It's not von Whatsit I'm worried about.'

'Daisy . . .' Bill hesitated.

'Do you want me to call them?'

He rolled himself in through the window and his feet were barely on the ground before Daisy's slap flipped his head sideways. The noise brought footsteps to a halt outside. The slap hurt. It was meant to.

'Two days fighting off that jerk,' she said. 'In a vile hotel that wasn't really open.'

'What jerk?'

The door opened and Captain Keller blinked to see them.

'What's he doing here?' Keller demanded.

'We were just talking about you,' Daisy said. 'My husband was using the restroom. He came back after you left.'

Bill put his hand to his face, and behind Keller someone laughed. Colonel von Neudeck pushed his way in and smiled ruefully at Bill's cheek. He bowed slightly to Daisy. Turning to Keller, he said, 'You didn't get my message?'

'What message would that be, sir?'

There was an insolence Bill hadn't heard before. The captain was performing for Daisy, Bill realized. Von Neudeck scowled. 'The one saying the general had rescheduled his flight.'

'He's here already?' Keller's voice lost its arrogance.

'Your absence was noticed.'

The captain turned grey.

'I regret', von Neudeck told Bill, 'that I'm going to have to abandon you. The general has called a second meeting.'

'Please tell him my house is at his disposal,' Bill said. 'Should he need it.'

'He'll need it,' von Neudeck said.

'We'll be off then,' Daisy said brightly.

'You're going home?' Keller's eyes narrowed.

'Yes,' Daisy said. 'We've decided to be civilized about all this.'

Von Neudeck's glance took in Daisy, the captain and Bill. But mostly it took in the slap mark on Bill's face.

'Very wise,' he said.

One of the general's staff was opening a hip flask, while his friends lit cigars. It was the cigars that gave Bill his idea.

'I don't suppose . . .' He hesitated. '. . . you have any spare?'

Von Neudeck looked surprised.

'Not that a man wants to beg.'

'You're out?' Von Neudeck smiled. 'Obviously, you're out. You wouldn't ask otherwise.'

He was turning for his office when von Hausen called.

'Give me a minute,' von Neudeck said tiredly. He went, and Keller followed, Daisy's departure apparently forgotten.

Now, Bill thought.

'Where are you going?' Daisy demanded.

Bill was inside von Neudeck's office before Daisy could object or anyone else notice. Nudging the door shut, he turned to the safes. Ignoring the green one, which was old and English, he crouched before the other and was grimly impressed.

It was formidable.

Two handles, two dials running from 0 to 100 set into a door that fitted precisely, with no gap for thermite to cut bolts, even if he had any.

With one eye on the office door, and praying Daisy would warn him if someone was coming, he spun a dial to reset it.

0—0—0—0

1—1—1—1

1—2—3—4

He ran through the obvious numbers, knowing the odds of getting lucky were almost as long as hitting three zeros in a row at roulette. He followed up with 10—20—30—40 and 20—40—60—80. Combinations he'd met more than once.

Had he known the model, he'd have tried its shipping combination, just in case it hadn't yet been changed. But he'd never seen a two-dial safe, never mind cracked one. And he could hardly risk being found with his ear to its dials. He was about to try another run of obvious combinations when Daisy coughed.

'Cigars,' she said loudly. 'It's bad enough William smoking them . . .'

Bill was at the window, dials wiped and set to where they'd been, staring at the staff cars in Connaught Square when von Neudeck entered. He seemed slightly surprised to find Bill waiting, but gestured to the humidor on his desk.

Bill chose a Montecristo Robusto.

'That's not enough,' von Neudeck said. 'Take several.'

Bill left the office with a heavy heart, six Montecristos and a clear picture in his head of von Neudeck's safes. One green, a known quantity and unlikely to present problems. The other squat and grey, decorated with a stencilled eagle, and unlike anything he'd cracked before.

71

Alderney, same day

'What were you after?' Daisy asked.

'The invasion plans.'

She stopped on the road to look at him.

'Are you serious?' she said.

'Obviously not.' Bill produced the cigars from his pocket.
'I wanted these. And I wanted a quick look around . . . Now.
Why this?' He touched his cheek.

'I felt like it. Besides . . .' Daisy shrugged. 'We needed to
be convincing.'

They stood on the outer edge of La Ville, with von Neudeck's HQ half a mile behind them. The shops on their way
through had been shut, the streets empty. The only person
they'd seen was a German soldier, who glanced idly but let
them pass.

'Now,' Bill said. 'Why did you let Keller manoeuvre you
into leaving with him? You could have refused. Made it a
point of principle. Said I should be the one to go.'

'You'd only just arrived.'

'They didn't know that.'

'Just as well,' Daisy said. 'You'd be dead.'

He wasn't going to get a straight answer, Bill realized.
Maybe Daisy had reasons for returning to Alderney. Reasons
beyond ransacking her husband's house. Given time, he'd
work out what they were.

'You might want to talk to the ghost,' he added.

'Ghost?'

'The one in the attic. White nightdress, gold crucifix, steals candles, only comes out at night. Spills wax when she's nervous.'

'Mignon?'

'She has a name?'

'Not sure it's her real one, though.' Daisy's smile was sour. 'She wouldn't be the only one around here, would she?'

72

Lisbon, same day

'You're letting me win,' Wallis said.

Frau Metz glanced at the growing pile of chips in front of Wallis and looked thoughtful. 'You prefer to win for yourself?'

'Always,' Wallis said. 'Wouldn't you?'

Wallis and Frau Metz were back in the high-stakes room at the Casino do Estoril at the German woman's invitation, less than a week after their first game. At least Frau Metz had more sense than to pretend Wallis's winnings were simply skill.

'Joachim's worried your husband will run out of money,' Frau Metz said. 'That its lack will force him to make the wrong decision.' She used von Ribbentrop's name with such ease Wallis was slightly jealous.

The chips in front of Wallis represented more than most men earned in a year. It was not that Wallis was spendthrift. It was not that her husband was poor. He simply liked money, large amounts of it. It made him feel safe.

We are the hollow men.

That applied to half his generation.

There was a darkness under their charm, a hollowness behind the solidity their fathers had. In her husband's case it was his father Wallis blamed.

'You were going to tell me about the will.'

'Yes,' said Wallis. 'I was.'

Frau Metz's timing really was uncanny, Wallis decided. She'd been wanting to talk about this and had had no one to talk to about it for ever. Wallis blamed her husband's father. His father, his family, and the War to End All Wars.

But mostly his father, and that bloody will.

'The old king was dead,' Wallis said flatly. 'No one wanted the new one parading his floozy. The reading was scheduled to take place in Sandringham great hall. My husband was so cross about my being excluded he almost refused to go, which would have been ridiculous. They were all there. Including his three brothers, his wretched mother, assorted lesser members of the family.'

Frau Metz held up her hand and Wallis bridled.

'We're being watched,' Frau Metz said.

A slightly saturnine man in an immaculately cut dinner jacket, which Wallis might have admired in another context, was staring at them. It was almost as if he wanted them to know he was watching.

'He can't hear us from here,' Wallis said.

'No. But he might be able to lip-read.'

'He might . . . ?'. Wallis sat back.

'We should continue this conversation tomorrow night,' Frau Metz said. 'That is, if your royal highness agrees.'

'What's to stop him coming back then?'

'I'll book a private room.'

73

Alderney, Wednesday, 10 July 1940

Stripping off her dress, Daisy changed into a swimming costume she didn't remember having left at Renhou and dived
into the early morning sea. It was colder than she expected,
which was the way she liked it.

She ploughed towards a distant rock, arms cutting into the
waves in a steady crawl. She knew exactly when to look up,
judged her roll perfectly and kicked off to give herself extra
speed for the return.

She made it from jetty to rock to jetty in 170 seconds,
which was close to her fastest. What she wanted to do was
drag herself on to the jetty below the terrace and dry in the
pale sun. Instead she made herself do it again.

Not as fast this time, but good enough.

Chest heaving, she hauled herself up, feeling her heart
race. A second after she'd stripped off, she looked up and
saw Bill watching from above.

Shrugging, she wrung out her costume, dried herself and
dressed. Then sat back, lit a cigarette and wondered whether
to consider him an enemy, a rival, a possible ally or an obstacle
to be removed. She'd thought him a looter that first day. But
his passport could have been William's if not for the photograph. He wore a copy of her husband's signet ring, and Mrs
Beecher, who guarded her position at Renhou like a dragon,
had obviously been briefed to expect him.

Yet he hadn't expected Daisy any more than she'd expected

him. He must be wondering why she'd covered for him. At least she hoped he was.

She intended to leave him wondering.

That was more than obsession, Bill decided.

More than Daisy burning off her fury at ending up in a deserted hotel in the company of Keller. It looked like a fitness regime. Not the kind recommended for women worried about their figures. More the kind prison hardmen used to avoid losing their edge.

He'd seen her naked, if only for seconds. What struck him wasn't how fit she looked but how dangerous. She hadn't covered herself either, when she realized he was watching.

He'd been the one to look away.

74

Alderney, same day

The ghost made an appearance before lunch.

Bill was heading along the footpath below Saye Farm, when the girl he'd seen with a candle gliding across the hall in Renhou fell into step beside him. Her English, which faltered when she started, got better as her confidence grew.

'I'm Mignon,' she said.

'I'm Sir William Renhou.'

'Madame said I should say hello.'

'Hello,' Bill said.

Mignon checked that she wasn't being mocked.

'Madame says you won't hurt me. I know you used to hurt her. She talked about that in the car. I know you used to hurt her a lot.'

Bill didn't have an answer.

Instead, he watched his ghost walk away.

75

Alderney, same day

'Don't you dare,' Daisy said.

Bill dragged his thoughts from Mignon cleaning silver at a kitchen table. It was an hour after lunch, which had been bread, fresh tomatoes and the remains of a roast chicken.

'Dare do what?'

'Involve Mignon in whatever's going on. She's not an asset.'

'I've no idea what you're talking about.'

'You know exactly what I'm talking about.'

'No,' Bill said. 'Believe me. I don't.'

When Daisy turned on her heels and strode for the library, Bill realized he was meant to follow. 'Why were you watching her?' Daisy demanded, the moment the door was closed.

Because she reminds me of my daughter.

Since that was obviously the wrong answer, Bill said, 'I was going to walk into town tomorrow. I thought she might like to accompany me.'

'Going where?'

'Island Hall.'

'You'd take that child to Nazi HQ?'

So much about Daisy didn't make sense. She looked the part, right enough. Blue-eyed, fair-haired, a gaze that held his. He could see her at Sir William's side at some Nazi do in Berlin. Why scruples about Mignon? And that, of course, led to the other question. 'Why didn't you give me up to the Germans?'

'You know why,' Daisy said.

Bill didn't.

'But now you're compromised,' he said.

'No,' Daisy said. 'I'm not. I just told them I was seeing what I could find out before handing you over.' She sounded as if she meant it too. 'Why would you drag Mignon to HQ anyway?'

'I need a copy of von Neudeck's key. I was going to take her in as cover, then keep von N. busy while she stole an impression.'

'Can you imagine what he'd do if he caught her?'

'I'll do it myself,' Bill said.

'You do that,' Daisy said. 'It will be safer for everyone.'

76

Alderney, same day

Bill was on the sea terrace with a whisky in his hand and evening coming in, when he realized he wasn't alone any longer.

'I'll get your key,' Mignon said.

'What if I say I have no idea what you're talking about?'

'Then you're lying. And you don't seem like someone who lies.'

'I've built a whole life on lying.'

'Is that true?' Mignon asked.

'Yes,' Bill replied.

'See,' she said. 'You're telling the truth.'

'Is there a point to this . . . ?'

'Yes,' she said fiercely. 'I'll get your key.'

'You shouldn't listen at doors.'

Mignon shrugged. 'You should check you're not being overheard.'

'No way,' Daisy said, when Bill mentioned it.

'I've already said that.'

'Find me clay to take the impression,' said Daisy, 'and I'll get myself into their bloody HQ and get you what you want.' Her smile was mocking. 'Unless you don't trust me?'

'And the price?' Bill asked.

'You tell me what you're really doing here.'

'When I've got a key.'

77

Lisbon, same day

'My ladies . . .'

A waiter had come to see if they needed more champagne. Frau Metz waved him away without Wallis noticing.

'The will wasn't what your husband was expecting?'

Of course, the poor darling hadn't been her husband then. She was still married to Ernest, and so far as the king's new subjects were concerned Edward was still sleeping his way through the wives and daughters of his courtiers. Another great British royal tradition that hadn't raised a whisper until Wallis disrupted it.

'No,' Wallis said, 'it wasn't. My husband inherited the crown but his brothers inherited the cash. He was forbidden to sell any of the royal possessions: the racehorses, the palaces, the paintings, his father's bloody stamp collection. He couldn't turn anything into cash on pain of having what he was trying to sell taken away. All of the trappings and none of the power. His mother and his brothers had him at their mercy. They knew that. He said his mother's expression when he stormed out of the room was triumphant. His brothers just smirked.'

'I had no idea, your royal highness.'

'No one does. His father treated him like dirt when he was alive, limited his money and kept him on a brutally tight rein. Nothing changed.'

'I'm so sorry.'

'It's so unfair. He's by far the best of them. I mean, look at his brothers. The new king has the charisma of a Croydon stockbroker. Gloucester's so fond of his fists he beat up his own equerry at the Duke of Abercorn's party. Georgie Kent was arrested as a prostitute after the police saw him and Noël Coward mincing through Soho in dresses. Believe me. That took some covering up . . .'

Frau Metz put her hand to her mouth.

'Quite,' Wallis said. 'There was a fourth. The simpleton. He died unexpectedly, which was convenient.' Any pretence they were playing cards had gone. Their hands rested on the table. The chips lay untouched.

'Your husband needs money?'

'Always. It helps him feel secure.' It also made him feel loved, but Wallis wasn't about to say that. Their conversation was one she'd been waiting to have. So far it was going better than she'd expected.

'Would it be crude of me to ask how much?'

'His brothers were each given three-quarters of a million in sterling. Over three million dollars. He was given a stamp collection he wasn't allowed to sell.'

'I'm sure Berlin could do better. If you think your husband won't be offended or misinterpret the gesture.'

'I'm sure he won't.' What she meant, of course, although Wallis wasn't about to say that either, was, *I'll make sure he doesn't.*

To General Sir Stewart Menzies,
Chief, Secret Intelligence Service (MI6)
From Sir Walford Selby,
His Majesty's Ambassador to Portugal

Date: Wednesday, 10 July 1940
<u>Secret</u>

The woman calling herself Frau Metz has been
identified as Helga von Bloch, the German military
attaché's niece. The man she describes as her husband
is Major Reinhold Berg, a senior Abwehr/intelligence
operative.

It is reported that Helga and Joachim von Ribbentrop
are lovers. This should not be considered definitive. That
claim is made for and by many Berlin society women. What
is certain is that her meetings with Wallis Simpson are not
innocent. Neither was her presence at the Casino do
Estoril on the night the Duke and Duchess of Windsor first
arrived.

To Admiral Canaris,
Chief of Abwehr/Military Intelligence
From Major Reinhold Berg, Portugal

Date: Wednesday, 10 July 1940
<u>Top Secret</u>

The matter in hand requires a draft on a Swiss bank
for 50,000,000 Swiss francs. I realize there are proper
channels through which this should be done, but may I ask
you to authorize this as a matter of utmost urgency.
We are within sight of achieving our aims.

78

Two soldiers with machine guns outside the hall's gates.

Two more at the front door.

Three roads meeting.

Daisy read Connaught Square in seconds, noting escape routes, defensible positions, hiding places. She'd been waiting for von Neudeck to leave. And, come lunchtime, he did, striding into the distance as if late for a meeting.

The gate guards watched her approach.

Maschinenpistole 40. Open-bolt, blowback-operated, fully automatic. An update to the MP 38 from the look of it. Daisy approved.

'Open it then.'

Her German was Berlin tinged, flawless. Her manner impatient. She caught the exact moment one guard glanced at the other.

He nodded and she was through.

The men at the front had just opened the door for her when she found herself facing a scar-faced sergeant on his way out. His eyes were drawn to her lapel. Daisy's usual Amerika-deutscher Bund badge had been replaced by one that was Berlin-made and solid gold, its swastika picked out in perfect red and black enamel.

'Lady Renhou,' Daisy said. 'I'm here to see the colonel.'

'Is he expecting you?'

'I certainly hope so.'

'Ah. Unfortunately he's left.'

'That's . . .' Daisy searched for the word. '. . . inconvenient. I'll wait,' she added firmly.

His eyes flicked again to her lapel.

She smiled. 'A present from Goering. We had lunch at Carinhall.'

The sergeant turned, leading her inside.

'You,' he said, pointing at a soft-faced boy in spectacles who seemed startled to find himself the object of their attention. 'Find Lady Renhou a chair.'

With that he was gone.

The boy's name was Otto, Daisy learned.

As von Neudeck's driver, his job was entirely pointless, since the colonel preferred walking and Alderney had few roads anyway. He seemed flustered by her announcement she'd skip the chair and wait in his boss's office instead.

'Civilians aren't allowed upstairs.'

'I'm hardly a civilian,' Daisy said, nodding to her lapel badge. 'Besides, I'm here at the colonel's request. Of course, if you'd rather I left?'

A woman in uniform bent over forms in the open-plan area outside von Neudeck's office. Without stopping, without waiting for Otto, who was still hurrying upstairs after her, Daisy strode to von Neudeck's door, put her hand to its handle and let herself in, quickly pocketing the key.

Five, four, three, two . . .

The door burst open and Otto hurried in, looking more flustered than ever.

'My lady, I'm sorry. You can't . . .'

'Wait in here?'

He shook his head.

'Then I'd better wait outside.'

Head down, the clerk doggedly kept checking the papers on her desk, comparing one column with another. When the clerk was done, Daisy stood noisily, making the woman look over.

'The restrooms?' Daisy asked.

Locking a cubicle behind her, she sat on the pan, removed a matchbox from her pocket and took a square of plasticine from inside. Pressing the borrowed key into the putty-like material, she put the impression into its box.

All she had to do now was return the key and get out of here.

'My lady . . .'

Von Neudeck was coming up as Daisy headed down.

'Ah,' Daisy said. 'Here you are.'

'You were looking for me?'

'I thought I should present my credentials. You saw my husband's. I realized you hadn't seen mine.' Her hand reached into her pocket for her passport, ignoring the matchbox with its precious contents.

'That's not necessary,' von Neudeck said. His voice was stiffer than Daisy expected. She realized a second later what he was looking at.

'You're admiring my badge?' She put just enough irony into her voice for him to glance at her. 'A present from Goering. I should probably be grateful it wasn't twice the size and encrusted with diamonds.'

Despite himself, von Neudeck laughed.

And that's a wrap, Daisy thought, as the iron gate clanged behind her.

In, out, job done. She felt surprisingly pleased with herself. It wasn't to last.

To Generaloberst Jodl, Chief of the Operations Staff,
Armed Forces High Command
From Reichsmarschall Hermann Goering

Date: Thursday, 11 July 1940
On the Record

     This is to confirm my view stated at this afternoon's
meeting of the High Command. It will take me 14 to 28 days
from today to achieve air superiority. After that, it is up to
the rest of you. Britain will be open for invasion.

79

Alderney, same day

Bill's first thought when he realized Daisy wasn't back was that she'd betrayed him. What if everything she'd said about finding out as much as she could before turning him in was true? She knew he wasn't Sir William. He'd admitted to needing the key to the CO's office at Nazi HQ. He'd quite obviously been landed by boat. That was three times as much as she needed to destroy him.

He felt sick. How much of a fool had he been to trust her?

Against that, what if she was in trouble because of him? What if the person in danger was Daisy? She wasn't the kind of person who'd take kindly to being worried about, but she was well over an hour late. And he was worried about her all the same.

He hoped to meet her on his walk into La Ville. But Rue de Beaumont was deserted and he reached the town having seen only goats, herring gulls, crows and a soldier on a BMW in the distance.

Neither of the gate guards looked at him strangely. The girl on the desk inside smiled as always. If Daisy *had* betrayed him, the news of it hadn't reached them.

'She was here,' the girl said. 'But she left.'

'Recently?' Bill asked.

'No, sir. Hours ago.'

*

'Where's Madame?' Mignon demanded.

'She'll be back,' Bill promised. 'In time for supper.'

'It's already supper time.' Mignon sounded frustrated. 'It's past supper time. She should be here.'

Mignon was right. Daisy should.

'I'm going to find her,' Mignon announced.

'No, you're not,' Bill said, remembering what Daisy said about not letting her outside. 'Certainly not at this time of night.'

Mignon glared at him.

'You can wait by the front steps.'

'The causeway,' Mignon demanded.

'This end,' Bill said. 'Not the other.'

Bill left Mignon and went to look for Mrs Beecher. He didn't find her, but Mrs Beecher found Mignon at a side door, shuffling her feet into walking shoes.

'Where do you think you're going?'

'To find Madame,' Mignon said.

'No you're not.'

Mignon's jaw jutted.

'You're meant to stay indoors,' Mrs Beecher reminded her. 'You know that. Madame's told you.'

'Just to the slope. Sir William said I could.'

80

Alderney, same day

Daisy knew how to stay still.

She was in a quarry near Saye Farm, waiting for whoever was following her to make a mistake. Her mistake had been entering the quarry in the belief she could escape through a fissure at the rear, which had been closed by a rock fall.

Slowing her heart, Daisy listened to the area around her. Herring gulls, but you could hear those everywhere; and crows, black-winged and raucous. She listened to the things that were there. For the things that weren't there but should have been.

The quarry was bigger than she remembered.

Big enough for hunter and hunted to play cat and mouse and begin to lose touch with which was which. What did the man following her want? That depended on who he was. Keller? It was obvious what Keller wanted from her two days fighting him off in the hotel. His rat-like little follower? The boy wouldn't dare. She wasn't sure who that left. Apart from everybody.

No one had seen her remove the key from von Neudeck's office. No one had seen her take its impression. No one had seen her put it back. She'd stake her life on it. Daisy smiled wryly. She was staking her life on it.

A darkening wall of rock guarded her back; a matting of bracken, brambles and thorn provided a barrier ahead. The palest ghost of a moon hung over the quarry's lip. Night was coming in.

In half an hour she'd make her move.

It was time.

Daisy's knees ached from crouching. Her ankles had pins and needles. She barely registered either as she rose to a half-crouch, blood returning to her heels. It was dark now, silent except for wind through scrub and the noise of waves breaking on a beach beyond the quarry entrance.

She was going to have to climb the quarry wall if she wanted to avoid confronting whoever waited at the entrance, which she didn't . . . but she'd got better at obeying orders and Mr Standish had been very clear about keeping out of trouble.

Pushing her foot into a gap in the rock face, Daisy reached for a handhold and dragged herself up, found a foothold and reached again, fingers closing on jagged rock just as her foothold began to give.

Dirt trickled beneath her.

She stilled, listening intently. All she could hear was the wind. She was halfway up now. More than halfway. She stared down into the quarry and saw no movement.

Finding a handhold, she checked her foothold more thoroughly this time, pushing down before trusting it. Only then did she reach up again, her fingers closed on a bush. Its roots tore and earth fell away.

Too loud. Too loud to miss. *Move it*, Daisy told herself.

Quiet was no longer relevant. It was about being quick. It didn't matter if she made a noise now. If someone was there, they already knew where she was. Mind you, if someone was down there, Daisy had a head start.

That counted.

Finding another foothold, she pushed herself up, fingers digging into dirt. It felt firmer this time. Stones tumbled as she lifted her foot but that no longer mattered. She was at the top. Rolling herself over the edge and straight under a low bush, Daisy froze as someone crashed through the undergrowth towards her.

Too noisily, far too noisily.

Her heart stopped as Mignon ran to the quarry's edge. Daisy was already rolling herself from under the bush, when Mignon froze. The child looked behind her, obviously terrified, and ran. A second later Daisy heard someone go after her. They were quieter, more practised, but Daisy heard them go.

No you don't.

Climbing to her feet, Daisy drew the knife she'd hidden in a makeshift sheath under her arm. Mr Standish's rules could go hang. Mignon was her *one saved*, the life she'd banked for her soul.

If they went after Mignon, this was war.

81

Alderney, same day

Spotting a rhododendron run wild beside a path, Mignon flung herself into it, crashing between dark branches that dragged like hands, and rolled down a slope to stop with a bump when she hit a ditch.

If she was lucky – if she was very lucky – her pursuer wouldn't realize.

She crouched in absolute darkness, trying to still her ragged breath and listening for her hunter. For a moment, she dared believe he'd lost her. Then she heard a rustle close by and backed away.

The hand that covered her mouth took her by surprise. She was down and smothered by a body before she knew it. Lashing out, she tried to knee her attacker, and bit at the hand clamped over her mouth.

'Ouch.' Her attacker pulled free. 'That hurt,' he hissed.

Mignon didn't recognize the voice.

'Stay low. Wriggle backwards.'

Mignon was about to ignore this, when a torch stabbed the brambles above her head and swept away to the right like a searchlight. It stopped at the end of its sweep and came back, passing over Mignon before sweeping to the left again.

'Trust me,' the boy whispered.

82

Field cap and jacket, silver-bladed knife. It was too dark to see if his jacket was *Splittertarnmuster* – camouflage – or not. When Daisy caught up with Mignon's pursuer he was prowling round a tight tangle of blackthorn, his torch stabbing at its branches.

Picking up a rock, Daisy threw it. She wanted to hurl it straight at his head. She didn't though. She reminded herself that the first thing she needed to do was lead the soldier away from here. And now he'd lost Mignon, Daisy had gone back to wanting to know who he was and why he was following her.

She *knew* she hadn't been seen taking the key.

Instead of braining him, Daisy looped her rock off to one side, and silently side-stepped several paces, dropping to a crouch and freezing. In the dark it was almost impossible to see a person who didn't move.

Turn around, damn you. Let me see who you are.

The soldier didn't. He stilled though, at the crash of the stone while he tried to work out where it had been thrown from. He was out by a half a dozen yards. A bit of Daisy wanted to kill him for going after Mignon. It was a big bit. Unfortunately, her orders were firm.

Lie low, don't act until activated.

Besides, on an island full of enemies, to kill one was to tell the others she was here. Rustling a bush intentionally, Daisy backed into the undergrowth and began to lead the man away. She'd deal with Mignon later. Wretched child.

83

Alderney, same day

It was bad enough not knowing where Daisy was.

Bill didn't realize how afraid he'd been for Mignon until she stepped on to the road and he slammed on the brakes, framing her in his headlights. The moon hung over her shoulder, reminding him his time was slipping away.

But it was the child he saw. 'Thank God,' he said.

Mignon stared at him.

'*I thought I said . . .*'

'I didn't go far.'

'I said the causeway.'

Climbing out, he put his hand on her shoulder and she flinched away.

When he opened the passenger door for her, she climbed dutifully into her seat and said nothing. She said nothing on the drive home either. Nothing as she rushed past Mrs Beecher and ran upstairs.

'What's going on?' Mrs Beecher demanded.

Bill shrugged. 'I wouldn't know.'

84

Alderney, same day

'Where's that bloody child?'

Daisy banged her way through the front door of Renhou, slammed it behind her and stamped across the hall, looking ready to punch out the first person to get in her way.

'Where have you been?' Bill demanded.

Daisy glared at him, then at the whisky glass in his hand.

'*Where have you been?* Just like old times,' she said. 'You're really getting into this role. Here . . .' She threw a matchbox at him. 'I imagine this is what you're worried about.'

Inside, dug into a square of plasticine, Bill found a perfect impression of von Neudeck's key.

'I owe you,' Bill said.

'You have no bloody idea how much.' Dirt smeared one side of Daisy's dress, her hands were filthy and her cheek scratched. He could smell sweat from where he stood. It was hard to miss the knife in her hand.

At least there was no blood on the blade.

Daisy turned to head for the stairs.

'Let Mignon be,' he said.

'Why?' Daisy said, stopping instantly. 'What's happened?'

'I don't know. I think she was scared for you. Really scared. She went to find you. I went to find her.'

'I ordered her to stay inside.'

'She's fifteen, fourteen. Whichever. What were you doing at that age?'

248

'You don't want to know.'

'There you go.'

Bill watched Daisy wrestle with going upstairs to shout at Mignon, and staying here to shout at him. 'If it's anyone's fault,' he said, 'it's mine. I told her she could go to the causeway.'

'The island's crawling with Nazis,' Daisy said furiously. 'What do you think they'd do if they found her?'

'It's not crawling with . . .' Bill stopped. He thought of Mignon's silence, her watchfulness, her almost painful awareness of everything going on around her. Sweet God, he'd been married to Miriam, and this child reminded him of the daughter he'd never seen. When did he become this bad at putting two and two together?

'She's Jewish?'

'Her father's in a camp. Her mother's rotting by some roadside. You really want Mignon to join her?'

'She wears a crucifix.'

'And she can say the Lord's Prayer,' Daisy said. 'I know. I gave her the one and taught her the other. It's not enough. She's not leaving Renhou again.'

'Daisy . . .'

'I'm going to tell her so.'

85

Alderney, same day

The door to Mignon's attic was locked. 'I'll force it,' Bill said.

'I've a better idea.' Daisy hammered on the door.

To Bill's surprise, Mignon opened it. Grabbing the girl by the shoulders, Daisy shook her viciously. 'I told you not to go out.'

Mignon's face was white with fear.

'Listen to me,' Daisy said. 'This isn't because you're a teenage girl. It's because they're Nazis. They killed your mother. They'll kill you too.'

Sobbing, Mignon turned and ran upstairs.

'*Daisy.*'

'God help me,' Daisy said.

One of the attics had been turned into a bedroom. A child's bed had been pushed against a wall, a chamber pot beneath. A circular window looked to the sea terrace and the rocks beyond.

'*Go away,*' Mignon told them.

'I will,' Bill promised. 'Once you tell me what happened out there.'

'*Nothing happened.*'

'That's not true,' Daisy said.

Mignon turned on her. 'You didn't come back,' she said furiously. 'You said you'd only be a while and you didn't come back.' Something flicked across Daisy's face. To Bill it looked dangerously like guilt.

'I'm sorry,' Daisy said. 'Now. What happened?'

Mignon's voice trembled. 'Someone chased me.'

'Who?' Bill demanded.

'I don't know. I didn't see him.'

'Did he see you?' Daisy demanded. 'Think carefully.'

'No,' Mignon said. 'Definitely not.'

Daisy sighed with relief.

'And the boy?' Bill asked.

'There was no boy.'

'I thought I saw . . .'

'There was no boy,' Mignon said crossly.

After they'd gone, Mignon ran through her escape in her head. Eddie, the boy who rescued her, had been on Renhou land with a crossbow, poaching Sir William's rabbits. She was hardly going to tell Sir William that, was she?

86

Alderney, same day

Trust me, the boy had whispered.

Mignon didn't trust anyone. Not really. But there was something about his voice . . . So she'd done what he said, backing along a darkened ditch. It was deep, the earth beneath her fingers sticky and sodden from a small stream.

Once she bumped into the boy, her bottom hitting his head. It was hard to know who was more embarrassed.

'We can stop now,' he said.

Their route had taken them under a wall of blackthorn to the middle of a ruined cottage. The clearing made by the cottage's floor was big enough to let in stars and sky. Reaching for a crossbow by a broken wall, the boy dug into his pocket, pulled out a bolt and yanked on a lever below the weapon's stock.

'It's loaded?' Mignon said.

'It is now,' he said. 'I'm Eddie.'

Mignon recognized him then. Narrow face, fair hair cut short. He'd crewed the boat when the Germans came. She'd watched through binoculars from her attic window.

'And I'm Mrs Beecher's niece,' she told him.

'Are you really Mrs Beecher's niece?'

'What do you think?'

'I think it's probably none of my business.' Behind the boy a shadow hung from thorns. 'Coney,' he said, seeing her gaze. 'The crossbow's mine too. My dad made it. He was good at making things.'

'Where is he now?'

'Dead.'

'I'm sorry.'

'My uncle's not dead though.'

Unexpectedly, Eddie put his finger to his lips. Both of them heard a car in the distance. Cars were rare on Alderney and this one came from Renhou.

When headlights stabbed the sky, Mignon stood to get a better look.

'He'll see you,' Eddie warned.

'I want him to see me.'

'Then you'd better go. His driving's improved, mind. Either that or he doesn't drink as much these days.'

'You know Sir William?'

'Me?' Eddie sounded amused. 'People like me don't know people like him. I poach on his land. He can't prove it and it's not like I take much.'

Stepping in, the boy gripped Mignon's shoulders and kissed her so clumsily she decided he probably hadn't done that before.

'You should go,' he said.

'I'm Mignon,' Mignon said.

The boy smiled. 'That's a nice name.'

She didn't care what Madame said. She was going to see him again.

From Abwehr HQ, Berlin
To Major Berg, Lisbon Embassy

Date: Friday, 12 July 1940
<u>Top Secret</u>

I enclose two passbooks for Credit Lucerne.

As you can probably tell from the pigskin finish and hand stitching, the first has been tailored to the duke's tastes. The second, as its white leather cover and gold clasp will tell you, is intended for the duchess. Please be sure to tell her that this account contains ten million Swiss francs, given as a token of our friendship. Also, be sure to tell her that this is the first passbook designed by Coco Chanel. She'll like this almost as much as the money. When these are given is almost as critical as what they contain. You have studied the duke. You know how much weight his wife's opinion holds.

Choose your moment wisely.

87

Portugal, Friday, 12 July 1940

'Probably Jewish,' Wallis told her husband.

'Really?' The duke examined the family arguing with the proprietor.

From the snatch of angry Portuguese it seemed they'd driven miles, and the mother was put out to find the hotel and its swimming pool closed.

'Look like locals to me.'

The pool had been freshly cleaned and two sun loungers put out. Side by side, but positioned so one was under a huge red parasol, and the other sat in the sun. Wallis had the one in the sun, obviously.

'The staff have been told?' the duke said.

'Yes,' Wallis said soothingly. 'They've been told.'

Specifically, they'd been told that the pool area was out of bounds, and if any photographs of the duke swimming found their way into the papers the police would become involved and none of them would work again.

'Oh, look.' The duke smiled.

A girl in a white blouse and black skirt was carrying a tray with a large jug of Pimm's, a saucer of salted almonds and an ashtray. She put them on a small table between the sun loungers, and curtsied.

The duke smiled benevolently.

Having waited for her to go inside, he checked there was no one else around to interfere with his enjoyment of the moment. Satisfying himself he and Wallis were alone, the duke kicked off his loafers, stripped off his shirt, fawn slacks and underwear, and dived naked into the pool, surfacing at the far end to turn swiftly and swim back again.

He had the body of a younger man. Whipcord thin and kept that way with a regime of exercise and diet. Wallis would join him later, when he'd got over his need to plough endlessly up and down the pool.

Two locals walked the slopes above the hotel. Suddenly unshouldering his shotgun, one of them fired and a bird stumbled on the wing, dead before the shot had echoed from the hillside. There seemed to be nothing that the Portuguese wouldn't shoot or eat, the Englishman thought dismissively. It was a miracle a single sparrow survived anywhere on the peninsula.

In the Englishman's pocket was an envelope he was to deliver to the hotel. It was cream, made from the finest quality bonded paper, and had the British royal coat of arms blind embossed on the back. On the duke and duchess's return to London, the king would meet them informally at Windsor for tea. The duchess would not to be presented at court as her husband wanted. Nor would there be any compromise on her title.

The man bringing this news expected to be shown into the duke's presence, although he didn't doubt the duchess, as Wallis Simpson was now styled, would be hovering like a malevolent witch at his shoulder.

What he didn't expect was to be turned from the door.

10 Downing Street
Whitehall

Friday

My Darling,

I told you I was to see His Majesty The King this
evening, and so I did. He asked for the truth of our
situation and I gave it to him. I told him it is all very well
my proclaiming Dunkirk a miracle in public, but in private
we must be realistic: 11,000 of our men lost or dead of
wounds, 14,000 hospitalized, 41,000 missing or captured.
2,472 lost field guns, 20,000 motorcycles, 65,000 other
vehicles, 377,000 tons of stores, 68,000 tons of ammunition,
147,000 tons of fuel, 440 tanks, 6 destroyers, 200 other
craft, 145 aircraft.

Although we will fight as no nation has fought before,
we cannot guarantee to turn back Herr Hitler's invasion
when it happens. I told His Majesty it was time for him to
move himself, his family and his court to Canada.

Dear God, I have never seen a man so angry. You'd
think I'd asked him to kneel at Adolf's feet. His Majesty's
best offer was to relocate to Edinburgh. Adding, damn it,
he'd only do that once London was directly threatened.

With fondest love,
W

88

Alderney, same day

'I couldn't find you.'

'I was busy,' Keller said flatly.

His English protégé nodded contritely, brought up short by the unexpected sharpness in his master's voice. Jimmy Todd was used to having his enthusiasm indulged.

'Should that man be using a torch?' he asked.

At the other end of Victoria Street the local policeman was setting off on his nightly rounds, the beam of his torch dancing across shop fronts.

'I'm sure it's fine.'

'Got it,' Jimmy said. 'The Germans don't need to bomb Alderney and the Brits won't bomb their own.'

'Well done,' Keller said. It was hard to know if he meant it.

From his place in the doorway of La Ville's only locksmith's, Bill watched Keller pull a silver cigarette case from his pocket. He offered one to his sergeant, before taking another for himself. As an afterthought, he offered one to the boy.

A moment later, the scar-faced sergeant lit Keller's cigarette, then his own, leaving the boy fumbling in his pockets for a light. Even now, twenty years after the Great War, trench lore held. *The first cigarette to spot an enemy, the second to aim, the third to fire.*

Either that, or the sergeant didn't like turncoats.

Jamming a shim, a paper-thin triangle of metal, into a padlock's shackle, Bill twisted and felt the lock click free. Two down, one to go. He was shimming a third when he realized the policeman was nearly on him.

Helmet on head, and truncheon at his side, PC Smith headed down Victoria Street as Keller and his sergeant headed up. They looked certain to meet right in front of the locksmith's Bill was breaking into.

Quickly, he told himself. Removing the padlock, Bill tugged the handle while trying to make no noise. The grill refused to shift. It wouldn't budge at all.

Shit.

Feeling with a lock pick between grill and frame, Bill found a heavy mortice he hadn't spotted that locked from the shop side. He wasn't going to make it. Not with soldiers and police almost on him in both directions.

He had to make it.

In desperation, he tried to lift the grill from its runners. His muscles locked, he felt the strain in his shoulders, and suddenly the entire grill lifted away. Bill staggered under its weight, metal grating on metal. The noise loud in his ears.

He saw the policeman hesitate.

Slithering through, Bill lowered the grill behind him as best he could and pushed himself into the darkest corner of the shop's entrance. His fingers closed on the matchbox in his pocket, ready to crush it. Daisy had . . . He wasn't sure what Daisy had. But he'd obviously almost got her into serious trouble.

He wouldn't put her at risk again.

Walk on, damn it. Just walk on.

The policeman knew he'd heard something. He wasn't sure what or where from. But he'd heard something. The torch beam flicked impatiently from side to side. Any second now . . .

The English boy sniggered.

'You do this every night?' Keller asked.

'Every night, sir,' the policeman said.

'Always at the same time?'

'And again, in two hours, then again two hours after that.'

'Against burglars?'

'Looters these days, sir.'

'Very commendable.' Stepping back, Keller saluted and, after a moment's hesitation, the policeman did the same. Maybe the boy's snigger finished him off, maybe it was Keller's barely hidden scorn. Either way, he'd had enough.

Shoulders stiff, he flicked off his torch and walked away.

Bill let himself breathe.

Keller had turned for the top of Victoria Street, and Bill was about to return to breaking in, when he realized he couldn't see Keller's sergeant. The man was in the shadows on the far side of the street, scanning shop doorways. It seemed the constable wasn't the only man to hear something.

Bill steadied his breathing and tried to stay entirely still.

The sergeant showed no sign of moving. A sniper in another life? Bill had seen men like that in the previous war. Able to focus for so long that they became almost invisible themselves.

The sergeant and Bill outwaited each other.

The man hadn't yet found the right door but he would.

Bill wished he'd brought a knife. Anything. Any one of his lock picks could take out a man's eyes, but for that he'd need to get close to a combat-hardened soldier who carried an SS dagger on one hip and a Luger on the other.

Bill was selecting the sharpest of his picks when Keller looked back.

'*Sergeant Hassel . . .*'

Hassel shrugged and turned away.

89

Alderney, same day

Inside the locksmith's, Bill found a lathe beside a window that overlooked an abandoned garden. There was enough moonlight through the uncurtained window to let him select a blank from a row of keys.

He'd darken it at Renhou. That way, if he was ever searched, no one would know it was newly cut, there being nothing like vinegar, ammonia and salt for adding age to a copied key.

Head down, Bill kicked the treadle and felt years fall away, as he remembered his time in Vienna before the start of the Depression, trying to earn a living as a locksmith. He'd tried more than once to go legit for Miriam, but his heart wasn't in it and she must have known it would never work.

Ten minutes later, Bill had a key that fitted his mould. Brushing brass filings from his fingers, he put back the lathe's cover and left the workbench as he'd found it – if a little less dusty. In Victoria Street, he lifted the grill on to its runner, snapped all three padlocks shut and checked both ways for the police.

It felt just like old times.

A half-moon hung over the chapel on Les Rocquettes, and lit the houses on the edge of La Ville. It was less than a month since Alderney had emptied and already their front gardens looked unkempt and overgrown.

Bill was almost safely back at Renhou when a Mercedes pulled up next to him.

'You're out late,' von Neudeck said.

'How on earth do you steer with only one arm?'

It was the right question.

'Get in.' Von Neudeck laughed and pushed open the passenger door. A mahogany and brass knob, fitted to the steering wheel, was the answer to Bill's question. In place of a gear stick, the Mercedes had a lever on the dash.

'Trouble sleeping?' von Neudeck asked.

Bill hesitated.

'It's two in the morning, William. I saw a man turn on to Route de Braye, thought it was you, decided not to check and then decided I should.'

'You know how it is.'

'Dreams?' von Neudeck asked.

'Not as often as the old days.'

That was the right thing to say too.

'I also walk,' von Neudeck said. 'When I can't sleep. Be careful though. If you ran into one of my patrols they might misunderstand.'

'Trouble?' Bill asked.

'A soldier thought he saw a man coming from a shop. Would have been a looter over from Guernsey had it been true.'

'It wasn't?'

'The place he identified was locked tight.' Von Neudeck smiled. 'I'm glad to have a chance to have a quick word. There's a possibility the British have put a spy or saboteur ashore.'

Bill tried not to freeze.

'In France,' von Neudeck said, 'British saboteurs kill collaborators first. If true, and this man were to decide that was you . . .'

'How reliable is your information?'

'More reliable than the report of a looter. The remains of

a canoe were spotted on the rocks at Les Étacs. By the time I sent a boat out the tide had taken them. It might be something. It might be nothing. Be careful. All right?'

'I'm being careful,' Bill said, meaning it.

'Good. In the meantime, let me give you a lift home.'

To Felix Frankfurter, Supreme Court
From Franklin D. Roosevelt,
President of the United States of America

Date: Saturday, 13 July 1940

Thank you for confirming the legality of my running for an admittedly unprecedented third term, should this be what I agree to do. I have arranged for the following to be put before next week's Democratic Party convention.

The President has never had, and has not today, any desire or purpose to continue in the office of President, to be a candidate for that office, or to be nominated by the convention for that office. He wishes in all earnestness and sincerity to make it clear that all of the delegates in this convention are free to vote for any candidate.

Darkness is spreading across the world and whoever leads America into the next four years faces a Herculean task. I have already asked Congress for a massively increased budget for military spending and this has not been without criticism.

I do not seek a third term as president but nor will I refuse to serve if called.

90

Portugal, Saturday, 13 July 1940

'Thank you for seeing me at such short notice,' Eberhard von Stohrer said. 'In fact, for seeing me at all. I gather your government has told you to avoid my company.'

The duke flushed but didn't deny it.

The duke, his wife and Germany's ambassador to Madrid sat in a café on the outskirts of Badajoz, a small city across the Portuguese-Spanish border. The duke wasn't meant to be in Spain, of course. But if his presence was discovered he'd say he'd wanted to see the site of Wellington's famous siege. The Iron Duke had taken Badajoz from an occupying French army in a ferocious battle, during the aftermath of which Wellington's troops slaughtered four thousand Spanish civilians. There'd been an equivalent and more recent slaughter in Badajoz when one of Franco's generals rounded up a similar number and machine-gunned them in the square. No one at the table was likely to raise that, though.

The Duke of Windsor was restless, and Wallis cross.

She'd hoped von Ribbentrop might come, even though his presence would have made things more complicated than they already were. Wallis had told her Portuguese maid, who she suspected was an English spy, that she and the duke were visiting the frontier fort at Elvas, five miles in the other direction and safely on the Portuguese side.

'Forgive me,' von Stohrer said, 'but I'm told you were fond of Tsar Nicholas. In many ways fonder of him than of your father.'

The duke's hand jerked in surprise and cigarette ash crumbled on to his sleeve. He stared at it in distaste.

'Darling, it's nothing.' Leaning forward, Wallis blew it away. She'd been wrong. Apparently, von Stohrer was capable of saying something that could catch her husband's attention.

'My godfather?' the duke said.

Along with his wife, his daughters and his son, the Tsar of all the Russias had been murdered by Soviet soldiers in a cellar at Yekaterinburg in the final months of the previous war. It was one of the scandals of the age. It was also something the duke had taken personally. He'd been fond of his godfather. His godfather had been fond of him. He certainly wrote kinder letters than anyone else in the family.

Damn it, now was not the time to get emotional.

The duke felt his lips tremble.

'It's just . . . von Ribbentrop thought you might want to see this, sir.' The German ambassador reached into a briefcase between them and produced a file. On the front was a hammer and sickle. The duke knew he wasn't going to like what came next. He didn't like it already.

'That's Soviet,' he said.

'You're right, sir,' von Stohrer said smoothly. 'It is.'

'They're animals. They're going to destroy the world.'

'That's what you said on the Côte d'Azur,' Wallis said. 'Remember? We were on our way to the beach and a servant ran out to say Britain was now at war with Germany. And you said that was bloody stupid, because the only people who'd gain were Jews and Bolsheviks. Fruity Metcalfe was there.'

'Ah, Fruity,' von Stohrer said. 'Now there's an interesting man. I remember photographs of your royal highness and Major Metcalfe in Tokyo in the 1920s, looking very fetching. You were wearing kimonos. There was someone with you.'

'Dickie,' the duke said. 'Dickie Mountbatten.'

Von Stohrer shook his head sadly. 'It's terrible,' he said. 'That we're fighting men like Dickie and Major Metcalfe.'

The duke nodded his agreement.

'This file,' he said. 'What's in it?'

'It might be best if you examined it yourself, sir.'

The first photograph showed the tsar sitting on a log in simple clothing, his wife behind him, his children either side. Five of them, aged twelve to maybe twenty-one.

The next . . . Christ, the man could have warned him.

The photographs beneath showed their bodies, blood-stained and disordered. A boy staring sightlessly at the sky. The final photograph showed a small pile of jewels beside the dresses they'd been sewn inside. The dresses were ripped to rags. The bare and bloody leg of a girl could be seen.

'*In God's name* . . .' The duke slammed the file shut. 'Why show me these?' he demanded angrily.

'The item you need, sir, is below that photograph.'

The duke flinched at the sight of his father's handwriting.

George V was not an imaginative man, or an intelligent one. He'd told his son that duty to empire, family and throne came before everything. Doing the right thing came before self-interest, no matter what the cost. He said it repeatedly and, in the prince's early years, reinforced it with a whip.

'My love, what is it?' Wallis demanded.

The duke almost couldn't tell her. If von Stohrer hadn't been there, he'd have been in tears.

'My father,' he said finally, his voice breaking. 'The bloody hypocrite wouldn't give my godfather exile. His own cousin. Nicholas wrote to him and he refused. The Romanov family died because my father was too gutless to bring them to London.'

'Why?' Wallis demanded.

'He was afraid of revolution,' von Stohrer said. 'Scared his own throne would be next. That having the tsar in London would remind his own subjects that monarchs could be overthrown. It was a risk he didn't want to take.'

'*The hypocrite. The bloody, bloody hypocrite.*'

The duke put his head in his hands and Wallis gripped his wrist.

'*Always do what's right. No matter what the cost.* How was refusing to help Cousin Nicholas doing what was right? You don't appease Bolsheviks. You fight them.'

'I agree,' von Stohrer said.

The duke glared at him. 'You've just signed a bloody non-aggression pact with the Bolsheviks. How can you possibly agree?'

'It let us invade Poland without interference. In return, we told Stalin where Trotsky was hiding. He's obsessed with arranging his assassination.'

'Why?'

'Who knows? Trotsky's bankrupt. Abandoned by his friends. He presents absolutely no threat. I imagine it's just settling old scores. They used to be comrades in arms. Now they want to kill each other.'

'See?' the duke said. 'All that dogma does something to their brains . . . This ten-year non-aggression pact. You don't intend to honour it?'

'Would you, sir?'

91

Alderney, Sunday, 14 July 1940

The air in the Ops Room was thick with cigar smoke and Bill wished General von Hausen would open the window. 'I imagine you'll be glad to see the duke again,' von Hausen said, sitting back in his chair and lighting another.

'Very glad,' Bill said. 'It's been too long.'

'And you think he'll be glad to see you?'

'I certainly hope so.'

It was all Bill could do to keep his voice steady. The game was up the moment the duke arrived. It was one thing to bluff the Germans, quite another to bluff a man who regarded Renhou as one of his oldest friends.

Bill felt sick just thinking about it.

He knew – how could he not? – as he'd known when he'd had a version of this conversation with von Neudeck at the start of the week, that the duke's first words would be: 'Who the fuck are you?'

How could they not be?

Standing, von Hausen put out his hand, which was a first. 'Thank you for coming in on a Sunday,' he said. 'And for talking so freely. The colonel was right to suggest we meet again.'

If von Hausen's politeness shocked von Neudeck, it unsettled Keller.

The general had seemed genuinely impressed by Bill's tales of drunken and promiscuous safaris. The bits that weren't outright lies Bill had filled with snippets from his SOE briefing at Arisaig, and from memories of features in the gutter press and general gossip.

'You're looking at the changes?'

He was smart, the general. Astute. Bill had thought his glance round the Operations Room had been subtle to the point of invisibility.

'Very smart,' Bill replied.

The general smiled.

A painting of Hitler had been hung next to one of Edward VIII. Apart from that, the room was as functional as you'd expect from a newly built command centre.

'A quick question,' the general said.

Bill tried not to tense.

'He changed?'

Bill thought of the duke's haunted face in the papers in the days after he gave up his throne. How could he not? 'Yes,' Bill said. 'He changed.'

'Wallis Simpson?'

'I would imagine so.'

'You're a good friend,' von Hausen said. 'Loyal. Careful with your answers. These are excellent qualities in a man.' He nodded at von Neudeck. 'The colonel will show you out. We'll meet again soon. In fact, I think it would be a good idea if you were here when the duke arrives.'

92

'That boy,' Bill said to von Neudeck, nodding to the unshaven youth in the foyer of the Island Hall. 'Why do you allow him to come and go?'

'The idea we have locals working with us makes Berlin happy. That makes the general happy.'

'I'm pretty sure my wife was followed the other night.'

Von Neudeck was shocked. 'You think it was him?'

'I've met boys like him before.'

'As have I,' the colonel said wearily. 'They come out of the woodwork like maggots. Always the same. Always wanting the same things. Always getting them. Keller suggested we put him on the payroll. Unfortunately, the general agreed.'

'You don't like Keller, do you?'

'He's intelligent. He's ruthless. He's worked hard to impress the right people . . . He'll be promoted soon enough. That's what he wants, along with one of these.' Von Neudeck tapped his Iron Cross.

'Being ambitious is enough to make you dislike him?'

'I haven't finished . . . His mother was English, so he feels the need to be more fanatical than everybody else. There's little to like.'

It was time to change the subject.

'It occurred to me,' Bill said. 'There should be a party to welcome the duke.'

'At Renhou? Hosted by you?'

271

Bill thought of the Wehrmacht safe on the third floor.

'I'd love to,' he said. 'But I think you should have one here first. As a matter of protocol. Perhaps invite the sheriffs and senior civilians from the other islands. Let the duke see that he's still loved.'

Bill watched von Neudeck think that through looking for flaws, and knew he hadn't found any when the man smiled.

'The general will like that,' von Neudeck said.

Bill smiled too. 'I'm glad. So will the duke be. Perhaps a dress rehearsal? A dummy run before he arrives? All of the guests, except him. That way you can iron out any problems early.'

And far easier to slip away unnoticed when the Island Hall was filled with strangers, and all the Germans, from von Neudeck's driver Otto through to the scar-faced sergeant and Keller, were tied up in red tape.

Hard-faced Guernsey islanders scowled at Bill, and one of them hissed as he passed. They were painting the hall's iron railings and scraping its cobbles clear of moss. The windows of the hall had been washed and the swastika banners now hung from newly scrubbed walls.

Guards with Schmeissers stood at the gates. A BMW R71 motorcycle/machine-gun sidecar combination was idling outside. There was no longer any doubt what this building was. The HQ of an occupying power.

To the Colonial Office, London
From Sir Henry Monck-Mason Moore,
Governor of Kenya

Date: Sunday, 14 July 1940

Further to Italian forces crossing into Kenya yesterday from their bases in Ethiopia: after fierce fighting, their
Somali forces have taken the British garrison at Fort
Harrington and the town of Moyale, and are pushing
inland.

I am despatching our East African Brigade to meet
them.

93

Alderney, Monday, 15 July 1940

There went Sir William, striding along as if he owned the road.

And to be honest, Eddie admitted, he probably did. He certainly owned the land either side of it. The girl lived down there. Eddie knew that now. She hadn't been at Renhou the day he brought the Germans to the house by boat, and Sir William, his wife and their housekeeper had shouted at each other.

Or, if she had, he hadn't seen her.

But she lived down there. She'd told him so. He'd watched her climb into Sir William's car to be driven back to Renhou the night someone chased her, and he'd known he'd see her again.

They'd met since, exactly twice.

Here, in the thorn-encircled ruins of the cottage, where they'd huddled together that night. She'd had to sneak out to meet him, and he wasn't allowed to tell anyone she existed. He'd had to promise her that.

Today was going to be the third time. He wondered how far she'd let him go. Farther than last time, he hoped.

It's not your fault, she'd said after their second kiss.

What wasn't? Eddie still didn't know.

94

Alderney, same day

'What's that?' Mignon asked.

Bill handed her the photograph of the Prince of Wales, and Mignon scowled at the dead rhinoceros under Sir William's raised foot.

'That's horrid,' she said.

Bill nodded.

'Then why do it?' she demanded.

I didn't, Bill wanted to say. Instead he shrugged.

The man Bill was pretending to be was heavily bearded, his eyes hidden by the rim of a pith helmet. Bill supposed he should be grateful that on recall to his regiment the real Sir William was required to start shaving again.

Mignon shut the drawing-room door with a slam and Bill heard her stamp upstairs. He imagined it would be lunchtime before she came down again. That left him holding the photograph.

It was meant to be of Sir William, a smug white settler, standing over a dead animal, with a backdrop of black porters he undoubtedly looked at daily and never saw; but it was really of the duke. Bill could see that now. The man's averted head, his careless smile. It wasn't that he hadn't known the photograph was being taken. He unquestionably had. His amused gaze as he listened to the planter's wife; her hunger as she gazed at him: this was theatre.

A performance all the more effective for looking as if the duke didn't know he was on stage, and wouldn't have taken it seriously if he had.

To Max, Lord Beaverbrook,
Minister for Aircraft Production
From Winston Churchill

Date: Monday, 15 July 1940
Confidential

     In the first six days of the Nazi campaign to starve us into submission by blockading these islands by air and sea their attacks have ranged from Dover to Aberdeen and from the Firth of Forth and the Norfolk coast to Plymouth and Yeovil.

     I am informed our losses are as follows:

Wednesday 10th
German – Aircraft 14, Crew 29
British – Aircraft 2, Crew 2

Thursday 11th
German – Aircraft 17, Crew 41
British – Aircraft 6, Crew 3

Friday 12th
German – Aircraft 9, Crew 28
British – Aircraft 5, Crew 4

Saturday 13th
German – Aircraft 6, Crew 11
British – Aircraft 6, Crew 5

<u>Sunday 14th</u>
German– Aircraft 3, Crew 3
British – Aircraft 1, Crew 1

<u>Monday 15th</u>
German – Aircraft 5, Crew 6
British – Aircraft 1, Crew 0

As you can see, the Nazis have no hesitation in sacrificing airmen or aircraft and, even allowing for our lesser losses, we do not have enough pilots or fighters to survive this level of attrition. Training must be accelerated, and production must increase. Resources will be reallocated and new factories set up. I am relying on you to make the second of these happen. It must happen immediately.

95

Alderney, same day

Bill was back in the library after lunch, looking at a Victorian floor plan of Renhou. The same rooms, in the same places, being used for the same things.

'Are you busy?' Daisy asked, putting her head round the door.

'Nothing's been changed.'

'Of course not. William was proud of that.'

Bill still didn't trust Daisy. Why would he? Her file at Arisaig had her down as a friend of Goering, married to one of Oswald Mosley's blackshirts. A man she'd abandoned to bolt into the arms of some swastika-eyed Parisian. And yet, she'd hidden Mignon, knowing she was Jewish, hadn't given him up to the Nazis, and had shielded him the day he found himself trapped the wrong side of a window at their HQ. One of those two lists made no sense.

'Can I help?' he asked.

'I can't find Mignon.'

'You've checked her room?'

'Obviously,' Daisy said sharply. 'She's not there.'

There was more to Daisy's sudden crossness than she was saying. Her voice was tight and her face unexpectedly strained.

'What is it?' Bill said. 'Tell me . . .'

'Someone's watching this house,' Daisy said abruptly. 'I don't want them finding Mignon.'

'How do you know?'

She glared at him. 'Reflections.'

'Field glasses?' Bill asked.

'Unless someone's after you with a sniper rifle . . . Where are you going?' she demanded.

'To check it out.'

'Don't get yourself killed.'

'Would you care?'

'Not particularly. Mignon might, though. She's begun to like you. God knows why.'

'And I her,' Bill said.

Daisy stared at him.

'I was married,' Bill said by way of reason.

'*She reminds you of your wife?*'

'We had a daughter.'

Bill watched Daisy's expression shift.

'Had?' Daisy said.

'Miriam took the child when she left.'

'*Miriam?* How old would this child be now?' Daisy shook her head. 'Don't bother answering that. Mignon's age, obviously. Whose fault was it your wife left?' She obviously expected Bill to blame everyone but himself.

'Mine,' Bill said. 'Entirely.'

He left the room before she could reply.

96

Alderney, same day

If anyone was on the hill, they had their target.

No one took a shot, and Bill found no one at the top. The furze was trampled though, and a Woodbine stubbed out on stone.

'Mignon.'

He stared round, wondering when she'd broken bounds, and how far she'd gone. He called again and realized he shouldn't be using her name.

Crows crowded the jagged crown of a ruined cottage, which was where scuffs in the grass led him. The gaze of the crows was harsh, and except for an occasional sideways glance, it wasn't on him.

It was fixed on something in the ruins.

Bill had walked twice round the ruin's shield wall of blackthorn before he realized the only possible way in was what looked like a badger run. Except Mrs Beecher had already told him Alderney didn't have badgers. Dropping to his knees, he edged his way through vicious thorns.

He was halfway there when the groaning began. Bill hesitated, not sure whether to go on or back.

'*Mignon . . .*'

There was a second's silence. Then the groaning started again, and the more Bill hesitated, the worse it sounded. Ignoring the thorns, he pushed on for a clearing in the centre. The boy from the boat lay on his side. He was clutching his gut, the stub of a crossbow bolt jutting from between his fingers.

He flinched as Bill approached.

'Stay still,' Bill begged.

Desperate eyes watched him.

'Take your hands away,' Bill ordered.

The boy shook his head, the slightest of movements.

'I need to see.' Reaching for his hands, Bill peeled them back, almost wishing he hadn't when he saw the sticky mess beneath. The bolt was buried in the boy's side and the leaf mould beneath him was black with blood.

'You're going to be fine,' Bill promised.

The boy's eyes were huge with tears as he stared at Bill, his face torn between hope and certainty that Bill had lied.

'Who did this?' Bill asked.

He opened his mouth, and then shut it.

'Tell me,' Bill said.

The boy almost shrugged. His face was desolate, his skin shiny and his eyes were going in and out of focus. His breathing was shallow and fast.

Bill was losing him.

'You,' the boy said. 'You must . . .'

'I must what?' Bill asked.

The boy was struggling to speak.

Bending closer, Bill listened carefully.

'Mignon,' the boy said. '*Mignon.*'

'Mignon did this?' Bill rocked back in shock.

The boy reached for Bill's arm and his hand fell away. Then strength left his fingers, his body shuddered and he slumped back.

Christ . . .

If the boy had a pulse, Bill couldn't find it.

He tried for a heartbeat, but the boy's skin was slippery and his flesh cold. Bill knew he should alert somebody, tell the authorities. He should drive the body to La Ville and contact von Neudeck, but he'd be answering questions for hours.

He didn't have hours.

It was Mignon he was worried about. Mignon he needed to protect.

Backing down the tunnel, Bill left the boy where he was. He was shocked to discover he was crying. For the dead boy, for Mignon, for the daughter he'd never known. Maybe even for himself.

97

Alderney, same day

'Have you seen Mignon?' Bill demanded.

'God. Your hands . . .' Daisy was in the hall.

'When was the last time you saw her? No, doesn't matter. Ask Mrs Beecher if she knows why Mignon sneaked out. And when.'

'What's happened?' Daisy asked.

'A boy's dead.'

'A German?'

'No,' Bill said. 'The boy from the boat.'

'Thank God.'

Daisy was so matter of fact Bill stopped.

'Can you imagine,' she said, 'if it was one of theirs? Any pretence of a truce would be forgotten. And it is a pretence. I drove here through Brittany. I've seen what they can do.'

And I stood at von Neudeck's side while the skin was stripped from the back of a simpleton with a whip, Bill thought. What he said was, 'I'll try the garage.'

'I've looked already,' Daisy said.

Think, Bill told himself. *Where would he go if he was her?*

Not to La Ville. It held Nazis. Not to Braye Harbour. More Nazis. And no boat would take her anywhere without a chit signed by some clerk at the Island Hall. She'd be frightened, shocked. Trapped on an island full of enemies. She wouldn't risk going far and this was the only bit of Alderney she knew.

What did amateurs do, when they did things like this? More times than not, they did the one thing you're not meant to do. They returned to the scene of the crime.

Bill ran up the slope and through furze, brambles and bracken to the thicket of thorns. The entrance was wider than he remembered, its dirt more churned than he recalled. His heart sank when the clearing came into view. Ahead of him was the same figure, curled around itself. Bill was readying to back away when something made him look again.

'Mignon?'

The girl didn't stir.

She lay, utterly still, where the boy had been.

For a moment Bill thought she was dead, but a pulse in her throat beat soft as a butterfly's wing, and her chest rose and fell, and he could feel her breath when he put his face close to hers.

'Can you hear me?' he demanded.

She gave no sign.

Blood crusted her dress and her knees and her face. Bill looked for the boy from the boat but he was gone, although Bill couldn't see where or how.

'Mignon. Talk to me.'

Not even a flicker of her eyelids.

Slipping his arms under her, Bill lifted Mignon up and headed for the thorns. He couldn't bear to drag her down the tunnel behind him, and he couldn't see how else to do this. She was lighter than he expected, her legs hanging limp as he tried to support them. Wrapping himself round the child to protect her, Bill looked for the most direct way through and started walking. His trousers were in shreds in seconds, the flesh beneath shortly afterwards. He'd have cried with pain but he was too far gone.

98

Portugal, same day

The Duke of Windsor was on his way out of Estoril casino when he spotted a man moving swiftly towards him through the crowd. It was not a particularly dense crowd, Monday evenings being less popular than others even in July.

'Oswald von Hoyningen-Huene, your royal highness.'

The man was in his fifties and wore a double-breasted suit that failed to hide his stomach. His jowls, thinning hair and ingratiating smile made him look like a seedy Home Counties estate agent.

He wasn't, though. He was Germany's ambassador to Portugal and had been since Weimar days. His survival into the Nazi era was down to his friendship with President Salazar, who ruled Portugal with the firmest of grips, and to his links with the highest levels in Lisbon society that Salazar's friendship gave him.

From habit, the duke glanced at the man's lapel.

No swastika pin.

'I'm not a Party member,' the baron said. 'I was one of Paul Hindenburg's staff and it's too late to change my spots now.' He named the German ex-chancellor so casually that the duke wondered whether it was intentional.

Hindenburg was the man who had brought Hitler to power.

'I'm in a hurry,' the duke said. 'What do you want?'

'How are you finding Portugal, sir?'

'It's hot. It's humid. It's too dusty. Wallis hates it.' The duke sucked his teeth. 'Better not tell your friend Salazar that.'

'And the gaming tables, sir?'

'Absolutely bloody.'

The roulette wheel had chewed up and spat out more of the duke's money in the last five hours than he could bear to consider. The casino had taken his marker, obviously. That wasn't the point. He didn't like losing and losing made Wallis cross.

Well, it made him cross, and that made him careful about not spending too much on other things, and that made Wallis cross. It was his bloody father's fault. Everything always was.

The baron stepped back, like a man about to say goodbye.

'I don't doubt we're being watched, sir. So I'll keep it brief. We accept unreservedly your unwillingness to be part of an invasion of your own country. What prince could possibly agree?'

'Certainly not this one.'

'Quite. We wondered if you'd had further thoughts about leaving Portugal? And finally, as a separate issue, we wanted to let you know we'd be willing to advance you fifty million Swiss francs, should they be useful.'

'Simply for returning to Spain?'

'If you could make your unhappiness with Churchill's refusal to negotiate a truce a little clearer that would help,' said the man. 'I believe *The New York Times* would be very interested in anything you might want to say.'

The duke smiled thinly. 'Anything else?'

'The question of Britain must be dealt with. If we're forced to invade and fight the island's inhabitants on their damn beaches, we will. If Churchill wants blood, toil, tears and sweat, he can have them. But that is his choice. Not ours. We don't believe it's your choice either.'

'Get to it,' the duke said.

'We still hope to agree terms. To sign a mutually beneficial alliance.'

'Against the Bolsheviks, when your damned Molotov-Ribbentrop pact falls apart?'

The baron glanced around, checking that no one was close enough to overhear. Several people were watching openly and one man at least, in a quietly expensive dinner jacket, had his gaze fixed on them in a way that reminded the baron of a hunter preparing to take a shot. 'I should be off,' he said.

'You should,' the duke agreed.

'There was one other thing.'

'There always is.'

'Berlin, at the highest level, was wondering if you would consider our entering Britain in your name? If we made it clear that we regard England as an ally momentarily led astray by a prime minister who didn't have his country's best interests at heart . . . ?'

At this, the Duke of Windsor spun on his heels and walked away.

A lesser diplomat might have thought that a bad result. Baron von Hoyningen-Huene had been negotiating complicated diplomatic deals his entire adult life. That the duke hadn't agreed was unimportant. That he hadn't rejected the suggestion outright, as he'd rejected every previous suggestion, was what mattered.

Berlin would be delighted.

99

Alderney, same day

Bill knocked clumsily.

'*Come in*,' Daisy called. When he didn't, she opened the door. Whatever she'd been about to say was silenced by the blood on Mignon's dress and her stillness.

'Is she . . . ?'

'No,' Bill said.

'Put her down there.'

The girl looked wax-like on Daisy's counterpane.

'Where did you find her?'

'Where the boy was.'

'Lying beside him?'

'He's not there.' Bill caught Daisy's expression. 'I mean it. He's gone.'

'Could he have crawled away?'

'He wasn't in a state to crawl anywhere.'

'You're sure he was dead?'

'He looked dead enough to me.'

'This is your fault,' Daisy said.

'How the . . . ? I'd never hurt Mignon.'

'You let her out that night. That must have been when she met him. You didn't say she'd been helped by an island boy.'

'I didn't know.'

'Now he's dead, and Mignon . . .' Daisy took a deep breath. Her glance when she stared at the bed was bleak. 'Who knows what the hell's happened?'

'Daisy . . .'

'Get out,' Daisy said.

'Let me stay,' Bill pleaded.

'I'm going to examine her.'

Bill stared down at the child, and didn't know how to look up again without letting Daisy see the tears in his eyes. 'I'm leaving,' he said.

Führer Directive No. 16
Date: Tuesday, 16 July 1940

<u>Preparations for a Landing in Britain</u>

As England, in spite of her hopeless military situation, still shows no signs of willingness to come to terms, I have decided to prepare, and – if other avenues fail – carry out a landing operation against her. The aim of this operation is to eliminate the English Motherland as a base from which the war against Germany can be continued, and, if necessary, to occupy the country completely.

The code name for this is Sea Lion.

Alderney, Tuesday, 16 July 1940

On Tuesday morning, a day after Bill carried Mignon into Daisy's bedroom, von Neudeck arrived by boat. This time his crew comprised two uniformed Kriegsmarine, who had orders to wait with the craft, and the island's policeman, who didn't.

'You've met Sir William?' von Neudeck asked.

'Met him?' PC Smith sounded surprised. 'No, sir,' he said. 'I've not.'

'Sir William doesn't mix?'

'Not with islanders.'

'There were visitors, though? Before the war.'

'Oh yes,' the policeman said in evident distaste. 'From London, and New York after his father died, for a while.' For an islander this counted as gossip.

'You have no reason to believe he'd do a thing like this?'

The policeman hesitated. 'I don't know enough about Sir William to answer.'

'There's no bad blood between their families?'

The policeman's glance was just short of contemptuous, his real feelings suddenly clear. 'I doubt the Renhous knew Eddie's family existed.'

'Is everything all right?' Bill asked.

'You know it's not,' von Neudeck said.

He ignored Bill's outstretched hand. That was warning enough.

'You were seen yesterday,' he said. 'Walking down the slope opposite your house with blood on your hands.'

'By whom?' Bill demanded.

The island's policeman leant forward. There was flint in his eyes. 'Is that the first question an innocent man would ask?'

'Innocent of what?' Bill demanded.

'I'll do the talking,' von Neudeck told the policeman. To Bill, he said, 'I assume this boy attacked you?'

'What boy?'

'*William . . .*' von Neudeck said.

'Dear God,' Bill said. 'Why would I do that?'

'I don't know,' von Neudeck said heavily. 'I thought perhaps he threatened you in some way. That you felt in mortal danger. That you were compelled to react. I don't doubt you had good reason to kill him. Now would be the time tell me what.'

Bill knew he was being invited to produce a valid defence, safe in the knowledge that it couldn't be contradicted.

'I didn't do it,' Bill said.

'He was stabbed,' the policeman said, 'and his lighter stolen.'

Von Neudeck scowled at that, obviously hearing the detail for the first time. 'What was special about this lighter?'

'It was made from the case of a round of .303 by his father in the last war. Eddie carried it everywhere.'

'Why in God's name would I steal a lighter?' Bill demanded.

'I don't know, sir. Why would you?'

'This is ridiculous.'

'You understand, sir, I'm going to require your fingerprints. Unless your German objects?' The policeman shot Colonel von Neudeck a spiteful glance.

'He won't,' Bill said.

'*William . . .*'

'I didn't kill the boy.'

'So, you have no objection to being fingerprinted?'

'None at all.'

Pulling out a large card with two rows of squares for Bill's fingers, PC Smith opened an inkpad. If the constable was surprised Sir William knew his way around fingerprinting, he didn't let it show.

'Satisfied?' Bill asked.

The man nodded.

'Then we're done . . .' Bill did his best to sound outraged. He wanted von Neudeck and PC Smith gone. He wanted them out of the house and off Renhou. He'd been seen walking down from the thorn thicket with blood on his hands. By one of the islanders, from the sounds of what von Neudeck wasn't saying. But he'd been empty-handed at the time. Not carrying Mignon.

'You really have no idea who did this?' von Neudeck asked.

Bill thought of Mignon, hidden in the attic.

'None whatsoever. I saw crows. There are always crows on this bloody island but these worried me. I heard a noise in the thorns and went to investigate, because someone's been watching this house. At least, so my wife believes.'

'William.' Von Neudeck's voice was sharp. 'We've talked about this.' Switching to German, he added, 'You need to take care. You know the islanders can't be trusted.'

'I'll be more careful.'

'And I'll say my goodbyes.'

Von Neudeck held out his hand and they shook.

All the same, Bill breathed a sigh of relief as he watched the boat depart. It wasn't his own fingerprints Bill was afraid of them taking.

It was Mignon's.

To All Editors, Immediate Release
From the Jewish Telegraphic Agency/
Overseas News Agency, New York

Date: Tuesday, 16 July 1940
<u>From our Paris correspondent</u>

Following the redrawing of the French border by
Germany, and Berlin's annexation of Alsace, news is
coming in that Jews in the city of Colmar in Alsace have
been rounded up, delivered in trucks to the revised border
and deported to France. The Vichy authorities have
responded by revoking the French citizenship of all
naturalized Jews.

Alderney, same day

The moon is your clock, Bill had been told at Arisaig.

Two weeks since this all started, less than two remaining. A young woman he felt responsible for was speechless with misery upstairs, and a woman he liked, but didn't trust, wasn't speaking to him. Bill was coming to hate the moon.

He didn't know Daisy was behind him on the terrace until she spoke.

'My husband despised this place.'

'Alderney . . . ?'

'Renhou.'

'And you?'

'At least Bluebeard's wife was imprisoned in a real castle. How did it go with your German earlier?'

'About as well as you'd expect.'

'You should have invited him to stay for a drink.'

'To stress my innocence? I wanted him gone before he could wonder who else might be in the house or if the boy had any last words.'

'Did he?' Daisy asked.

'No,' Bill said firmly.

However dark Daisy's thoughts were, Bill imagined his were darker.

How long would it take the Wehrmacht to cross those waters? How long to blitzkrieg their way to Edinburgh or Aberdeen? Maybe they wouldn't bother going that far. Maybe they'd just take London and the English Midlands. Set up a Vichy state beyond. Would we really fight them on the beaches?

He doubted it. No one else had.

You know the islanders can't be trusted.

This one certainly couldn't.

He'd held his temper around Keller, controlled his face around General von Hausen, swallowed his contempt for von Neudeck's belief he was one of them. All the pieces were where Bill needed them.

He'd even reached an agreement of sorts with Daisy. One based on a reluctance to upset each other's apple carts. Yet, right here and right now, his biggest concern was small and parochial and much closer to home. He couldn't help it if Mignon reminded him of a daughter he'd barely known.

'I'm going to talk to Mignon.'

'I don't think that's a good idea.'

'Please,' Bill said.

'Now there's a word I don't imagine comes easily.'

102

Alderney, same day

A hurricane lamp stood on a table. The stub of a candle sat on a saucer beside Daisy's bed. The window was open and Bill could hear waves dragging on shingle. Mignon didn't stir when they entered.

'She thinks it's her fault,' Daisy whispered. 'Whatever happened. Whatever she did. Whatever was done. Whatever she's not telling us.'

'It's not,' Bill said.

'I know it's not. But she thinks it is.'

'Mignon?' Daisy's voice was gentler than he'd ever heard it. When she went to sit on a stool beside the bed and reached for Mignon's hand, the gesture was almost tentative. 'Sir William needs to talk to you.'

'Bill,' said Bill.

Mignon's glance dismissed not simply Bill's words, but the world and her room, Daisy's worry and the food she wouldn't eat and which Daisy hadn't let Mrs Beecher in to collect. She was crying. Silently.

'Listen to me,' Bill insisted. He knelt by the bed and put his hand on to her shoulder, feeling the slow sobs shaking her body. Whatever had happened out there, whatever she'd done . . . It wasn't fear or guilt that had reduced Mignon to this white-faced shell. It was loss.

'It hurts,' he said. 'It hurts every time.'

Mignon looked at him.

'Eddie's not the first person you've lost, is he?'

The child's howls filled the house so suddenly that Mrs Beecher came rushing to Daisy's room to hear the tail end of a list that included Mignon's mother, her father, a brother, and a boy in Antwerp she'd loved more than life.

When Bill told Mrs Beecher what was going on, she put a hand on his shoulder for a second, to steady herself or steady him, Bill wasn't sure which. Slowly the howls gave way to gulping sobs.

'Best leave her to Lady Renhou,' Mrs Beecher said.

An hour later Daisy found Bill on the terrace, staring at the sea.

'How did you know?' she demanded.

Drawing on his cigar, Bill blew out smoke that drifted like a miniature Milky Way. His thoughts had kept looping back to Vienna. Now he'd remembered his distress the evening he returned to find Miriam gone, he didn't know how to forget it again.

'I know what loss looks like,' he replied.

'Who doesn't? What are you doing out here anyway?'

Bill held up his glass.

'What's that?' Daisy demanded.

'Whisky.'

'Horrible stuff,' she said, taking his glass.

'I should get to bed,' she said later.

Daisy showed no sign of going though, and Bill shifted on his stone bench to make space. She gave him back the empty glass and went to stand at the balustrade instead. Her free hand gripped its mossy top as she stared into the darkness.

'You can see France from Alderney's other side,' Bill said. 'But we're too far from Britain to see it from here.'

'Your country, not mine.'

'How's Mignon?'

'Sleeping,' Daisy said, her voice instantly softer. 'She cried herself out, which was probably the best thing that could happen.'

'Young love,' Bill said.

'Is that meant to be as callous as it sounds?'

Bill thought of Annie McLean dead at sixteen on the top floor of an Edinburgh slum. 'It wasn't meant to be callous at all.'

Daisy grunted.

'We should go to our beds,' Bill told her.

'You're . . .' Daisy hesitated. 'Different around Mignon. Kinder.' She said it reluctantly. Sounding exasperated. 'The hurt shows.'

They went in together, brushing against each other as they passed through the French doors. Bill shivered at a shock-like static and saw Daisy turn. Her hand reached up to grip his head and pull it down.

Her kiss was hard, almost cold.

'That means nothing,' she said, pushing him away.

Bill dreamed of Daisy, falling into fitful sleep unsettled by her kiss, and half wondering if unsettling him was the point of it. He woke from dreams of meeting Miriam in Glasgow and their life in Vienna. A girl he'd loved enough to marry, and who'd loved the baby he gave her enough to leave him.

103

Alderney, Wednesday, 17 July 1940

'You. Now.'

The man dragged from his bed by German guards blinked and looked terrified. His friend was rolling out of a second bunk when a soldier pointed a rifle at him. The soldier's snarl suggested he'd have no trouble pulling the trigger.

'You can't just . . .' There was a rifle inches from Jerome's face.

'We can,' the corporal told him. He nodded to the soldiers holding Georgie, who bundled the huge man out of the door.

'At least tell us why you're taking him.'

'He's being arrested.'

'For what?'

'Murdering a local boy.'

'He'd never. He wouldn't hurt a fly.'

'He tried to kill the colonel.'

'That was an accident. He didn't kill Eddie. He was with us the whole time.'

'How do you know when it happened?' The corporal stared at Jerome, inviting him to answer. When he didn't, he sneered. 'Feel free to confess. If you helped him.'

'When are you bringing him back?'

'We won't be bringing him back. Once he's confessed, he'll go to trial. It's up to Colonel von Neudeck after that.' The soldier shrugged. 'Be grateful he hasn't already been shot.'

104

Portugal, same day

'A small token,' Miguel Primo de Rivera said. He placed a wicker basket on the tiled table in front of the duchess.

'How lovely.'

Inside were two bottles of the finest Codorníu, too warm to be drunk immediately, four bottles of vintage Rioja, a large slice of Manchego wrapped in greaseproof paper, a large loaf of bread and a dozen freshly picked oranges.

'From my own grove.'

'So kind of you,' Wallis murmured.

'You'll forgive me for bringing cheese from Spain. I thought you might miss it. Not that Portuguese cheese isn't good in its own way.'

'I was sorry about your brother,' Wallis said sombrely.

Miguel's brother, José Antonio, founder of the Spanish fascist party, had been put against a wall and shot four years earlier. 'Bolsheviks, Jews and anarchists,' de Rivera said. 'The same people who started this war. My brother had political immunity. They ignored it.'

'I heard,' the duke said.

'Your majesty . . .'

'It's royal highness,' Edward said. 'At least it is these days. You'd better tell me why you're here. I don't imagine you drove all this way to bring me lunch.'

'Generalissimo Franco is worried for your safety.'

'I doubt the Germans will attack me.'

'It's not the Germans who worry him. His excellency begs you to return to Spain where he will put a palace and armed guards at your disposal. He fears that if you do not take suitable precautions your life is at risk.'

'You're saying London will hurt me?'

'Do you intend to return?'

'That is a grossly impertinent question. Of course I intend to return. It's my country.'

'His excellency has heard you refused.'

'There are matters of protocol that still need settling.'

De Rivera's gaze slid to Wallis, who was standing stony-faced, listening to the men talk around her. Their eyes met.

'And if they're never settled?' de Rivera asked.

'*De Rivera . . .*' the duke said.

'With respect, sir. The Portuguese are your brother's allies. They will return you, whether you want to be returned or not.'

'They're hardly going to kidnap me.'

'No, sir. They'll send guards and escort you to the plane. They will do it very politely. Very apologetically. But they will do it. At the very least, consider the generalissimo's generous offer.'

'I'm safe enough here.'

'*Darling . . .*'

'No,' Edward said. 'I'm not discussing it. I refuse to believe my own brother would have me harmed. This is an absurdity.'

'It won't be your brother,' de Rivera said. 'It will be Churchill. With respect, you know this. You are in danger. Your time is running out. This is not absurdity, sir. This is the reality of your situation.'

The duke refused to meet his gaze.

In the Englishman's opinion, the only decent thing about being based in Lisbon was that it allowed him access to the

Casino do Estoril, where the Duke of Windsor also liked to play. But for all the Englishman liked testing the odds, he wouldn't have put his own money on the duke obeying orders to come home.

Slowing on his approach, he stared at the Casa de Santa Maria, with its swimming pool and perfect view of the long bay. He doubted the duke was even paying Espírito Santo rent.

A Mercedes was parked out front.

Pulling off the road, the Englishman slung his car under a fig tree, leaving it not quite hidden but not too obvious, and reached for his field glasses.

In the garden behind Casa de Santa Maria the duke and another man sat at a table while Wallis Simpson prepared Caesar salad. Properly, he was interested to see, using anchovy paste mixed with Dijon mustard, pulped garlic, ground parmesan, splashes of olive and rapeseed oil, and finally a crust of dry toast.

It wasn't really her culinary skills that interested the Englishman, or the frugality of the duke's appetite either. It was Miguel Primo de Rivera, unofficial bag man to General Franco, and an old friend of the duke's from his earlier, more carefree days.

He doubted their meeting worked in London's favour.

London would have to be told, and would undoubtedly add it to the duke's debit list, which grew longer by the day. Matters had not yet reached a point where Churchill was prepared to order drastic measures; but if he did, then drastic measures would be taken. Adjusting his Walther PPK, the Englishman buttoned his tropical-weight Savile Row jacket, and sighed.

He didn't doubt he'd be the one to take them.

To War Office, London
From Adjutant to General Sir Clive Liddell,
C-in-C, Gibraltar

Date: Thursday, 18 July 1940
<u>Urgent</u>

We are under attack from French aircraft.
Spanish radio declares this the opening salvo in
France's response to the 'underhand' sinking of the
Bretagne at Mers-el-Kébir and says France threatens
increasing and greater aerial damage in the days ahead.
Our anti-aircraft guns are holding the French
bombers at bay but the fleet and our harbour are their
obvious target. General Liddell asks for reinforcements.

To General Sir Clive Liddell,
C-in-C, Gibraltar
From War Office, London

Date: Thursday, 18 July 1940

      Please ensure that your staff understand you are not under attack by French aircraft. Nor is this France's response to a British naval manoeuvre. These are Vichy planes and this is a Vichy response. The Free French Government in London condemns this attack unreservedly.

      As you must already know, such reinforcements as we have are required for Malta, which is under far worse attack from the Italians. Should reinforcements become available they will be allocated as needed.

      Gibraltar's position is noted.

HQ Alderney
The Channel Islands

Thursday, 18 July 1940

My dear Sir William,

I'm sorry I had to call on you in such a fashion the
day before yesterday. It is obviously important that my
administration is seen to uphold the rule of law. I'm sure
you understand my position.

Investigation by my staff has established that the boy was
killed by one of the labourers brought over from Guernsey.
A sordid tale that it might be better for everyone not to
investigate further. Since the man in question is mentally
deficient, has confessed to the murder and this is quite
clearly a civilian matter, I intend to leave it to the local
authorities in St Peter Port to pass sentence.

I'm glad the issue is closed.

Yours,
Ernst von N.

To: Sir William Renhou, Knight of Renhou

105

Mrs Beecher was already up and making jam when Daisy came down the next morning. The housekeeper didn't glance round from her stove, just stirred her bubbling mixture a little harder.

'The electricity's gone,' Daisy said.

'That's because the generator's broken.'

'Have you seen . . .' Daisy hesitated. '. . . My husband?'

'He went out an hour ago.'

'Did he say where he was going?'

'Not to me. He might have told Mignon he was off to find the generator a new fan belt. They had a bit of an argument. Mignon wanted to join him.'

'Impossible,' Daisy said.

'Quite,' Mrs Beecher said. 'But there are ways to say things. And *absolutely not* isn't the way with a girl Mignon's age.'

'Why jam?' Daisy asked. 'Why now?'

'Waste not, want not. I remember the last war. It was going to be over by Christmas. It wasn't . . . Will you take Mignon when you leave?'

'Bill asked that too.'

Mrs Beecher raised her eyebrows.

Daisy shrugged. What else was she meant to call him?

On the surface he was just another Brit, hiding being a shit behind a veneer of manners. But then he was pretending to be William, and that was her husband to a tee. For all Bill's black gaze and barely restrained fury there seemed to be more to this version than that. Watching him carry Mignon into the house had been a revelation. She'd felt the fury burn away as he passed, the girl seemingly lifeless in his arms. In that moment he'd been someone else entirely.

A man she'd had no idea was in there.

106

Washington DC, same day

Standish turned from the window to examine the man who'd entered his office at the Department of Unintended Consequences.

'Good crossing?'

'I flew, sir.'

'Thought you were quick.'

'You ordered me to fly, sir. At least, your initials were on the note.'

'That's possible,' Standish admitted. In Ohio, being born with his inclinations made being 'reserved' advisable. He found being inscrutable harder.

'What did you find out?'

He watched his visitor pick at the question.

'About what?' he asked finally.

'Start with Lilly,' Standish said with a sigh.

He listened carefully to what his man had to say about Lilly Black's death, the Duke of Windsor's subsequent movements, the number of groups shadowing the duke and who might be first to make their move. Written reports were useful, but sometimes you had to look a man in the face and watch his eyes.

Lilly's death had hurt this man. It had hurt Standish too.

'Tell me again about de Rivera.'

What had the Englishman watching the meeting from a distance been there to observe? And on whose behalf had the brother of the Spanish fascist party's martyred founder visited the duke? Franco's, Hitler's, his own?

Franco's price for allying himself with Berlin and invading Gibraltar had been high enough to make Hitler baulk. That was either very greedy or very clever. The possibility that Franco would support Hitler with words but not soldiers was to be encouraged.

'And the duke?'

'He's drinking heavily, exercising obsessively and injecting cocaine. He's not sleeping either. His wife is worried.'

'I'm not surprised she's worried.'

The duke was between a rock and a hard place, and one or the other would crush him. It might take a bullet through the window to focus his mind. Standish hoped London could be relied on to arrive at that realization for themselves, rather than go for the simpler, more finite, bullet through the head.

'I'm sorry about Lilly,' Standish said. 'I know you were close.'

'Sir . . .'

Assets in the field weren't allowed to fraternize, but it happened, and Standish's words were meant to do more than express his sympathy. They were to remind his visitor he had no secrets.

'What are you doing next?'

'I was rather expecting you to tell me that, sir.'

'I think a holiday is in order.'

'A holiday, sir?'

'Somewhere quiet. The English Channel Islands are meant to be delightful at this time of year. The weather's mild and the flowers are in bloom. Apparently, Jersey's lovely. But I'd try Guernsey. It's quieter.'

'Haven't they just been invaded?'

'I'm sure you'll find the Germans welcoming.'

His visitor was watching him carefully.

Standish pushed a file across. Inside was a passport, return tickets to France, a press card, and a leather wallet full of English pounds, American dollars and German marks.

'You'll be travelling as Mr Peel. Newly employed by *The New York Times*. You'll be staying at the Hotel Grande. You're carefully neutral but lean towards Berlin. You're there to write a news story about the occupation. A positive story. One of which they will approve. While there I'd like you to deliver this . . .'

Standish put a leather case on his desk.

'Am I allowed to ask what's in it?'

Opening it, Standish revealed loops for pens, a pop-up blotter with a compartment for writing paper, envelopes and cards beneath. There was a fountain pen, two silver-topped ink bottles held in place with straps, a leather diary, an address book and a jotter with a little pencil in its spine.

The stationery was new and of excellent quality.

'This is for Daisy Renhou. Daisy Black as was. A birthday present. She'll be expecting it. Your flight's this afternoon.'

'Where do I find her?'

'You don't. She'll find you.'

If Standish's visitor minded being summoned across the Atlantic to act as a courier, because that was what had just happened, he didn't let it show; and if the case was heavier than its contents suggested, he didn't let that show either.

107

Portugal, same day

Wallis found her husband in the courtyard that afternoon, fussing over a little two-seater sports car. He was wearing a hacking jacket, new jodhpurs, a cap and tan riding boots.

'Where are you going?' Wallis's voice was sharp enough to set the Duke of Windsor's mouth into a tight line.

'For a ride.'

'By yourself?'

He glanced around as if to say *do you see anybody else*, finished buckling back the hood of the MG T-Type coupé and yanked open the driver's door.

'Where did that come from?'

'The embassy.'

She waited.

'The British embassy,' he said heavily. 'It was delivered first thing. Apparently, the ambassador thought I might like it.'

'It probably records everything you say.'

For a moment, the duke seemed intrigued, then he shrugged, almost regretfully. 'I'm not sure that's possible.'

Wallis knew when to avoid an argument. She disliked losing and from the set of his face this wasn't an argument she'd win. She stepped closer and gripped her husband's arm, because gripping his hand was too obvious and in this mood he was quite capable of pulling away.

'We're in this together,' she said.

Her husband hesitated.

'You can say it,' Wallis said. 'It might be best if you did.'

'I have bloody Berlin on one side and London on the other, and they're yanking me in opposite directions. I'd happily be shot of both of them.'

'Do you mean that?'

'A bit. Hitler's going to win, you know. Whatever I decide, he's going to win. He always does. The ambassador sent me Churchill's Fall of France speech. "Upon this battle depends the survival of Christian civilization." Pompous shit.'

'Darling . . .'

'I'm cross.'

'Obviously. Did the ambassador say anything else?'

'It was the note. He hoped I'd like the car. It represents the very best of *British* engineering. He also sent copies of the old bastard's more recent speeches. He thought they might interest me . . . If you believe Churchill, he's single-handedly going to save the world from darkness.'

'You don't believe him?'

The duke ran his hand through his hair. 'Obviously not. The first time the Luftwaffe bomb London the entire bloody country will fold.'

Wallis sighed. 'You're right,' she said. 'A drive might blow those cobwebs away.'

'Don't you wish we were somewhere else?' the duke asked.

'I don't mind where we are,' Wallis said. 'So long as I'm at your side.'

The duke put his hand over hers, holding it in place for a second. Then he climbed into the MG, pulled the door shut with a satisfying thud and started the motor. It wasn't large as engines went but the car's frame was ash, the bodywork light and the sports version came with twin carbs and a high tune.

It growled fruitily as it pulled away, and Wallis's mouth twisted as she watched dust rise from the back wheels. She needed to telephone Baron von Hoyningen-Huene and have a word. She hoped the German ambassador was in.

108

Alderney, same day

Whoever lived at Fort Clonque before the war would be horrified by the changes a month of abandonment had brought.
That, and the fact their castle had acquired a squatter. Two trac-
tors stood by its gatehouse, one in pieces. How they'd been
brought across the causeway Bill had no idea. A rusting AJS
motorbike leant against an inside wall. Its rear wheel had been
removed.

A goat grazed in front of a Victorian gun encampment.
The fort's curtain wall secured one half of its compound.
Nothing but a drop to the sea secured the rest. As there was
no sign of human life, Bill hammered a tyre iron against the
motorbike's detached wheel.

A dog howled in answer.

'All right. All right,' someone shouted.

An unshaven man clutching a whisky bottle pulled back a
canvas that closed off an arch. Beyond him was a workshop
of sorts. The man shouted. The dog kept barking.

'They said in town you might have a fan belt,' Bill told him.

'Did they now? Who did you say you were?'

'Renhou,' Bill said. 'William Renhou.'

'Are you indeed?' The man whistled. 'You'd better come in.'

Bill wondered if the man was drunk, given how bleary-
eyed and unshaven he was, but his swaying seemed more
habit than inebriation.

'You have a fan belt?'

'In here.' Pulling back the canvas, he ushered Bill through.

Bill heard him gulp down the last of his brandy.

'Perfect timing,' the man said, raising his bottle.

It smashed into the side of Bill's skull, and the dirt came up to meet him.

To All Agencies
From Trans-Ocean News Service,
Berlin Office

Date: Friday, 19 July 1940
<u>Immediate Release</u>

In a speech to the Reichstag today, Herr Hitler stated:
'Mr. Churchill for once believes me when I predict a great empire will be destroyed, an empire that it was never my intention to destroy or even to harm.

'I do realize that this struggle, if it continues, can end only with the complete annihilation of one or the other of the two adversaries.

'Mr Churchill may believe this will be Germany. I know that it will be Britain. I am appealing once more for common sense. There is no reason why this war should go on. If, however, Mr Churchill insists, I shall have relieved my conscience in regard to the things to come.'

109

Alderney, same day

'The charge is murder . . .'

'And treason,' Bill heard Jerome say. 'Treason, treachery, framing Georgie, and being a filthy fascist. And murderer.' He kicked Bill in the guts and Bill almost spewed into the sack someone had pulled over his head.

'Right, bastard's awake. Get him upright.'

Hands dragged Bill to his feet.

'Let's just hang him.'

'We have to try him first.'

'Drowning would be better. The Nazis will know he's been executed if they find him hanging. We can't risk that.'

'What makes you think we'll leave a body?'

Five or six men stood around him. Bill hadn't known there were six islanders left on Alderney, and then he realized there weren't. These were Jerome's crew from Guernsey, plus a couple of locals.

'The priest's arrived,' someone said.

'Let him wait,' the scrapyard man replied. 'I want a word with his lordship first.' He dragged the hood from Bill's head and Bill discovered he was still in the workshop, only now the workshop was lit and it was dark outside.

'Hold him still.'

A knife sliced the rope tying Bill's wrists, and when the scrapyard man grabbed his forearm, Bill realized too late what he intended. He fought, but the men held him too tightly and he felt his hand pushed into the jaws of a vice.

'Right. Let's see the bastard confess.'

'Christ, Pete.'

'We know he did it. What's the problem?'

'Don't,' Bill said.

'Want to confess?'

'To what?' Bill demanded.

Jerome punched him in the gut.

Bill would have doubled over but his other arm was in a half-nelson, and he could only watch helplessly as the scrapyard man began tightening the vice with easy twists of the handle.

'Last chance,' he said.

'I saved Georgie's life.'

The man twisted the handle half a turn. Twisting it again, he grinned when Bill groaned in pain. 'Confess to killing the boy.'

'I didn't . . . Don't,' Bill begged.

'Don't what?' the scrapyard man demanded.

'Break my hand.' How the hell could he crack a safe with a ruined hand? Assuming he was still alive at the end of this. That was the bit he needed to worry about.

'I'm going to whip him before we hang him,' Jerome said.

'Are you going to confess?' Michael, the barman from Braye, asked.

Of course he wasn't. They'd take his confession as real and kill him without even the pretence of a trial.

'You've got the wrong person.'

'Who killed Eddie then?'

Bill thought of Mignon, and of Eddie's terror as he gasped out her name. Bill didn't know why she'd kill someone she so obviously liked, and he didn't know how to ask, and he'd told Daisy there'd been no last words.

He couldn't even tell these people the child existed.

'I don't know,' Bill said.

'Fuck this,' the scrapyard man said.

A half-twist of the handle had Bill screaming as a knuckle popped. He was sobbing from an unholy mix of pain, frustration and rage. How could he complete his mission now? What was the point of him even being here?

'I didn't fucking do it,' he shouted.

The scrapyard man reached for the handle. 'I don't believe you.'

'*That's enough.*'

Jerome pushed Pete aside and loosened the vice. The hood went back over Bill's head and his wrists were dragged behind him.

'Best get him up there,' Jerome said. 'They're waiting.'

110

'All rise,' a voice said.

Around Bill people began to stand.

'Why is he hooded?'

'To stop him escaping.'

'If he tries to escape you can shoot him.' The voice was young, well spoken, and not as assured as it sounded.

There was silence from the crowd as Bill's guards obeyed. Bill stood in the middle of a circle of some sort, swaying with the effort of not falling over. In front of him stood a young priest.

'I'm Clack,' he said. 'I've been asked to adjudicate.' His eyes widened as he took in Bill's state. 'Who did this?'

'He fell,' the barman said. He'd shaved for the occasion and found himself a jacket. His gaze was hard when it turned it on Bill. 'We're going to hang you,' he said, looking Bill up and down.

'What did I ever do to you?'

'I'm Eddie's uncle,' Michael replied.

'I'm sorry about your nephew.'

His punch caught Bill in the gut, and the scrapyard man grabbed Bill before he could fall, holding him steady so Eddie's uncle could land another.

'Enough!' the Reverend Clack said.

They disagreed, but they let him go all the same.

The SOE lieutenant who'd trained Bill would know what to

do. Bill didn't doubt that. Unfortunately, Bill didn't. He was standing in the gaze of a full moon, at the highest point of Fort Clonque, in a shamrock-shaped depression designed to let the British shoot French invaders if they tried to scale the walls. Wisps of cloud drifted overhead, and at least a dozen hard-faced Guernsey islanders were ranged round him. There wasn't one of them who wouldn't be happy to see him hang.

III

Alderney, same day

'How do you plead?'

'To what?' Bill asked. He meant his answer to be forceful but his voice was weak and it came out as a croak, barely audible to those watching.

'Speak up,' the priest said.

'Plead to what?' Bill demanded.

'You are charged with the murder of Eddie Duplain. A child, and the framing for murder of George Bisson. How do you plead?'

'And treason,' the scrapyard owner insisted.

The young priest sighed. 'And treason,' he agreed tiredly.

'The punishment for treason is death,' the man said. 'Treason and treachery and murder. The verdict must be death.'

Several voices muttered agreement.

'What's your part in this?' Bill asked the priest.

'I'm your judge.'

'I don't recognize this court.'

'Not German enough?' Eddie's uncle asked.

The young priest stared at Bill, his face clear in the moonlight. 'You are Sir William Renhou. You are charged with murder. How do you plead?'

Bill's first instinct was to say he wasn't Renhou. But how could he, when any one of the Guernsey islanders could be a Nazi plant?

'I'm not a killer,' Bill said.

Reverend Clack stared at him. 'You're an ex-soldier, I'm told. You're wanted by the British authorities for the murder of your own ADC. Of course you're a killer. You'd be wise to take this seriously.'

I am, Bill thought.

He'd seen courts like this in action. In the trenches, and among British prisoners in a German camp in the last war, and in civil prisons back home. Evidence was irrelevant and logic there to be ignored. Kangaroo courts reached the verdicts they'd decided in advance.

'Can we talk alone?' Bill asked.

'You can talk to me here. How do you plead?'

'Not guilty, obviously.'

'You deny killing Eddie?'

'Sir William was seen.' Eddie's uncle pushed himself forward. 'I've told you,' he said to the priest. 'He was seen. He has to hang.'

'Mr Deslandes——' the priest said.

'Or shot. I don't care which.'

'You'll have your chance to speak later,' Clack said, sounding sympathetic. 'But it's his turn now. We have to do this properly.'

'Why should we?' Jerome protested. 'He had Georgie tortured.' The other Guernsey islanders erupted in furious agreement. Any louder and they'd bring the Germans down on them. 'And then framed him for murder.'

'Accident or not,' Bill said. 'Your man almost killed their CO. London's orders are for you and the invaders to get on as well as possible. Those are their orders too. If they weren't, he'd be dead and so would you. *All of you*. Besides, I've already written to ask for his release.'

'Why would you do that?' Jerome demanded.

'Because he didn't do it.'

*

'I think,' the priest said, 'we should concentrate on this boy. It's said he poached regularly on Renhou land and that you're known to be unforgiving. How do you plead to that?'

'I've told you. Not guilty, obviously.'

'And I've been told, repeatedly, you were seen coming from the thicket where his body was found. You walked away without even looking back.'

'Are you my judge?' Bill demanded.

'I've said that already.'

'Only you seem to be doubling as my prosecution and a witness too.'

'A boy died,' Clack said angrily.

'Then his killer is still out there, isn't he?' Bill stared around the amphitheatre, meeting the gaze of a dozen men in the moonlight. 'Unless, of course,' he added, 'He's here . . .'

It took a minute for the Guernsey islanders' fury to subside.

'You were seen,' Michael said. Eddie's uncle was frustrated by Bill's refusal to engage with this damning piece of evidence.

'That doesn't mean I did it.'

'Explain how that's possible,' Clack said.

Bill knew he was being offered a chance, and he wished that he could explain, starting with the fact that they were all on the same side, but it wasn't that simple.

'I found him in the thicket.'

'He's lying,' Eddie's uncle shouted.

'Quiet,' the young priest snapped. 'Unless you want the Nazis to find us.' Turning to Bill, he said, 'And you just left him there?'

'He was dead.'

There was an ugly murmur from the crowd.

'So you went home?'

'Yes,' Bill said, 'I went home.'

'To telephone the authorities?'

'There is no telephone at Renhou.'

'Then why go home?' Clack demanded.

The priest noticed Bill's hesitation and his tone hardened. 'You found him, you realized he was dead. You went home. What then?'

'I went out again.'

'Why?'

The islanders were watching Bill.

'It would be best if you answered,' the priest said.

Not for Mignon, Bill thought.

Acceptance Speech at the Democratic National Convention by President Franklin D. Roosevelt for a 3rd Term as President of the United States of America

Friday, 19 July 1940

My conscience will not let me turn my back upon a call to service.

The right to make that call rests with the people, through the American method of a free election. Only the people themselves can draft a president. If such a draft should be made upon me, I say to you, in the utmost simplicity, I will, with God's help, continue to serve with the best of my ability and with the fullness of my strength.

112

Alderney, same day

Bill's safest option was to say he wasn't Sir William, that he was an SOE agent landed from a submarine to steal Nazi invasion plans. Unfortunately, he doubted they'd believe him, and it didn't solve who'd killed the boy, or deal with Georgie's whipping and the fact he'd been framed.

The priest was beginning to look worried.

'Renhou,' he said. 'If you have anything to say I suggest you say it. Otherwise, these people will have no choice but to—'

'*What have you done to him?*' The voice blazed with outrage.

Its owner stalked into the centre of the moonlit circle with a crossbow gripped in her hands. When Eddie's uncle stepped forward, she pointed it at his stomach. The entire crowd froze.

'That's . . .' he started to say.

'I know whose it is. He taught me to load it too.'

The man dismissed, Mignon turned to Bill and her eyes filled.

'I'm sorry,' she said. 'This is all my fault.'

'No,' Bill said. 'It's not.'

'Who's this?' the priest demanded.

Mignon swung her weapon in his direction. 'Did I say you could talk?' Her anger burnt in the moonlight as her gaze dismissed him too.

'You didn't come back. Madame said you would and you didn't.'

'Where's Daisy?' Bill demanded.

'Here,' Daisy said. 'Hot on this brat's heels.'

Mignon bit her lip and the crossbow trembled.

The double-barrelled shotgun Daisy carried was loaded but broken open. She looked convincingly furious at Mignon for leaving the house, with Bill for being stupid enough to find himself in this situation, and with the crowd for forcing her to do this.

'I'm taking Bill back,' she said.

'You're—' The scrapyard man shut his mouth when Daisy snapped the shotgun shut and turned both barrels on him, her finger already tightening on the trigger.

'You think for one second I wouldn't kill you?'

The men either side of him stepped away.

'Very wise,' she said. Her smile flinty.

The young priest was glancing between Mignon and Daisy. He seemed mesmerized by their weapons and their certainty.

'What Sir William won't tell you—' Mignon said.

'*Don't*,' Bill said.

'What he won't tell you is why he went back to the house. Why he went out again. He won't even tell you what he was doing when he found Eddie. He was looking for me. He won't tell you because he thinks I killed Eddie and he doesn't want to betray me.'

There was an instant hubbub.

'I didn't,' Mignon raised her voice. 'He didn't either.'

'Who did then?' Eddie's uncle demanded.

'A German,' Mignon said. 'It's obvious.'

'Eddie was waiting for me,' Mignon said. She stood for a moment, looking shamefaced. 'He was hiding in the ruins overlooking Renhou. Whoever stabbed him didn't expect him to be there. I don't know if Eddie surprised them or they surprised Eddie. But he was stabbed to stop him talking. He must have been.'

Bill could see the priest trying to work out how old Mignon was. Whether he was dealing with a young woman or a child.

'You're friends with Eddie?' he asked.

'Eddie helped me. I was being chased. We hid . . .'

Mignon stopped, stricken. Bill knew it was because he was hearing things he hadn't heard before. He doubted Daisy had heard them either.

'You hid . . . ?' Clack prompted.

'We hid where Sir William found Eddie. The ruins became our den.'

'How do I know you're not lying to protect Sir William?'

Bill had a first name now. A small shift in the wind but a shift all the same. He didn't blame the priest for being sceptical. As everybody kept saying, Bill had been seen Lady-Macbeth-like with blood on his hands.

'I wouldn't,' Mignon promised.

'You wouldn't what?' Clack asked.

'Lie about Eddie.'

'Why not?'

Mignon's mouth trembled.

Bill could see Daisy biting her lip. She saw him looking and turned so that he couldn't see her eyes well up. That was unexpected. Discovering she had emotions.

'You liked this boy?' the young priest asked. He sounded bemused.

Mignon nodded.

Walking across the redoubt, Daisy put her arm round the girl's shoulders and Mignon leant into her. 'Mrs Beecher's niece went out,' she said. 'She's not allowed out without a grown-up's permission. Not with soldiers on the island.'

331

She was speaking to the priest; everyone else might as well not have been there. 'My husband went looking for her. He found Eddie instead.'

'What drew your husband to the cottage?'

'He saw crows and heard groans.'

'Eddie was alive?'

'He was already beyond saving. My husband hurried home to see if Mrs Beecher's niece was there and left the moment he realized she wasn't. He was frightened for her. When he reached the ruins, the body was gone.'

'And he found this girl?'

'Where Eddie had been.'

That caught everyone's attention.

'What was she doing?' the priest demanded.

'Lying there.' Bill's voice sounded hollow even to himself. 'On her side, eyes wide and utterly still. Blood all over her from the bracken. I thought she was dead. For a second, I thought she'd been killed too.'

'It's all my fault,' Mignon said.

'No,' Daisy and Bill said, together. 'It's not.'

113

Portugal, Saturday, 20 July 1940

'Darling . . .'

'I know what I'm doing.' The duke accelerated out of the corner, the 1,300-cc engine of his two-seater MG growling as its back wheels skittered; and then the road straightened out and the duke roared up an incline, dropping down a gear as he approached another bend.

'"A touch of blood." That's Lawrence of Arabia, you know. "A skittish motor with a touch of blood in it is better than all the riding animals on earth."'

'He died in a crash.'

'That was on two wheels. This has four.'

Changing down, the duke took the hairpin too quickly, laughed as he fought the steering wheel, and crested a hill thirty seconds later fast enough to lift all four wheels from the road.

'I shouldn't have let you have that last whisky.'

The duke laughed again, although Wallis's expression suggested she wasn't joking. Settling slightly, the duke took a series of downhill bends with ease, reading the road perfectly and only touching his brakes now and then.

He had a decision to make. One that had been eating at him for days. He knew Wallis wanted him to throw in his lot with Berlin. Most days that was what he wanted too. But he couldn't bring himself to say it.

Behind the wheel of the MG it didn't matter though. The

ambassador was right. It really did represent British engineering at its finest. In this car he felt himself alive.

'Nearly there,' he said, as close to an apology as he was going to get.

They'd agreed to meet Oswald von Hoyningen-Huene. Their cover would be that they'd driven to a famous beauty spot for a picnic, only to find the German ambassador already there.

'Here we go,' he said.

The duke indicated a car in the distance and hit the accelerator, braking as he went into a slight corner and accelerating hard out of it.

'Darling.'

'All good . . .'

The duke stepped on the brakes as he swung into the lay-by. Nothing. He stepped on them harder, but his MG failed to stop. As he swung back on to the road, Wallis grabbed the door handle and the ambassador jumped back. Below, a huge lorry turned the corner, heading straight for the MG.

They were going to crash.

114

The duke dropped down a gear, and then another, hearing his motor scream. Yanking up his handbrake, he changed down one final time, and the MG shuddered to a halt. Its brake pedal was tight to the floor. Von Hoyningen-Huene was already hurtling down the road behind him.

'My God. Are you all right?'

The German ambassador opened Wallis Simpson's door and helped her out, keeping his hand under her elbow until she found her balance. The duke let himself out the other side. He was shaking.

'Let me handle this, sir.'

Striding towards the lorry the MG had scraped past, the ambassador indicated that its driver should climb down. A short and intense conversation followed, which ended with the ambassador pulling out his wallet and emptying hundreds of escudos into the man's hands. Having pocketed them, the man walked to the rear of his lorry and stared at its scarred paintwork, then at the gouge in the red dirt bank, obviously wondering how the MG had got through.

'He'll say nothing,' von Hoyningen-Huene promised. 'Now, sir. What happened?'

'My brakes failed. They were a bit spongy yesterday. Not like that though.'

'My driver's an excellent mechanic. Would you let him take a look?'

'I'd be delighted,' the duke said.

The duke, Wallis and Oswald von Hoyningen-Huene sat in the shade of a Saracen olive tree on fold-out stools. In front of them was a wicker basket.'

'Another glass of Riesling, sir?'

The duke cast a glance at his wife, then shook his head. 'Best not,' he said. 'It will only give me a headache.'

'Here we go,' the ambassador announced. The duke's MG was being reversed up the road. 'If you'd give me a moment.' He stood with his chauffeur for a while, listening intently and considering the damage to the side of the little coupé.

'Is it drivable?' the duke asked, when he returned.

'Sir. How long have you had that vehicle?'

'A day or two. Why?'

'And you bought it in Portugal?'

'It was a present.'

'From a friend?'

'What's going on?' The duke's voice sharpened.

'Could someone have got at it? Perhaps when you were parked in Lisbon or Estoril?'

'I haven't taken it to Lisbon or Estoril.'

'There are tiny holes in each of the brake hoses. It was only a matter of time before your brakes failed totally. My man says you're lucky to be alive.'

Wallis put her hand to her mouth.

'I don't believe it,' the duke said.

'What don't you believe, sir?'

'That the British embassy would—'

'It would solve all their problems,' Wallis said. 'Wouldn't it? Very neatly. Me, you, our refusal to do what we're told.'

'*Wallis.*'

'My love.' His wife's voice was shaking. 'I love you. I'm scared. I don't want to end up over the edge of a cliff.'

'It was a gift from your embassy?'

'Yes,' the duke said. 'It was a present from my embassy.'

The ambassador looked sombre and said nothing for a long time. 'I think,' he said finally, 'now is the time to ask yourself who your real friends are. Are they the people who did this, or are they those of us who'd keep you both safe?'

'Can you keep us safe?' the duke demanded.

'Of course,' the ambassador said. 'We can keep you safe and we can give you back your life, your country and your throne.'

'And in return?' the duke asked.

'We ask simply for your friendship.'

The duke put out his hand. 'You have it,' he said.

115

Guernsey, same day

A thin-faced island doctor, with a stethoscope round his neck and pens in his top pocket, a clipboard in his hand and spectacles perched on his nose, woke Bill by shaking him harder than necessary.

Bill blinked at the splint on his right hand.

'You need to take this off,' he said.

'I've no intention of taking it off.'

'I'll do it myself.'

'Then you deserve to be crippled.'

'Where am I?'

'In hospital. On Guernsey.'

'Why?'

'Your wife insisted. The Germans agreed.'

'My wife . . . ? How badly am I injured?'

'You'll live. You have a visitor.'

'Show her in.'

'I told your wife to come back tomorrow. And he can show himself in.' The doctor turned to leave but then changed his mind, standing back against a green-painted wall instead.

'You can go,' von Neudeck told him.

'I'll stay.'

'I'd like some painkillers,' Bill said, 'if that's allowed?'

The doctor shot him a scowl and turned on his heel, leaving the ward door open to indicate he'd be back shortly.

'This is dreadful timing,' von Neudeck said.

It hurt to snort. 'In what way?'

'London's appointing the Duke of Windsor governor of the Bahamas. We know that Churchill intends to have him killed the moment he boards the ship. Either that, or the moment he lands.'

'That's ridiculous.'

The colonel shook his head. 'Oh no,' he said. 'That true. The duke's told Churchill he won't leave until his brother grants his wife a royal title, receives her at court and adds her to the Civil List. Hell will freeze over first. But it gives him an excuse to refuse to get on their bloody ship.'

'Why would he go to the Bahamas?'

'Ah, here are your painkillers.' Von Neudeck stepped back to give the doctor room.

Having dropped his pills twice, Bill thanked the doctor a third time, and fumbled the glass of water, tipping half of it on his hospital pyjamas.

'Now,' von Neudeck said. 'What happened?'

'I fell,' Bill said.

Von Neudeck wasn't the only one to look shocked.

'You have a hairline fracture to your skull,' the colonel said. 'A broken knuckle and a badly bruised hand. You're missing a back tooth. You have cracked ribs, a black eye and a split lip. You'll be pissing blood for a week.'

'It was a bad fall,' Bill insisted.

'*Sir William*,' von Neudeck said.

'How's Daisy?'

Von Neudeck blinked. 'The only reason you're here is your wife rattled the gates of my HQ so furiously the guards decided to call me. She demanded that you be brought to this hospital immediately. I gather that you two might be getting on better than before?'

'A little,' Bill admitted.

'I'm glad. Now. You tell me what really happened.'

The doctor was watching, obviously trying to work out why Bill wouldn't oblige. In a way Bill's next question was meant for both men.

'Would you?' he asked.

'I thought we were friends?'

'We are. In as much as we're allowed to be. All the same, it was a fall.'

Colonel von Neudeck stared at the doctor. 'In your opinion,' he said, 'is it possible that these injuries could be the result of a fall?'

'It's *possible*,' the doctor said after a long pause.

'What are your chances of falling again?' von Neudeck asked.

'Slight,' Bill said.

'You're certain of that?'

'As certain as any man may be.'

116

Guernsey, same day

In the time it took the doctor to show von Neudeck out, Bill stole a stethoscope and a pair of latex gloves from a medical cart just outside his door. He'd need them for what came next. Although how he could crack their safe with a fractured hand . . . He wondered how close Daisy was to trusting him. Close enough?

Or did he have some work still to do?

117

Five German bandsmen with enough braid to be generals filled the stand in Guernsey's Cambridge Park, which was only a minute's walk from the Hotel Grande, and five minutes from the hospital where Bill was being treated.

'Look,' Mignon said.

'Let's sit for a bit,' Daisy suggested.

Mrs Beecher had chosen Mignon's clothes for her. She wore a very ordinary dress and looked like any other island girl. All the same, Daisy had to hold her hand to stop her flinching when soldiers walked past. Now Mignon's presence was known, Daisy wasn't letting her out of her sight until she'd worked out how to handle that.

'Can we sit at the back?' Mignon asked.

She chose the deckchairs and Daisy paid the sixpence asked. Then she dug in her pocket for change, nodded to an ice-cream cart, and sent Mignon to buy cornets – two if she had enough change, one if she didn't. The moment she was gone a man slipped into her abandoned seat.

'Reception gave me your note,' he said.

'What are you this time?'

'A journalist.' His business card, introducing him as a stringer for *The New York Times*, was no more real than the one he'd given her a month before describing him as a US trade representative at the Paris embassy.

'Covering the happy occupation?' Daisy asked sourly.

'Something like that,' he said. The man deposited a pretty-looking writing case between the deckchairs and tapped it three times with his little finger. The agency signal that he'd be leaving it there.

'You'll also need this.' He unhooked a press camera from his neck, balancing it on the writing case.

'I already have a camera,' Daisy said. 'A fifth of that size.'

'Oh. This doesn't take photographs. It would be best if you didn't lend it to anyone or try to look inside.'

'What does it do?'

'Point it in the right direction and press the shutter. It's good for one use and Mr Standish's tests show it can last for up to seven minutes.'

'*What does it do?*' Daisy said crossly.

'Lets you see in the dark. Call it a late birthday present. There's some rather elegant notepaper in that case should you want to send the boss a thank-you letter. Now. There's talk about your husband. You didn't say he was back.'

'He's not my husband.'

'I believe your divorce is not yet through?'

'The man you're talking about is not my husband,' Daisy said heavily. 'He's simply pretending to be.'

'Why would you let him?'

'Because . . .' Daisy hesitated. 'My alternative was to give him up to the Germans. Who'd have shot him. And don't think I didn't think of that.'

'London wouldn't have been happy.'

'I'm not sure I care.'

'He's a Brit saboteur?'

'He's a Brit something,' Daisy said. 'I'm not sure exactly what.'

'Then I suggest you find out.' He heaved himself from the deckchair. 'I'd better go. Your chaperone's back.'

'Who was that?'

'Nobody,' Daisy said.

Mignon looked sympathetic. 'The change wasn't enough.'

Daisy eyed the two cornets she was carrying.

'He let me have them anyway.'

At a nod from a bandmaster with an absurd moustache and a chest full of gold braid, the musicians readied themselves and launched into a waltz.

'Very clever,' Daisy said.

Mignon stopped licking her ice cream. 'The players?'

'Yes,' said Daisy, meaning that too. The music was light, bouncy. Even the islanders who'd scowled to see a German band setting up mellowed as the concert went on. If the soldiers had launched into a military march it would have been different. But they didn't: they started with Strauss and went on to Rossini and Offenbach, finishing to a smattering of applause. The normality of it all was disarming.

Intentionally so.

Mignon pointed at Daisy's untouched ice cream. 'Are you going to eat that?'

Obediently Daisy passed it over.

To Generalfeldmarschall Walther von Brauchitsch
From Adolf Hitler, Führer

Date: Sunday, 21 July 1940
<u>In Confidence</u>

You will advise me on the feasibility of launching a blitzkrieg attack on the Soviet Union this autumn in the immediate aftermath of the fall of Britain. Aim for the immediate destruction of at least 200 Soviet divisions with less than 100 divisions remaining.

If I find the report satisfactory, you will present it to the High Command of the German Army and I will set a date for an autumn attack.

I am naming this Unternehmen Otto.*

* Name later changed to Barbarossa.

118

Portugal, Monday, 22 July 1940

Pulling into the forecourt of Casa de Santa Maria, the Duke of Windsor killed the engine of his newly repaired MG and sat back with his eyes closed as he listened to its engine cool. It was Monday, late afternoon, the sun was bright, the breeze gentle and everything was set for a perfect evening. The garage Eberhard had recommended had beaten out the panels, repainted the bodywork, replaced the brake hoses and checked over everything else just to be sure.

He just wished he didn't feel so discontented.

When the duke opened his eyes again, Wallis stood beside the car smiling.

'Look.' Wallis held up a tiny leather-bound booklet and the duke bent closer. Behind it was one bound in white leather.

'That one's mine,' she said, seeing his gaze.

Taking it, he flipped it open and froze. 'I didn't agree to take their money,' he said crossly. 'I said I'd consider it.'

'They must have misunderstood.'

'You opened my post?'

'They came in one package. Addressed to both of us.' Her voice was sharp. It wouldn't hurt him to see that she was upset. Her husband held up his hand in apology. 'That's a bank book too?' He nodded to the one she held.

She handed it across.

'Ten million Swiss francs?'

'They gave you fifty.'

There were a dozen things he could have said. Wisely he said none of them. Instead, he looked thoughtful. 'You know this means we're committed, don't you? London will go insane if they find out.'

'Then they'd better not. I wouldn't trust the English not to shoot us. At best, they'll bundle us into a van and fly us off to some thinly disguised jail.'

'I'm English.' The duke's voice was mild.

'Your mother was a German princess. Your father's surname was Saxe-Coburg-Gotha, until he changed it to something suburban to keep a bunch of ghastly little newspapers happy.'

'Oh God . . .' The duke ran his hand through thinning hair. 'I need a drink, a Chesterfield and another drink.'

'Come to bed.'

He raised his eyebrows.

'You're feeling frayed,' she said. 'At least we can talk there.'

'You really think I should throw in my lot with Berlin?'

'It's not my place to say. My place is at your side.' She reached for his hand. 'Wherever that is, I'll be happy. What I need to know is, do you think you should?'

'This war should never have happened.'

'Of course it shouldn't,' Wallis said tartly. 'It's ripping Europe apart. It's already ripped it apart. I'm not sure what Churchill thinks letting Britain be ripped apart too achieves.'

'The only people who will do well out of it are the Bolsheviks.'

'And Jews,' Wallis said. 'They do well out of everything.'

'Most Bolsheviks are Jews anyway.'

'You're right,' Wallis said. 'If it wasn't ridiculous, I'd think Churchill was on their side. As for your brother . . .'

'He's a fool,' the duke said crossly. 'Always was. If he wasn't, he'd have ordered his government to make peace by now.'

'You've decided?'

'I'm going to Berlin next week.'

'The Germans have asked you and you didn't tell me?'

'They don't know yet. I've only just decided. Herr Hitler always struck me as a reasonable man. I'm going to demand we negotiate face to face.'

'He will need to know what you have in mind.'

'I'll write this evening.'

'And what will London say?'

'Nothing,' the duke said. 'They're not going to find out.'

119

Alderney, same day

Mignon was in her room and Bill safely downstairs and having his bruises fussed over by Mrs Beecher. Both of which suited Daisy fine.

Shutting her bedroom door with a sigh of relief, she flicked open a cut-throat razor she kept in her bedside locker in case of need, and turned to the writing case she'd collected on Guernsey.

'Here goes,' she said.

Raising the lid, she ran the razor across the stitches holding the various compartments in place. These lifted away as a single unit, as she'd suspected they would.

Putting the collection of paper, envelopes, silver-topped ink bottles and assorted fripperies down on her bed, she cut the seams securing the false bottom beneath and lifted it away.

'Pretty,' she said. 'Very pretty indeed.'

A broken-down rifle nestled in cut-away foam. Its barrel, mechanism and screw-in silencer had been gun-metal blued. Its rear stock, forestock and furniture were Bakelite or polymer and, where possible, hollow to reduce the weight. Even the telescopic scope was synthetic. It had been supplied with two clips of . . .

. . . 7.92 × 57-mm Mauser.

Standard German issue. She liked that touch. Five rounds in each. Daisy wasn't sure why. She only ever needed one shot.

Leaving the clips where they were, she dropped to a crouch and arranged the parts on the bed in front of her. It took her sixty-three seconds to put the rifle together and twenty-eight seconds to field-strip it back to constituent pieces. The next time she was faster on the build, and knocked a full five seconds off the breakdown. The third time, she put the parts together with her eyes shut, faster than she'd built it the first time. Raising the rifle, she dry-fired before opening her eyes again.

It felt off balance.

Field-stripping her new toy one final time, Daisy found a plug in the rubber plate that fitted against her shoulder. It unscrewed to reveal a small but empty compartment. A steel barrel on a polymer stock would throw out the balance. It was obvious when you thought about it. Filling the compartment with sand would fix that.

Daisy smiled.

To Joachim von Ribbentrop,
Reichsminister of Foreign Affairs
From Oswald von Hoyningen-Huene,
Reich Ambassador to Portugal

Date: Tuesday, 23 July 1940
<u>Top Secret</u>

To be encrypted, then carried by courier. No transmission
by wire, no copies to be made or kept.

     The Duke of Windsor has asked for a personal
meeting with the Führer. He understands entirely, how
could he not, that the Führer is busy and if this request
is granted that it is the duke who will need to travel. I
suggested a telephone call on a secure line but the duke is
insistent that the meeting must be as equals, face to face.
We already know the duke prides himself on his ability to
'read' other men and has told the duchess that he will base
his final decision about how firmly to ally himself with the
Reich on how receptive the Führer is to his concerns.
     He has asked for a guarantee that he will be allowed
to return to Lisbon if that is his choice. He asks that this
guarantee is given by the Führer personally.
     In my opinion, the fact he asks for this meeting
indicates that, to all intents and purposes, his decision is
made. He simply wishes to preen in the glory of being
taken seriously. A politeness that London refuses to
accord.
     I await instructions.

To War Cabinet
From Winston Churchill

Date: Tuesday, 23 July 1940
<u>Restricted</u>

We must abolish the use of 'Local Defence
Volunteers' as a term, with immediate effect. Their
nickname of Look, Duck & Vanish is now in use by everyone
from the housewife at the village pump to the man on the
Clapham Omnibus. It sends exactly the wrong message.

We will not look, duck and vanish. We will wait, stand
and fight.

We need something that tells this country what we're
fighting for: our mothers, our wives, our children; the
family hearth and the respect of those who come after us.

I suggest Home Guard.

120

Alderney, Tuesday, 23 July 1940

Bill felt Daisy's gaze on him as he watched Mignon plant purple pansies in a trough on the terrace. When he turned, her expression was unexpected. If he didn't know better, he'd have said it was almost kind. The moment Daisy saw him notice, she shrugged.

'This came for you.'

Bill slit the envelope and pulled out a piece of card. It was an invitation to von Neudeck's birthday party. Across the back was the colonel's promise that he'd understand if Sir William felt too unwell to attend.

'I'm not going,' Mignon said.

'You're not invited,' Daisy said. She smiled at Mignon. 'Mrs Beecher's making a cake if you want to lick out the bowl. Unless you're too grown up for that.'

Mignon went.

All I have to do, Bill told himself as he went in to supper, is go to the party, get into von Neudeck's office, crack his safe and get the invasion plans off the island. There was a submarine due in six days' time with orders to collect him.

He'd conned von Neudeck into believing he was Sir William. He'd managed to wangle an invitation into their HQ so he didn't even need to break in. He was a safe-cracker. This was what he did for a living.

How hard could it be?

The answer, of course, was close to impossible given his injured hand. He needed help, and the only person he could ask was sitting across the table watching him from the corner of her eye. He had no idea how to even frame the question.

Daisy and Bill ate alone in the dining room that night.

It was a quiet meal and a simple one. Mrs Beecher had found a ham and made a potato salad. There were Bath Oliver biscuits and blue cheese scooped from the heart of a Stilton she kept in the cellar.

They drank a claret too heavy for the weather and too good to be wasted on people only drinking because it was there. Having delivered supper, Mrs Beecher said she'd move Mignon back to her attic.

'Do it another time,' Daisy said.

'Madame?'

'Leave her in my room for now.'

Mrs Beecher seemed ready to object, then her face softened, and she nodded to herself as if warring halves had somehow reached agreement. 'You're probably right. I might take her cocoa.'

'Is that the beginnings of a truce?' Bill asked, the moment the door shut behind Mrs Beecher.

Daisy scowled.

'I'm not being nasty,' Bill told her.

'He was a shit,' she said fiercely. 'A real shit. You have no idea how much of a shit he was. And she took his side, every single time.'

Alderney, same day

They went up the stairs together, Daisy hesitating outside her old room where Mignon lay sleeping. 'You're not going to put her at risk again, are you? Because I'd go to von Neudeck and turn you in myself rather than that.'

'I'd deny it.'

'Bill. It's not a joke. I used her as cover to get here. I told myself anywhere was better than a city full of Nazis. I intend to keep her safe.'

'*Daisy.*'

Before Daisy could reply, the door opened and Mignon peered out, a blanket wrapped round her shoulders. 'You shouldn't argue.'

'We're not arguing,' Bill said.

'It sounds like arguing to me.'

'We're talking,' Daisy said. 'Go back to bed.'

Mignon did.

Bill followed Daisy up the next flight and watched her slow as she approached her temporary room. Turning, she said, 'Are your reasons for being here worth putting the rest of us at risk? No . . . Are they worth putting Mignon at risk?'

Bill knew what his answer should be.

'No,' he said. 'I'm not sure they are.'

'Do you mean that?'

Bill thought of Eddie, blood-covered in the bracken; of

Mignon's howls of grief for those she'd loved and lost, her courage facing down the kangaroo court at Clonque.

'Yes,' he said, 'I do. She's in danger on this island.'

'At the very least,' Daisy replied, 'we need people to think she's gone.'

Bill hesitated. 'Whose side are you really on?'

'America's,' Daisy said firmly.

'Which side is that?'

'We're still deciding. Well, the president is.'

'Between England and Germany?'

'Between neutrality and war. Why ask now?'

Bill showed her his hand. 'I'm going to need help.'

'Doing what?'

'Cracking von Neudeck's safe.'

Daisy looked both ways along Renhou's upper corridor, as if suddenly expecting to see Nazis, and held open her bedroom door.

'Finally, we get to it,' she said.

Alderney, same day

There was enough room at the window for them to stand side by side without touching. Bill could feel the heat of her, and smell sea on her skin. He was aware of her bed behind them. More aware than he liked to admit. It was all he could do not to glance back.

'Lilly died a few days before I arrived,' Daisy said suddenly

'Who did?'

'My sister. In a way she's why I came back.'

'I'm sorry.'

'Me too. More than I ever imagined. Now, who do you work for?'

'I don't know. Not really.' Bill felt her shift, and said, 'That's the truth of it. I was due to hang. A man offered me my life in return for this.'

'You're a murderer?'

'No. But that wouldn't have saved me.'

'You're not a soldier?'

'A long time ago. In the trenches.'

'That much of what you told von Neudeck is true then? You really fought at the front in the Great War?'

'And watched friends die, their memory betrayed, and nothing improve.'

'You sound like a communist.'

'They wouldn't have me,' Bill said.

It was an old joke and a tired one, and only half a joke

anyway. He'd never been able to put his sense of betrayal at what followed the war into words. Annie's death in the Old Town slums. The riots in Glasgow. London sending in its tanks. The hunger marches and starvation.

'If you're not a spy,' Daisy said, 'what are you?'

'What does this have to do with your sister?'

'Everything,' she said. 'At least I'm beginning to think so.'

The knot in Bill's gut was something he hadn't felt in years. Shame. Shame at coming back from the trenches when better men died. Shame at pushing Annie's baby into Mary's arms in a Cowgate pub all those years ago. Pushing it into her arms and running. As he'd been running ever since.

'Who are you?' Daisy demanded. 'Really.'

He considered lying. Of course he did. Lying was second nature. He'd spent twenty years being everyone but himself.

'You can tell me,' she insisted.

Bill didn't want to. But he knew he would.

'Your turn,' Bill said. They were in bed by then, mostly clothed and having done about half of what people who go to bed usually do. 'I'd been told you were a fascist sympathizer.'

'William's politics weren't mine. The Rat's neither.'

'The Rat?' Bill asked.

'No one who matters. A man came to see me in Paris and I saw him again the day before yesterday in Guernsey. He works for the president.'

'And you work for him?'

'I work for the man he works for.'

'How did that come about?'

She half turned, her face lit by the candle on her dressing table. The wind through her bedroom window was warm and the sound of the waves hypnotic. For a moment, she looked like someone else. Someone much younger.

'My father felt girls should be able to defend themselves. He came to regret that in my case.'

'Boyfriend trouble?'

'Of a kind. Lilly's though. Not mine.'

'What happened?'

'I served three years for manslaughter. My mother told everyone I'd had a breakdown, which was her version of events. When I came out, my father suggested I might want to move to Paris for a while. Sending family reprobates to Paris to get them out of the way was all the rage back then.'

'But Lilly stood by you?'

'She was furious. I think' – Daisy's mouth twisted – 'she thought I'd been presumptuous. If he was going to be shot it should have been by her. Still, it led to a job I wouldn't have been offered otherwise.'

'What do you do?'

Daisy smiled. 'I kill people,' she said.

123

Alderney, Wednesday, 24 July 1940

It was dawn, with the curtains in Daisy's room rippling in the early morning wind. Daisy and Bill woke in each other's arms.

'I need a swim,' Daisy said, rolling away.

'Can I ask a question first?'

Her face grew wary.

'Are you here to kill Hitler?'

She shook her head.

'The duke?'

'Not him either.'

'You promise?'

'I swear it,' she said.

'When did you start to trust me?' Bill asked.

'I don't trust you,' she said.

'You know what I mean.'

Daisy thought about it for so long Bill knew she'd either tell him the truth or not answer at all. 'Your face,' she said finally. 'When you carried Mignon in. That was when I knew you weren't simply using us.'

'I am simply using you.'

'Then you'd better ask properly, hadn't you?' Daisy said. 'Whether I'll help you with this safe. Given you're not going to be able to open it on your own.'

To Oswald von Hoyningen-Huene,
Reich Ambassador to Portugal
From Joachim von Ribbentrop,
Reichsminister of Foreign Affairs

Date: Wednesday, 24 July 1940
<u>Top Secret</u>

To be encrypted, then carried by courier. No transmission
by wire, no copies to be made or kept.

      The Führer is pleased to award you the Order of the
German Eagle, with Diamonds, Special Class. I send my
own congratulations. The decision to send the duchess her
own bank book was inspired.
      Please tell the duke that Herr Hitler would be
delighted to see him. That we will make immediate
arrangements, and that the duchess is obviously included
in this invitation. The meeting will be in Berchtesgaden at
the Eagle's Nest, which I believe was not completed at the
time of the duke's last visit. Please make sure the duke
understands this is the location the Führer reserves for
meetings with foreign heads of state.
      You are to give the duke, in the Führer's name,
absolute guarantees for his freedom of movement. In fact,
you may guarantee anything he asks. Once we have him
here, of course, here is where he will stay. It is to your
credit that he comes of his own accord, without us needing
to action Operation Willi: Colonel Schellenberg's plan to
spirit him out of Portugal before the English can.

124

Alderney, same day

'My God,' Daisy said. 'Look at that.' She pulled to a halt in Rue de l'Église and stared at a row of staff cars parked on the approach to the Island Hall. The distant sound of a waltz said von Neudeck's party had already started.

'Brought over by ferry?' Bill suggested.

'Or in one of their bloody landing craft.'

Bill counted five Mercedes-Benz, a lean and positively dangerous-looking sports car of a type he didn't recognize, and a Hispano-Suiza. Daisy, being Daisy, parked in front of the Suiza, which had the lines of a fighter plane and was racing green.

'Wonderful, isn't she?' a voice said.

They turned to find Colonel von Neudeck striding towards them. The enthusiasm in his voice was at odds with the strain in his eyes. He did a double take when he saw what Bill was wearing.

'You came in uniform?'

'Your invitation said Formal Dress.'

Sir William's wardrobe had provided a striking scarlet coat and high-waisted black trousers as worn by Guards officers. Gold-edged epaulettes announced the real Sir William's rank, and bullion badges his regiment. Bill also wore a row of Sir William's medals in miniature. A foreign order of knighthood hung from his neck.

'Very striking.' Von Neudeck's smile looked forced. 'The general will be pleased.'

The general might be but Bill wasn't. It had been Daisy's suggestion and it was a good one, but that didn't mean he liked it.

'Légion d'Honneur?'

Bill shrugged. 'Pulled a wounded boy from a foxhole at Verdun. Turned out to be some general's son.' As likely a reason as any. Unless the real Sir William had been given it for being on staff. That happened. Bill scowled.

'Are you all right?' von Neudeck asked Bill.

'My husband's not good with crowds at the best of times.' Von Neudeck nodded to Bill's splinted hand.

'And now's not the best of times?' He patted Bill's shoulder, took Daisy's hand to kiss, but changed his mind, kissing her on the cheek instead. 'You look as beautiful as ever,' he said.

'Is that car yours?' Daisy asked.

'If only . . .' Von Neudeck smiled. 'It's a present for a special visitor.'

Daisy glanced at the Island Hall.

'Who is not yet here,' von Neudeck said.

'When is he due?' Bill asked.

'Any day now, I'm told.'

Ushering them towards the gates, von Neudeck winced at the bunting, blazing uplights and bright red banners either side of the portico.

'You'll be glad when this is over?' Bill asked.

'Beyond glad,' von Neudeck said, sounding old.

'Everyone we invited said yes. I imagine they felt obliged. Farmers, bank managers, the doctor who treated you. We've shipped in the Sheriffs of Jersey and Guernsey, obviously.

Even the Dame of Sark is here. You know she took two days to surrender, then demanded we wipe our boots on the way in? Dreadful woman.'

'Not the birthday you had in mind?' Daisy said.

'One mustn't complain.'

'On the contrary,' Daisy said. 'One must, frequently.'

Von Neudeck laughed. 'Come on,' he said. 'The general's probably wondering where you are. Luckily he's in a good mood.'

Bill looked interested.

'He brought an intriguing letter.'

'From the Führer?'

'To the Führer,' von Neudeck said. 'Come on. I've said enough.'

'We're in,' Bill whispered as they were ushered through the door.

Daisy snorted. 'Getting out is usually harder.'

125

Alderney, same day

There were lilies in huge vases either side of the door and an oak table against a side wall laden with magnums of Krug in silver buckets; five of the bandsmen from Guernsey sat in a far corner playing Strauss.

It was resolutely normal and civilized.

Like von Neudeck, General von Hausen wore a Blue Max. Its cross was gold, inlaid with blue enamel, *Pour la Mérite* written round its edge.

'A memento,' he said, catching Bill's glance.

'We should let you go,' Daisy said.

Von Hausen glanced to a sharp-faced woman Bill suspected was the Dame of Sark. He sighed. 'You're right,' he said. 'Duty calls.'

'Men,' Daisy said as he walked away. 'Endlessly impressed by trinkets.'

'That's unfair.'

'Your Legion d'Honneur was the first thing von Neudeck noticed. The first thing the general commented on. They're your enemy, technically you're theirs, but you're all still impressed by each other's medals and uniforms and scars. Now look at the women. Most of them can't wait to get away.'

'And your husband,' Bill said. 'Did medals impress him?'

'He lived for them,' Daisy said.

*

The English boy at the table had champagne ready when Bill and Daisy reached him. Taking a glass, Daisy downed it and held it out.

'Hurry up,' she demanded.

The boy scowled.

'Keller's little attack dog,' Daisy muttered, switching to German. 'The more he beats him the more loyal he becomes.' As she and Bill walked away, she tipped the contents of her fresh glass into an aspidistra.

'They gave us the good stuff,' Bill said.

'Krug for the VIPs. Cooking champagne for the rest. It's probably looted from some vineyard in France.'

'It's still good,' Bill said.

'It's still looted. Now, how do we do this?'

Bill liked that *we*. 'Feel ready to take me up to the balcony?'

'Now there's an offer I don't get every day.' Leaning in, she kissed his cheek. A dozen people noticed and von Neudeck raised his glass. Daisy returned the salute.

'Let me get you a refill first,' Bill offered.

'So I can drown another pot plant?'

'Or tip it off the balcony on to a sentry below.'

She laughed, and a dozen people noticed that too.

Their plan was to leave the party late, drive home slowly and be so obviously drunk that should the Germans discover they'd been robbed, which they shouldn't for a while, he and Daisy would already be above suspicion.

'We're on,' Daisy said.

Bill hooked his arm through hers and together they headed for the stairs. A fresh-faced lieutenant stepped in their way; they'd run through how to do this before arriving and they were expecting that.

'The party's down here,' he said.

'I need some air.' There was a petulance to Daisy's voice

Bill hadn't heard before. It was put on, just like her irritation. When the lieutenant straightened up, Bill knew who was behind them.

'Sir William,' von Hausen said.

'General.'

'Can I help?'

'That car,' Daisy said. 'The green one. It's beautiful.'

'You think he'll like it?' The general caught himself, wondering how to take the words back, but there was no need.

'He'll love it,' Bill said. 'Although he'll complain about the lack of decent roads to race round.'

Von Hausen laughed. 'We'll give him his own back, soon enough.'

The general waved the lieutenant aside and glanced up the staircase. It was a grand staircase in a very small way. A toy staircase for a toy mansion, in a toy island for a toy king.

'This is very kind of you,' Daisy said. She smelt of Chanel and wore a gown that plunged at the back. Her evening bag was tiny and beaded. The overall effect was risky, elegant and slightly devil-may-care.

She's good at this, Bill thought.

The general was having trouble tearing his gaze away.

'You're sure it's all right?' Daisy asked.

Daisy and Bill went up together watched by the whole room and in particular by the general who, when Bill glanced back, was paying particular attention to Daisy's derrière. The door to the balcony was held back by a metal stay that Daisy kicked up with her heel, letting the door snap shut behind them.

126

Stripping off Sir William's mess coat, Bill tossed it into a corner of the balcony and threw his Legion d'Honneur on top. No point in making himself more of a target than need be.

'Gloves and stethoscope?'

Daisy held up her bag. 'An hour, you said?'

'Should be enough.'

'Then we're on.'

The balcony doors were just visible from the dance floor below so they kept low and tight to the far wall of the landing just in case. It was empty, the stairs to the floor above hidden by a fire door. Daisy stopped with her hand on its handle.

'We didn't agree what to say if someone saw us.'

'*I'm looking for the colonel.*'

'It's his party. He'll be where his guests are. How about, *We're looking for somewhere to fuck!*'

Her gaze was challenging. They hadn't yet, not quite.

But Bill wanted to and she knew it.

'Come on,' she said. 'That's our line. This isn't the time to get prissy.' This was a very different Daisy. The boredom and sneer were gone. This version was focused, impatient. She was enjoying herself.

'I'll go first,' Bill said.

'Bad idea.' Daisy nodded to his injured hand. 'Not sure how much use you'd be in a fight with that.'

'We're not here to fight.'

'Probably just as well.'

Following her through the door, Bill felt it swing behind him, and caught it just in time. The door at the top mirrored the one they'd just used, and Daisy opened it slowly, listening for footsteps or voices. The waltzes from below were muted now, the creaking of water pipes more obvious.

The Ops Room had been painted an institutional green and filled with rows of steel desks, map tables and chalk boards. More desks than von Neudeck had staff, many more. It seemed Hitler really did aim to launch his invasion from here. A single desk near the edge had a lamp lit.

'Bugger,' Bill said.

Daisy shrugged. 'I'll deal with it. If necessary.'

He'd ask how but Bill had a feeling he already knew. This version of Daisy wasn't simply enjoying herself: this version was dangerous. He recalled her fury when tricked into leaving with Keller on that first day; and a bit of him knew he was lucky to still be alive. Daisy could so easily have decided things would be simpler with him out of the way.

Pulling the key from his pocket, Bill prayed it would fit. Habit made him try the handle first and it opened easily. The bloody thing wasn't locked.

Daisy laughed.

'After all that,' Bill said.

'You have no idea,' Daisy said, thinking of the scar-faced sergeant.

Bill and Daisy were still smiling when Bill turned to where the safe should be and discovered it was gone.

Communiqué: German High Command

Wednesday, 24 July 1940

<u>Immediate Release</u>

In an attack this evening off the South Coast of England, one of our high-speed motor boats sank an enemy merchant ship of 18,000 tons off Portland with its torpedoes. No injuries were sustained on the Reich's side.

127

Alderney, same day

'*Was zum Teufel?*'

Von Neudeck's driver rose from a crouch, leaving the bottom drawer of the filing cabinet he'd been using still open. He shifted slightly, trying to see who stood behind Bill.

'Don't mind me,' Daisy said, shutting the door behind her.

'You shouldn't be here.'

There was no politeness, no sir or madam. Otto's words were stripped of everything but shock. His skin had gone pale.

Daisy moved towards him and Bill shook his head.

'We were looking for . . .'

'. . . a place to fuck,' Daisy finished for him.

'And,' Bill nodded to the humidor, 'the colonel said I could take a couple of those.'

'There are cigars downstairs.'

'Not like these.' Bill knew he was delaying the inevitable. They'd been seen. The safe was missing. Their plan was unravelling around them. There was only one way this encounter could end. It was just . . . Bill felt a miserable sense of recognition. Otto was probably the only person on Alderney who minded being here more than he did.

Daisy was waiting. She knew that he knew the boy couldn't be allowed back downstairs, ever. Unless . . .

'I'm Abwehr,' Bill said.

The young man froze. The German High Command for Military Espionage, Counter-intelligence and Sabotage was a

371

power in its own right. Ruthless, dedicated, feared. It even ignored Hitler's direct orders on occasion.

'My mother was German,' Bill said, borrowing Keller's childhood and reversing it. 'Why do you think the colonel trusts me?'

'He knows you're here?'

'As I said, he told me to help myself to the good cigars.'

Otto was considering this when they all heard a woman laugh outside.

'I'll just see who that is,' Otto said.

He tried to sidestep them and, before Bill could stop her, Daisy reacted. One hand to Otto's jaw, her other to the back of his neck. She jerked his head so savagely he crumpled. She caught him before he hit the floor.

'One of us had to do it,' she whispered.

Lowering Otto quietly, she put her ear to the door.

'A man and a woman, screwing.' She waited a handful of seconds. 'Christ,' she said. 'That was quick.'

There was laughter, then drunken footsteps charging down the stairs.

'Let's get out of here,' Bill said.

'Don't forget the door,' Daisy reminded him. He hadn't. He locked it on his way out, watched Daisy put the key in her bag. They left Otto where he was.

128

Alderney, same day

No one was waiting on the balcony to find out where they'd been. Bill's mess jacket remained in the corner. Daisy's cigarettes balanced undisturbed on the balustrade. They'd been gone less than ten minutes, leaving a dead boy in an office behind them.

'Any bright ideas?'

Daisy's voice was bleak enough to make Bill reach for her hand.

He tried not to mind when she jerked away. He looked at their balcony, the swastikas on the façade either side of them, the staff cars in Rue de l'Église, and the soldiers with submachine guns in the square. Then he looked at Daisy, sitting right on the balcony's edge, head down as she lit a cigarette.

'Is everything all right?'

Daisy jerked at the sound of von Neudeck's voice, and Bill felt himself freeze, fighting to keep his expression normal.

Don't let him suspect anything.

From his wariness the colonel was wondering what he'd walked in on.

'Ah. Colonel . . .' Bill said.

'I'm sorry,' Daisy said, over the top of him.

As Bill watched, she came back to life. It was the danger. Her lightning-quick glance at Bill was replaced for the colonel with a trembling smile.

'I've been out of sorts since my sister died.'

Von Neudeck sounded puzzled. 'This was recent?'

'Very recent,' Daisy said.

'It's the reason my wife came back,' Bill said. 'She'd gone to Paris . . .'

'So I've been told.'

Von Neudeck's voice was studiedly neutral. So much so that Daisy gave a second smile. 'My husband and I were going through a bad patch.'

'And now . . . ?' he asked

There was something dangerous in Daisy's gaze. 'Oh,' she said, 'I like this version much better.'

Daisy might find the colonel's unexpected appearance exciting. Bill didn't. He was only too aware of a murdered German soldier one floor above. And God knew where the safe he was meant to crack had been taken.

'You came to find us?' Bill asked.

'Yes. The buffet's about to begin. There's plenty, so Lady Renhou should only join us when she's ready. I'm going to borrow you though. The general's abandoning us for Berlin. He wants to say goodbye.'

'The safe's here,' Daisy said, the moment Bill returned.

'You found it?'

'We had the right room. We just looked in the wrong place.' She was grinning, deservedly pleased with herself.

'What made you go back?'

Daisy indicated the swastika banners, the uplights to the newly renovated HQ, the Mercedes-Benz lining Rue de l'Église. 'I looked elsewhere first. It wasn't in the Ops Room, nor the side rooms. The rooms down here can't be secured. None of this makes sense if it's not here at all. Your people knew it was going to be here.'

They weren't his people, but Bill let that go.

Daisy was right though. At no point had SOE had any doubt about where Bill would be sent. It was never the Channel Islands. It was always Alderney. *The stepping stone.* Hitler's choice.

Fat holes low down in the wall showed where someone had unscrewed the missing safe. The faintest traces of brick dust on the far side of von Neudeck's fireplace said someone had recently decided it was worth fixing the green safe to the wall.

Bill deducted the thickness of the green safe's sides from its overall size, and realized it would just about be possible to squeeze the grey safe inside it.

Bastards.

To Winston Churchill
From Admiral Sir Alfred Dudley Pound RN,
First Sea Lord

Date: Wednesday, 24 July 1940

News is coming in of a Nazi attack on a French
repatriation ship off Portland, carrying 1,300 French naval
officers and men returning from Britain to Vichy France
under the terms of the Armistice. That is, on-service men
who have effectively surrendered as ordered.

The French Government had been informed in
advance of our intention to repatriate these men aboard
French ships. She was flying the French flag, and had
French colours painted on to her deck and sides. She was
fully illuminated and had her navigation lights burning.
There could be no doubting her nationality or neutrality.

Upon receipt of her distress signal, I ordered four
British destroyers to proceed at once to the scene. I will
let you have the number of survivors when I have it.

129

Portugal, same day

'In a moment, darling.'

Wallis smiled at her husband and indicated the darkened pool. The housekeeper had the evening off. One of the maids had gone to late Mass; the other had gone to bed; the cook had retired to her room.

'I have some things to do.'

She watched the duke stride to the springboard, shuck off his shirt and climb out of his slacks, standing naked for a second before diving in. A moment later he was ploughing down the pool, his stroke strong and his kick steady. A flash of white buttocks in the darkness as he turned and he was off again.

Heading indoors, Wallis settled herself by the telephone. The operator at the switchboard for the German embassy answered immediately.

'Frau Metz,' Wallis demanded.

'May I ask who it is?'

'A friend.' Wallis spoke English, because that was what she spoke. Maybe it was the strangeness of this which made the woman operating the German embassy's switchboard connect her call without question.

'Frau Metz,' Frau Metz announced.

'It's me,' Wallis said.

'Ahh. Of course. Did you like the Chanel bank book?'

'I adored it,' Wallis said, real warmth coming into her voice. 'I carry it with me.'

'I'm glad. How can I help?'

'I think he's getting cold feet.'

There was a silence at the other end. Wallis wondered if she'd been too colloquial, and was about to phrase it another way, when Frau Metz said, 'I see.'

Wallis wondered if she did.

'What do you think should be done?' Frau Metz asked.

'I'm going to suggest we return to Spain.'

'I have a better idea,' Frau Metz said. 'Why don't I ask the ambassador to drop over? He can be very persuasive.'

130

Alderney, same day

'Turn the dial,' Bill ordered.

'How many times?'

'It doesn't matter. We're just resetting it.'

The office door was locked behind them and their backs were to Otto's body. Daisy was wearing the surgical gloves that Bill had stolen in Guernsey, and he had the stethoscope.

The Victorian safe was a model he'd met before.

'Right,' he said. 'Let's try something.'

He had Daisy turn the dial four times to the left and stop when 50 aligned with the diamond-shaped marker on the hour, if you treated it as the face of a clock. Asking her to turn it the other way, he watched it come to a stop.

Daisy sat back.

'Try the door,' he said.

'It can't be that easy.'

'It isn't, usually. But safes get left on shipping combinations more often than they should. This one's been on a single-digit factory setting for fifty years, waiting for a lock-smith to reset it.'

The safe inside was something else entirely.

Was there a patron saint of safe-crackers? If there was, no one had told Bill, but a swift look at the second safe convinced him he'd need divine help.

Kneeling in front of it, Bill crossed himself.

The most common superstition says you clear the tumblers

by spinning the dial a set number of times, before returning it to zero. Only then should you begin work. That's what they are. Superstitions. But the man Bill learned from always crossed himself, and turned the dial five times, so that's what Bill did.

'Ready?' he asked.

Daisy nodded. 'What do I do again?'

Putting the disc of the stethoscope he'd stolen in Guernsey beside the first dial, Bill inserted the earpieces and told Daisy to turn the dial counter-clockwise.

'Slowly,' he said.

She scowled.

He was listening for two clicks close together. The first slightly louder, which meant just about audible, the second faint enough to be its echo. He had Daisy reset the dial to zero, move it on three numbers, and start again.

And then again. And again.

'How long is this going to take?' she whispered.

'Longer than it should, if we stop to talk.'

'At least tell me what you're doing.'

Trying to open a hideously difficult safe and get out before I'm caught, arrested, tortured and shot, Bill thought. What he said was, 'Working my way round the dial, three shifts on every time, to find a number.'

The first was 10. The second 80.

On a good night, downhill with a back wind, he could open a difficult safe in an hour. But forty minutes had passed since they went to the balcony; fifteen since they came up here again. Night was starting to fall; they couldn't turn on the lights and the question was how much longer could he and Daisy realistically hide.

Not much longer, and not much longer wasn't enough.

Removing his stethoscope, Bill went to the locked door and listened for footsteps.

'Did you hear someone?' Daisy whispered.

'I'm thinking.'

Returning to the safe, he said, 'Ten, eighty.'

Daisy's eyes narrowed. 'That's what you've got so far?'

People like patterns, so something about those numbers nagged him. He got the first one at the point Daisy reached the second.

'A,' he said.

'H,' she told him.

They wouldn't be that stupid. Then again, perhaps he meant fanatical. Half of von Hausen's entourage looked as if they'd hang their own children to order. Knock the zeros off and they had 1 and 8, which read as A and H in a simple alphanumeric swap of numbers for letters.

Adolf Hitler.

What would a Nazi choose next?'

Perhaps . . . no, 80, 80 for Heil Hitler was too obvious.

Besides, the Kellers of the world were puffed up with their own intelligence. A simple number/letter switch felt insultingly simple. What if the AH was coincidence, and it was the 1 and 8 that mattered? 18?

'What numbers do people usually use?' Daisy asked.

'Well, o–o–o–o, 1–1–1–1 and 1–2–3–4 are the idiot choices. I tried those the day I begged cigars from von Neudeck.'

'No,' Daisy said. 'I mean, how do people pick their numbers?'

'The year they were born. The year their child was born. The year they married.'

'Try Hitler's birthday.'

'I don't know it.'

'The twentieth of April 1889.'

'God. How do you know that?'

'We were invited to his fiftieth. We were breaking up by then. William went.'

Not bothering to listen for the clicks, Bill had Daisy turn the dials, wishing he could do it for himself.

It wasn't 1889.

Bill tried variants, replacing 90 with 9, and 80 with 8 and it made no difference. The combination was still wrong. Bill tried the lower dial, just in case it worked there. It didn't.

He'd have to do it the old-fashioned way. Only, finding the safe gone, being dragged off to say goodbye to the general, then needing to get the other safe open first meant he didn't have time to do it the old-fashioned way.

Not before darkness came in, and someone came to find out where the hell he was. Besides, he knew that 1 and 8 mattered.

'What other dates in the 1800s would be important to Germans?'

'Try 1871,' Daisy said. 'The year the Kaiser was crowned.'

'Don't tell me. You were at that party too.'

She smiled sourly. 'I have the best manners, education and alibis that money in Boston can buy. Now, let's hurry it up.'

'Return it to zero,' he said, 'then five times to the left and stop on 10. Now, four to the right and stop at 80. Three left and 70. Two times to the right and stop on 10 again. One final time to the left until the dial stops.'

She did, and Bill could almost taste the tumblers turning inside the door. He reached for the upper handle and it was still locked. Feeling sick, he tried the lower one, expecting little and felt it shift, hearing bolts retract. Daisy's education and his experience had saved them time they didn't have.

'One down,' Daisy said.

If the formation of the Kaiser's Reich was the first date, what would the second one be? Obviously not 1918, the Kaiser's fall. The rise of the Third Reich from the Kaiser's ashes?

That bunch downstairs were arrogant enough.

Resetting the lower dial, Bill had Daisy run rapid clockwise and anti-clockwise variants of 1933.

She struck gold.

Twisting the handle, Bill yanked back the door and Daisy reached inside. No invasion plans, no official files, no books of codes or cyphers. Nothing.

The sodding thing was empty.

To Winston Churchill
From Admiral Sir Alfred Dudley Pound RN,
First Sea Lord

Date: Wednesday, 24 July 1940

The vessel attacked off Portland was the French liner
Meknès. To reiterate, she was sailing at night with full
navigation lights and was clearly marked as neutral. This
is not an act of war; it is an act of barbarism.

According to survivors she was intercepted by a
torpedo boat. The Germans machine-gunned her without
warning. The passengers and crew were given five minutes
to take to the lifeboats. She was then torpedoed and sank
inside of five minutes.

The number drowned is put at 400.

In my long career in the Royal Navy I have never come
across a case where an enemy combatant attacked a
clearly marked neutral vessel belonging to a country with
which it had recently agreed terms. In my opinion, this
tells us everything about how the Nazis treat those they
have defeated. May I respectfully request you bring this
outrage to the attention of the House of Commons
tomorrow?

131

Alderney, same day

Daisy ran her hand over the floor of the safe in disbelief, feeling for a hidden compartment. There wasn't one.

In desperation she tried the sides and then under the top, her fingers closing on an envelope at the back. Peeling away Scotch tape, she pulled it out and let its contents spill across the floor. Nude photographs of the prince, pornographic letters to his first mistress, photographs of him in a Japanese brothel, further letters in which he ranted about his father's cruelty, the new king's stupidity, the new queen's lack of taste, class and intelligence . . .

'My God,' Daisy said. 'They've been collecting this stuff for years.'

The real gold was the notes, personal letters and memoranda that formed the milestones on the ex-king's recent road to treason. The last of these was by far the newest. If those before had been damning, this was worse.

Casa de Santa Maria
Lisbon
Portugal

Monday, 22 July 1940

Dear Herr Hitler,

As you rightly pointed out at the time, letting my brother take the throne was a mistake on my part. It has become increasingly obvious that the only way to keep Britain safe, and its empire intact, is for me to claim them back. An armistice between our countries must be signed as swiftly as possible. I would request that all further negotiations on this are between us and take place face to face.

Yours,
Edward Rex & Imp.

To: Herr Adolf Hitler, Führer and Chancellor of the Reich

132

Alderney, Wednesday, 24 July 1940

'Oh fuck,' Bill said.

133

Portugal, same day

'Sir, this is a delicate matter . . .'

'Then get to it,' the duke said crossly. He had no doubt that Oswald von Hoyningen-Huene was about to ruin his late-night swim.

'A few months ago you said goodbye to Raffaele, Baron di Vituso, when he was still Mussolini's ambassador to Paris. You both had a few drinks and I believe you were free with your confidences.'

The duke tensed. All taste had gone from his Chesterfield and it no longer mattered how beautiful the view was. 'Vituso asked me a leading question,' he said, 'at a point when I was angry, upset by my family's cruelty to my wife, and it's possible I answered too honestly. I don't see how this is your business.'

'It's been suggested you might be planning to delay your visit to Berlin.'

'Good God, a few days at most. Next week simply isn't convenient.'

'I see,' von Hoyningen-Huene said.

The duke sat back, stubbed out his Chesterfield and lit another, letting its smoke drift into the night sky. Wallis had been as surprised to see von Hoyningen-Huene as he had. She'd suggested the table by the pool and that was where the two men now sat, with a bottle of Scotch unopened between them.

'What's this about Vituso?' the duke asked eventually.

'Unfortunately, Raffaele taped your conversation.'

The duke's stomach lurched. No man should have his private conversations made public. He thought back to the heavy leather case Vituso had been carrying. Bastard. The man was meant to be his friend.

It didn't help that in the last forty-eight hours he'd found himself wrestling with whether his decision to side with Berlin was right. A man was allowed to think things through, wasn't he? He really shouldn't have told Hitler he was prepared to retake his throne. And he certainly shouldn't have let Wallis persuade him to take Berlin's money. Although, God knows it had helped, and giving him money was substantially more than his bloody brother was prepared to do. And if he didn't save Britain from crashing defeat, who would?

Hitler would win. He always did. Common sense, never mind self-interest, said choose the winning side. He'd be able to influence things if he retook his throne. That had to count for something, surely? He'd certainly have more influence than any of the French fools who'd let their country be driven into the dirt before trying to make a deal. He was going to side with Berlin. Of course he was. He just needed a few more days to square that with his conscience.

Let his brother go and be Governor of the Bahamas.

All the same, von Hoyningen-Huene's arrival had made him cross. 'You're planning to blackmail me. Is that what you're saying?'

'God forbid,' the ambassador said, obviously shocked. 'That's the last thing I intend. I was there when your car almost crashed. I'm the one trying to keep you safe. I will do everything I can to ensure you're not embarrassed. You are England's last king. And its next one.'

The duke smiled at the irony. 'But there are those who would embarrass me?'

'Himmler,' von Hoyningen-Huene said. 'He always goes for the biggest lie, the nastiest move, the worst interpretation. You've met him. It's in his nature.'

The duke shut his eyes, blocking out the view and what remained of the man's words. He was less successful at blocking his memory of that last evening in Paris, when the Italian ambassador had appeared to pay his respects and they'd ended up having a whisky together. Several whiskies.

Vituso was a good listener. The duke could remember the exact point they'd moved off politics on to personal tastes. Some of Vituso's tastes were exotic. He wasn't the only one. And then there was his note to Hitler. God knows what London would do if that ever got out.

'Now,' von Hoyningen-Huene said. 'About Berlin . . .'

The duke opened his eyes and the world and its problems made an unwelcome return. 'What do you have in mind?'

'Frau Metz will be in touch.' Reaching for the whisky, von Hoyningen-Huene tore away its foil, pouring them both a slug and pushing a small jug of water across the table. 'Here's to your reign,' he said, raising his glass. 'Himmler's jealous. You realize that, don't you? That's what this is about. He's jealous that Herr Hitler respects you.'

134

Alderney, same day

'Damn it,' Daisy said.

'What?'

She tapped Otto's body with her foot. 'I'm a fool. I should have knocked him out, tied him up, dragged him up to the roof and only killed him at the end.'

'Why would you be on the roof?' Bill demanded.

'Because', Daisy said, as if it was obvious, 'I have less chance of being seen throwing him off the roof than pushing him out of a window.'

Bill put his head in his hands.

'Don't be like that,' Daisy said.

Otto had committed suicide, apparently. Hating military life, unhappy at where he found himself and miserable to be away from his Berlin friends, he'd hurled himself into the courtyard in the middle of a party, unable to take any more.

'You have to admit it sounds plausible,' Daisy said.

Bill hated to agree.

The Ops Room was empty. A louvre window in its ceiling was clearly visible. Dragging a desk across, Daisy clambered up. 'I'll go first,' she said. 'You pass him up.'

Bill looked at the splint on his hand and shrugged.

Scrambling up in a flash of thigh, Daisy swore as her hip caught on the catch. A moment later she was through. Leaning in, she told Bill to hurry it up.

Lifting Otto was harder than he expected.

'Got him,' Daisy said. Grabbing the body under its arms, she dragged it through the window and out of sight. 'Check the forecourt,' she ordered.

'For what?' Bill asked.

'Witnesses.'

Apart from the guards on the gates, the courtyard was empty. The guests not on the dance floor must be in the gardens at the back.

'All clear,' he told Daisy.

'This won't take a moment.'

Bill heard rather than saw Otto's body hit the cobbles. A gate guard shouted, instantly hushed by his companion, and Bill saw the gates pushed open and the guards run inside. The first pulled off his jacket to throw over Otto's head, and Bill stepped back as Keller's sergeant came into view.

A moment later Keller was there.

He barked an order and the guard took back his jacket, then picked up Otto's feet as his colleague grabbed Otto's arms, and between them they hurried him away.

'What's happening?' Daisy said, appearing beside Bill. She seemed barely out of breath. Bill drew her closer and she let him. Together they watched the scene unfold. The sergeant had a fire bucket in his hand and was tossing sand over the cobbles where Otto's head had been.

'You've locked the safe?' Daisy checked.

'Aye,' Bill said. 'Both of them.'

'Then it's time to dance,' she said.

135

Alderney, same day

The music was slow and candles lit the room now that night had fallen. If anyone noticed that Daisy's silk dress was slightly ripped at the hip, and they probably did, they were too polite to look openly or mention it.

The party was nearing its end, and the officers brought over from the other islands were at the drinks table hammering what was left of the champagne. The younger ones were laughing a little too loudly, the older ones smiling indulgently. A group of four subalterns, with their arms round each other's necks, so drunk that they could barely stand, broke into a Nazi drinking song and had to be hushed by a more senior officer.

'Keller hasn't told them, has he?' Daisy whispered.

'No,' Bill said. Even a private found dead at a party would put a slight dampener on things. Instead, island couples danced, German officers drank, farmers in badly fitting brown suits stood around wondering how soon they'd be allowed to leave.

Everything seemed normal. Dangerously so.

'The question', Bill said, 'is why . . .'

'Because,' Daisy said sourly, 'he thinks he can use it to his advantage. Or because telling the others would render him vulnerable in some way. That's all it ever is with men like that. Believe me, I know.'

And I'd have been one of them, Bill thought.

He stepped in closer and Daisy wrapped her arms round his neck and held him for a second. He could smell Chanel

No. 5 and feel her body against his. When he tasted the salt on her neck, she shivered. He imagined she was acting and hoped she wasn't.

Anyone watching would have thought them tired, a little tipsy and entirely comfortable with where they found themselves. They were behaving disgustingly like a couple freshly in love. When the music stopped, Daisy pulled Bill towards a chair. 'Let's sit this one out,' she said.

He followed, seating himself so she could sit on his knee.

Turning, she tugged at his bow tie until its ends hung loose. 'That's better,' she said. 'I've always loathed Mess Dress.'

She caught his surprise.

'William loved it. All that glitter. All that gold. He'd have lived in it. And yes, it really was that simple. He could have loved spaniels and by the end I'd have kicked them on principle.'

'Were you ordered to marry him?'

'No. It was entirely self-inflicted. Sometimes I just get a little too deep into the part.' She snuggled in and anyone looking would have thought she was kissing Bill's ear. 'Another drink,' she said. 'Then home James and don't spare the horses . . .'

When Bill slid his hand down her spine, she stilled for a moment and then kissed him for real. 'We could skip the drink,' he said.

'We should be seen drinking this one.'

Von Neudeck appeared the moment they stood. 'I do hope you've enjoyed yourself,' he said. His voice was strained.

'Are you all right?' Bill asked.

The colonel's gaze slid to Daisy, who let go of Bill's hand. 'I was about to get myself another drink anyway. What would you like, darling?'

'Whisky,' Bill said. 'If they have it.'

'If they haven't,' von Neudeck said, 'or it's not good enough for Sir William, then the cognac is particularly fine.'

'You've just conquered France,' Daisy said, deadpan. 'So yes, I imagine it is.' She walked away and both men watched her go.

'Without being rude,' Bill said, 'and without wanting to presume on our tentative friendship, *is* everything all right?'

'My driver's dead,' von Neudeck said flatly. 'He collected you from the house a couple of times. You won't remember him.'

'Of course I do. What happened?'

'Suicide from the sound of it.' Von Neudeck kept his voice low. 'He was bullied badly by the men. It didn't help that Keller made his contempt obvious. You'll have noticed Hassel, Keller's NCO. His face is unmissable. He was particularly vicious. I've told Keller that if that's proved I'll have Hassel court-martialled.'

There was something the colonel wasn't saying.

'You were fond of Otto. Weren't you?'

'I thought he'd be safe here. At least safer than anywhere else. He was a friend . . . a friend of my son's. A good friend.'

'You don't talk about your family.'

'No,' von Neudeck said. 'I don't.'

They were saved from unpicking that by Daisy returning with three brandy tumblers. 'It was cooking whisky,' she said. 'I brought this instead.' She handed one to the colonel, one to Bill and raised her own.

'Happy birthday,' she said.

They downed their glasses in one, and von Neudeck thanked them for coming, although his birthday had obviously been anything but happy.

'Who's driving?' he asked.

'My wife is,' Bill said, holding up his damaged hand.

'Take care to avoid ditches,' von Neudeck said.

136

Alderney, same day

Parking the Humber in front of the hut where it usually lived, Daisy nodded to the causeway. 'We've left it too late.'

It was almost midnight and the water was high. The moon showed over Aldoy Head, lighting the waves a canoe would cross in five days to take Bill away. He'd been trying to work out when to tell Daisy. She must know his time was almost up.

'Get wet or use the dinghy?' Bill asked. His splinted hand made rowing impossible. That made the decision hers.

'I'm not sure I can row in this dress.'

'Take it off,' Bill said.

'I'm being serious.'

'So am I.'

Holding her evening bag above her head, Daisy waded into the water with Bill following. The sea was warmer than he expected and rose to his hips, Sir William's mess jacket hanging heavy where it dragged in the gentle waves. Bill was climbing on to dry land when he glanced over.

'You're staring,' Daisy said.

'You'd be staring if you were me.'

If the sea had soaked his uniform it had rendered Daisy's dress invisible. The silk clung to her and followed every curve and muscle from her hips down.

'Wait,' Daisy said.

Bill stopped. Instantly on guard.

He was still searching for the danger when Daisy reached up, pulled his head down and kissed him hard. When she stepped back, she was grinning.

They met no one in the hall, for which they were grateful, and crept up the stairs like a couple of teenagers trying not to be seen.

'My room,' Daisy said.

This time she didn't fold her clothes. Simply tossed her bag into a corner, stepped out of her knickers, and draped her sodden dress over a chair. Reaching for him, Daisy tightened her fingers.

They kissed, fucked and came before reaching the bed. And having reached it, they did all three again to check it was as good as they thought it was the first time.

'Beginners' luck,' Bill said.

'We're hardly beginners.'

'You know what I mean.'

137

Washington DC, same day

Wednesday, 24 July 1940 was the day Charles Standish III, head of the small group who'd spent the previous three years watching the movements of Wallis Simpson and the Duke of Windsor, discovered there was a bigger group whose job it had been to take his reports, mesh them with information from other equally small and misnamed departments and pass it up the line.

It was, he had to admit to himself, a bit of a shock.

'Everyone reports to you?'

The middle-aged black woman behind the desk smiled.

A rare occurrence, although Standish didn't know that.

'Not to me, personally. And not really report. Information comes in. We introduce it to other information.' She spoke about the information as if it was alive. In a building filled with mess, her office was unnervingly tidy. A dozen piles of paper, all with absolutely straight edges. A row of books organized by colour first, then size within colour. Pencils of exactly the same sharpness.

'I find mess painful,' she said, seeing his gaze.

Standish reddened.

'Oh, don't worry. I'd have been worried if you didn't notice and it would have made me wonder if we had the right man.'

'For what?'

She smiled a second time. 'For whatever it is you do. Now, tell me a little about your man's visit to Daisy Renhou in Paris.'

'How do you . . . ?'

'From the ambassador. He really should have cleared it with us first.' She hesitated. 'I'm sorry about Daisy's sister. Lilly, wasn't it? The file mentions you were close.'

Standish nodded bleakly.

'What's she like?'

'Daisy? They're twins. Identical.' He thought about it. 'She pretends to have no morals and to have discarded all scruples, but that's untrue. She's more like Lilly than she knows. Can I ask why?'

'You can ask . . .'

Pushing back her chair, she left the office and Standish went to the window to watch workmen roofing over a classical courtyard to create a huge room that would presumably house more shelving.

'And it seems I can answer.'

The woman retook her seat. 'We have a problem. London sent their man to the islands about the time you ordered Daisy to return. They're rubbing along after a fashion. Needs must, I imagine.'

'That's the problem?'

'A problem,' the woman said. 'Not the problem. The problem is rather more serious. We knew that Lilly threw herself from the roof. We've just discovered that the German captain who was on the roof when she killed herself is now on Alderney.'

'He'll know who Daisy is?'

'I imagine he's known from the start.'

138

Bill woke to bright sunlight, Daisy asleep beside him and Mignon in the doorway. Her eyes were wide with fright. She very carefully didn't look at either of them. 'Soldiers are coming.'

'Have they seen you?' Bill demanded.

'No.' Mignon shook her head.

'Up to the attic now,' he said. 'Hide yourself and lock the door from inside. Remember to remove the key this time. Why isn't Mrs Beecher dealing with this?'

'She's out,' Mignon said flatly. 'And you're . . . here.'

'Where's von Neudeck?' Bill demanded.

Keller's eyes narrowed at the question. 'I'm in charge of this investigation,' he said tightly. 'Berlin's orders. The colonel has agreed.'

'What investigation?' Bill said.

'Where's your wife?'

'Why?'

'Answer the question.'

Bill laughed. It wasn't a wise move, because the captain's face tightened. Instinctively, Keller glanced at the sergeant who'd accompanied him. And his face tightened again when he saw Bill notice.

'She's upstairs,' Bill said.

'Get her,' Keller ordered.

Bill glared at him.

'If you'd be so kind.'

'What's this about?' he asked when he got back.

'Where's your wife?'

'Getting dressed. Now, answer my question.'

'You know what this is about,' Keller said.

'No. Believe me, I have no idea.'

To War Cabinet
From Winston Churchill

Date: Thursday, 25 July 1940
<u>Restricted</u>

Waves of up to 50 Junkers Ju 87 dive-bombers have launched a full-scale attack on merchant ships and destroyers in Dover harbour. Anti-aircraft guns have been engaged and RAF fighters scrambled from bases across the South Coast. I have already received reports of losses on both sides. I have no doubt they are trying to break our resolve before they invade.

They will not succeed.

You will receive more news when I have it.

139

Alderney, same day

A soldier stood beside the French windows to the terrace; others guarded the doors to the kitchens, library and hall. Bill watched Daisy check her escape routes in a lightning glance.

He thought her shoulders sagged slightly.

All of the soldiers carried Schmeissers, ugly machine pistols with folding metal stocks. And they looked battle-hardened, wary. Their scar-faced sergeant stood at Keller's side.

'Good morning,' Daisy said.

Keller's gaze raked her. Like a predator finally closing on its prey. 'I'd like you to come down to HQ.'

'Why?' Daisy demanded.

'A quick chat.'

Daisy gazed at the soldiers covering the exits. She looked grimly amused. 'You could have sent a note,' she said lightly. Bill alone noticed how fiercely she dug her nails into her hand.

'You will accompany us.'

'I'm sure whatever you need to say can be said here.'

'Did you know fingerprints can be lifted from human skin?' Keller shrugged. 'Of course, it helps if the body is fresh. Although forty-eight hours is still possible. The fresher the better, though. And, of course, our corpse is very . . .'

'I've no idea what you're talking about.'

'I doubt that,' Keller said.

'Tell me,' Bill said. 'If you won't tell my wife.'

'I'd be happy to. Sprinkle aluminium powder on to the flesh, blow it off and there you have it. Perfect prints from human skin. The skin needs to be clean, of course. Luckily our corpse was finicky about such things. His type often are.'

Bill scowled. 'Try making sense.'

Keller's voice hardened. 'A German soldier was murdered last night. The colonel, being him, jumped to the wrong conclusion. He decided the man killed himself. He even tried to blame Sergeant Hassel here. Luckily, I was able to step in. You understand that I'm Abwehr? Here to keep an eye on things?'

Well, that explained a lot.

'Are all members of German intelligence experts in fingerprints?'

Keller ignored the question. 'I examined the body,' he said flatly, 'looking for evidence rather than jumping to conclusions. Our dead man had his neck broken. There is a clear thumbprint at the corner of his jaw.'

'Why pick on Lady Renhou?' Bill asked. 'Why not me? Why not one of your own? Assuming any of this stuff is true. I mean, look at my wife. Can you think of anyone who looks less likely to kill?'

Keller looked. His gaze wasn't kind. 'The thumbprint is too small to be yours or mine.'

'It could be a child's,' Bill said.

'That's absurd,' Keller said. 'There were no children at the party.'

'Von Neudeck's party?' Bill asked.

Keller nodded.

'God,' Daisy said. 'This is ridiculous. I'm going to call my embassy.'

'From where?' Keller asked.

'La Ville. There must be a working telephone.'

'I'm afraid I can't allow it.' He nodded to his men. 'I'm placing you under arrest for the murder of a German soldier.'

'You have no proof.'

'I have your thumbprint.'

'You haven't taken my prints. It could be anybody at that party. God . . .' Daisy's voice was mocking. 'It could be your precious Dame of Sark.'

'So like Lilly,' Keller said. 'Identical twins, I believe. Why would I need yours when I have those I took from your sister's body?'

Daisy went for Keller before Bill could stop her.

Her strike just missed his throat, but the follow-through from her elbow smashed into his jaw and he lurched back. He'd have died from her next blow, if Sergeant Hassel hadn't grabbed her from behind.

Keller's punch doubled her over.

A soldier clubbed Bill before he could even reach the man. Rolling over, he found himself facing a Schmeisser, and the corporal holding it looked ready to pull its trigger.

'Christ,' Keller said, clutching his jaw. 'Bring them both.'

'Bill's not part of this.'

'Part of what?' Keller demanded.

'Whatever you think this is.'

Keller turned to Bill. 'Were you with your wife last night?'

'You know I was.'

'The entire time?'

Out of the corner of his eye, Bill saw Daisy shake her head. The tiniest gesture, accompanied by a glare. 'Not the entire time,' Bill admitted.

'How much of it?'

'Identical twins don't share fingerprints,' Bill said. 'So I've read. How can having Daisy's sister's fingerprints help? Leaving aside that all this is absurd.'

'You're right, of course,' Keller said. 'About the fingerprints. But they're closer than fraternal twins, much closer than mere siblings, and infinitely closer than strangers. How long were you and your wife apart?'

'Bill went to say goodbye to General von Hausen,' Daisy said, before Bill could reply. 'I stayed on the balcony. He took a while to return.'

'How convenient for you,' Keller said.

At a nod, Keller's men closed around Daisy and the sergeant manhandled her through the hall to the main door. A *Kübelwagen* was visible in the distance, parked behind the Humber.

'Bill,' Daisy said suddenly. 'I left my evening bag on the back seat.'

'Your evening bag?' Bill asked.

'How touching,' Keller said. 'How homely.' He waved his hand for Hassel to take her away and turned to find Bill glaring at him. 'Something you want to say?'

Bill stepped in close. 'You hurt her and I'll make you pay. Even if I have to go to Berlin and face Herr Hitler myself.'

'Ah, Sir William finally shows his famous teeth.'

'I mean it,' Bill said.

'I'm sure you do.' Reaching out, Keller gripped Bill's hand as if to shake it, and squeezed the splint until Bill shuddered in pain.

'It's unwise to annoy me,' Keller said. 'You should remember that.'

Sweeping his other hand up, Bill locked his fingers round Keller's larynx, a fraction away from crushing it. 'And Hitler and von Hausen need me more than they need some half-English lackey. You'd do well to remember that.'

The captain stepped back, nursing his throat. 'I will kill you,' he said. 'When you're no longer useful. That's a promise.'

'If I haven't killed you first.'

140

Portugal, same day

The famous art nouveau façade of Joalharia do Carmo, the prestigious Lisbon jewellers, was black with silver lettering and had been since the boutique was founded in the early 1920s. A stone arch elegant enough to belong to a very exclusive theatre framed its front. A heart-shaped coat of arms crowned with a coronet hung above its door. The windows were draped with silk to give its clientele privacy.

It was exactly the kind of place the Englishwoman across the street would have expected Wallis Simpson to shop. Penny Moony had been watching Joalharia do Carmo in the reflection of a milliner's window for the last half-hour.

Her orders were to follow the duke and duchess, record whom they met and make brief notes about anyone she didn't recognize. It had sounded easy enough, but she'd spent her day fighting crowds and dodging trams. No one at the British embassy had factored in Wallis Simpson's inability to stay in one place for longer than five minutes. This made the length of time she'd been in that jeweller's all the more suspicious.

Penny decided to wait where she was.

Wallis had been less than friendly that first night at the casino, and Penny knew she had no more chance of looking like she belonged in Joalharia do Carmo than she had in a high-stakes room at the Casino do Estoril.

141

Alderney, same day

As Bill watched the *Kübelwagen* disappear, Mignon materialized at his side. He put his hand out to stop her going through the door and stepped in front of her to hide her from anyone watching. Reaching back, he found her hand and held it tightly.

'You're meant to be hiding,' he said.

'What will they do to her?' Mignon asked.

'Nothing, yet.'

Bill hoped he was right. Berlin needed him to babysit the duke. At least they needed Sir William. He'd refuse to do it unless they released Daisy. Obviously, it was complicated by the fact that he wasn't actually Sir William. And that Daisy had committed the crime she was accused of . . .

But it was a start.

'Is Mrs Beecher back?' Bill asked.

Mignon nodded. 'She came in through the kitchens when she saw their car. She's prising the back off an old sideboard in the attics to put it in front of a hatch in case I need somewhere to hide. She says she'll get you breakfast later.'

'I don't need breakfast. I need to talk to the colonel. Please tell her she's not to tidy Madame's bedroom. And you're to stay hidden.'

'She's not to . . . ?'

'Never mind,' Bill said. 'I'll tidy it myself.'

The wardrobe in the room Daisy now used was dark, old and unnecessarily tall, like most of the furniture in Renhou.

Bill lobbed Daisy's evening bag up there, with the envelope still inside, watching it land on top in a puff of dust next to a writing case.

My bag. I left it on the back seat.

She hadn't. She knew she hadn't. He'd watched her raise it above her head, carry it across the flooded causeway and toss it into that corner, before . . .

BIll's glance took in Daisy's torn dress and Sir William's uniform, and then, because he couldn't help himself, the crumpled bed. There might be a worse time to discover he was in love but he doubted it. The way her chin went up, the way she bristled when the sergeant gripped her upper arm. She'd marched across the causeway unaided. Bill just wished she hadn't reminded him of an aristocrat going to the guillotine.

His duty was obvious . . . Get the envelope into British hands without putting himself or the prize he'd been sent to secure at risk. Daisy Renhou was a foreign agent who'd fallen foul of local risks. Not his problem.

Not London's concern. Bill knew what he was *meant* to do. And he knew he'd be doing the opposite.

'I'm sorry, Sir William. The colonel is busy.'

'Tell him it's urgent,' Bill had insisted.

The Wehrmacht stenographer on the desk in reception at the Island Hall disappeared up the stairs and took her time to return. 'He sends his apologies, Sir William. He's on the phone to Berlin. Perhaps you could come back later?'

'I'll be back,' Bill promised, turning for the door.

The English boy from the borstal smirked as he watched him go.

To War Cabinet
From Winston Churchill

Date: Thursday, 25 July 1940
<u>Restricted</u>

Today's wave of attacks on Dover by Ju 87 dive-bombers shows no signs of abating. Although both Naval and Merchant Marine shipping have taken damage, greater damage has been prevented by our fighters, who have successfully intercepted the enemy and inflicted heavy casualties.

Current losses:

German – Aircraft 21 (with another 12 probable + 3 to anti-aircraft fire)

British – Aircraft 7

That the Luftwaffe is willing to take losses of 3:1, possibly 5:1, shows the seriousness of Hitler's intention to rid the Channel of British shipping and clear our skies ahead of invasion.

Two B-class destroyers, HMS *Brilliant* and HMS *Boreas*, sent to investigate a *Schnellboot* incursion also came under attack. The *Boreas* was hit, with 15 killed, 29 wounded, and damage to its decks. The *Brilliant* took a hit, without casualties.

Both destroyers are being towed back to Dover.

142

Alderney, same day

Nothing in the back of the car.

Bill knew there wouldn't be. Walking to the Humber's boot, he yanked it open. A spare wheel, a jack, a tool box containing spanners, pliers and a radiator hose. Exactly what he'd expected to find. Removing them, Bill lifted away the carpet to find bare steel beneath.

What had Daisy been trying to tell him?

He tipped up the front seats and found nothing, felt down both sides of the leather back seat to no avail, then yanked the seat away. A shotgun hid beneath, half-a-dozen 12-bore cartridges beside it. The gun stank of cordite and needed cleaning. There were cartridges in both breeches. One had been fired, quite recently.

Bill's guts lurched.

He wondered if Daisy realized how much she was trusting him. Then realized she must do.

In his head was Mrs Beecher's comment about Daisy having returned twice to Renhou. *I'd been at my sister's in Jersey until someone said you were back. They were wrong. It was Lady Renhou. She returned at the end of May, emptied her room of everything valuable, told me I was fired and left.'*

Where would *he* hide a dead body in a hurry if he had to?

The petrol cans in the last of the cellars were far too tidy given the state of the cellars before it, which were clogged with furniture and decades' worth of abandoned items. Dragging the first few rows of cans out of the way, Bill found more four-gallon cans behind them and shifted those as well. Five minutes later he hit what looked like an old trunk. It took another ten minutes to clear the cans on top of it and drag it free. By then, Bill was dripping with sweat, and not simply from exertion.

William E. H. G. Renhou was stencilled across the top.

Kicking it open, Bill stepped back, gagging at the stench.

A canvas-wrapped mummy rested on a sea of slime. An area the size of a shotgun blast stained its upper half. Rough sisal was tied where its shoulders, hips and knees might be.

Slashing the canvas with his pocketknife, Bill freed a hand that was more bone than flesh. It wore a signet ring identical to his own.

What was it Welham had said? Renhou hadn't been among those returned from Dunkirk, nor on any of the lists of prisoners taken. Dead ADC or not, officially he was down as missing in action, presumed dead. *Presumed.*

Sir William had made it home from the war after all.

To General Sir Stewart Menzies,
Chief, Secret Intelligence Service (MI6)
From Sir Walford Selby,
His Majesty's Ambassador to Portugal

Date: Thursday, 25 July 1940
For Your Eyes Only

SS officer Colonel Schellenberg has arrived in
Lisbon.

He is on our embassy's 'Watch & Inform' list so this
should be regarded as formal notification of his arrival. He
is, friends at the US embassy tell us, charged with
activating Operation Willi. As yet, we're told, they do not
know what this might be. My feeling is that they know
more than they are saying, which suggests Washington
might already have information on this.

Perhaps we should enquire?

143

Alderney, same day

'God, what a mess . . .'

Colonel von Neudeck reached for his hip flask, flipped up its lid and swallowed a mouthful before passing it through his car window. He'd been driving out to Renhou when he spotted Bill, walking into La Ville.

Bill swallowed without tasting. Handed the hip flask back.

Fort Albert loomed to one side, crowning the slope like the medieval fortress it wasn't. Bill stared unhappily at the hill as von Neudeck struggled with what he wanted to say. Bill knew he wouldn't like it, however much the German sweetened his words. In the end von Neudeck didn't bother.

'I'm going to say something you won't like.'

'Don't let that stop you.'

'Would you say you've been getting on better with your wife than before you went away? That you've become closer?'

'What are you really asking?'

'It's just . . .' Von Neudeck looked uncomfortable. 'It's possible she may have been using you. Reports had you at each other's throats. They had you both drunk, unfaithful or worse. Have you stopped to ask yourself why she suddenly likes you now?'

'The first time we met, she told you I wasn't me.'

'A marital tiff. Very convincing.'

'Christ,' Bill said. 'I love her.'

'That doesn't mean she loves you,' von Neudeck said. 'Believe me. It happens all the time.'

Bill scowled and von Neudeck sighed. 'I wouldn't want to believe it either. But I've been on to Berlin. They have files. Abwehr files. Her sister was an American spy.'

'That doesn't mean she is.'

'Her father too. Espionage runs in that family. It's their trade. I realize this must be a huge shock, and von Hausen has told me to say he understands, he wants you to know he doesn't hold you responsible for her crimes.'

'*Von Hausen?*'

The colonel was taken aback by Bill's shock. 'A German soldier is dead,' he said stiffly. 'Surely you'd expect the general to be involved? Keller has orders to wrap this up fast. Before—'

'Keller's Abwehr,' Bill said.

'*He told you that?*'

Bill nodded. 'You didn't know?'

'I'd guessed,' von Neudeck said. 'I just didn't expect you to know. The general flies in on Monday and we're expecting the duke on Tuesday. Von Hausen's promised Berlin nothing will mar his arrival. The issue must have been dealt with by then.'

'*Dealt with?*'

'This isn't a local boy being stabbed,' von Neudeck said. 'This is the murder of a German soldier at an official party. In our own headquarters. Just days before the arrival of an important ally. We can't just frame an islander.'

'My wife will be tried . . . ?'

'By the general.'

'And then?' Bill asked.

'If guilty she will be shot.'

Bill hadn't thought he'd feel despair like this again. 'Washington will go mad,' he said eventually.

'No. They will accept it. How can they not? She will have

been tried and convicted of murder. A murder she will have confessed to. If the wife of a German officer murdered an American soldier on American soil do you think Washington would overlook it?'

'You can stop this.'

'No,' von Neudeck said. 'I can't. Nor can you. It's out of our hands.'

'Tell General von Hausen I refuse to help. I'll insult Wallis Simpson as a gold-digging whore. I'll call the duke a traitor to his face.'

The colonel actually flinched.

'Tell him,' Bill ordered.

'I'll call Goering.'

'Goering?'

'It's his bloody fault I'm here. Let him sort this out.'

To Admiral Sir Alfred Dudley Pound RN,
First Sea Lord
From Winston Churchill

Date: Thursday, 25 July 1940
<u>Secret</u>

Coal is essential for the functioning of our factories, the powering of our ships and the very survival of these islands. Following this morning's near total destruction of a coal convoy by Stukas, all future convoys will sail at night.

I am also mindful of last night's iniquitous attack on the Meknès, when she was running at night with full lights. Our convoys will run dark, run silent and will not set sail in daylight. This is a direct order. There will be no exceptions. We are fighting for our lives. We cannot sustain our current losses. Things must change.

Please instruct all convoy leaders accordingly.

144

'Confess,' Captain Keller demanded.

'To what?' Daisy's voice dripped contempt.

'You killed Otto.'

'I don't even know who Otto is,' Daisy said. 'You expect me to know the name of every soldier on this island? Don't be ridiculous.'

'We know you did it.'

'You know nothing of the sort. My guess is you did it and you're trying to pin it on me. *Liked* Otto, did you?'

His slap was hard.

Daisy smiled. 'Thought so.'

'We have your fingerprints.'

'You haven't taken my fingerprints.'

'We have your sister's.'

'I don't have a sister,' Daisy said bitterly.

The cellar under the Island Hall was dark, dank and stank of dust. There was a chair, a desk, a light. She was on the wrong side of the light, obviously enough.

Daisy sneered. 'You're so predictable.'

She wouldn't be able to hold out when they began properly because nobody did, and even the best broke after three days. Her only hope was to delay, fence verbally and hope Bill was working up a plan.

'Why did you kill him?'

'Kill who?'

'Answer the question.'

'What question?'

'What did Schultz know that you couldn't let him reveal? How did a woman like you entice a man of his proclivities on to the roof? Indeed, why the roof? So many unanswered questions.'

'This is nonsense.'

'I've known you were a spy from the start.'

'You have the wrong sister,' Daisy said. 'I quarrelled with both Lilly and my father over marrying Sir William . . . It's been years since any of us have even talked. I'm a member of the German American Bund, for God's sake. My husband's a friend of the Duke of Windsor. I've met Hitler – in Berlin,' Daisy added, pressing her advantage. 'Wallis Simpson was there. Hell, Reichsmarschall Goering, Himmler and Speer were there. You can ask them. They'd put Speer in uniform. He was furious. You know how he likes his suits.'

She was talking too fast, giving too much detail.

All she had to do was add, *You have to believe me*, and they'd know she was lying. Daisy forced herself to stop, and leant back. The sergeant gripping her shoulders to keep her in place let her. He, at least, was impressed with her tale of parties with high Nazi functionaries in Berlin.

'All this in the company of the famous Sir William?' Keller said.

'Yes.' Daisy kept her reply simple.

'Who seems so changed he could almost be someone else.'

She managed a smile, although her gut lurched. 'Wonderful, isn't it?' she said. 'The thing is, you really need to check all this with Berlin. The duke will want to see me when he arrives. Wallis too. We're friends.'

'What do you know of that?' asked Keller, sounding put out.

'Von Hausen told me.'

She said the general's name lightly enough to sound

convincing. The longer she kept Keller talking and the more she gave him to think about, the less likely he was to start hurting her. But he would start, eventually. His type always did. When it came to things like that, Keller and her late husband had a lot in common.

145

Portugal, same day

'There's a ring in the window,' Wallis said, 'An emerald, with diamonds either side.'

'Ah.' The jeweller smiled slightly and nodded his approval of her taste. 'A particularly fine example of a reverse Ceylon. It belonged to Sri Vikrama Rajasinha, the last King of Kandy.'

'That's Ceylon,' the duke told her. 'Well, part of it.'

The jeweller brushed a tiny speck of dust from his immaculate black suit. 'Most of the truly impressive rings from the subcontinent come with a claim that they belonged to some maharaja or other. In this case it's true. There's a portrait of Sri Vikrama Rajasinha that shows him wearing the ring.'

'Wasn't he mad?' the duke said.

'Either that, sir, or entirely wicked.'

'I'd like to see it,' Wallis said.

'Certainly, senhora.'

She had no doubt he knew exactly who she was but was doing a good job of pretending he didn't.

'If you'd like to take a seat.'

Crossing the room, he opened a door to reveal a private room, with a mahogany table and three red-cushioned and gilded chairs. The woman occupying one of the seats scrambled to her feet.

'Your royal highness.'

'Frau Metz.'

'I'm sorry I wasn't here when you arrived.'

The two women air-kissed briefly and then Frau Metz curtsied to the duke.

'We've met,' Wallis told him. 'Enough times to dispense with protocol . . .' She stopped at a knock on the door and the jeweller entered with a black velvet tray on which rested the last King of Kandy's emerald ring.

He bowed slightly before leaving.

'It's beautiful,' Frau Metz said.

'You didn't notice it in the window when you came in?' Wallis sounded slightly disappointed.

'I used the rear entrance.'

'Very wise,' the duke said. He glanced at the ring. 'I suppose we're going to have to buy this thing?'

'*Darling!*'

'It would help secure their discretion,' Frau Metz said. 'Although, obviously, few jewellers are more discreet than this.'

The duke pulled a face.

'Of course,' Frau Metz said, 'my embassy would be delighted to present it to your wife as a token of our friendship if you'd agree?'

Wallis looked hopeful.

'That would be generous,' the duke said. 'Now, let's talk about what we need to talk about.'

'Given the delicacy of the next few days, the ambassador believes the less contact you and he have the better. I have his full confidence, and if it helps in this matter, I'm friends with Joachim von Ribbentrop, as your wife knows.'

If Frau Metz noticed the duke's mouth tighten, she didn't let it show.

'I am to say your flight for Berlin will leave at six p.m. on Sunday, three days' time. Having packed only what you need, you must drive that little English car London gave you to the lay-by by the pines where you stopped this morning.'

'You have someone following me?'

'We have reason to believe the English intend to kidnap you. We're doing our best to ensure that doesn't happen.'

'*Good God.*'

'Quite, your royal highness. You should be there by three o'clock. If you could have Senhor do Espírito Santo's cook prepare a picnic basket for a late lunch, and perhaps make reservations in town for supper – that would help convince the spies the English have in your household of the innocence of your drive.'

'What happens at the lay-by?'

'You change motorcars, sir. Your car is found abandoned, no one knows where you've gone and you'll be airborne before anyone finds out.'

'You'll know,' the duke said.

'But we'll also have people out searching for you. So, nobody will know we know. We will search as frantically as anyone else. It will be very convincing.'

'Berlin gives guarantees?' the duke said. 'I negotiate only with Herr Hitler?'

'You have his word.'

'Very well.' The duke's nod was abrupt.

'Now . . .' Frau Metz nodded towards the door. 'If you'll let me sort out the matter of this ring?'

'Thank you,' Wallis said, slipping it on her finger.

Frau Metz smiled. 'It suits you.'

146

An hour passed, possibly less. The light in Daisy's eyes made thinking impossible. The noise of the generator and the heat of the cellar had given her a headache. She supposed she should be grateful they hadn't yet tied her to the chair.

Keller wanted his confession. Daisy imagined he wanted it before he telephoned Berlin to check on her boasts. Perhaps as a trophy. Perhaps as an insurance policy.

'We know who you are,' he said.

'Daisy Renhou,' said Daisy. 'It's hardly a secret.'

'What you are, then.'

'An American.'

'You say that as if you expect it to save you. You think we're stupid? Your president is selling weapons to the English behind our backs. Your country has just passed an Act to double the size of its navy. Are these the actions of someone neutral?'

Opening a briefcase, Keller pulled out a photograph.

Two women sat in a café on the Champs-Élysées, talking. 'I'm sure you recognize yourself. The other woman is your sister. Who liked to call herself Gretchen Schmidt, among other names. I thought you said you were estranged?'

'We were. That was taken years ago.'

Keller turned over the photograph. 'Three years ago.'

'We met the once. We didn't get on any better than before.'

'Your sister operated between France, Spain and Portugal. We'd had our eye on her for a while, before she decided to throw herself off a roof rather than answer my questions. Do let me know if you're planning to do the same.'

'We're in a cellar.'

'I'm sure I can find you a roof.'

'*Captain Keller* . . .'

Von Neudeck stalked to where Daisy sat, moved the light out of her eyes and turned her cheek to the side. His thumb traced a bruise and felt her lip.

It was bleeding.

'She fell,' Keller said.

'A few slaps,' Daisy said dismissively. 'The odd punch, a sly hand inside my blouse and a twist of my breast. Nothing you wouldn't expect from a thug.'

Keller's lips tightened.

Without a glance, von Neudeck pushed the sergeant out of his way and helped Daisy to her feet.

'Thank you.' Daisy's smile was shaky.

'Did you kill Otto?'

'Of course not,' she said.

'Do you know who did?'

'No.' Her voice was unsteady. 'It wasn't me, though. I'm an American citizen. I have friends at the embassy in Paris. My family have friends in Washington. Our countries are not at war.'

'Yet,' Keller said.

Von Neudeck turned to Keller. 'I've just had a word with Marshal Goering,' he said. 'Remember him? He's not happy with the way you're handling this. You personally. In fact, he's very disappointed. He expects General von Hausen's staff to show more discretion.'

Keller was white. Either with fear or fury.

'Sir,' he said. 'The general would want—'

'The general isn't here,' von Neudeck said flatly. 'I am.'

'May I go home?' Daisy asked.

For a second, she really thought he might say yes.

147

Alderney, same day

'What do you want?' Hassel demanded. He looked Mrs Beecher up and down. Mrs Beecher hated him already.

'I've brought Lady Renhou some things.'

'She doesn't need anything,' he said, blocking the police station door. That was where the colonel had moved her ladyship. Mrs Beecher knew this because the new Sir William had told her.

'Yes, she does,' she said firmly. 'It's her time of the month. You know what that is, surely?'

The sergeant glared. He was one of those glowering thugs who'd burn the world down given half a chance. She'd met his type before.

Mostly they needed a good slap.

'I need to search your basket.'

'Of course,' Mrs Beecher replied. 'You'll find a file for the prison bars, a revolver and a rope to climb down.' She met his stare. 'I've brought underwear, *serviettes hygiéniques* and a dress. Feel free to rummage.'

'And that?' He pointed at her brown paper bag.

'Supper,' Mrs Beecher said. 'Chicken sandwiches, apple pie, a piece of Dundee cake. Try not to steal it all.' She pushed it at the man, and he almost took it too.

'This way,' he barked.

Beyond the lobby counter was a door. He led her through that to a room piled high with boxes. It was impossible to tell if they were just arriving, leaving, or had been taped up and forgotten about months earlier. On the wall, a fading photograph of George V in royal robes stared sternly.

'Down here.'

He yanked open a door to reveal darkness. Flicking on a torch, he stamped his way down concrete steps to damp cells in a cellar. Grudgingly, he lit a hurricane lamp.

Lady Renhou sat up from her cot, blinking.

'You can't keep her down here like this,' Mrs Beecher protested.

'They can keep me anywhere they like,' Daisy said flatly. She already had dark circles round her eyes and her cheek was swollen.

The cellar was low and dark, lacking even strip windows.

'She's brought you women's things.'

Mrs Beecher removed the dishcloth she'd used to cover her wicker basket and Daisy's eyes widened at the sight of sanitary pads.

The sergeant was staring.

'Want to take a closer look?' Mrs Beecher asked. The man swore, turned on his heel and stamped out, his boots heavy on the concrete stairs.

'Be careful,' Daisy said. 'He's dangerous.'

'He's a Hun,' Mrs Beecher said. 'I've dealt with them before.'

'How is . . . ?'

'Sir William?' Mrs Beecher asked.

'Bill,' Daisy said.

'Furious. Brooding.'

'Tell him not to do anything stupid.'

'He's in love with you. I'm not sure it will do any good.'

*

On her way out of town, Mrs Beecher met Keller. At a flick of his hand, the English boy who behaved like his shadow went to stand by a wall.

'What are you doing?' Keller demanded.

'Taking a walk,' Mrs Beecher said. 'It's a free country. Well, it was.'

Keller scowled. 'Tell your master I'd intended to visit. Unfortunately, I've been summoned to Berlin and fly out first thing tomorrow. I'll be back Monday in time for Lady Renhou's trial though. Tell him I'm looking forward to that.'

148

Alderney, same day

Being loved gives you strength. Loving gives you courage.

Daisy's father had told her that, quoting some Chinese sage given to firing off aphorisms and winning battles with equal regularity. Bill had doubted it when she said it, but now he knew it to be true. He wasn't proud it had taken this long to find two people he loved enough to make it so.

He was on his way to see the scrapyard man at Clonque because he had to start somewhere and he couldn't think what else to do.

The scrapyard dog hurled itself at the rusting fence and choked when its chain brought it up short. Climbing to its feet, it shook its head, drew in a wheezing breath and glared at Bill. It was judging distances, working out if its chain would let it reach Bill, something it should have done at the start.

It was hard not to see a moral in that.

Bill was heading for the groundsheet rigged as the workshop's curtain when it was drawn aside before he could reach it. His gaze dropped to the scrapyard man's hands: he couldn't help it. This time round he wasn't carrying a bottle, although his fists were clenched.

'I never paid you for the fan belt,' Bill said.

The scrapyard man blinked.

'Then again, your customer service left something to be desired.'

The man's gaze went to Bill's hands in turn. He relaxed when he saw Bill was unarmed. For all the stone walls of Clonque that rose like cliffs, the fort looked substantially less threatening in the afternoon light.

'I need your help,' Bill told him.

That was unexpected enough to get his attention.

149

Alderney, Friday, 26 July 1940

Friday dawned and an He 111 on Alderney's runway boosted the power to its starboard propeller and made a turn. It was the transport model, with its bomb bay replaced by a four-seater compartment. Its departure was watched from the control tower by Luftwaffe officers, and more quietly through the fence by Jerome, the foreman of the Guernsey work party. He crouched low in the scrub and practised saying he was gathering early mushrooms.

They didn't give his men enough food. Obviously he needed to supplement it. Jerome had a handful of field mushrooms in a basket as proof. As for the scrapyard man, Pete was halfway to Telegraph Tower, sitting on a boundary stone that separated his family's field from his neighbour's.

He had a folding .410 in his jacket. If anyone asked, no one had told him shotguns were now illegal. Standing, Pete suddenly screeched like a hawk. And a crow watching from a post fell silent and started cawing again, angrier than ever at being fooled. It was his signal they were no longer alone.

'Here we go,' Bill said.

Taking the brandy he'd been promised, Pete nodded to where Jerome was hurrying up the path towards them.

'They freed Georgie,' Jerome said.

'I'm glad. How is he?'

'Built like a horse, which helps.'

Bill nodded. 'I'm sorry all the same.'

'You wanted to meet?'

Bill kept it simple. 'First point, I'm a British agent. I'm here on a mission. Second point, I didn't injure the boy.'

'We thought . . .'

'I know what you thought. Third point, My wife's been framed for murder. I'm going to spend today on reconnaissance, and break her out tomorrow night. My house is the first place they'll search. I'll need help hiding her.'

'You'll need help getting her out,' Jerome replied.

To Sir Walford Selby,
His Majesty's Ambassador to Portugal
From General Sir Stewart Menzies,
Chief, Secret Intelligence Service (MI6)

Date: Friday, 26 July 1940
<u>For Your Eyes Only</u>

Re: Operation Willi

It seems likely the Nazis intend to stop us removing
HRH The Duke of Windsor from Portugal, should it come
to that. In view of this, London has decided to combine
forces with Washington to deal with this situation should
it arise.

Elizabeth Moore, an American operative, will be
joining you on secondment from Roosevelt's Office for the
Coordination of Intelligence, or whatever they're calling it
this week. You are to accord her full access and every
courtesy.

To SIS Desk, Lisbon
From Sir Walford Selby,
His Majesty's Ambassador to Portugal

Date: Friday, 26 July 1940
<u>Confidential</u>

    Ian, I know your opinion of women and Americans,
but Elizabeth Moore comes highly recommended and it is
important we 'play nicely'.
    Remember this.
    WS

150

Bill didn't doubt the shotgun he'd found inside the Humber was a good one. He was going to ruin it all the same.

'Do we have a saw?' he asked.

Mrs Beecher was in the kitchen, washing up after breakfast. Mignon was drying.

'What kind of saw?' Mrs Beecher asked.

'A sharp one.'

When she returned it was with a selection. Bill chose a hacksaw, a fretsaw and a long and slightly rusty ripsaw.

'I'll be in the billiards room,' Bill told her.

Using the edge of Sir William's billiard table as a workbench, Bill gripped the shotgun by its beautifully engraved action and hacked away its stock, rounding off the pistol grip. He hacked away both barrels to leave himself with a stubby sawn-off. It was as crude as it was dangerous.

'That looks nasty,' Mrs Beecher said. She held a tray with coffee, biscuits, milk and sugar, which she put beside the saws. 'Do you want the other one?'

Bill remembered the shotgun Daisy had been brandishing at Clonque. He hadn't seen it again after that night.

'They're a pair?'

'Perfectly matched,' Mrs Beecher said proudly.

Five minutes later, she put a leather gun case on the billiard table's green baize. *Gebrüder Merkel* was embossed on its top.

'It was in Lady Renhou's old bedroom. I noticed it when cleaning. Seems a pity to ruin both.'

Bill met her gaze.

'Then again,' she said. 'Needs must.'

'Do we have any of those metal eyes you put door hooks into?'

When she came back, Bill had just hacked off the second stock. She stood watching while he shaped the back of the pistol grip.

'I'm beginning to see why they sent you, sir.'

She left Bill to saw off the barrels and screw eyes into the grips of both weapons. And they were weapons, for all they'd begun as a perfectly matched pair of German 12-bores. If he put a short length of clothesline through the clasps, hung the sawn-offs round his neck, and positioned them under his coat on either hip, most people wouldn't even notice they were there.

Not something he'd learned at Arisaig, whatever Mrs Beecher thought. It was a trick he'd picked up from an Afrikaans bank robber in Dar es Salaam the year Miriam left and he decided to travel. It had taken him another year to realize it didn't matter how far he went, he'd always take himself.

151

Portugal, same day

The luncheon party at Casa de Santa Maria was breaking up and Wallis's guests were heading to their motorcars, some in a better state to drive than others.

The duke had noticed the way Miss Moony, the younger and slightly less plain of the two women from the British embassy, had watched his wife's every move.

Wallis had that effect on some women.

Admiration, he imagined.

'Sir. If I could have a word?'

It was the black-haired chap with the immaculately cut tropical suit and the knowing glance. The duke wasn't entirely sure he liked him but at least he knew how to dress.

'Savile Row?' the duke asked.

'Of course, sir.'

'Very smart.'

That was the point at which he should have said thank you; instead he looked round to check they weren't over-heard. Not that there was much fear of that. The British ambassador was busy helping Miss Moony into his Rolls-Royce with a little more attention than necessary. The less attractive of the embassy girls had already helped her-self in.

'I hope you enjoyed luncheon,' the duke said.

Apparently, the man found something about the question amusing. 'Oh yes,' he said, 'I haven't enjoyed a meal this much in years. Now, you mentioned a picnic. I wondered if you'd like company?'

The duke frowned. 'Wallis and I . . .'

'Like to be alone? Understandable at a time like this. If unwise . . .'

'Unwise?' There was sudden frostiness in the duke's voice.

'Have you run into a Colonel Schellenberg recently, sir? Say, on one of your other picnics? He's Hitler's top assassin.'

'I'm not in the habit of knowing assassins.'

'Very sensible.' The man leant in, his voice suddenly hard. 'As things stand, sir, if Schellenberg doesn't kill you, we will. Alternatively, we can keep you safe. You have a choice to make. If I were you, I'd choose wisely.'

The duke jerked back.

The man was staring at him. It was a dark, entirely unforgiving gaze and one that made the duke shiver. 'Go to the Bahamas,' the man said. 'Take your wife.'

'*I don't know who you*—'

'Sir,' the ambassador said, appearing unexpectedly at the duke's side. He looked between the men. 'Everything all right? Ian?'

'Absolutely,' the man said. 'We were saying goodbye.' He bowed slightly to the duke. 'I do hope not for good.'

152

Alderney, same day

'I'm taking a walk,' Bill said. 'Don't wait up.'

'Like your walk last night?'

'Exactly like my walk last night.'

'Measure twice, cut once,' Mrs Beecher said knowledgeably. 'I was in the ATS, wasn't I? Last time round.' She smiled. 'Say hello to Madame.'

To the Editor, *Dover Express*
From Alfred Duff Cooper,
Chief, Ministry of Information

Date: 27 July 1940
<u>For Immediate Attention</u>

     I am told you have asked questions about the sinking of a destroyer in Dover harbour this afternoon. As you're probably now aware, HMS *Codrington* was deployed on patrol duties in the Channel and was undergoing maintenance when an enemy bomb broke her back.

     The idea that a British ship can be sunk in a British harbour by enemy dive-bombers is one that will alarm your readers. As such, it should not be reported. No reference should be made to it now, or in the future. No reference may be made to deaths or the salvage operation.

     Thank you for your cooperation.

153

Portugal, same day

'Darling . . .'

'I mean it,' the duke said.

He'd expected his wife to be furious. She wasn't. She was shocked. He doubted anyone had ever told her she could only take one suitcase before.

'I can't possibly . . .'

'You don't have a choice.'

He'd seen her white with rage at not being able to take two full dinner sets, her furs and her hairdresser with her when they left Paris. Now was when she should explode. It was late on Saturday night, the house they'd borrowed from the Espírito Santos was quiet, their guests had gone and he'd just told her to pack a single bag. They were leaving.

'Darling. What's going on? You're scaring me.'

'You have to trust me.'

He was drunk, but not that drunk, and not too drunk to drive. If he could just get out of here and keep going, he'd be safe. They both would. The world would feel cleaner and clearer in the morning, less soiled. The duke felt his eyes brim, and turned away to hide the tear he couldn't stop escaping.

He was a king, for God's sake. Life wasn't meant to be like this. Bloody, bloody people. He'd only invited them to be civil and lull the British embassy into thinking everything was all right, of course.

They'd threatened him.

Well, one of them had.

As things stand, sir, if Schellenberg doesn't kill you, we will.

What was that if not an outright threat? *Alternatively, we can keep you safe.* Did that ghastly little man really think he was the only one saying that? Damn them all. Franco had promised him safety too. Let the generalissimo keep his promise.

I'll take Beigbeder up on his offer, the duke decided. Borrow the Spanish castle. The one with the Moorish gardens. Wallis will like it there . . . I'm happy enough to reclaim my throne with Hitler at my side. But if that's what he wants, he can say it to my face. Let him come to me.

Shakily, the duke reached for a whisky decanter and changed his mind. He'd been drinking since lunchtime. Another glass and he wouldn't be able to drive straight. He reached for a packet of Chesterfield instead, remembering to offer one to Wallis.

'What's going on?' Wallis said. 'If you don't tell me I can't help.'

'No one can help.'

From a moment, she looked mutinous.

'I mean it,' he said. 'I'm between Scylla and Charybdis. One or the other will destroy me.'

'What and what?'

'A rock and a hard place.'

'Darling. What's this about?'

'We should go,' he said. 'I'll tell you when we're driving. You need to pack first. Tomorrow will be too late.'

'You'll tell me now.'

'When I'm driving,' he repeated.

The road to the Spanish border was dark and almost deserted. The duke drove with his roof up, his headlights off and his sidelights on. The sky was black enough for stars, and the moon in its last quarter as sharp as a scythe. The night wind through the window of his green MG was warm and scented with scrub and herbs and smoke from his cigarette.

'You can't see,' Wallis protested.

'I can see well enough,' he assured her. Dropping a gear, he turned on to a dirt track and began climbing.

The Buick was too well known. He'd chosen the MG because it was small and recently filled. For reassurance, he'd jammed a two-gallon jerry can behind the seats, ignoring Wallis's complaint that gasoline would make her clothes smell.

Setting his back against red leather, the duke peered through his windscreen. No lights ahead, no lights coming up behind, nothing resembling a roadblock. He'd been right to take the long way round. Maybe they'd been lucky. He was owed some luck.

'Tell me,' Wallis said. Her voice was tight.

'That dreadful man at luncheon,' the duke said.

'The one with the naval cufflinks?'

'Never trust a man who doesn't give his surname,' the duke said fiercely. 'It's always a bad sign.'

'What about him?'

'He was only pretending to be drunk. I watched him. He spent the entire meal with a glass in his hand and barely took a sip.'

'What's this got to do with leaving in a hurry?'

'Everything,' the duke said. 'At the end, he came up, pretending to be tipsy, and asked if I'd run into a German called Schellenberg. And then the bloody man leant in, as if to say something in confidence, and said I'd do well to stay away from Schellenberg. Because the way things were going, if Schellenberg didn't shoot me, he would.'

'Good God,' Wallis said.

'Utterly inappropriate. He then said, as if he'd just thought of it, that being a good boy and going to the Bahamas was probably my safest bet.'

'*He said that?*'

'More or less. Well, I'm not going. We're going to Spain. We'll borrow that palace you liked the sound of. Colonel Beigbeder can keep us safe.'

'Don't you want your throne back?'

'Obviously I want my throne back. I've been thinking . . . I'm entirely happy for Hitler to be at my side when I enter London. All the same, he can come to me.' The duke glanced in the mirror. 'We're being followed,' he said.

'Are you sure?'

He slowed down and the car behind them kept its distance. When he slowed again it slowed too.

'I'm certain.'

154

Portugal, same day

The headlights were still behind them, and the duke felt his shoulders tighten inside his lightweight jacket. He owed the prickle of sweat under his hair to more than the night wind. The Spanish border must be close now. Stamping on the accelerator, he felt the little MG shudder like a boat in a storm.

Wallis glanced back. 'They're gaining,' she said.

She was right. They were too. The MG was light and fast, and the best in its class, but the open-topped tourer following was infinitely more powerful. It had been waiting for this point, the duke realized, feeling suddenly sick. The last of the straight road was gone, leaving a tight climb through the hills ahead. He had a terrifying vision of his little car being pushed over the edge. Of the MG sliding down the slope to explode below. He could see flames, feel the heat on his flesh.

'*Darling . . .*'

Tearing his attention back to the road, the duke wrestled the wheel, feeling something in his shoulder pull as he fought a tight bend, rocks sharp enough to rip the bodywork apart just inches from his window.

He was in the wrong gear and he felt the engine lug, hammering like a boiler until he dropped down two gears, hearing it scream as he took another turn. The big car was right behind him now, its headlights blinding in his mirror.

As the track unwound, the tourer chasing him roared, lurched forward and began to draw alongside.

'There isn't room,' Wallis protested.

The duke knew that. He had jagged rocks to one side and a bigger, obviously more powerful motorcar on the other. When it nudged in, he jerked on the steering wheel, the MG scraping rock as he tried to get away.

'*Darling!*'

It was only stamping on the brakes that stopped him ploughing into the bigger car as it swung in front of him. Deceleration flipped Wallis forward, and for a horrified second, the duke thought she'd slam into the dashboard. At the last moment, she shielded her face and took the blow on her arm.

'Christ,' the duke said.

His wife was sobbing. Her hands gripped her elbow.

In the open-topped motorcar ahead, a woman in the back seat turned, produced a revolver and pointed it at him.

No shot came.

Instinctively, the duke slowed, increasing the distance between them, but the woman shook her head and gestured him closer.

'Do as she says,' Wallis begged.

The duke had been intending to. His little coupé was too slow to outrun them, the road too narrow to turn. They could try reversing, but the road's edges were crumbling and there was a sheer drop to one side. He doubted he'd make a good job of it in the dark, half-drunk while being shot at.

'She's signalling,' Wallis said.

The woman was pointing to the left. As the tourer passed a turning, it stopped and she indicated they should take the turn. A rough track, barely wide enough for a motorcar, faced them. The duke edged his MG up it, finding himself halted a dozen paces in by an iron gate. The gate was padlocked.

There was nothing for it but to turn off his engine. Behind them the tourer growled as it nosed its way up the track, stopping tight behind them. A second later its headlights went out.

155

Portugal, same day

In the silence that followed, the duke could hear crickets, wind through gorse and the creak of pine trees. It was a beautiful night to die. Except they weren't going to. At least he didn't think so . . .

'If they were going to kill us,' he told Wallis. 'They'd have done it. Besides, I imagine we're more use alive.'

'Who are they?' she demanded.

The duke shrugged. 'I have no damned idea.' He ran his hand through his hair, making himself presentable, straightened his tie and tried to smile. The first man out of the car held a rifle. Instead of pointing it at the duke, he scanned the hill above them and turned to take a hard look at the road they'd travelled and the horizon beyond.

Only then did he glance at the duke. It was the bastard from the luncheon party. The one whose words had set him running.

'Sir,' he said.

'You again.'

'Yes, sir. Me again. The name's Fleming.'

'What in God's name are you doing here?'

'Trying to keep you safe, believe it or not. We're taking you home.'

'You're . . . ?'

'Well, I'm not. She is.' Fleming stepped aside so he could see the sharp-faced woman who'd held a gun on them. She glanced once at the duke, then leant against the tourer and lit a cigarette. She showed no interest in joining them.

As the duke watched, a second woman clambered from the front and stood slightly unsteadily.

Wallis gasped. 'That's my Piguet dress,' she said crossly, 'and my Dior jacket.'

'You'll get them back,' Fleming promised.

'Fleming. What's going on?'

'We are, sir,' Fleming told him. 'Penny and me. You're going back. For the purposes of the rest of this night, we're you.'

'You're me?'

'We're both of you.' He gestured to the second woman, who came over and dropped an awkward curtsy. It was Penny Moony, whom they'd last seen being helped into the ambassador's car. Her hair had been cut and dyed to make her look as much like Wallis as possible.

'That's my ruby necklace,' Wallis said.

The woman didn't reply.

'I said . . .'

Dropping her cigarette, the woman leaning against the tourer ground it underfoot and headed over. She moved almost lazily.

'Problem?' she asked.

'No problem,' Fleming assured her.

'That's good.' Her accent was American. She stared at the duke and dismissed Wallis with a glance. 'I'm Liz,' she said. 'You almost met a friend of mine a few months back. Her name was Lilly.'

'Almost met?'

'You won't remember.' Nodding to Fleming, she said, 'You two need to hit the road. I'll take our lovebirds home.'

The duke opened his mouth to object.

'There's no way we or the Brits are letting you return to Spain. Nor are we going to let you be Hitler's puppet. You'll get on that ship to the Bahamas and like it.'

'I can't get on that ship,' the duke protested. 'Berlin says London's going to have me killed.'

'They're lying,' Liz said. 'But you should know that the day you land on Alderney – and that's where they'll be taking you, by the way – is the day she dies.' Liz jerked her head towards Wallis. 'Do you want to be king that badly?'

'They'd never do that.'

'No,' Liz said crisply. '*We* would.'

Even Fleming was slightly shocked.

'We have someone in place,' Liz said, 'with a single task. Kill your wife. It's called leverage. If I were you, I'd let me drive you back to Lisbon and deliver you to the Brits. Safer for everyone.'

156

Alderney, same day

The moon was within days of disappearing. Bill's time was up and his real job was done. All he had to do was get the evidence of the duke's treachery back to London and he'd have kept his side of the bargain. His slate would be clean and he could have his life back. But what was that worth if Daisy wasn't in it? And then there was Mignon.

He couldn't just leave her here.

It was half an hour to midnight, long after curfew.

'You should let me do it,' Jerome said. He didn't even bother to say hello. Simply stood from where he'd been crouching by a stile.

Bill shook his head.

'You could be the one to hide her,' Jerome protested.

'Renhou's the first place they'll look . . .'

And after tomorrow night I'll be gone.

That wouldn't give him long enough to hide Daisy. He wanted her free from prison, and Mignon and her properly hidden more than anything; certainly more than he wanted to get himself to London with the contents of that safe.

'All the same . . .'

'Look,' Bill said. 'What would you do?'

They walked on in silence.

'You think the Nazis will be expecting us?' Jerome asked eventually.

'Wouldn't you be?' Bill replied.

157

Alderney, same day

The bells of St Anne's were striking midnight. The police station on New Street lay ahead. La Ville felt haunted by its lack of inhabitants.

'This is far enough,' Bill said.

As the bells faded to silence, the local policeman left on his rounds, truncheon swinging from his belt. He marched past the alley where Bill and Jerome waited in the shadows, without noticing them.

'Hang on. That's . . .' Jerome started to say.

Pete from the scrapyard was reeling down Victoria Street, oblivious to the curfew, with what was left of Bill's bottle of brandy in his hand. He shied when Jerome stepped out of the shadows.

'What the fuck?' Pete peered into the darkness. 'Who's with you?'

'Who do you think?' Bill said. 'Do you know who's in the police station?'

'Only one way to find out,' Pete said.

'Wait . . .'

It was too late. Having tripped on the police-station steps, Pete propped himself against its door and hammered to be let in. Seconds later he fell through. A minute passed, then another. Bill was beginning to get worried when the door swung open, and Pete staggered out, muttering under his breath. He peered around him and set off in the wrong direction.

'Christ almighty,' Jerome said.

Since following the drunk was going to be a lot easier than persuading him to come to them, Bill and Jerome set off after him. They caught up in Rue de l'Église. It wasn't hard. Pete was on his knees, staring at the shards of the bottle he'd dropped.

What was left of Bill's brandy was mixing with dirt.

'There's that Kraut,' he said, wiping his chin on the back of his hand as he climbed to his feet. 'The shiny-faced bastard. He's expecting trouble. That English kid is with him, wearing Nazi cast-offs. Little shit.'

'He's expecting trouble?'

'The sergeant? Got a gun on a strap round his neck.'

Schmeisser. Five hundred rounds a minute, thirty-two rounds a magazine. Very nasty, very fast and very dirty. Bill had the woman at Arisaig to thank for knowing that.

'Did you see Lady Renhou?' Jerome asked.

Pete shook his head. 'The cells are underground. I should know, I've been in them often enough. I got through to the back though, until that Kraut came up from below waving his gun. Wanted to know what the noise was about.'

'What did you tell him?' Bill asked.

'Told him I'd lost my dog and wanted to report it. He said I was drunk.' The man spat. 'Told him he'd be drunk if he'd lost his dog.'

Despite himself, Bill laughed.

158

Alderney, same day

The policeman was returning from his rounds when Bill whistled. The first couple of bars of 'Colonel Bogey'. The man froze and looked round slowly; Bill whistled another few bars. PC Smith looked the very picture of a flatfoot, chin thrust forward and shoulders squared as he stamped towards them.

'They're waiting for you. You must realize that.'

'It's crossed my mind,' Bill said.

'*Crossed your mind* . . . Their sergeant keeps checking his sub-machine gun and then his watch. I think he was expecting you earlier.'

'Me specifically?'

'Can't think who else it would be.' He glanced at the sawn-offs half hidden by Bill's coat. 'Fire those and every Nazi on the island will hear you.'

'They're a last resort.'

'A knife would be better. A big one.'

Jerome opened his jacket to reveal a machete.

'You do know, don't you,' the policeman said, 'what the Waffen-SS did to the Breton village that killed a German sergeant?'

Bill didn't, but he could imagine. Women and children die as easily as men, and armies tend not to keep count of dead civilians. Despite himself, he felt for the policeman. If the Nazis won, he was a turncoat.

If they lost, he was a collaborator.

In a just world, the islanders would be grateful for the buffer he provided between them and the occupiers. In practice, they'd despise him for doing what London ordered: keeping calm and carrying on.

'Does Sergeant Hassel eat at the station?' Bill asked.

'Never seen him eat at all, sir. He sleeps on a cot in the cell next to Lady Renhou's. He's barely left the station since she arrived.'

Bill's heart sank. He needed ten to fifteen minutes when Hassel was absent, PC Smith was on his rounds and the quisling boy was the only one on guard. He'd been hoping Hassel came and went to HQ.

'He *must* leave, surely?' Damn it, Bill had seen him leave. The previous evening, on reconnaissance, he'd definitely seen the sergeant returning from somewhere.

'Well, he drops back to his billet most nights.'

'For supper?'

'For the widow.'

It wasn't a pretty tale or a rare one. The woman was French, and the sergeant had brought her from Normandy. Bill doubted he treated her well, and he doubted the villagers would treat her much better if she ever returned.

'How long does he go for?'

'An hour, at most. He locks the boy in, locks me out, and takes the keys.'

'Good,' Bill said. 'We'll wait.'

'He's just come back.'

Bill's heart sank.

Tomorrow was the last night before General von Hausen came back and Daisy was tried, found guilty and shot. After that came the submarine, and Bill's boat on the beach. Bill couldn't afford to leave it until tomorrow. He'd spent all day working himself up to this. Yet what choice did he have?

Sawn-off shotguns or not, he couldn't get past a man with a Schmeisser, which could clear a room of anything living in seconds. Not without a real risk of getting Daisy killed. Tomorrow was leaving it too late. Yet tomorrow was what he'd got. Bill felt haunted by the waning moon.

159

Portugal, Sunday, 28 July 1940

It was an hour before dawn. In that half-light which looks black when seen from inside a lit room, and close to daylight outside, Colonel Schellenberg stood beside a Spanish customs hut with his field glasses trained on the road.

As the distant car drew nearer, he recognized it as the racing green MG he'd been told to expect. He checked the soldiers with sniper rifles hidden on the roof of the hut. Although he'd been told to expect a chase, he could see no pursuers.

'Don't show yourselves,' he said.

Had they been German there'd be no problem, but they were Spanish and not technically under his control.

'Only shoot if I order,' he added.

The locals glanced at each other, but nodded.

'It will be faultless,' the customs post's chief promised, coming out of his hut and staring for a second at the approaching sports car.

'It had better be,' Schellenberg replied.

The MG had reached the Portuguese side of the border. Its canvas hood was up and its windscreen thick with dust. Schellenberg could just make out the couple inside.

What was delaying them?

The driver was being questioned, which wasn't what Schellenberg needed. What he needed was the Portuguese to inspect the couple's papers, come to attention, salute smartly and wave them through.

What if he was warning them?

They might now be parked out of sight, but the arrival of a Spanish army truck, an Interior Ministry motorcar and a German diplomatic limousine could hardly have been missed.

No scandal. Berlin's orders were clear.

Irrespective of what the duke wanted, he was to be delivered to Berlin immediately. General Franco had already agreed to this. Schellenberg wondered how serious an incident it would create if he ventured on to Portuguese soil to snatch them. He didn't want to be the man who brought Portugal into the war against the Fatherland, not this close to victory.

'Sir . . .'

'I'm aware.'

The door of the MG snapped open and its driver climbed out.

He wore a fedora pulled low and dark glasses. He said something the Portuguese customs officer didn't like, because he scowled and indicated towards the hut. When the driver reappeared he was pushing his wallet into his jacket. A jacket that was as immaculately cut as the German would have expected. His fedora was tipped below one eye.

Enough, Schellenberg thought.

The barrier on the Portuguese side rose and the MG entered that dead space between customs posts. The Portuguese barrier descended before the Spanish one could rise.

'Slowly,' Schellenberg muttered, as the bar went up.

The fools were being too enthusiastic. He watched the MG edge forward and felt almost physical relief. The snipers would have their telescopic sights fixed on the road the car had travelled down. There was no pursuit to be seen, though. Nothing could stop what was about to happen.

'Right,' he said. 'Let's get them.' Striding to the driver's side, Schellenberg dropped to a crouch. 'Welcome to Spain, your royal highness.'

A total stranger stared back.

160

Alderney, same day

The waiting was the worst. In the Great War, Bill had the daily 'hate', three minutes of free-fire fury every morning to burn off the anxiety of knowing he was alive while not knowing how long that would last.

He woke early, too early, and not simply from light through his bedroom window. He made himself weed a flower bed he'd never see again because either he'd be dead or on a submarine home. He trimmed a rambling rose and did his best to repair a dry-stone wall. Anyone on reconnaissance would have fallen asleep from boredom.

Looking up, he saw Mignon was waiting for him to notice her.

'You're meant to be inside,' he said.

'I brought you tea.' She put the cup on a stone table with a bang. He waited for her to go, but she stayed put. 'Madame didn't do it,' she said fiercely. 'She wouldn't. They're lying. The sergeant did it, the one who chased me.'

Bill froze. He couldn't help it.

'He chased you . . . ?'

'The night I met Eddie. He didn't see me.'

'You didn't say.'

'You didn't ask,' Mignon said. 'I thought I'd imagined him. That mouth. That terrible face. Then he came here with that German captain to take Madame away, and you and Madame were . . .' She was crying.

'The sergeant did it,' she said fiercely.

'Yes,' Bill said. 'I think that sergeant did it too.'

'I'm sorry,' Bill said as Mignon turned to go.

'For what?'

'Everything.' He put his arms around her and hugged. For a heartbeat, she held herself rigid, then she leant her head into his chest and hugged him back.

'I'd better go inside,' she said.

Picking up a cutting from the rose Bill had pruned, she tossed it on to a bonfire he'd only just lit, leaving him to watch the rising smoke turn grey. The bonfire, the sky overhead, the girl who could have been his daughter. He felt as if he'd briefly been given someone else's life, only to have it taken away again. And knew, without wanting to believe it, that, at best, he'd only really been borrowing it.

161

Portugal, same day

The pair from the British embassy knelt in the dust on the Spanish side of the border with their hands behind their heads, staring at the back of a customs hut. They'd been kneeling there for what felt like hours.

But they were still alive. That was a start.

Telephone calls had been made, and men in suits had arrived to glare at them. They were out of sight of the Portuguese side, but Fleming had given the Portuguese officer a telephone number and money to keep an eye on what happened, and Fleming didn't doubt he and his men were watching.

They'd certainly been there to watch the infamous Colonel Schellenberg drag him from the MG and throw him into the dirt. That was the most dangerous point. It reassured Fleming that the Portuguese were near enough to hear shots, because that made those shots less likely.

'Name?' Schellenberg had demanded.

'Smith,' Fleming had said. 'Mr and Mrs Smith.'

And here he was again. Stamping out to repeat his question.

'I've told you already,' Fleming said. 'Mr and Mrs Smith. We're English. We're going away for a quiet weekend.'

'Your real names?'

Fleming sighed. 'Passport. Inside jacket pocket.'

The German dug his hand into Fleming's jacket, swearing at what he found. Fleming's passport was diplomatic and gave him immunity – at least it was meant to.

'You won't like mine either,' Penny Moony said. She jerked her head towards a handbag lying in the dirt.

'It's a serious offence to lie to customs,' one of the Spaniards said.

'I didn't lie,' Fleming said, climbing to his feet and helping Miss Moony to hers. 'Well, not much. I certainly didn't do anything improper like show you false papers. Our few days away are quite improper enough. It's simple, really. We work together at the embassy in Lisbon and we're friends, good friends. We're trying to stop our other friends finding out.'

'Why not find a hotel in Portugal?' the Spaniard demanded.

'Because', Miss Moony said patiently, 'we're trying to be discreet.'

'This is absurd,' Schellenberg said.

'Really?' Fleming said politely. 'In what way?'

'That car . . .'

'Beautiful, isn't she? I swapped her for the weekend with a friend. He's borrowed my Aston Martin.'

'You're not taking this seriously,' Schellenberg said.

'I'm taking it very seriously indeed,' Fleming said. 'As, no doubt, are our Portuguese friends, who will be taking notes. I imagine they've been making some telephone calls of their own.'

The Spaniard scowled. 'You expect us to believe this nonsense about running away for a few days?'

Fleming gave his companion a quick glance and she smiled. They'd done what was required and what happened now was up to the Spanish.

'It might be best if you did,' Penny said.

'Why?' the Spaniard asked.

'Because we're diplomats, with diplomatic credentials, in a neutral country, and, fairy stories aside, our embassy knows exactly where we are. We will telephone them from the next town to confirm we're safe.'

'You won't be going to the next town,' the Spaniard said.

'And why not?' Miss Moony demanded. Now was where things could get really nasty. The ambassador had warned her and Fleming of the risk they were taking and asked them to confirm in writing they took it willingly.

Unconsciously, or not, the Spaniard had turned his back on Schellenberg, already distancing himself from the German's failure. 'Because', he said, nodding to the Portuguese side of the border, 'I'm sending you back.'

162

Alderney, same day

The day thou gavest, Lord, is ended, the darkness falls at thy behest . . .

It was strange the things you remembered from childhood. Bill's last day on Alderney was indeed gone, and darkness falling. Slipping the lanyards for his sawn-offs over his head, he settled the guns at his sides and slid himself into a three-quarter length coat. Waiting for this evening to arrive had been one of the hardest things he'd ever done. Mignon and Mrs Beecher eventually deciding it was best to leave him to brood on his own.

The tide was rising, the causeway half flooded as he crossed it to head for La Ville, one eye on the radium dial of his Rolex to check he was on schedule, his other looking out for enemy patrols.

Jerome was by the gate to the flower garden behind Rue de l'Église, which was where Jerome was meant to be. He was watching Constable Smith walk his beat. The island's policeman stopped at the gate and didn't so much as glance in their direction.

'He left five minutes ago. I'm going home. You're on your own.'

He stamped off towards Connaught Square.

'Right,' Bill said. 'The widow.'

'You should let me do it . . .' Jerome spoke with the dogged determination of a man determined to do the right thing.

'I'll do it.'

'Then you might want this.' Jerome pulled a length of cheese wire, fitted with toggles either end, from his pocket. 'I made it this afternoon.'

'Thank you,' Bill said.

On their way to the sergeant's billet at Crabby Bay, Jerome spoke of nothing much in urgent whispers. Bill wasn't surprised. In the trenches, his friends had talked of sisters, mothers, families and brothels behind the lines, wins at cards, the rats, the lice and rain. Everything except what was coming. Death, and the violence it rode in on.

Bill was expecting both that night.

163

Alderney, same day

A huge man stepped from the shadows of a boathouse above the shingle. Pete, from the scrapyard, appeared behind him.

'Georgie decided he wanted to help.'

The big man nodded.

'Your sergeant went in fifteen minutes ago,' Pete added.

'You followed him here?'

'It seemed like a good plan . . .'

'A very good plan,' Bill agreed.

Pete glanced at Bill's hand. 'You want me to do this?' As apologies went, two offers to kill someone on his behalf in one evening was bittersweet.

Bill thanked Pete and said he'd do it himself.

Almost exactly thirty minutes later, the front door to Hassel's cottage opened and the scar-faced SS sergeant stood framed in its light. The man shut the door behind him, waited for his eyes to adjust, and turned for the slope to the road.

Bill stepped back into the shadows.

When he glanced round, Jerome, Pete and Georgie were gone.

For a moment, Bill thought he'd lost Hassel as well; then he saw him again, silhouetted against the night. He was younger and fitter, and far harder than Bill had ever been. If the sergeant hadn't found his way blocked by a drunken argument, Bill would have been left behind.

The scrapyard man was swearing at Jerome, who was snarling back in *Dgèrnésiais*, while Georgie watched from the side. Even if there'd been room to go round, none of them should have been out and the sergeant didn't like being ignored.

'Curfew,' he barked.

'Fuck your curfew,' the scrapyard man replied.

'Yeah,' said Jerome. 'Fuck it sideways.'

The sergeant grabbed Jerome's throat, and Jerome swung a punch that Hassel blocked, landing a vicious jab of his own to Jerome's kidneys. As the sergeant swivelled to kick out Jerome's jaw, he was barged aside.

'No, you don't,' Georgie said.

The sergeant was going for his pistol when Bill stepped out of the darkness, a sawn-off shotgun in his hand.

'You,' the sergeant said.

'Yeah,' Bill said. 'Me.'

He raised his shotgun and Hassel charged, grabbing its barrel and twisting it out of Bill's hands. Bill ducked his head a split second before the lanyard would have strangled him, feeling it scrape free. Turning the weapon on him, Hassel yanked the trigger.

He looked puzzled when the 12-bore just clicked.

'Empty,' Bill said.

Flipping the weapon round, the SS sergeant swung it like a club and Bill dropped under the blow. Landing on his knees, Bill drove his fist into Hassel's groin, slamming his elbow into the man's throat as Hassel jack-knifed.

Lieutenant Fairbairn would be proud.

Standing unsteadily, Bill slipped his makeshift garrotte over Hassel's head, pulling it so tight the toggle cut into his injured hand. The man arched backwards, instinct making him grab for the cheese wire. A split second later, training kicked in and his elbow jabbed back, catching Bill's ribs.

Bill gasped, breath rushing from his lungs.

Hassel missed Bill's groin with a swung-back fist. Then his fingers swept up as he went for Bill's eyes, and Bill's fear of being blinded killed the man. The garrotte sliced flesh as Bill jerked back, Hassel's feet kicked, and then the gargling stopped as he shat himself.

Dropping Hassel to the ground, Bill dug in his jacket for the key and found Eddie's trench lighter too. Made from a fired round of .303, it had obviously been taken as a trophy from the murdered boy.

'Bastard,' Bill muttered.

Lifting Hassel's pistol from its holster, he took the man's SS dagger as an afterthought, leaving its sheath on his belt.

When he looked up, Jerome was staring.

'The shotgun wasn't loaded?'

'First barrel empty,' Bill said. 'Second full.'

'He could have killed you then?'

'Only if he'd pulled the second trigger. We need to get him off the road.'

'No,' Jerome said. 'We need to do this properly.' Pointing to one of the upturned boats, he told Georgie to drag it down to the water's edge and come back for the body.

'I'm glad he's dead,' Georgie said.

'I'm glad he's dead too,' Jerome told him.

When Bill and Jerome left, Georgie and the scrapyard man were still discussing whether to wrap the sergeant in an anchor chain or put stones in his pockets.

164

Alderney, same day

The sergeant's sidearm was a Pistole Parabellum, otherwise known as a Luger, and it felt unnervingly familiar in Bill's hands. He offered it to Jerome.

'Get caught with this and they'll shoot you,' he said.

'They'll shoot me anyway,' Jerome replied.

Alderney was too open, too un-wooded and too empty of inhabitants for unsilenced gunfire. They both knew that. With a curfew declared and enemy patrols out, the sound of a shot would be heard across the island.

'Last resort,' Bill stressed.

Their luck held on the road back to La Ville. They saw no one on Route de Braye, although they spotted two soldiers as they neared the police station. The soldiers didn't see them and Bill was content with that. There'd be killing enough soon. Digging into his pocket for Hassel's key, Bill reached for the police-station door.

'Ready?' he said.

Jerome showed his machete.

'Cover me,' Bill said. The time for talking was over.

165

The reception area was empty.

Lights were on at the rear. An empty bottle of Schultz-Weisse beer stood on an otherwise empty desk. A filing cabinet had three drawers open. The door down to the cells stood wide.

Bill shut the door from reception, gesturing Jerome to follow, and headed for the stairs. There was absolute silence from below. No voices. Not even the shuffle of footsteps. He went down slowly, with Jerome behind him.

Bill put his finger to his lips.

Gripping his dagger, he pushed on the lower door, peered round it, and swallowed a gasp. Keller's protégé was on his knees, his head yanked back. Daisy stood behind him, holding one of Renhou's kitchen knives to his throat.

'God bless Mrs Beecher,' she said. 'That woman thinks of everything.' If she was surprised to see Bill, she didn't let it show.

'He decided to question me,' she added. The boy on his knees had wet himself. 'I'm in the middle of explaining why that's a bad idea.'

Bill told Jerome to take the boy upstairs and find any files related to Lady Renhou. He and his wife needed a word. As an afterthought, he nodded to Jerome's machete. 'Remove his head if he gives you trouble.'

It was Bill's casualness that convinced the boy he meant it.

'What happens now?' Daisy demanded.

'We get you away from here.'

'After that,' Daisy said crossly. 'I mean after that.'

Bill's answer was interrupted by a crash from above. He'd reached the bottom of the stairs when Jerome appeared at the top, clutching his jaw. Keller's protégé was behind him. The boy smirked as he raised a Schmeisser. Jerome's machete was missing.

'Little shit said Lady Renhou's paperwork was—' Jerome fell as the boy hit him with the Schmeisser's stock.

'*Did I say you could talk?*'

Bill caught Jerome before he could crash into a wall.

'Your knife and those shotguns on the table.' He watched as Bill dutifully did as he was told.

'Now your pistol,' he said to Jerome.

Jerome pulled Hassel's Luger from his belt and put it beside the sawn-offs. He and Bill backed towards Daisy at a jerk of the Schmeisser. Daisy was looking murderous. 'Should have let me kill him,' she muttered.

'I thought you were teaching him a lesson?'

'All lessons end.'

'*Shut up.* All of you.'

The boy jerked his machine gun towards the cells, and Bill and Jerome obediently backed towards Daisy, who refused to move. The boy was turning his Schmeisser on her when they heard footsteps above . . .

166

The boy glared at Daisy and gripped his weapon tighter, glancing uneasily at the steps. Someone was at the top listening. The upper door shut firmly, and they could hear steps on the stairs.

'Ah,' von Neudeck said, shutting the lower door. 'Here we all are.' He held up the machete. 'I did wonder where this came from.' He smiled at the boy with the Schmeisser, looked slightly puzzled to see Jerome, and bowed slightly to Daisy.

Turning to Bill, he said, 'I was going to drop by your house, but I thought this might be where I'd find you. What with it being the night before your wife's trial.'

'You set this up?' Bill said.

'Yes and no. I mean, it was always going to be tonight, wasn't it? Given it wasn't last night, which would have been more sensible. What with Keller gone and the general arriving tomorrow. It must be time for you to leave. Surely? I mean, now you've cracked the safe and stolen the treasure . . .'

He gave a wintry smile.

'Does Keller know about that? I suspect not. But with him you can never be quite sure. Intelligence, ambition and absolutely no morals. He and the Party were made for each other . . . Did you do that?' He nodded to the blood trickling slowly down the English boy's neck.

'No,' Keller's protégé said. 'She did.'

'Should you even be down here?' von Neudeck asked him.

'I was going to question her.'

'Did Captain Keller ask you to?'

'He didn't say I couldn't.'

'A true barrack-room lawyer's reply.' Walking to the table, von Neudeck picked up the nearest sawn-off and looked at its butchered stock. 'Gebrüder Merkel,' he said sadly. 'Finest gunmaker in Europe. Matched pair too.'

He jerked the weapon at Jerome, Daisy and Bill to indicate that they should move away from the boy. Then he jerked it again, to say they should back into a corner.

They did as he ordered.

Putting the first gun down, he picked up the second. 'Such beautiful engraving, and the tightest tolerances in gunmaking. I have a pair at home.' He caught himself. 'I used to have a pair,' he said. 'Mind you, I used to have a home.'

He pointed the gun at the ceiling and pulled its first trigger.

It didn't fire and a pin didn't fall.

Looking surprised, he raised its muzzle to his nose and sniffed. 'Unfired,' he said. 'But also uncocked. So, either uncocked and unloaded. Or fired once already, on to an empty chamber.' Breaking the gun, he checked its breech and flipped it shut before anyone could move. 'How interesting.'

'Ernst,' Bill said.

Von Neudeck stopped. 'You know,' he said. 'That's the first time you've called me by my name. I always called you Sir William but you never progressed beyond my rank. I always knew, you know.'

'Knew what?' Bill demanded.

'That you weren't Sir William. I met him, you see, years ago. He was with His Highness when the Prince of Wales questioned me. He told me who my questioner was. A prince pretending not to be a prince and a one-armed, recently gassed young German officer pretending not to be afraid. He was beautiful, you know, back in the day. The prince.'

'I've seen the photographs.'

'Oh, you had to meet him to really feel it.'

'You've known all along?'

'Oh yes. It was impressive. The way you walked into that room at Renhou, headed for the safe and pretended to fumble its dial. Then produced a share certificate for a copper mine as evidence that you were you. Nicely English, nicely eccentric. And pretending to fumble the dial, a neat touch.'

'What gave me away?'

'Something about the eyes. Right colour obviously. But not nearly cruel enough. Then someone broke your knuckles, didn't they? After that, you and Miss American Spy had no choice but to team up. Quite the pair.'

Daisy scowled. 'I've no idea what you're talking about.'

'Of course you do,' von Neudeck said. 'You helped him crack the safe and steal its contents. Contents the Reich will happily kill, torture or blackmail to see returned. So much turns on them, you see.'

'She had nothing to do with any of this,' Bill said.

'How sweet,' von Neudeck said. 'Lying for the woman you love. Makes a change from lying to the woman you love.' He turned to Jerome. 'That's how it usually works, isn't it?'

Jerome wisely didn't answer.

'What now?' Bill asked.

Von Neudeck put down the shotgun he was holding, picked up the other, broke it open to check the load and flicked it shut.

'Now,' he said, 'is where it gets messy.'

Pivoting, he pointed it at the boy and pulled both triggers. The first pin hit an empty chamber, the second the brass primer of a 12-bore cartridge. Heavy shot blasted the boy into a side wall. The Schmeisser he'd been holding hit the floor.

Noise filled the cellar.

'He was a vulgar little shit,' said von Neudeck when the noise settled to ringing silence. 'His type always are.'

167

Alderney, same day

'They had my son,' von Neudeck said, half emptying his glass.

The unused shotgun lay on his lap, and a half-empty bottle of cheap brandy stood on a table in front of him. Jerome having gone upstairs with orders to find alcohol, and a warning that the colonel would kill Bill and Daisy if he didn't return.

Jerome now stood by the wall, Daisy beside him. Bill sat at one end of a table, with von Neudeck sat at the other. 'Drink up,' the colonel said.

Bill shook his head.

'Need a clear head for what comes later?' Von Neudeck blew out his breath. 'Yes, I suppose you do.'

'They had your son,' Bill nudged.

'In the camps. Outraging public decency. They found him in a public lavatory behind the Hauptbahnhof with another boy. He was a pervert, you see. Their words. He was in the camps and I was in disgrace and under house arrest in a rotting little castle in Prussia I couldn't afford to repair. And then Goering made me an offer. Well, it was more of an order. Go to Alderney and wait for the duke. If necessary, remind him who you are. So here I am. Why wouldn't I be? The Nazis terrify me. They represent everything I despise. Keller's kind gave us this war.'

'Your kind gave us the last one.'

'And we paid the price. Don't tell me we didn't.'

'When was your son arrested?'

'Three years ago. I'd retired by then, my daughter was married and my wife dead. I was skulking in the castle. Selling off cottages and fields to get by. I couldn't find a job, you see. The wrong kind of German.'

'What kind's that?'

'The kind that likes French wine, reads Jewish novelists, listens to Russian composers, votes for the wrong party . . .' Picking up his brandy, von Neudeck emptied his glass, banged it back on the table and gripped the shotgun, although Bill hadn't tried to move.

'This is where it ends,' von Neudeck said.

'You said *had*,' Bill said. 'They *had* my son. Who has him now?'

'God has him,' von Neudeck said. 'They told me he was still alive. That they'd release him if I gave up his friends and did what they wanted. They lied. They arrested his friends and hanged them as traitors. They didn't like Hitler, you see. All of them were executed except one. Otto. They sent him with me as a reminder . . .'

'Of what?'

'What happens to people who don't toe the line. It's all Goering's fault. The prince told Goering he remembered me. Goering decided it would be a nice touch if I was here to greet him. And so here I am.'

'You can't be certain your son's dead.'

'Oh, I can,' von Neudeck said crossly. 'The moment I was back in uniform I contacted the camp to ask. To them he was just a number. They didn't connect us because for them he had no name. I got a note back from a clerk saying he'd been dead two years.'

'Otto was the other boy behind the Hauptbahnhof?' Bill asked.

Von Neudeck picked up the shotgun. 'I knew you'd get there in the end.'

Before Bill could move, von Neudeck put the muzzle under his own chin, yanked the second trigger and jerked backwards, his chair going over as the back of his head disappeared. Brains, blood and fragments of bone smeared the brick behind him. Trapped within the cellar walls, the noise was deafening.

168

Alderney, Monday, 29 July 1940

Somewhere beyond Alderney's edge a submarine was preparing to surface. Some poor bastard had already been given the job of fetching him. Bill needed to get back to Renhou, retrieve the evidence about the duke, wrap it in something watertight, and get himself to his rendezvous below Aldoy Head.

'Check the way,' he told Jerome.

The Guernsey islander nodded. He had sense enough to know what Bill wanted to talk to Daisy about.

'You're leaving,' Daisy said.

'No. You are.'

'*Bill* . . .'

'I'm serious.'

'We can talk about it later.'

'Daisy. This is it. There is no later.'

'What about you?' she demanded. 'What about Mignon?'

'She's the best of the reasons I need to go back to Renhou.'

'She will be in her attic. Mrs Beecher will be in bed. The lights will be out, because it's after midnight. A slice of cake will be waiting for you on the kitchen table.'

Bill wanted to believe Daisy, but von Neudeck's suicide had shaken him.

'Anyway,' Daisy said, 'I can't take your place. You're the one they sent. Tell Mr Standish to tell President Roosevelt there's no evidence. He should tell the world I'm innocent. He'll know I'm not. All the same, tell him to make a fuss. Get it out there on CBS and NBC. Washington needs to pressure Berlin.'

'What if they don't manage it in time?'

'I'll be hidden,' Daisy promised.

'Where?' Bill demanded.

'Christ, does it matter? In the church tower, in a cave, in one of the ruined cottages on the cliffs. I'll take Mignon with me. We'll survive. Surviving is what we do.'

They found Jerome at the causeway, which was still underwater, although the tide had now turned. He had the dinghy waiting.

'I'll row,' he said.

He rowed well, as you'd expect from an islander, and they were nearing the jetty at Renhou when Daisy suddenly froze. Bill looked for what she'd seen.

Mignon scrambled to her feet.

'Throw me the line,' she shouted.

Dipping his oars to slow the boat, Jerome stowed his oars and turned to ward off the approaching jetty. Their dinghy came to an abrupt halt.

'Why are you still up?' Bill demanded.

'I was worried, wasn't I?' Mignon snatched at the bow rope.

Catching it, she looped it twice round a post and burst into tears. As she did, a figure stepped from the shadows and put his pistol to her head. Bill should have realized her voice was strained. Should have noticed she didn't ask why Jerome was there, or even greet Daisy.

'I'm sorry,' Mignon sobbed. 'I'm sorry.'

'We've been waiting for you,' Keller said.

169

Alderney, same day

Three things happened at once.

Pushing the dinghy back as far as its bow rope allowed, Jerome tipped himself sideways into the water – at which Keller took his pistol from Mignon's head and fired into the darkness – and Daisy rose from her seat to go for him.

'I'll kill her,' Keller warned.

His pistol was back at Mignon's head.

The girl was crying loudly.

'Mrs Beecher's niece,' Keller said. 'You think I'm stupid? You think I didn't know you were hiding a Jew? You were lying from the start. All of you . . .'

He turned to look for Jerome but the water was black and all they could hear was waves on rock. In the aftershock of a shot they shouldn't have been able to hear that, but Keller's pistol was silenced. A second later they heard faint splashing and Keller fired a second time.

The splashing stopped.

'Drag the dinghy in,' he ordered.

Bill reached for the rope and did so, wrapping it a couple more times round the post to keep it tight. He took his time and tried to look unflustered.

'Help your wife then,' Keller said.

Bill helped Daisy out and followed.

'You should have lied,' Keller told Daisy. 'You should have said Otto was blackmailing you. I'd have believed that of the little shit. Instead, you left me to wonder what reason you might have to kill him. That was a mistake. I'm going to need the contents of the safe.'

'What safe?'

Keller back-handed her.

'Christ,' she said. 'You're as predictable as William.'

Mignon glanced at Bill.

'Apparently, that's not William,' Keller said. 'I'd begun to wonder.'

170

Portugal, same day

The air was hot, even for Portugal. The wind had dropped and the pre-dawn was sticky with tomorrow's rain. Walking through the firs towards Salazar's hunting lodge felt and smelt like walking through a sauna fully clothed.

Fleming's Walther PPK felt heavy in its holster. Six rounds of .32 automatic, one already in the breech. Kill the duke, or not . . . It all turned on a telephone call. He'd be glad when this was over.

This time round there were no grand cars with flags on the bonnet, no swimming pools or elegant sweeps of beach. He could only imagine how Wallis Simpson was taking being locked down on a hilltop in a squat stone hunting lodge chosen for being defensible against Nazi attack.

A pair of SOE men guarded the rear gate. Two more patrolled the road below. Those were the ones you were meant to see. There were others, hundreds of others, mostly Portuguese special forces, hidden in the trees.

António de Oliveira Salazar, the hundredth prime minister of Portugal and its de facto dictator as leader of the Estado Novo, had taken the warning that Germany intended to abduct the Duke of Windsor seriously.

Fleming had met George VI, the duke's younger brother, and found him to be entirely trustworthy, if a little unimaginative. But even with that said, this whole business between the brothers had been handled extraordinarily badly. Fleming was a patriot and a royalist, like most men of his class, but he couldn't help feeling the British royal family were notoriously bad at learning from mistakes.

Although, so far, they'd kept their heads.

Unlike the French. Well, mostly.

The duke sat alone in the little courtyard, a cigarette in hand. Despite it being the wrong side of midnight, he didn't seem surprised to discover he had a visitor.

'Always you,' he said.

Fleming nodded. 'Always me.'

'Remind me of your name?'

'Fleming, sir.'

'Of course.' The duke reached for his coffee cup and found it empty. Fleming couldn't help but notice that his hands trembled.

'Does the embassy know you're here?'

'It was the embassy that sent me.'

The duke looked slightly shocked. 'I'd fetch some more coffee,' he said. 'But I'm not sure there's much point, is there? At least you waited until Wallis was asleep.' His face was haunted and his eyes empty. It was like looking into a tragedy mask and realizing there was no actor behind.

'Do it then,' he snapped.

'Sir . . . ?'

'Hurry up.' His voice was waspish.

The ex-king was a man unused to holding in his emotions, at least in recent years. And yet, as he turned his head to stare into the distance, he was a man with every emotion held so tightly in check that the air around him almost vibrated.

'Christ,' the duke said, 'if you're going to do it . . .'

Unexpectedly, given how fiercely he'd have said he despised the man, Fleming felt pity as well as a shock when he realized

485

the duke knew why he was here. Fleming prided himself on not lying, except to women or in the line of duty . . . and this was very definitely duty.

'I'm not here to kill you, sir,' he promised.

'You're not?'

Not yet anyway. Maybe not at all. Time will tell.

171

Alderney, same day

Keller stood with his back to Renhou's fireplace, a cigarette in his hand. He seemed entirely at ease, his tone almost conversational. If not for the silenced Beretta and the cat-like way he watched Bill, they could have been acquaintances at a club. Mignon, Mrs Beecher and Daisy lay face down on the carpet with orders not to move. Mrs Beecher was in her dressing gown.

'Don't worry,' Keller said. 'They're behaving.'

Bill tried not to stare.

'You looked sombre, you glanced at this' – Keller lifted his Beretta – 'you turned to check that your wife, her stray and your servant were behaving. Except she isn't your wife, is she? Because you're not Sir William. And yet, you seem willing to die for her. Interesting.'

Keller drew on his cigarette.

'And you *are* going to die. I'm sure you realize that.'

'We're all going to die,' Bill said.

Keller scowled. 'Now's not the time to get philosophical,' he said.

Until that point, he'd had the look of someone who finally had what he wanted: everyone around him under his complete control.

'You're convincing though,' Keller said. 'Right age, right physical shape, right height, strong facial likeness. And, of course, that withdrawal, which can be regarded as unease, haughtiness or damage, depending on how one wants to take it. Very English, whichever it is.'

'You'd know better than me,' Bill said.

Keller glared at him and Bill smiled.

It had been a throwaway jibe, based on von Neudeck's dislike of the man. What was interesting was how fiercely Keller reacted. 'Your mother was English, wasn't she?' Bill said. 'I think the general might have mentioned it.'

That was a lie, obviously.

Keller's face hardened. 'I never lived there.'

'He said you were born in Brighton.' It was von Neudeck who'd told Bill, obviously. But Bill wasn't about to tell Keller that.

'My father took me when I was tiny.'

'If you say so.'

Flipping open a silver case, Keller thumbed a cigarette, snapped the case shut and returned it to his pocket; then he dipped his head to a lighter. He made the action look effortless.

'You never went to Berlin, did you?' Bill said.

Keller smiled thinly. 'I'd like a drink,' he said. 'Which of your whiskies would you recommend?'

Mrs Beecher began climbing to her feet.

'Not you,' Keller said. 'He'll get it.'

When Bill returned, Mignon was crying, muffled sobs she was trying to smother. 'He kicked her,' Daisy said.

'I told her not to move.'

'You were standing on her hand.'

'Did I say you could talk?' Keller demanded.

Crouching in front of Daisy, he wrapped his fingers in her hair and lifted her head from the floor. When he put his pistol to her forehead, Daisy closed her eyes and Bill thought for a second that he'd pull the trigger, but instead he let her head drop. 'No,' he said, 'I don't think I did.'

'I'm going to kill you,' Daisy said.

Keller laughed. Taking the glass Bill offered, he raised it in a toast. 'So many wasps in one trap. Madame exposed as a spy and a thief, you exposed as an imposter and an enemy of the Reich, von Neudeck disgraced by his sheer credulity . . . As for Reichsmarschall Goering, who put Neudeck in place, he *will* be embarrassed. Admiral Canaris will see to that, with General von Hausen's help, of course.'

'This trap was General von Hausen's idea?'

Keller bristled slightly. 'What? Pretend to fly out, wait for you to free your bitch, catch you on your return? No, my idea entirely. The general merely agreed . . . Now.' Keller indicated Daisy. 'She should be behind bars. Do you want to tell me why she isn't? I'm surprised my sergeant was that careless.'

'He sees a woman.'

'Ah, the widow. You waited until he went? That was wise. The English brat?' Keller shrugged. 'Well, he was always disposable.'

'I don't imagine he knew that.'

'His kind never do.' Keller sniffed his Talisker and took a sip. 'Right,' he said. 'Tell me where she hid it.'

'Hid what?' Bill asked.

Turning to Mignon, Keller fired.

172

Alderney, same day

Screaming, Mignon rolled away, clutching her hand. Blood flowed from its edge, where Keller's shot had ripped flesh below her little finger. She was sobbing uncontrollably now.

'Flat to the ground,' Keller ordered.

The girl made herself lie still.

Stepping over her, Keller walked to where Mrs Beecher lay, pointed the muzzle at her leg and made a pffft sound, exaggerating the silence of a suppressed shot. Then he turned and stared at Daisy as critically as any biologist examining an animal he intends to dissect.

'So many targets,' he said.

'You want von Neudeck's place? Is that what this is about?'

Keller's face darkened and he stepped in close, leaning until his face almost touched Bill's. 'Is that what you think of me? Is that who you think I am? Someone who'd settle for *this*?' His wave dismissed Renhou, Alderney and the other Channel Islands beyond. 'This is a staging post, a stepping stone. I intend to be at Hitler's side when we conquer England.'

'Your mother was English. He won't like that.'

Keller snarled, 'My father was entirely German.'

The mention of his mother had focused Keller's anger, which was fine because it was meant to. If anyone was to act as a lightning rod for his fury it had to be Bill. Besides, manipulating people was what Bill did – had been what he did. There was a way out of this. There had to be.

Keep him talking, Bill told himself.

The longer Keller talked the longer Bill kept them all alive. Then again, the longer he talked the less time to reach the submarine. He looked at the Beretta in Keller's hand. Its built-in suppressor. The unswerving certainty in Keller's eyes. And he knew the man had no intention of letting any of them leave Renhou alive. This was simply Keller indulging himself, enjoying his power.

Feed his ambition.

'That's how this works?' Bill asked. 'Retrieve what was stolen and General von Hausen will give you a place at Hitler's side?'

Something flickered across Keller's face.

It was lightning fast, and the speed with which the man bit down on it said that it mattered. Bill had sat across poker tables from people that studiedly expressionless. It usually meant their hands weren't as good as . . . Suddenly everything slotted into place for Bill as cleanly as tumblers aligning inside a safe door. He smiled.

'Von Hausen doesn't know it's missing, does he?'

Yanking back its hammer, Keller depressed his Beretta's trigger, only keeping the hammer from falling with his thumb. 'You told von Neudeck you had a daughter,' he said. 'Does Mignon remind you of her?' Mignon's whole body tensed. Bill had always known she'd be the one the captain would shoot first.

'Well?' Keller demanded.

'Let her up,' Bill replied. 'Let them all up.'

'You'll give me the contents of the safe?'

'I'll give you everything.'

Daisy was first on her feet and she hurried to Mignon, who was shaking too badly to stand on her own. Wrapping her arm round her, Daisy turned for the door.

'Where are you going?' Keller demanded.

'She's wet herself. She's bleeding.'

'Revolting child.'

'You'd wet yourself if some thug shot you.'

'You realize, of course, that if you or your Jew tries to make a run for it, I'll kill our fake Sir William here, and then hunt you both down? It won't be—'

Pushing Mignon from the drawing room, Daisy shut the door behind her before Keller could finish. Bill thought Keller would call them back but instead he scowled.

'Women. They understand nothing.'

'Should I make tea?' Mrs Beecher asked Bill.

'Coffee might be better,' Bill said.

'Very good, sir.'

'Just us,' said the captain, turning to Bill. 'I imagine you armed yourself while fetching my whisky. I suggest you put whatever you took on the table.'

Bill opened his mouth to deny it.

'Let's make a deal,' Keller said. 'You deny it. I find something. I kill the first person to walk through that door.'

Bill put his kitchen knife on the table.

'Very sensible. Anything else?'

Bill shook his head.

'Quite certain?'

'Yes,' Bill said. 'Quite certain.'

It was only after Keller smiled that Bill remembered the blood-crusted garrotte rolled like a guitar wire in his pocket. The thought of Keller realizing whose blood it was made him glad that the captain was feeling infallible.

The door opened, and Daisy was the first through it.

'What?' she demanded, when both men stared.

173

Alderney, same day

Bill needed Keller out of Renhou.

Away from the girl who reminded him of his daughter and the woman he wished was really his wife. Away from Mrs Beecher, who'd made being ordinary extraordinary by turning behaving as if everything was normal into an act of heroism. Bill had two things going for him. First, most of the Germans on the island believed Keller was in Berlin; von Neudeck certainly had. And secondly, Berlin didn't know their safe was empty.

That was Keller's weak point. All Bill had to do was figure out how to use it. 'If you could chase up that coffee?' he told Daisy.

He thought she'd tell him to do it himself. Then she went, stony-faced and tight-shouldered, leaving Keller, Mignon and Bill alone. They waited, then waited some more. It was Keller who moved first, Bill and Mignon following. The kitchen was empty, its garden door open. They were about to head out, when Daisy came back, a hurricane lamp held high.

'The bloody woman's gone.'

'Where?' Keller demanded.

'Somewhere else,' Bill said. 'If she has any sense.'

A kettle was boiling on the range. An open tin of Nescafé had a teaspoon dug into its middle. Digestive biscuits waited on a plate. The captain looked from the tray to the door, then turned his attention to Bill, who'd glanced at his Rolex.

'Expecting company?' he asked.

When Bill hesitated, Keller's eyes narrowed.

'I'll do you a deal,' Bill said.

'You're in no position to negotiate.'

'You don't know what I'm offering,' Bill said. 'The contents of the safe, an Iron Cross, promotion – two promotions – a place at Hitler's side.'

'What's to stop me winning those myself?'

'My way's quicker. But it comes at a price.'

'And what is this price?'

'My wife is allowed to leave Alderney.'

'She's not—'

'For the purposes of this she is. She's also an American citizen, and America is currently a neutral country. She has friends in Washington and diplomatic immunity. You don't want to be the person who brings America into this war.'

Keller looked thoughtful. 'And in return?'

'You get back everything stolen. That gives you the Duke of Windsor. It gives you the Duke of Windsor standing at Hitler's side, and you and your Abwehr general in the entourage behind. Now I'll tell you how to get your Iron Cross . . .'

'Don't,' Daisy said. 'You can't do this.'

Keller smiled. 'It seems he can.'

Daisy and Keller returned together from collecting the envelope, watched by Bill and Mignon from the hall. Daisy's face was white with anger, Keller's smug. He weighed the envelope in his hand.

'Should I read it?'

'You don't have time,' Bill said.

'Of course I do. I have all the time in the world.'

'No,' Bill said. 'We need to move.'

Keller looked amused. 'Who says you're going anywhere?'

His Beretta was pointed at Bill's heart. 'What's to stop me killing you?'

Mignon was obviously wondering the same.

'Because you need me to signal to a submarine. This is where you earn your Iron Cross. If I don't send the signal, a canoe won't set out to collect me, and you'll never be the hero who captured a British commando as he came ashore to spirit away the contents of a German safe.'

'Christ, Bill,' Daisy said. 'Whose side are you on?'

'Mine.' He smiled at Keller. 'Just think of it. Capturing a commando, preventing critical information falling into London's hands, thwarting Churchill's personal plans. It'll be the Iron Cross First Class with Oak Leaves. You'll be famous.'

174

Portugal, same day

'So,' the duke said. 'Why *are* you here?'

He had the drawling upper-class accent one would expect. It was Fleming's own, although he had to work a little harder to maintain it. And Fleming doubted he'd ever quite manage that unmistakably patrician air of languid boredom, which had descended the moment the Duke of Windsor decided Fleming wasn't about to kill him.

'Look around you,' Fleming said. 'There are special forces everywhere. You can't see them but that's the point. The longer you delay leaving for the Bahamas, the greater the Nazis' chances of reaching you. And you *are* leaving for the Bahamas. As of now you have no choice.'

'Look—' the duke said.

'We're waiting for a telephone call,' Fleming said, talking over him. 'What happens next depends on that call. It's going to be a long night.'

'The Bahamas are my best option?'

'Believe me, sir. You'll like the other options less. We've reserved a suite on the SS *Excalibur*, with ten cabins for staff and men to keep you safe.'

'My prison guards, you mean.'

'They're there to keep you safe.'

'Why *not* shoot me now?' The duke ran a tired hand through his hair. 'A suite, a dozen cabins. It all seems a little elaborate. Surely now's simpler than waiting until I'm at sea?'

'No one wants you dead, sir.'

Not unless we have to.

The duke smiled thinly. 'You haven't met my sister-in-law, have you?'

175

Alderney, same day

Fuck this, Daisy thought, pushing her tongue against her cheek. Keller's punch had been hard. Still, at least the bastard hadn't shot her.

Life had taught her pragmatism.

She tried her wrists. They were tied as tight as she expected. Houdini would have had a key up his sleeve. She wasn't Houdini, but she was trained, and had forced her knuckles together and kept her wrists apart as much she could when Keller wrenched her hands behind her back.

That in itself wasn't enough to get her out of this. Although it would help in the escape, provided she was bloody-minded enough to keep at it, and didn't mind exhausting herself – and losing half the skin on her wrists.

Express pain, the manual said.

She'd winced and gasped as Keller yanked her bonds taut. He'd liked that, obviously. She'd groaned in agony as he lashed her to the chair, yanking his rope tight across her chest, even as she tensed her arms and made her shoulders as broad as possible. Keller had tied her ankles last.

He'd been in a hurry. That was the best thing she had going for her. He'd needed to get to the headland and needed to get there fast. The submarine would go if it didn't get the signal soon, Bill kept telling him.

By the end, he was practically shouting it.

He could have got her killed. Bill probably didn't realize

that the quickest way to incapacitate a prisoner was not having a prisoner in the first place. She'd have killed Keller if the positions were reversed. Unless she had a use for him later.

Maybe he had a use for her?

If only as a sacrificial victim for General von Hausen to condemn. That thought didn't fill her with joy. Gritting her teeth, Daisy began working her hands free.

It hurt. It was always going to.

176

Alderney, same day

'He's going to kill us,' Mignon said. 'The moment you've signalled. You know that, don't you?' She and Bill were climbing to Aldoy Head, trying not to get caught on brambles or trip in rabbit holes in the half-dark.

Dawn was an hour away, maybe a little more.

How long would it take to reach the top? Five minutes. Ten? Not long for Bill to make a move that would save them, or mess up and prove Mignon right. He would save Mignon and Daisy. He had to. Even at the cost of saving himself.

'Did you hear me?' Mignon hissed.

'I heard you,' Bill said.

'More father-daughter endearments?'

Bill was doing his best to ignore Keller and the pistol he held at Bill's back. In reality he knew exactly where Keller was, and had the Beretta's pressure to remind him. The torch Bill had taken from Renhou was turned off.

It wasn't much of a club and precious little use against a pistol but it was what he had, and his tale of needing to signal the submarine had bought them time. Time was everything. Bill had no doubt Keller intended to kill them. The man wasn't bothering to pretend otherwise.

'When is this submarine due?'

'Now,' Bill told him. 'It's out there waiting. If it doesn't get a signal soon, it will go home.'

'And come back tomorrow.'

'No,' Bill said. 'This is one time only. If I don't signal tonight, they assume I'm dead and the mission aborts.'

'And what was your mission?'

'To steal that envelope and deliver it to Churchill personally.'

'I don't understand,' Mignon said, sounding sad. 'I thought you were good. Why are you telling him this?'

Keller wanted to say London couldn't have known about the envelope. That Berlin had kept it secret, but here Bill was . . . 'I *knew* you were a spy,' he said.

'You knew nothing of the sort. If you had, you'd have arrested me on the spot. And I'm not a spy. I'm a thief. A good one.'

'You're not military intelligence?'

'They were going to hang me for murder.'

Bill heard Keller suck his teeth. Beside him, Mignon shifted away.

177

Twisting her wrists, Daisy felt the rope dig into her flesh as she fought to loosen it. Sisal stretched. Not as much as she'd like but enough. Her wrists were rubbed raw, most likely bleeding.

Pushing one hand down, she tried to make the other as narrow as possible as she pulled it up. Rope scraped across already raw skin.

It hurt. She couldn't bear to admit how much.

Almost there.

Daisy had been telling herself this for the last five minutes. It had to be close to being true. She yanked again, refusing to give in to the pain. She could do it. More importantly, she needed to. She had to.

She wasn't going to wait for Keller to come back and do whatever he had in mind for her before putting a bullet through her head or fixing a show trial where the outcome would be the same. Besides, Mignon and Bill were up there.

Either they'd need her help, or they wouldn't.

But they were going to get it. Whatever.

Yanking one wrist against the other and no longer caring about the pain, Daisy gritted her teeth and fought against Keller's knots, feeling one of her hands finally begin to work free.

178

'This is high enough,' Keller said.

Mignon stopped, her hand on a bush to hold her steady, one foot on a rock, the other trying to find a grip on the dirt. Bill was behind her. She waited to see what he would do.

'No, it's not,' he said. 'We have to signal from the top. If it's not from the top the canoe won't launch.' He gripped his torch like a talisman. The horizon was a fraction lighter, but the stars were thin, and the three of them stood in shadow.

'If you're lying . . .' Keller said.

'You'll shoot me.'

Keller grunted in agreement.

You'll shoot me anyway, Bill thought.

He put his hand to Mignon's shoulder and felt her flinch.

'Trust me,' he whispered.

He hoped she heard.

The top of the hill was close, fifteen paces of path, rock and thorn. Mignon might be able to escape into the gloom if he told her to run. It was unlikely Keller would miss him though.

He could hear crows cawing, disturbed by their arrival. Above them a hawk screeched, frighteningly near. The crows fell silent, then started cawing again, angrier than ever.

'Hurry up.' Keller's voice was tight, his patience fraying.

When Mignon gasped, Bill thought she'd twisted her ankle.

'Hurt yourself?' he asked.

'No . . . Yes. Doesn't matter.'

Before Bill could ask what was wrong, Mignon reached the top, stepped to one side and held out her hand for him. Bill saw them then. Aldoy Head had grown a half-circle of standing stones.

Bill was still making sense of that when Keller pushed him out of the way, and Bill cannoned into Mignon, who tripped.

Now or never.

Spinning round, Bill swung his torch like a club, catching Keller a blow to the head that he half ducked, his training kicking in. Staggering backwards, the German found his balance, raised his Beretta and fired.

Muzzle flash lit the gloom.

Mignon flung herself sideways, the cliff's edge crumbling beneath her feet, and she dropped from sight. Her cry could be heard above the crack of Keller's silencer and the fall of stones on the beach below.

Her scream for help was almost a relief.

Bill was hurtling for the edge when Keller grabbed him. Pushing his pistol under Bill's jaw, Keller ground its silencer into Bill's throat.

'Let her fall,' he ordered.

'If she does,' a standing stone said, 'you die too.'

Raising a crossbow, Eddie's uncle pointed it at Keller's heart.

179

Alderney, same day

Daisy raced for Renhou's front door but changed her mind, grabbed a pair of binoculars from a cupboard in the hall and swerved for the main stairs, taking them two at a time. She'd be too late to change whatever was happening, unless she could change it from here. Even if she wasn't, she needed to know what was going on before rushing in.

In her bedroom, she yanked away the inner compartment to her writing case and scattered rifle parts across her bed. Her hands ached, her fingers hurt, her wrists were missing half their skin. She didn't let that get in her way. It took her seconds to snap the sniper rifle together, jack a round into its breech and fix its scope.

It took her longer to fix the weird camera she'd been given to the top of the scope, and wire it to the camera case, which was really its battery.

Faster, she told herself.

She was still cross with herself for not having practised that properly when she reached the top of Renhou's lone turret and scanned the headland. She could see figures in the half-light, more of them than made sense.

The binoculars brought them closer.

Bill, Keller, Mrs Beecher, the uncle of the boy Mignon had liked.

Where was Mignon?

Seven minutes, Mr Standish's courier had said. That's how

long the battery would last. How should she know when to start looking? Maybe she shouldn't have tipped gasoline across the floors of the cellar and set candles on petrol-soaked rags.

Maybe that should have waited.

If she didn't start looking, she wouldn't know. Setting aside the binoculars, Daisy lifted the rifle, put the scope to her eye, fingers reaching for its switch.

180

Alderney, same day

Keller's mistake was to remove his pistol from Bill's jaw. As he turned to shoot Eddie's uncle, Bill grabbed his wrist, grasped the Beretta with his other hand and twisted so savagely bones broke.

Now they both had hands that didn't work.

Slamming his forehead into Keller's face, Bill yanked the pistol from his fingers and hurled it over the edge before Keller could grab it back. Then the captain was on him, Keller's ruined hand hanging limp but a dagger already in the other.

He stabbed at Bill, who stumbled back.

Keller's next slash was for Bill's throat. It was devastatingly fast and Bill only just ducked away. He came at Bill and Bill twisted to one side.

'Save Mignon,' he begged.

Eddie's uncle ran for the cliff edge and dropped to his knees. Mrs Beecher abandoned her place in the standing stones to join him. These were the people she'd gathered, Bill realized. She must have raced from the kitchen to Braye, then down to where the Guernsey islanders slept.

When Keller slashed again, Bill blocked, stepped back and kicked at Keller's broken fingers. Luck was with him. Keller gasped and Bill kicked again, missing this time. Keller's reintroduction to pain had unnerved him.

He began backing away, knife in hand.

The standing stones formed into a circle around them.

'No you don't,' one of them said. The scrapyard man had a wrench dangling at his side. When Keller slashed at him, the man laughed. He wasn't worried or flustered. If anything, he seemed to be enjoying himself.

'You'll be shot,' Keller said.

'He killed your sergeant, Sir William did. He's going to kill you now.'

'You're lying.'

'It was a nasty death.'

Keller stabbed savagely and the man grinned.

'You've been played,' Bill told Keller. 'The submarine's out there, right enough. It didn't need signalling though. Not from the beach and not from here. And Pete's right, you know. Whatever happens to the rest of us, this is where *you* die.'

Keller flung himself at Bill.

The man had flipped his dagger, so that it trailed from the edge of his hand, almost slitting Bill's throat as it swept past. 'I'm going to gut you,' Keller said.

He meant it too.

Bill could feel the gaze of the scrapyard man, sense the other Guernsey islanders at the cliff edge. They were waiting to see how this ended. Bill knew how it ended. It ended in death. The question was whose.

Pete could have split Keller's head with his wrench, the priest from St Anne's could have clubbed him with the knobkerrie he carried, Georgie could probably have picked him up one-handed and thrown him off Aldoy Head. Hell, Eddie's uncle could have already nailed him with the crossbow.

They didn't though. They wouldn't. They were here to witness.

This would be allowed to run its course.

Keller was younger and better trained. But the scrapyard man's boast that Bill had killed Hassel had shaken him. He'd also started keeping his injured hand out of Bill's way. In that they were even. Bill's injured hand throbbed from where he'd blocked Keller's earlier blow. Until tonight Bill had hoped his killing days were done. If he got out of this alive, then God willing, they would be.

They circled each other in silence.

The world around them fell away. The end was close. They both knew it. Only one of them would crawl away. Maybe not even one.

The captain held his blade at groin height. It was near impossible for Bill to see unless he took his gaze from his face, and harder still to stop. Keller put all his strength into his next blow, ripping his dagger up in the hope of opening Bill to the ribs. Cut an enemy like that and he'd slip on his own guts. Bill escaped, but only just.

Stepping forward, Keller stabbed again.

181

Alderney, same day

As the darkness lit to a luminous green, the figures on the headland jumped into focus, unnervingly bright. Mrs Beecher and the priest from La Ville; a man Daisy thought was a Guernsey islander; another she didn't recognize. They filled her cross hairs one after another. She could have killed any with a single shot.

Mignon. Where the hell was Mignon?

She looked for Bill and found Keller. He was holding a knife and his face said he intended to use it. He had the look of a man readying to strike. Before she could pull the trigger, Bill lurched into her sights.

They were circling, she realized. Both intent on killing the other while watched by men standing round them.

Men who insisted on getting in the way of anything resembling a clear shot. It was a brutal fight, and Bill looked to be losing. The quickest way to save him was take out all the onlookers to give herself a clean shot.

She didn't know them; she didn't owe them anything. She had enough rounds to do it. Daisy's finger tightened on the trigger but she stopped herself. Bill would be upset. Even if she did it to save him.

Mignon? Where was . . . ?

There was no time to worry about that. Keller jabbed, and Bill only just stumbled back in time to avoid a wound that would have opened him from groin to chest.

Get out of my way, damn you.

She didn't want to kill the onlookers to give herself a clear shot, but she would if she had to. Daisy knew herself well enough to know that.

182

Alderney, same day

Just in time, Bill saw the blow coming.

Grabbing Keller's wrist, he held it away from him as he slammed his forehead into Keller's face again, stunning himself and feeling the man's nose break.

The Abwehr captain reeled back, blood pouring into his mouth.

Finding his balance, he stabbed at Bill to keep him back. Bill grabbed for Keller's wrist, but Keller was waiting. He was younger, fitter, fighting for his life . . . Battle-hardened more recently, better trained too. Sweeping Bill's feet from under him, he followed Bill down, his dagger yanked free from Bill's grip, his arm already raised to plunge it home.

Bill saw the blow coming.

Then blood exploded from Keller's hand and the dagger spun away. The bullet passed through Keller's fingers, taking the knife with it before anyone watching even heard the sound of a muffled shot.

Both men staggered to their feet.

Bill didn't know where Daisy had fired from. He didn't care.

This time he didn't hesitate. He slammed his elbow into Keller's throat as Lieutenant Fairbairn had instructed. Lifted his arm and chopped the nape of Keller's neck. The man went down and was trying to kneel when Bill kicked him in the side of his head, rolled him on to his front, knelt astride him and yanked his head back until he heard his spine snap.

183

Alderney, same day

The rocky ledge on which Mignon balanced narrowed at both ends before falling away to the beach below. The bramble she gripped was making her fingers bleed. 'Every time I move, the roots shift. I'm scared.'

'The bullet didn't hit you?' Bill said.

'I felt it go past.' Her laugh was shaky. 'Like a wasp. I thought I was dead. I thought he was going to kill you.'

'He tried. I need you to hang on.'

'*I'm trying.*'

There was a flash of the Mignon he remembered in her voice. Bill felt someone put a hand on his shoulder. It was the padre from St Anne's.

'Your wife's here,' he said.

'Look after Mignon,' Bill said. 'I'll be back.'

Bill reached Daisy a few seconds before flames burst from the ground-floor windows of Renhou, turning its granite walls pink. She seemed barely out of breath, despite having run up the slope, and she was grinning.

'All that gasoline,' she said. 'How could I resist?' She hesitated. 'You understood what the shotgun meant? You found the school trunk?'

Bill nodded.

She'd set fire to a house she loathed, with the half-mummified body of her equally hated husband inside. Bill imagined she regarded it as a fitting end to both.

'Where's Mignon?' she asked.

Daisy lost her smile the moment he told her.

Mrs Beecher knelt in tears, looking frantically from the house she'd served since she was a girl, to Mignon on a ledge twelve feet below, unable to save either. Bill retook his place, moving Mrs Beecher aside gently.

Aldoy Head glowed with the flames that had begun to consume Renhou. The building was ablaze. The oak panelling in the hall undoubtedly walled with fire, the curtains in the drawing room burning, the heraldic beasts on the great stairs bathed in flame. It wouldn't be long before the roof caved in.

It wouldn't be long before the Germans arrived either.

Von Neudeck, Otto, Keller, his sergeant and the quisling boy were dead. The other Germans on this island might not come, but the flames were rising and the fire would soon be fierce enough to be seen in Guernsey. It was probably already visible in France. Someone would raise the alarm.

'I've sent for a rope,' the priest said.

'It won't get here soon enough,' Daisy replied. She gripped Bill's shoulder. 'Look at her,' she said. 'She's shaking so badly she can barely balance. She hasn't got the strength to climb a rope if we had one. One of us has to go down.'

184

Alderney, same day

'Undo my splint,' Bill said.

Daisy took his hand, found the start of the bandage and unwound it, discarding the splint that kept his hand rigid. Flexing his fingers, Bill tried not to wince.

'I want everyone's belt,' he shouted.

It took those around him a second to realize what Bill intended and then they were scrambling to join their belts together into a rope.

'That won't hold both of you,' Daisy muttered.

'It won't need to.' Wrapping one end of the makeshift rope round his injured hand, Bill lowered himself over the edge and felt for a foothold, feeling grit scrape free and hearing Mignon cry out.

'To the side,' she said.

The men holding the belts shifted, and Bill crawled sideways, until he was no longer directly above her.

'There's a foothold to your left,' Daisy called.

She was leaning out so far Bill was worried she'd fall.

Moving his foot as she directed, Bill found rock and braced himself as the men above lowered more belt and he felt for a foothold below that.

'The ledge is shifting,' Mignon said.

'Hang on.'

'*I'm trying,*' she said. '*I'm trying.*'

Bill felt for a handhold, moved too quickly and almost lost

his balance, yanking on the belts to catch himself as he gasped in pain. The side of the cliff was lit by flames from Renhou, and Bill could see how far he'd fall. He said a prayer for those taking up the tension above.

'Hurry,' Mignon begged.

Bill found a foothold, a handhold, and then . . .

He tried to step down and the belts jerked him back. Looking up, Bill tried to work out where it had snagged and realized it hadn't. The men above had simply run out of makeshift rope.

'Move closer,' Bill shouted.

'The first man's too close already.'

'I'll do it.' Stepping into view, Georgie took the belt from the others, wrapped one end round his fist, and fed the slack over the edge. Bill saw his shoulders set as he readied to take Bill's weight.

'Hurry,' Daisy said.

'How much more belt have we got?' Bill asked.

'Lots,' Georgie said. The man released a little more and Bill stepped down to Mignon's ledge. It was even narrower than he'd imagined.

'Careful,' Mignon said.

The ledge started crumbling under the extra weight, rocks tumbling into the sea below. Bill held tighter to the belt, and heard Georgie grunt with pain. The man's back must have been in agony.

Stretching for Mignon's hand, Bill stepped sideways.

'We can do this,' he said.

She smiled and her fingers touched Bill's, and he saw the point she realized the bramble she clung to had pulled away. He heard its last roots rip, heard the dirt tumble beneath her feet, and the people above him cry out . . .

185

Portugal, same day

'All right,' the duke said finally. 'I'll accept that Bertie's wife hating me doesn't mean Bertie wants me shot. But you know, Winston would if he thought he could get away with it.'

'Sir . . .'

'He had a go, you know. On the road out of Paris. Damn nearly succeeded. Bloody round of .303 passed right between us.'

'That wasn't London,' Fleming said forcefully. 'And nor was the problem with your brakes. Even von Hoyningen-Huene was shocked by how close he came to killing you. His men had tampered with them to give you a scare.'

'Really?'

'Really,' Fleming promised.

'Well, there it is.' The duke looked at his Omega. 'I know it's ridiculously early but I might have some breakfast.'

Inside the house a telephone began ringing. President Salazar's own. It sounded unnaturally loud. No one went to answer it, because everybody inside had been told that if the telephone rang, they were to leave it alone.

'I'd better get that,' the duke said.

'It's for me,' Fleming said.

He unbuttoned his jacket on his way in, picked up the telephone's receiver and sat himself on a chair.

'Yes,' he told the operator. 'I'll hold.'

As he waited, he removed his Walther PPK from its

holster, screwed on a short silencer and rested his weapon on the table. If he had to do it, he'd do it fast, the moment he returned. The duke wouldn't even see the shot coming.

'Yes,' he said. 'It's me.'

Fleming listened carefully, then asked his contact in London to repeat what he'd just said.

'You're certain? The package has been collected. I can stand down?'

Satisfied that this was the case, he stood up, put the receiver back in its cradle, and breathed a deep sigh of relief. He didn't know if killing an ex-king counted as regicide. He'd been hoping not.

Having removed its silencer, and put his Walther PPK back in its holster, Fleming went to order breakfast for the duke. Fleming had opinions about breakfast. To be worthy of that name, it needed to include black coffee, bacon, eggs, scrambled not fried, marmalade and toast.

On his way to the kitchens, he decided to order some for himself too.

186

"'I am the resurrection and the life, saith the Lord. He that believeth in me, though he were dead, yet shall he live: and whosoever liveth and believeth in me, shall never die . . .'"

It would be untrue to say the graveyard at St Anne's was crowded. The patch between the transept and the chancel on the north side was busy though. The freshly dug grave looked raw, the coffin newly made and hastily varnished. All of those who'd been on the cliff three nights before were there and some who weren't.

The priest was waiting for them to settle.

The coffin had been carried from the church and placed on canvas straps that would be used to lower it into the ground. All that remained were the Prayers of Commendation and Farewell, and the Committal itself.

Mignon's funeral was almost over.

It shouldn't have been Christian. But Bill, Daisy and Mrs Beecher had decided to ignore that. What mattered was that a funeral happened. Eddie's uncle had shined his shoes. Pete from the scrapyard wore an old tweed jacket stretched tight across his shoulders. Washed and shaved, he looked like a different person.

Just as the priest was about to begin the Commendation, a Mercedes flying a swastika drew up on Victoria Street. The man who climbed out struggled with the gate for a moment, then straightened up and headed for the grave.

He was dressed sombrely, as befitted a man at a funeral. A simple field marshal's uniform, with loden cloak and the bare minimum of decorations.

'May I . . . ?'

Bill moved aside to make room.

As the priest began his celebration of Mignon's life, Reichsmarschall Goering stood at ease, his hands behind his back. Bill doubted very much Mignon would have recognized herself in the kind, obedient and thoughtful island girl she'd apparently been. After the Commendation came Prayers of Farewell, then the coffin was lowered on its straps and the straps pulled away.

Within a few minutes the only people left were Daisy, Goering, Bill and the priest, who was muttering private words over the grave.

'You look younger without the beard,' Goering said.

'Thank you,' Bill replied. 'You came especially for this?'

The field marshal was obviously tempted to say yes, but the truth won out. 'I'm siting a Luftwaffe HQ and listening post at La Ville. And, to be honest, I just wanted to stand on conquered British soil. I thought, since I was already here, I might as well . . . Obviously, Berlin think I'm in Paris.'

'Obviously,' Bill said.

'Who would have thought it?' said Goering with an unnerving smile.

Bill waited for him to elaborate. Instead, he turned to include Daisy in the conversation and his face was suddenly mournful.

'I'm so sorry about your château. That must be such a blow. Entirely destroyed, I'm told. Barely an outer wall standing.'

'If that,' Daisy said.

'And about the girl, obviously.' Goering glanced apologetically at Daisy before turning back to Bill. 'Ernst told me that you had an indiscretion when younger. There was a child, a girl. It's not unheard of for such indiscretions to be taken into the family. Discreetly, of course. I wondered if perhaps . . .'

Bill looked away. Goering didn't take it amiss.

'Ernst von Neudeck murdered,' Goering said. 'His driver, your girl. Renhou destroyed, papers stolen . . . The Abwehr insist they couldn't have known Keller was a British agent, that he'd steal papers and flee. I disagree. The Führer disagrees. Keller's mother was English, you know. There will be changes. Permanent changes. Admiral Canaris is disgraced. The Führer has told von Hausen he's lucky not to be shot.' Goering smiled. It was a very wide smile.

'And the duke?' Bill said.

'It would have complicated things, you know. Having to behave. Having to pretend that it was all being done in his name. Now, when the invasion happens, it will be cleaner. Much cleaner.'

'You mean messier,' Daisy said.

Goering smiled. 'For a while.'

'So, you don't need me here after all?' Bill asked.

'Need you?' Goering said.

From Daisy's expression, she was wondering where Bill's question was heading. He wasn't quite sure, but he didn't doubt she'd interrupt soon enough if it took a direction she didn't like.

'It's just . . .' Bill said. 'I'd like to travel.'

'We'd like to travel,' Daisy said firmly.

'Where?' Goering sounded interested.

Anywhere but here.

'Casablanca,' Daisy said, before Bill could reply. There was a steely glint in her eye. 'We've always fancied Casablanca.'

'Always,' Bill agreed.

Reichsmarschall Goering lit a cigarette without offering Bill or Daisy one. He drew deep and stared at the church wall. His mind was on other things. 'You saw no evidence of an affair? Your girl and Keller.'

'*She was a child*,' Bill said sharply.

'You'd have known if anyone did?'

'Yes,' Bill said, 'I would.'

'You believe Keller tried to make her go with him?'

'I can see no other reason he'd drag her down to the beach. I'm assuming he *was* picked up by submarine?'

'So we believe.'

Goering shifted uneasily and Bill waited.

'It was the priest here who identified her body?'

'I couldn't,' Bill said simply.

Goering obviously wanted to know how badly she'd been battered. From the look on his face he'd been told it was horrific.

He held his peace.

Berlin wanted the deaths on Alderney and Keller's disappearance hushed up as thoroughly as possible. It was better that way. Sir William and Lady Renhou leaving for warmer climes was simply a bonus.

187

Alderney, same day

The evening news from the BBC for Thursday, 1 August was reassuringly matter of fact.

The Norwegian turncoat Vidkun Quisling had travelled from Oslo to Berlin to pay homage to Hitler. The Norwegian king in exile, Haakon, had urged his people to continue their resistance to the Nazi invaders. French soldiers in Marrakesh were refusing to accept Vichy rule. Nazi bombers had been turned back over the Midlands by British fighters. Britain had suffered some shipping losses in the Channel. A contingent of exiled Czech pilots were forming up into their own fighter squadron. Britain stood ready to meet any invasion. The Duke of Windsor had embarked on a steamer in Lisbon in readiness to take up his duties as Governor of the Bahamas.

188

Marrakesh, Thursday, 15 August 1940

'Really?' said Bill, when Daisy was done explaining.

'Really,' Daisy replied. 'You asked if I was there to kill the duke and I promised you that I wasn't. That was the truth of it. The absolute truth.'

'You were after the duchess all along?'

'If we killed the duke, we killed one of yours. If we killed Wallis, we killed one of our own. It was an easier call. Although your lot would probably have got the blame. At least from Berlin. That's not the point . . . They feed off each other like vampires. Kill one and you destroy the other.'

On the afternoon that Sir William and Lady Renhou arrived in Marrakesh from Casablanca they checked into La Mamounia and took the sultan's suite. They were in Marrakesh because the house they'd bought in Casablanca was being redecorated. That night, Bill lay in bed and stared at the ceiling fan.

'What are you thinking?' Daisy asked eventually.

'About Mignon.'

Daisy's hand found his and gripped tight. She rolled in close but it was simply to hold him. The heat in Morocco, even at night, was such that she quickly rolled away again and threw back the sheet.

'I'm going to adopt her,' Bill said.

Daisy laughed. 'Of course you are,' she said.

Mignon was arriving next week. Flying out under a new name from London, via Lisbon. On a mail plane that would undoubtedly hold its full consignment of n'er-do-wells and spies.

189

Marrakesh, same day

In that room at La Mamounia, two weeks after Mignon's funeral, in the space between waking, sleep and dreams, with a fan thudding overhead and Daisy drifting off beside him, Bill remembered Mignon's hand reaching for his and the sound the roots made when they ripped free.

Even thinking about it made him shiver.

'Please,' she'd said.

'*Reach.*'

Her fingers had found his and slipped away.

He'd grabbed for her, no longer caring if he fell too, and felt Mignon's hand close on his wrist. The makeshift rope had jerked and Georgie, with the lacerated back, had grunted as the buckles and leather belts strained, and Bill had half dragged, half helped Mignon back to the ledge.

They'd stood there stunned.

The ledge was tiny. The belts had stretched and the strip of leather wrapped tight round Bill's fingers had cut so deep he could see purple, but he and Mignon were alive and that was more than he expected.

Above, Daisy was issuing orders, demanding people hurry, while Mrs Beecher reassured her that they *were* hurrying. It seemed that real ropes had arrived. Catching one thrown down to him, Bill wrapped it round Mignon's waist and knotted it tight.

'I wish you weren't going,' she said.

He yanked on the rope to tell them to pull her up.

'I'm not going,' Bill promised.

'You're not?' The rope tightened and Mignon began to lift away.

'No,' Bill said. 'You are.'

Things moved swiftly after that. The second Bill was at the top he began delegating jobs and after a moment's hesitation people started doing what they were told.

'The Nazi was a British spy,' he said.

Georgie opened his mouth to object and Eddie's uncle nudged him. 'Not for real,' he said. 'It's pretend.'

'We're going to need a coffin,' Bill said.

'Be simpler to dump him at sea,' Eddie's uncle objected.

'It's for Mignon.'

Daisy stared at him.

'She's dead,' Bill told Daisy. 'We're going to bury her.'

Eddie's uncle grinned. 'You mean, you're going to bury the captain and tell the Huns it's Mignon?'

'I'm going to need a coffin, a suitably grim death certificate, a police report that states that having murdered his colonel and an English boy he'd recruited to the auxiliaries, Captain Keller came to Renhou, set fire to the house, tried to persuade Mignon to leave for London and dragged her out at gunpoint when she refused. My wife and Mrs Beecher witnessed this.'

'Where were you?' Daisy demanded.

'With him.' Bill nodded to the priest.

'Things you needed to get off your conscience?' Daisy asked.

'Who hasn't?' Bill said.

A few of the work party were still trying to make sense of Bill's words, but not Mignon. She'd got it from the first.

Taking the envelope from Keller's jacket, Bill pushed it at her. 'This is your ticket out of here.'

Daisy, Bill and Mignon hurried to the beach.

A canoe was there, half hidden behind black rocks below Aldoy Head, the man beside it crouched low. He was watching Renhou burn.

'Christ,' he said. 'What happened?'

'It's a long story,' Daisy told him.

'*You didn't sink,*' Bill said.

There was enough relief in Bill's voice to make the petty officer pause. 'We filled one of the torpedo tubes with oil, sir. Blew it, went silent and sat it out on the bottom for what felt like days.'

'You need to get away from here.'

'I know, sir. You're so late I've been back to the sub once already. The skipper sent me in again when we saw the fire. You'd better say your goodbyes.'

'Come on,' Bill told Mignon.

They waded into the sea together.

'I can't take both of you, sir. My orders . . .'

'You have only one passenger,' Bill told him. 'It's not me.' He half lifted, half helped Mignon into the canoe. 'My daughter has an envelope for Churchill that he wants, desperately . . . Understood?' He helped turn the canoe and pushed it into deeper water.

'Wait,' Mignon said.

'We'll see you very soon.'

Mignon's hand reached for his as it had on the ledge, and then the petty officer dug his oars into the waves and Mignon laughed as the gap widened. Bill watched until the canoe was out of sight.

Acknowledgements

This novel is built around a bricolage of dates, places and facts culled from history books, timelines, local papers, national papers, memoirs and *Hansard* . . . In the age of the internet, a random photograph from Tripadvisor and a faded map called in from a library are equally important, and with this book, more than any other, I've sometimes felt like a caffeine-fuelled spider bot!

In particular, Wallis Simpson's *The Heart Has Its Reasons* was at least as important for what she didn't say, as for what she did; while John Lewis's *A Doctor's Occupation*, Roy McLoughlin's (ed.) *Living With The Enemy*; and the documentary series *The Channel Islands at War* were invaluable for introducing me to the words of those who had lived through the German occupation of those islands.

My thanks to Braye Beach Hotel for the week I spent taking endless photographs of Alderney's forts and coves and bays, when not typing frantically in their bar. And also thanks to the Alderney Museum in St Anne's for letting me shelter there when the rains came down.

A tip of the hat to Jonny Geller at Curtis Brown for fixing the contract. Rowland White at Penguin for buying the book. Viola Hayden, at Curtis Brown, for sane advice and listening to the occasional rant. Ruth Atkins, also Penguin, for a great (and blessedly concise) set of editorial notes. Sarah Gabriel for work on early drafts. Richenda Todd for a superb copyedit, and Nick Lowndes at Penguin for managing the process, liaising with design and keeping everything moving.

More than ever, a book is a collaborative process, and I've been lucky.

Finally, Sam, as always.

Thank you.

Edinburgh
February 2021

He just wanted a decent book to read ...

Not too much to ask, is it? It was in 1935 when Allen Lane, Managing Director of Bodley Head Publishers, stood on a platform at Exeter railway station looking for something good to read on his journey back to London. His choice was limited to popular magazines and poor-quality paperbacks – the same choice faced every day by the vast majority of readers, few of whom could afford hardbacks. Lane's disappointment and subsequent anger at the range of books generally available led him to found a company – and change the world.

'We believed in the existence in this country of a vast reading public for intelligent books at a low price, and staked everything on it'
Sir Allen Lane, 1902–1970, founder of Penguin Books

The quality paperback had arrived – and not just in bookshops. Lane was adamant that his Penguins should appear in chain stores and tobacconists, and should cost no more than a packet of cigarettes.

Reading habits (and cigarette prices) have changed since 1935, but Penguin still believes in publishing the best books for everybody to enjoy. We still believe that good design costs no more than bad design, and we still believe that quality books published passionately and responsibly make the world a better place.

So wherever you see the little bird – whether it's on a piece of prize-winning literary fiction or a celebrity autobiography, political tour de force or historical masterpiece, a serial-killer thriller, reference book, world classic or a piece of pure escapism – you can bet that it represents the very best that the genre has to offer.

Whatever you like to read – trust Penguin.